Raves for
XAVIER KNIGHT/ C. KELLY ROBINSON

The Strong Silent Type

"Compelling."

—*Booklist*

"Remarkable . . . Four-and-a-half out of five stars . . . I absolutely loved the characters and the . . . mystery and suspense."

—RAWSISTAZ Book Club

The Perfect Blend

"Fast-moving, true-to-life, and most entertaining . . . Robinson is a wonderfully talented writer who captured my attention on page one and kept it until the very end."

—Kimberla Lawson Roby, *New York Times* bestselling author of
Too Much of a Good Thing

"A winner! Terrific and entertaining, with a rhythm that draws you in . . . Robinson is truly one of the most gifted new writers in the industry today."

—Victoria Christopher Murray, bestselling author of
A Sin and a Shame

more . . .

"A perfect blend of humor, drama, and emotion."

—Gloria Mallette, bestselling author of *Shades of Jade*
and *The Honey Well*

"One read you will not want to miss . . . What a story! . . .
Robinson flaunts his literary skills and spins a tale of
love and family that is emotionally riveting and highly
entertaining."

—Tracy Price-Thompson, bestselling author of
Chocolate Sangria and *Black Coffee*

No More Mr. Nice Guy

"Robinson handles his subject matter with plenty of attitude.
As in his debut, brisk plotting, snappy vernacular, and resilient
characters keep things entertaining . . . this spunky title will
please fans of E. Lynn Harris and Omar Tyree."

—*Publishers Weekly*

"Highly recommended."

—Book-Remarks.com

Between Brothers

"Not since Spike Lee's *School Daze* and the much-loved sitcom
A Different World has the black experience on campus been
this intriguing and, at times, funny . . . *Between Brothers* is a
spirited tale."

—*Essence*

The Things We Do for Love

XAVIER KNIGHT

GRAND CENTRAL
PUBLISHING

NEW YORK   BOSTON

Copyright © 2008 by Xavier Knight
Reading Group Guide copyright © 2008 by Hachette Book Group USA, Inc.

Grand Central Publishing
Hachette Book Group USA
237 Park Avenue
New York, NY 10017

Visit our Web site at www.HachetteBookGroupUSA.com.

Printed in the United States of America

Book design and text composition by SDDesigns

First Edition: March 2008
10 9 8 7 6 5 4 3 2 1

Grand Central Publishing is a division of Hachette Book Group USA, Inc. The Grand Central Publishing name and logo is a trademark of Hachette Book Group USA, Inc.

Library of Congress Cataloging-in-Publication Data

Knight, Xavier, 1970–
    The things we do for love / Xavier Knight.—1st ed.
        p. cm.
    ISBN 978-0-446-58238-4
    1. African Americans—Fiction. 2. Christians—Fiction. 3. Gospel musicians—Fiction. 4. Christian gay men—Fiction. 5. Spouses—Fiction. I. Title.

PS3568.O2855T48 2008
813'.54—dc22   200703440

*Dedicated to the memories of
Victor Robinson and Winzle Wilson,
beloved uncle and grandfather*

Acknowledgments

An odd sensation hums inside as I write the acknowledgments page for my sixth published novel. Am I thanking everyone as "Xavier" or as "C. Kelly"? I guess at the end of the day, I am simply God's creation, brought into the world through Chester and Sherry. So as I try to follow the KISS rule, here goes.

I give thanks to Jesus Christ, my Lord and Savior, for giving me the opportunity to now write books that openly portray characters struggling to reconcile their human frailties with their faith. My career in publishing has often reminded me to lean on my faith in you, but there is no greater privilege than to use my God-given gift for your glory.

Kyra, my partner through so many growing pains, a wonderful mother to Miss K, for constant support and love from day one. Kennedi, you are a walking, giggling, and beautiful answer to prayer, and Daddy now knows that no book can compare to the joys you bring! Alexis, for paving the way to parenthood for "Uncle C and Auntie Ky"—we are so proud to see you growing into such a talented little lady! To Mom, Dad, Russ, Barrett, and Shelli, what can I say that I haven't said in past publications? I love y'all! Russ, thank you for sharing a journey that opened my eyes and helped inspire this story. My thanks for years of love and support, as always, go out to all members of the Robinson, Alford, and Grimes families.

Pastors Daryl and Vanessa Ward of the Omega Baptist Church, thank you for providing spiritual nourishment to our entire church family, even during a crisis that may have stopped other pastors in their tracks. Many thanks as well to the hundreds of Omega members and personal friends across the country who continue to support my work.

My career has continued in large part thanks to the ongoing support of book clubs, journalists, readers, and publishers. You know who you are, and you are not forgotten. To the dozens of authors who helped welcome me into the industry, you are always in my thoughts and prayers. Some of you are still riding the bestseller lists with what looks like ease (I know, it's never as simple as it appears), while others like me have faced temporary or even permanent "sabbaticals." May we never forget that as long as we write our best work and pursue our dream, we win regardless of what the "in crowd" or chattering classes say.

My specific thanks to those in the industry who specifically helped get this book into your hands. Elaine Koster, for loyal service and insightful advice. Karen Thomas, for believing in my talent. Latoya Smith and the Grand Central Publishing team, for having a little patience when the pace of life keeps me from answering your questions and reminders as quickly as I should. Victoria Christopher Murray, your enthusiastic validation of this book, when it was in proposal form, was clear proof that I was on the right track. Kimberla Lawson Roby and Jacquelin Thomas, thank you both for recent exchanges that helped me realize that I was "gone but not forgotten" during my vacation from the literary scene.

Finally, if you have purchased this book, thank you for spending precious dollars on the fruits of my labor. May you be entertained, enlightened, and most importantly, blessed!

The
Things
We Do
for Love

Prologue

In the days after the truth about their son was revealed—the type of truth that takes lives and destroys marriages—Dionne and Jesse Law had plenty of time to dwell on memories. Happy, humorous, heartwarming memories, the ones that keep you moving forward when your heart asks if it could just stop beating and be done with it all, please. Though neither spoke a word to the other in those darkest, bleakest hours, they each drew on one shared moment in time.

Jesse Law and Dionne Favors met three times before either had a romantic thought about the other. Their second run-in occurred in the community bathroom of Truth Hall, one of the freshman women's dorms on the campus of Dionne's alma mater, Howard University. It was eight minutes after five on a dark fall Thursday morning. For her part, Dionne, who had been awake all of three minutes when she stepped into the shower room, wore a loose, rumpled housecoat painted with images of clouds and sunlight, a favorite she'd received from her father on her fifteenth birthday.

Jesse, on the other hand, was buck naked.

"Ohmigod! E-excuse me!" Stumbling backward, preparing to run from the shower room, Dionne squeezed her eyes tight and clawed desperately for the nearest towel rack. She knew it had been right there, just to her left when she first stepped onto the shower area's greasy tile floor. She hoped it hadn't gone anywhere.

"Whoa, sis!" The naked man's shout told Dionne she'd missed the mark, a hint confirmed by the sudden sensation of flight as the grip of her flip-flops gave way and her feet went out from under her. Her eyes still shut—she wasn't prepared for another flash of the brother's forbidden if admirable birthday suit—Dionne instinctively held her hands out, hoping to slow her fall.

"I got you." The mystery pervert's voice had a hoarse, scratchy sound, and it was literally in her ear now. It helped, though, that his tone was so calm and soothing. Realizing she had never smashed into the tile, Dionne slowly released the pressure she'd exerted on her right eyelid. Once she had a limited view of her "savior's" face—his eyes and nose were plenty—she stopped, keeping the other eye slammed shut.

When he had her fully right side up, the brother took a step back, his eyes full of laughter as he peered at Dionne through the humid, steamy air engulfing them. "You're okay, right?"

"Um, yes, yes, um, yes." Dionne scolded herself as she nodded her head like an obedient child, one eye still closed and her arms folded as if she were the one showing off her goods right now. She just wanted this . . . thug . . . to get to stepping and get off the dorm's premises. As a senior resident assistant who had never once entertained a male in her room, Dionne took great pride enforcing the dorm's rules about fraternization. All men had to be off the premises by midnight, and in recent years security cameras had been placed throughout the halls to ensure that violators and their hostesses were captured and appropriately penalized.

For most of the administration, the curfew was simply a quaint device to encourage respect between the freshman males and females, but Dionne liked to think that anything she did to dampen her peers' sex lives was to their spiritual benefit. Many of these girls who currently had little use for God would someday fall to their knees, say the gospel prayer, and walk the aisle of a church. If she could minimize their fornication, at least they'd have a little less sin weighing them down on that special day.

All the more reason why she had every reason to be disgusted and indignant with this show-off who'd accosted her, treating himself to a shower in the girls' bathroom just because he could. Dionne knew the type; not only had he probably spent the night banging headboards with some misguided coed, he was happy to further flaunt his "creeping" abilities by rinsing himself off in plain sight of everyone, including women like her who respected themselves.

Dionne decided she had no business cowering like some wallflower in front of this brother. *He* was in the wrong, not her, and it was time to act like it. "Do you have a towel?" she asked suddenly, snapping the words purposefully.

"Aww," the trifling brother replied, his tone taking on a rebellious edge. "I'm not harming your virgin eyes, am I?"

His perceptive language caught Dionne off guard and she inhaled sharply, unable to breathe until she heard him turn and grab something off the very rack she'd swung for and missed. "I'm decent now, beautiful," he said, pointing to the beach towel wrapped snugly around his hips.

"You have no business being in this facility at this hour, least of all in the bathroom," Dionne said, an index finger aimed toward the man's Adam's apple. She had both eyes open now, and kept her tone steady and firm while fixing her gaze—for the most part—to his light brown eyes, high cheekbones, and thick, tapered eyebrows. "Whose room are you staying in?"

"Hey, baby," the brother said, fanning the air with his hands. "Be cool, okay? You don't need to worry about that. Look, I'm not even a student at Howard, all right? I wasn't hip to this curfew business in the first place."

"You're not a student?" Dionne nearly took a step back in self-defense. There had been rapes in the dorms before, primarily by men from outside the HU community, vagrants who had broken, entered, and done unspeakable things. Dionne had gotten up early this morning to meet an evangelism team over in Southeast DC; she had no intention of becoming a statistic today.

Reading the anxiety on the sister's face, Jesse had raised his hands over his head. "It's not that kind of party," he said, his voice lowered further. "Seriously, all you need to do is let me roll out of here ASAP. My tour bus hits the road in an hour. I miss it, my manager will kill me."

Dionne first cracked a smile, both relieved by the brother's assurances of innocence and amused by his claim of having a "tour bus," but then the stranger's familiar features finally hit her. "You're kidding," she said, her arms crossed and her insides frosting over again. "Are you Jesse Law?"

He grudgingly assured her he was, and Dionne found herself reliving the previous week, when every "worldly" girl she'd known chattered on about the young hottie the Homecoming Committee secured for the week's biggest concert. At the time, Jesse Law was an undeniable star—as he and Dionne faced off in the shower, two of his recent singles were perched on *Billboard*'s R&B Top 10—but he wasn't exactly keeping Usher up at night. His albums reliably went platinum, his videos got play on both BET and MTV, but odds were that wouldn't be true five years from now. Whether Jesse Law realized it or not, his songs—and from what Dionne could see, the boy himself— just weren't all that special. Like most church girls, she had fallen as a Howard freshman for one of his early singles ("I Got It All"), but had found his musical charms much easier to resist than true-but-twisted talents, such as Prince or R. Kelly.

Having mentally cut the brother down to size even as her eyes flitted over his hairy barrel chest, broad shoulders, and tight waistline, Dionne pulled her housecoat tighter around her. "I'll make you a deal, Brother Law—"

He cleared his throat, twitched as if annoyed. "Brother?"

Dionne cracked a smile, glad to feel the balance of power finally shift. "Come on, Jesse, it hasn't been that long since you stepped foot inside a church, has it?" Around the time she bought his first CD, she'd been into Jesse Law just enough to know that he was the baby brother of the Laws, one of the most talented families in gospel music. A trio of his older sisters—predictably named the Law Sisters—had recorded and toured the country regularly for the past fifteen years, and his older twin brothers, Larry and Harry, spent the Eighties giving the Winans a run for their money before Larry left to pastor a Nashville church. "I know you haven't forgotten your church home training," she said, her tone playful, although she was serious.

Jesse had lost patience with this sister. Before she'd signaled her knowledge of his family history, he'd viewed baby girl with a charitable eye. She looked a hot mess at the moment—her rumpled housecoat looked like it had been stored in a time capsule, and her misshapen pink shower cap was proof this girl had no boyfriend to impress—but she was tall, long-legged, robustly built without being overweight, and her piercing brown eyes had an intriguing power. Then, of course, there'd been the glimpse of breast and nipple she'd inadvertently flashed when she lost her step. Her spiritual taunting, however, drained such lovely sensations from Jesse's memory bank. She didn't know him like that; he was a hot second from pulling rank and telling her to get out of his way. "You letting me go or not, Miss—"

"Favors," Dionne replied, extending a hand as she heard her parents' northern Tennessee accents reflected in her own. "Sister Dionne Favors. The deal I'm offering, Jesse, is that I'll let you go your merry way if you'll let me pray with you. Promise I'll make it quick."

Jesse cursed under his breath, then ran both hands through his fine waves of jet-black hair, which were cut into a high, rounded fade. He didn't have time for this silliness; not only would it be a pain to call for a cab from an undesirable part of DC, but he knew the girls he'd spent the night with were still in their room awaiting his professions of love, and that would require a few minutes of finessing itself. Eager as he was to bolt past Dionne, though, some force—either the God whose existence he now doubted, or his stepmother's loving influence—took hold of him, told him to humor this square but cute girl. "Go for it," he said, taking her hands.

As they drew closer, Dionne felt the tight brown curls atop her head dampen beneath her shower cap, but she ignored the sweat beading on her forehead, plowing into her prayer. "Lord," she said, suddenly feeling self-conscious about the deepness of her rich alto voice, "we thank you for the very real talents you have blessed Brother Jesse with. We know that you gave him those talents, along with such a blessed and spiritual family, Lord, for a reason. Father, help Jesse to eventually see that you've called him to do more than shake his butt on stage and sing about the flesh. Show Jesse his way, Lord, so he can serve you in a way that makes you, as well as his family, proud. Amen."

"That was cute," Jesse said, unable to muzzle himself as Dionne opened her eyes. "May I go now?"

"Fine," Dionne said, letting her arms hang at her sides. His patronizing remark angered her, but she needed to show this brother some Holy Spirit love instead of being openly defensive. "You kept up your side of the bargain. I never saw you in here, okay?"

"You're first-class, sister," Jesse said, leaning in and planting a kiss on her cheek. "For the record," he whispered, keeping his lips poised inches from her ear, "you don't really know me well enough to pray for me. We could always do something about that, though."

"You know," Dionne replied, a rush of warmth spreading throughout her chest, "I said you could go, Jesse. I don't need to be disrespected."

"Who said I was being disrespectful?" Someone coughed in the hallway, and Jesse paused long enough to make sure the girl wasn't joining them. "Sounds like you think I'm some rebel without a cause, some loser who broke ranks with my 'sanctified' family for the hell of it."

"I don't—I don't—look." Dionne was starting to doubt her sanity. She couldn't remember when she'd been this tongue-tied. Aside from a slight acne problem, she had to admit Jesse was as handsome as his fans imagined him to be, but he wasn't her type. At least not in theory. "I don't know you, obviously, but you may as well know, I've seen you in action before. I know you've always been into things that wouldn't make your parents proud." As a true fan of the Law Sisters especially, Dionne had read enough articles in *Gospel Today* to know that Jesse's mother, Mama Frankie Law, still served as minister of music at Greater Light of the Cross Church in Hyattsville, Maryland. It was the same legendary church where his father, Phillip Sr., had held the same role before flipping his Cadillac in a fatal wreck on the Beltway, when little Jesse was still a child.

Jesse's brow furrowed as he clamped his hands against the sides of his waistline. When his towel slipped just enough to reveal a patch of hair Dionne had no business viewing, he did nothing to cover himself. "So you're an expert on my parents, huh?" If it was any of her business, he'd tell her that the woman she guessed was his mother, the saintly woman who had raised him from the age of seven on, was no blood relation. But then, if she didn't know that much, she was more clueless than she'd ever know. And that was before even touching on the hellish hypocrisies Jesse had seen during a childhood immersed in the Black church and gospel industry. It amazed him that anyone his age could be naïve enough to take the "church" game seriously.

Dionne knew the conversation was starting to spiral, but she was helpless to slow the pace of their jousting now. "That other time we met," she said. "It was a few months before your first CD came out, after my junior year of high school. Teen Night at the Ritz." Although she had been a proud square from Silver Spring's most privileged neighborhood, Dionne had practiced the apostle Paul's exhortation to "be all things to all people," even in her teens. It was the only reason she'd spent time in hostile environments, like those DC nightclubs. By accompanying some of her more emotionally vulnerable friends on their forays into such lust-driven, alcohol-fueled environments, Dionne had helped several of them pick up the pieces after disastrous one-night stands, abusive encounters, or verbal beatdowns from the same smooth talkers who'd swept them off the club floors.

Dionne crossed her arms as she stared Jesse down. "I don't imagine you remember a girl named Paula Rogers? I was sitting to her left when you walked up on us and started macking it to her at the Ritz."

Jesse smirked, although his insides snarled. "Did I take her home? Or just out to my car for a little ride?"

"You had your fun for a few weeks before throwing her away," Dionne said, shaking her head. She still recalled how much she'd been in denial that night. She knew that preachers' kids—and as the baby of a family of gospel legends, Jesse was close enough to being one—could be a trip, but she'd hoped that the Laws were such a special family that they hadn't produced any rebels. The minute young Jesse had accosted them, though, the last dregs of her innocence were shredded. Jesse had entered the club and immediately been treated like ghetto royalty, receiving back pounds and hugs from a row of notorious drug dealers, professional carjackers, and petty thieves. Combine that with his intimidating swagger and the hungry leer he directed at every attractive female in the place, and Dionne had sensed Jesse was running as fast as he could from his family's legacy.

Pawing at the damp mound of hair on his head, Jesse bit his lower lip, frustrated at himself for trying to remember a shred of information about Dionne's friend, this Paula chick. All he'd need was a little tidbit to shut the self-righteous girl up, convince her he was a genuine human being. No matter how much he scanned his mental database, though, he came up empty; he was no saint now, but in those days there had just been too much weed, liquor, and women for him to have stored Paula away. It was time to go; he'd already wasted a good ten minutes with this cranky do-gooder.

"I'm out," he said, flinging away the towel and grinning when Dionne gasped despite herself. He didn't need his hostess's towel, anyway; her room was two doors down from the bathroom. "By the way," Jesse said, turning over his shoulder in the bathroom's doorway and flexing his buttocks for Dionne's horrified benefit, "you might try to get a little bit of this into your life. I'm sure any number of brothers would happily provide it." He turned back toward her, facing her with himself fully exposed and smiling when she shut her eyes again in horror. "Don't sleep, Dionne. It might cool you out some, help you mind your own business." He strode away, laughing loud enough to wake the entire dorm, not knowing his flexing buttocks and dangling manhood would linger in Dionne's fevered dreams for weeks to come.

Two years passed before Dionne experienced the pleasures Jesse paraded before her that day in the shower, pleasures they just barely postponed until their explosive wedding night in an Aruban honeymoon suite. When she flung her drenched, glowing body back against the bed's slick, matted sheets, Dionne had thanked God in prayer for blessing her first time. Jesse had been even more nervous than her about how well they'd ultimately fit together, but he had been gentle, thoughtful, and attentive in a way that helped his new wife open up like a blooming flower eager for rain.

So many things changed during their journey from the girls' shower to the honeymoon suite; far more happened before their marriage found itself peering over a cliff with a pack of raging lions on its heels.

First Jesse's record label dropped him after one failed CD, spurring a wilderness period where he accepted a friend's offer to make some cash "off the books." That adventure ended with an early-morning shoot-out in the parking lot of Greenbrier Mall, an episode jarring enough to lead Jesse to the friendly embrace of Coleman Hill, a young DC-area gospel singer. As Coleman convinced Jesse to rekindle his interest in songwriting and the childhood faith he'd abandoned, he also dragged his struggling friend to an Atlanta conference for young Black Christians, a conference that Dionne, fresh out of Howard School of Divinity, had helped coordinate.

Their paths crossed the second night of the conference, and before they knew it, not only had their testy conversations led to numerous late-night phone calls, but Dionne had dumped David, her straight-laced, reliable boyfriend, and accepted Jesse's tentative invitation to the movies.

Seven years into their marriage now, the memory of those days felt like ancient history. In that blink of an eye, Jesse had confronted his past with his wife's help, separating the abuse he'd suffered in the church from the love Jesus held for him. Helping Jesse through the very real traumas in his past opened Dionne's eyes, transforming her from a self-righteous Holy Roller into an empathetic, perceptive listener whose effectiveness in ministry had tripled. After using the last bits of his celebrity to earn a music degree from Howard in exchange for serving on the faculty, Jesse had put his talents to work for God, starting up the gospel group Men with a Message, with his old friend Coleman.

Even more impressive to Dionne's family—her parents had been slow to forgive her for throwing the goody-goody David overboard for a rebel without a cause—Jesse had successfully leaned on God to stay sexually faithful to his wife, making the most of one lover after years of going through a dozen every six months. And while her commitment to her ministry—running a Christian school in Southeast DC—was already rock solid, the sight of Jesse's spiritual growth had deepened Dionne's faith. She was confident that with God's help, she could save even the most hopeless child from his or her environment.

At their seventh anniversary party, just before all hell broke loose, Coleman, the Laws' dear brother in ministry, summed up the conventional wisdom. "Some folk just get together," he had said, tipping his glass of sparkling apple juice toward them as he stood on the expansive oak deck of the couple's new home, surrounded by dozens of family and friends. "Not these two," Coleman had continued. "When you look at the special way God uses their talents for His glory, you know He *put* them together."

Good friend that he was, Coleman had respectfully left one fact about God's involvement in their marriage unspoken: for a faith that spoke of the importance of couples being fruitful and multiplying, the absence of children was a hole Dionne always knew would test their bond. Even she, though, never dreamed how ferocious the test would be, nor how their individual failures of judgment would dump fuel onto an already volatile situation. The wounds were deep enough, the scars insistent enough, that years later they would record it all for little Samuel Law's eventual knowledge. For while they agreed not to tell him the truth while he was a child, they knew he would eventually demand it.

1

Jesse

I 've thought this through all night. I'm keeping the baby." Vanessa's voice had backbone as she said those words. A tremor escaped between a syllable here and there, sure, but that only made sense, given what was at stake. My son's mother was trembling with fear, but her tone told me she was unquestionably up to the task.

Sliding another notch lower into the leather driver's seat of my BMW sedan, I pulled my cell phone back from my ear before responding. "Vanessa, slow down," I said, my eyes darting across the dimly lit, vacant alley. Her statement filtered menacingly through my soul, which hummed with the words *you knew this was coming*.

I cleared my throat before saying, "I didn't understand you. What did you just say?" Odds were, she'd just repeat herself, but you never knew. In my B.C. (Before Christ) days, I'd backed many an indignant sister off me by simply daring them to repeat the very line they'd saved up for weeks, the one they'd thought would devastate me for sure: *I already had the abortion. I know you're seeing that tramp. He was better than you, anyway.* Sometimes even, *She was better than you, anyway.*

No matter how seemingly powerful the line, I usually found their delivery weakened with repetition, until I finally turned it around on them to get the outcome I wanted. And now more than ever, with my wife's mental and emotional health on the line, the outcome Vanessa was talking about was 100 percent unacceptable.

"I never wanted this child before," Vanessa replied, stealing some of my fire right off, "but that was before he started growing inside me."

I decided to play it cool, stifling a chill as I began applying the same charms I'm told my daddy employed on his many women back in the day. "It's a miracle, isn't it?" I asked, my tone hushed. "I can't think of clearer proof of God's work."

"Oh God, Jesse," Vanessa said, sniffing back what sounded like a tear. "You know me—a cynic to the end, a scientist before all else. Before now, the science of maternity was academic—I didn't really get it, not the way a mother does. But having this little life inside me . . . I know I'll never be the same. I might even be a better doctor when all's said and done."

"I don't doubt that, Vanessa, I really don't," I replied, my heartbeat quickening as the bright headlights of a red Mazda 6 lit up the opposite end of the alley. "You're going to grow as a result of this experience," I said into the phone, though my gaze focused on the slowly approaching vehicle. "We all will. You, me, and Dionne too." My precious wife's name had a metallic taste whenever I spoke it in front of Vanessa; may God forgive me, but I had gradually convinced myself that she and Dionne occupied two mutually exclusive realities.

"I'm not looking for a fight," Vanessa said after a few moments of unbearable silence. The Mazda had rolled to a stop less than fifty yards from me, but thanks to the tinted windows on the driver's side, I had no clue who was inside. "I know you and Dionne will make perfect parents to the right child someday, but, Jesse, this is my baby. Nothing we've agreed to the past few months changes that—"

"This is *our* baby, Vanessa," I said, cutting in before her statement could take root. In truth, I felt the child belonged to Dionne and me exclusively; left to her own devices, Vanessa had nearly sacrificed this developing life on the altar of her demanding medical career. "We have to decide his future together, okay? That's all I'm asking."

"I'm not going to promise I can just walk away from him," Vanessa replied, her words now forceful again. "I'm not the same woman you started sleeping with six months ago. I get it now; this is a real human being inside me, one who should grow up knowing his true mother's love."

My attempt to come off disengaged was betrayed by the vibrations in my voice, and I struggled to keep my tone level. "The baby will have Dionne's mothering love," I replied, turning away abruptly when the Mazda's driver's side door popped open suddenly. "He won't lack for anything. Trust me."

Vanessa's weary sigh almost made we wish my son could have two mothers. "It's not like I don't appreciate all you two have been through." During the several weeks in which Vanessa and I had battled over how to handle the pregnancy, I had reluctantly shared the spiritual trials Dionne and I endured throughout our six-year attempt to become parents in the way we'd thought God intended. The rigidly scheduled sex routines and positions, the humiliating fertility checkups; the shattering diagnosis of Dionne's conception-blocking health complications, and, finally, the four near-miss adoptions, most of which fell apart during that harrowing period when a birth mother could still change her mind. Now we were in a place I'd never imagined in my worst nightmare, and even still it looked like this child—my own flesh and blood—might slip away. But then, I wasn't going to let that happen.

As I massaged my heated brow, I decided to wait another day to nudge Vanessa back to the other side of the line. The harder and more immediately I pushed, the more I'd just get her back up. Better to bide my time, especially given how many practical facts were on my side. Between her remaining years of residency and the fact she had no extended family willing to help her, single parenthood would severely complicate Vanessa's hard-earned path toward a medical practice.

"Why don't you get some sleep," I said to her, my tone suggestive but subdued again. I finally risked a turn back toward the Mazda and was oddly relieved to see the exact person I had expected, Angie Barker. "The guys and I have to catch a plane to the Stellar Awards in Nashville tomorrow," I said to Vanessa while waving to Angie. "I'll call you from the airport, okay?"

"Okay," Vanessa said, the tightness in her voice softening. "Good luck in Nashville." She paused, then sheepishly said, "Even with all I know, Jesse, I still believe in what you guys do." My contemporary gospel group, Men with a Message, was up for five Stellar Awards and there were rumors about Grammy nominations.

I heard Vanessa's compliment, but stifled any response. She was too smart not to know how much the contrast between my "calling" and our clandestine relationship wounded me. No, her words were a warning shot across my bow: getting my son from her wasn't about to be easy.

Angie was leaning against her driver's side door when I emerged into the chilly night air, her arms crossed, though her full lips were spread wide in a wicked grin. "Ooh, somebody's gotten up in your grill for real," she said, eyeing me with a look of amused intrigue. "You got that look in your eyes from the old days, Jesse, like that time you pulled your nine on Tony Jefferson and them at Chicago's." She stepped forward and pinched at the left shoulder of my bomber jacket. "Should we, uh, do this another time? I don't want you to hurt a sister."

My emotional mask sliding into place, I popped a stick of Big

Red into my mouth before extending a friendly hand. "This is the perfect time, Angie," I replied. "You know whenever you call, I come running."

"Oh sure," she said, edging closer into my personal space. Even from underneath her black suede coat, the rise and swell of her healthy breasts were noticeable. Sizing me up from the shelter of her stylish black-framed glasses, Angie touched a hand to my cheek. "Haven't seen you up close in years, old friend, just been reading—and occasionally writing—about you. You look good."

Even with everything weighing on me—tomorrow's high-profile trip to Nashville, Dionne's upcoming, high-stakes interview for a ministerial position at a megachurch in Columbia, Maryland, and, of course, Vanessa and the baby—my human flesh was eager to return Angie's compliment. Mentally calling on Christ for restraint—an exercise I still required several times a day, even after years of mostly monogamous marriage—I settled on a safer route. "How about you?" I said. "You look like you hit the gym regularly yourself. I bet folks fall out when they hear you have a twelve-year-old." If memory served, Angie had gotten pregnant about a year after our breakup, when we were a couple of punk teenagers.

"Aw," she replied, grinning and placing a gloved hand to my chest before respectfully removing it. "That's so *sweet* of you, now, Jesse." At five foot eleven, she was just an inch shorter than me, but she crooked her neck as if struggling to make eye contact. "Is the industry gossip true? Has Jesus really changed you?"

My heart did another flip as I gave a false smile. "It may not make the most entertaining story for an award-winning journalist, but it's the truth." Angie broke into music journalism by trailing top gospel performers across the country. In the early days she'd stalked the likes of Kirk Franklin, Hezekiah Walker, and Commissioned, from coast to coast, getting in their faces with a warm but determined smile until they gave her a few minutes of time. Eventually she developed a wide network of contacts and a reputation for publishing deeply personal and provocative profiles of artists from not just the gospel world but rap, R&B, and jazz. Her talents had been displayed in *Ebony, Essence, Billboard, Savoy*, even *Rolling Stone.*

As a result, when I'd told the other members of Men with a Message—Coleman, Micah, Frank, and Isaac—about her six voice messages, they'd forced me to return her call. "You treat her real nice, now," my boy Micah had told me as they stood over me earlier that same morning. Generally the most mature group member and our most prolific producer, Micah's eyes had a strangely giddy quality when Angie was on his mind. "What she can do for our career—or, I mean, what God can use her to do for our career! J. Law, you cannot mess this up!"

Micah's attitude might not have been so enthusiastic if he'd known the rest of the story. Angie wasn't just an objective journalist interested in a young, increasingly popular gospel group; she and I had what you might call "history." We'd met as teens illegally hitting the DC club scene. She ran with a group of fine, wannabe-down sisters from suburban Virginia, while I hung tough with what I'll call a shadowy group of brothers from my Northwest DC neighborhood. At the time I was the equivalent of crack to a black girl trying to escape the shackles of suburbia, so I had Angie's number—as well as my hand up her shirt—within minutes of our first meeting.

Angie startled me out of my thoughts when she suddenly armed her car's alarm system. Hopping in place at the sharp, chirping sound, I yanked my car door back open. "Why don't we talk in here?"

The sound of Angie's alarm hadn't just scared me, because right then a dog two stories overhead began barking to beat the band. Casting a gaze toward the dog's yips and yaps, Angie crossed her arms again. "You ashamed to be seen with me?" She swept an arm toward the other end of the alley. "You know, I realize you're still a bit famous in your own right, but most of the kids out there are trying to have fun on a Friday night. Ain't nobody looking at you, Jesse Law." The alley was at the west end of the popular U Street Corridor, an area populated by a stew of college kids, twenty-something professionals, and locals who weren't disgusted by the sight of spoiled, pampered kids.

"Refrain from the very appearance of evil," I said, shaking a finger playfully, and knowing she'd catch the scriptural reference. "All it takes is one mouthy fan to spread rumors of seeing me hanging with a beautiful woman other than my wife. No sense encouraging mess."

"So what angle would you take if you were writing a profile of your group?" Angie was in my passenger seat now, her legs crossed at the ankles and a BlackBerry device in her lap. "There's so many directions we can go—the amazing sales numbers of you guys' last two CDs, the secular radio play you've been getting down South, and then there's, of course, everyone's personal stories." She bit her lower lip in a slow, tempting fashion that made the filthy man in me wish we'd actually slept together back in the day. At the time my only experiences had been with Ms. Melissa, an older divorced woman at my church. For the three weeks that Angie and I dated, I guess we were too busy juggling other dates and dodging our parents' discipline to make time for sex.

"The most intriguing story, of course," Angie said now, "is how you made the transition from solo R-and-B star to member of a gospel group. That's a very rare career path."

"Only in God's plan could it make sense," I acknowledged, laughing for the first time in what felt like days. Although I had grown up in a house full of gospel performers, I was the rebel. For five heady years I'd been perched a couple rungs below where Bobby Brown was before me, and where Usher has since prospered. Three platinum

CDs, one People's Choice Award, five American Music Awards—not too shabby. The end of the road, of course, had come quickly and cruelly, and by twenty-two I'd pretty much been handed my walking papers.

"So that's what I'm envisioning for the story," Angie said. "We'll get the widest audience this way, a combination of the group's gospel fans, as well as fans from your 'worldly' days. You're the hook, Jesse: how a bad boy became good."

I fought the urge to kick my old friend out of the car right then; her constant references to my blighted past had me thinking my fears and paranoia about her intentions might be justified. I decided to shortstop the suspense, cut to the quick. "Is there something on your mind, Angie?" I asked, turning and facing her head-on. "I mean, let's get to the point. I'm not even the group's real star. Why did you call me instead of Coleman?" Built like a linebacker, Coleman had an overpowering, penetrating voice that matched his intimidating size. In baseball terms he was Men with a Message's cleanup batter, our home run king. Put him in front of a live audience, and he'd have any haters subdued in seconds, literally blown over with emotion as he rocked them with exhortations of God's power and grace. He was the group's only indispensable voice; if he ever accepted any of the solo deals being thrown his way, we'd be in major trouble.

Angie was still considering my attempt to call her bluff, her hands folded in a way that made her look oddly submissive. "I don't know how much I should say at this stage of the interview," she said, her eyes on her lap for the first time. "I don't want to come off like I'm threatening anyone. I want to base the story around your own journey, in the most positive way possible." She finally raised her gaze back to mine and placed a hand on my knee. "Okay?"

Emotions raged and warred inside me. While I caught the hesitation in Angie's voice when she mentioned the idea of "threatening anyone," I knew she had a platform God could use to tell the story of my salvation. It had been quite a path, a transition from a youth spent fleeing the hypocrisies of the Christian faith—ones my late father embodied simply by fathering me with a drug-addled white woman half his age, while my stepmother and half siblings slept peacefully a few houses away—into a life-changing relationship with Dionne that seeded, watered, and nurtured the presence of Christ into my very soul.

While my salvation was a very personal matter, Dionne was the unmistakable catalyst. The lasting mystery for me will always be that it took that third time we met, at a conference in Atlanta, for me to realize just how beautiful she was.

By the time I stole Dionne from her boyfriend, I not only had prayed to accept Christ, I felt the first frightening stirrings of a call to use my musical talents again, though this time for a more noble purpose. I wasn't really built for the gospel industry—my singing voice has always had a soft quality that's more Ralph Tresvant than Johnny Gill, more Babyface than Luther. When I really look at my role in Men with a Message, my voice is secondary; it's the lyrics of the songs I write that touch people's hearts. Not that I keep score, but I've noticed that while people fall out in the aisles during Coleman's songs, they're more likely to come forward for prayer when I'm front and center. As a result, I'm at ease being the pseudoheartthrob (yes, even "saved" women notice a handsome man) and the brother who peels away my listeners' outer shells, the one expressing the fears and scars they're tempted to hide from others.

Once I'd poured out most of this history to Angie, I peered over at her as she furiously typed shorthand into her PDA device. "We should wrap this up soon," I said, feeling spent both from reliving the past and from anticipating my next phone call with Vanessa. "I have an eight-thirty date with my wife. She's expecting a romantic night, since we'll be apart for the next week." After the Stellar Awards taping, the group was hitting the road to a couple of Gospel Fest concerts on the West Coast.

"That's fine," Angie replied, shrugging and still typing. "Are you okay finishing up via phone?"

"Sure," I replied. Clearing my throat, I tapped her left wrist. "Before I give you a formal go-ahead on all this, though, there's still the question of what you meant earlier."

Angie had gone shy again. Her chin still tucked toward her bosom, she asked, "What did I say earlier?"

"Something about threatening the group?"

"I wanted to save it for last," she said, gripping me with a steely stare now. "I have no intention on being shallow with it, Jesse, but someone in your group is facing some pretty explosive issues in his private life."

My fists clenching defensively, I began to picture Angie's article on the screen of my mind, and it was all about me. All about how I'd soared to the top of the record charts during a rebellious youth. All about my proclaimed salvation and years spent singing God's praises, for paychecks that were whispers of what I'd once earned. All about my betrayal of my wife, fathering a child with another woman and planning to pass him off as our adopted son. It was a pitch-perfect "Whatever happened to . . ." tale, a story of how I just couldn't get right after tumbling from the spotlight and the "real" record charts.

None of the more humanizing elements of the story—my shift from a youth spent sexing any female who had two legs to my years of fidelity with Dionne, the unpredictable way in which my relationship with Vanessa had developed, the fact that I'd ultimately saved a life she was ready to extinguish—would make it into print. I would be neatly and cleanly exposed as a sham, another hypocrite, just another faded star who'd sought face-saving solace in religion's questionable bosom. In one fell swoop I was sure to lose Dionne and the baby, while capsizing the careers of my brothers in ministry. Eight years of Christian living, up in smoke.

I was choking. I don't know on what, but something was lodged in my throat and I couldn't get it out. Slamming my fists on the dashboard, tears squirting at the edges of my eyes, I saw Dionne's face flash across my mind, followed by Vanessa's and a vision of what my son might look like when he was born. Something kicked inside me and I pushed out a violent cough just as Angie reached for me.

"I—I'm fine," I said, jerking away from her as I wiped spittle from my mouth. "Get out of my car," I said finally, once I had caught my breath. My stare pinning her where she sat, I held on to my steering wheel as if my car were being rocked by an earthquake. "I'm not playing with your 'gotcha' journalism." I'm not sure that I meant it—given the stakes, I'm sure I had my price. At that moment, though, I was in no mood to negotiate.

The car was deadly silent for what felt like hours before Angie sighed several times and opened her door. Shifting away from me, her voice still low, she didn't even look back as she spoke. "So you know," she said, her voice a near-whisper, "I wasn't even talking about you."

2

Dionne

efore my eyes were opened, I spent most of my days trying to save others. I know what you're thinking: *Girl, you're an evangelist—of course you should be trying to get folks saved.* Slow down. I'm not saying I didn't put in plenty of time sharing the Gospel, but I spent almost as much time trying to save folks from themselves. On this particular early evening, that often futile pursuit had me stranded an hour from home, trapped at the mercy of my childhood friend Suzette Hill.

We were on a stretch of Thirteenth Street near Logan Circle, a block that had seemingly dodged the rampant gentrification of recent years. The high-rise apartment building Suzette had disappeared into reminded me too much of Sutton Plaza, a glorified housing project I lived in during my sophomore year at Howard. Even under the evening's dusky skies, I had noticed the building's greasy, grimy exterior, the faded off-white paint, and the frequent rows of boarded-up windows. As I stood outside the front entrance, arms crossed as I waited on Suzette, I stepped aside constantly to steer clear of small bands of aspiring gang members, strolling prostitutes, and the occasional john. Across the street a group of anxious teenagers massed around a bus stop, playfully shoving and taunting each other.

With the sound of the kids' taunts and whiz of heavy traffic filling my ears, I dared another impatient glance at my watch. I hadn't wanted to stay cooped up in the car, but the mild winter evening air still held a nip of chill and I was shivering in my vinyl trench coat. Suzette had promised to be inside only a second, and at this point she'd had me out there for five minutes. I turned toward the apartment's entrance, ready to drag my girlfriend outside by the hem of her weave, when I heard my name.

"Reverend Dionne?" The young sister had slipped up beside me just that fast, a pleasant smile on her pretty, ashy face.

Sizing her up and blinking my eyes at her outfit—loud orange high heels, a black windbreaker barely concealing a tight aqua blue skirt magnifying the size of her trim but muscled hips, and an unruly blond wig—I flashed what I'm sure was an awkward smile. "Carly? Oh Lord, girl, come here."

We embraced, and as I cradled the girl's head against my neck, I nodded to myself when pungent marijuana fumes seeped from her pores into mine. *You answer in your own time, Lord,* I reminded myself. *Not our concept of time, but yours.*

Carly stepped back from me, but kept her hands glued to mine. "Look at you, Reverend, lookin' all fine!" She was smiling from ear to ear, no sense of shame or embarrassment on her keen, perfectly proportioned facial features. "You lost some more weight, didn't you?"

"I have kept up with aerobics class lately," I replied, appreciating the compliment. Jesse and I had first started working out together a year after we married, but I had never tried to keep up with the punishing regimen he followed to keep his physique trim. Eventually, though, my competitive nature led me to raise my own game, lengthening my workouts, taking on weight training, and attending grueling ninety-minute aerobics classes on my own.

"Where are you living now, Carly?" I kept an easy smile on my face, but searched my young friend's face for some acknowledgment of how this all looked. We stepped back underneath the shabby awning hanging over the apartment's front walkway, which was lit by a single hanging lightbulb, just as another trio of hookers passed, two of whom took lingering glances at Carly. I resisted the urge to warn them to leave her alone and get their own houses in order while they were at it. Hadn't the hookers been run out of this area by now?

"I'm staying with my cousin Parnell right now," Carly said once the other girls moved on. "It's cool, you know," she continued without meeting my eyes. "He work nights and don't mind watching Maisha for me. So I earn my living during the day, get home before he leave, and it's all good."

As I stared back at Carly, in my mind's eye she reverted to the struggling teen mother I ministered to a year earlier. The wig molted and fell away, leaving only her attractively clipped natural hairstyle; the loud, tight streetwalker's uniform was replaced by a cute track sweat-suit; and her ashy face was suddenly freshly buffed and oiled. She had always been a beautiful girl, both inside and out.

With the unpleasant discussion of her life over for the moment, Carly looked at me anew. "Your skin glowin', Reverend," she said as a smile spread across her face. "You think you finally pregnant? I know you and that fine Mr. Jesse gonna have a beautiful baby someday."

"Nothing's promised, child," I said, taking one of her hands and stroking gently. "Not even to the righteous." It wasn't simply a lesson I'd read in the Bible. Seven years of struggle had done the job, kicking my butt hard enough to convince me that a seemingly simple, common dream was pretty much out of my reach. "If the doctors know what they're talking about, my skin's not glowing because of a baby."

Carly's eyes popped wide. "You not sick, are you?"

"Oh no, I'm fine," I replied, realizing I might have made things sound worse than the reality. I might never bring another life into this world, but at least I had my own health. "Actually, between you and me," I whispered, pulling Carly's head close to my shoulders, "I do expect to become a mother soon. We're adopting."

Carly reached forward to hug me again, and this time she acted like she wouldn't let go. "I am *so* happy for you, Reverend Dionne," she said, dampening my blouse with her tears. "You-all gonna make some awesome parents."

"Well, we're putting it in God's hands," I said, my hands twitching suddenly. "If it's His will"—on our four previous adoption attempts, it hadn't been—"everything will work out and we'll bring the baby home in a few months. Keep us in your prayers." Ignoring the racing of my pulse, I tried to ease into my question. "Now, how can I pray for you, baby?"

"Just remember me when you get on your knees, Reverend," Carly replied, squeezing me again before letting go. She raised her eyes to mine. "I know you mad at me, but I'm not gonna do this forever."

"Carly, honey, I'm not mad," I said. As a youth minister with nearly ten years of on-the-street experience, I had counseled and mentored too many troubled teens to think they all responded to tough love. Some needed a boot up the butt, sure; others, like Carly, were precious flowers, delicate creatures so deeply damaged by hostile environments that they required painstaking, patient, and repetitive nurturing.

"What I want you to know, honey," I said, "is that you don't have to do *this* for even one more day if you don't want to." It wasn't planned, but the next thing I knew, the Spirit hit me and I said, "You can come home with me tonight. My friend drove me here, but she owes me. We can drive by your cousin's, get Maisha, and head on out to Maryland right now."

I can't help wondering if Carly would have gone for it with a few minutes to consider, but right then Suzette came bursting out of the apartment's front entrance. Built like a feminine tank, my girlfriend barreled past both me and Carly. "Dionne, let's go," she shouted, patting my shoulder as she bustled toward the side parking lot. It was like she didn't even see Carly.

I watched Suzette sashay her full figure a few more steps before I cleared my throat. "Excuse me. I'm having a conversation here, Miss Thing. I waited on you plenty while you were in there, so cool out a minute, please."

Carly's kiss to my cheek was so quick, it didn't register until I turned from Suzette to see my young friend stepping into the busy street. "See you, Rev," she whispered, blowing a kiss before checking both ways for traffic.

I stood watching Carly zigzag across Thirteenth as a grumpy Suzette sidled back over to me, a pocket-sized vanity mirror in her hand. "Well," she said, her tone indignant as she checked her lipstick and the look of her fresh flip hairdo, "excuuuse me for interrupting your attempt to hire a hooker."

"Now, see," I replied, flashing her a look, "poorly thought-out comments like that will get your husband fired when you become a first lady." I enjoyed teasing Suzette, who was one of the most vivacious and uncensored Christians I'd ever known, about the ways she'd have to tone herself down if Coleman, her husband of five years, ever followed through on his interest in becoming a full-time pastor. Even though the gospel group he had formed with my husband, Jesse, was a rising success, Coleman was clearly blessed with the skills of a natural preacher.

Once I explained exactly who Carly was, Suzette took the face-cracking news with a surprising dose of humility. "My bad, girl, I know that must not have been easy," she said after she'd started up her

Buick Lucerne's engine. She braved another look in my direction before pulling out into the street. "Did you ever tell Jesse about her?"

"Jesse and I have no secrets," I said, exhaling to release the butterflies her question raised. "I pulled back just in time, Zette." I had only myself to convince of that, of course. I hadn't followed through, but for a dark period in my life, I'd come dangerously close to breaching Carly's trust.

Throughout her pregnancy with Maisha, Carly had insisted desperately that although she was scared about her ability to be a responsible mother, she fiercely loved the little life growing within. For me, however, suffering the latest wounds of besetting childlessness, that hadn't been enough. Before I knew it, I had used my influence over this "baby having a baby" to convince Carly to give Maisha to me and Jesse. The only thing that saved all of us—me, Carly, and the baby—was a luncheon that Jesse had with Carly and me. By the time he had finished quizzing her, my husband had taken me into our bedroom, hugged me close, and whispered into my ear. "Carly wants that baby, sweetie, and God gave the little one to her, not us." Jesse said this, his voice wet with tears. "If I know that, I know you do." He held me back at arm's length, his eyes bucking me up with strength. "This is not the one for us, baby." Face-to-face with my flesh, with the emotional influence I had unfairly wielded, I had collapsed into Jesse's arms, unable to believe how I had violated my ministerial calling.

Though I knew I'd been forgiven, I whispered another confession before changing the subject with Suzette. "So what treasure did you glean from our little adventure tonight?" Besides saying it had something to do with Coleman, my sister-friend still hadn't explained just what type of mission she was on. The only thing she'd stated, repeatedly, was that it was a make-or-break issue affecting her and Coleman's marriage. Because Jesse and I had been the matchmakers for the two of them, I felt obligated to support her in this murky hour of need. While I was there for moral support, I knew good and well that my prayers were worth more than my physical presence, and I couldn't pray without some idea of what was happening.

"Look, Dionne," Suzette said finally, after staying silent for a minute, which was totally unlike her. "Maybe it's best if I just build my case and hold my cards until I have clear proof. Once I have you sold, I know I'll be ready to confront Coleman about all this." She slapped the steering wheel with forced playfulness. "You think I'm crazy," she said, "but I got a step closer tonight to proving my husband is on the down low."

"Suzette, Suzette," I replied, my tone just below a shout as I threw up my hands. "Will you stop jumping to conclusions? You can't talk like that about your husband—the father of your kids, for goodness' sake—without real evidence." From everything I knew of Coleman Hill, I couldn't conceive of Suzette's suspicions having any basis in reality. I was convinced this was a case of protective perception; Suzette feared her handsome, buff husband was having an affair and—in an age when J.L. King and Oprah had sisters fearing that every gay brother lay in wait to deceive them into bed—she preferred to believe her husband was the latest example of this "new" phenomenon. No way he could just be the typical brother who'd taken up with a more attractive, sexier woman, right?

Checking my look in the mirror on the overhead sun visor, I repeated the counsel I'd given my friend the first day she brought her suspicions to me. "You and your husband need to have a long talk before you play detective anymore, girl. He may have perfectly good explanations for what you think are signs of trouble."

"Please," Suzette replied. "Coleman and I have talked plenty. We always end up in the same place—the river of Denial.

"You want to know what I found out in that godforsaken, flea-bitten apartment?" Suzette's eye contact didn't waver, even though my eyes narrowed at the sound of her profanity. "Don't get 'holier than thou' on me, Reverend. I'm being real here, Dionne." She squeezed her eyes shut suddenly, as if wishing something away. "I've followed my husband to this place six different times in the past month," she said, her voice hollowing out as she raised a hand in testimony. "He always comes over here late in the afternoon, comes straight over from the studio. This is while he tells me he's laying down tracks with Jesse and the boys." She turned back in the direction of the apartment, though we were several miles away now. "He's making music with someone back there, and the only occupant of the apartment who signs Coleman in is some *man*."

"You're jumping way ahead on this, Suzette," I said, crossing my arms as she barreled through a stoplight, making me question her competence for driving right now. "There's any number of perfectly innocent reasons Coleman could be meeting with this guy."

Suzette's eyes flashed with disdain, though she kept them focused on the road. "The girl at the front desk says this guy he was visiting— Adrian Wilkes—works for the Republican National Committee, some sort of political strategist. What the hell does a politician have in common with a gospel singer, huh? Why they holed up in an apartment together for an hour or more at a time?"

"Suzette," I said, drawing my back up slightly, "do you hear yourself? The language, the anger, all when you have no real facts even. Do you trust your husband, or don't you?"

"Look." As Suzette braved a quick glance at me before turning back toward the road, I sensed God's spirit there, calming my spunky sister through my words. "It's not like I didn't hear the talk about Coleman back before we married, and it's not like we didn't talk about it then. But I can't wipe it out of my mind, Dionne."

I felt the strength of my argument lose steam as I considered Suzette's reminder. Coleman had first cut his chops on the gospel scene as a member of several of Kirk Franklin's different groups: the Family, God's Property, Nu Nation. I couldn't keep them straight, but Coleman had been a member of pretty much every one. From there, he'd become one of the most popular background singers for top-tier gospel artists, before finally forming Men with a Message and recruiting Jesse as the group's high tenor.

Anyone who heard Coleman sing knew he was going to be big, huge—a star who'd eventually be spoken of without the use of a last name. Maybe that was why tongues wagged about the brother's love life even when he was a relatively unknown background singer. As a minister who attended more than my share of gospel shows, I knew a fair share of people in the business and heard constant chatter from "gospel groupie" types who found Coleman's goody-two-shoes act suspicious. Not only did he not have a girlfriend, he had quickly developed a reputation for firmly rejecting girls who offered him their bodies, usually throwing in a heavy, scalding dose of quoted Scripture along the way. In an industry where every performer sang about sexual morality, but few practiced it, such steadfastness got you branded as one of two things: fanatic or homosexual.

In my personal experience as a sexual square, one accustomed to seeing my dates go bye-bye when I talked about saving myself for marriage, I had been tagged as the fanatic, a brand that hurt in my teens, but became a badge of courage once I hit my twenties. I guess God blessed me that way; I outgrew the usual desire to be "down" and "cool" pretty quickly, and never needed my ego stroked by misguided boys trying to take my treasure. I took pride in being known as the type of girl guys planned on marrying and raising babies with—I didn't need the dating-game nonsense, all I wanted was a good man and two or three healthy children in my life. At least I had the man.

As a fellow square, though, Coleman had been tagged with the "gay" brand, one inflicted with whispers, unfounded rumors, and innuendo.

By the time Jesse and I got serious as a couple, we were so tired of hearing him slandered that my husband finally asked Coleman point-blank whether it was true. For our money, Coleman's insistence that he was "of course" straight—combined with his eventual courtship of Suzette and the three beautiful stair-step children they quickly conceived—was all the convincing we needed. After all these years, though, it seemed Coleman hadn't quite sold his own wife.

For the rest of the drive back to Suzette's—where I had parked my car—we discussed those mean-spirited whispers of years before, comparing notes on exactly what we'd heard. "You just can't know what it's like," Suzette said, once we'd taken a seat in her massive great room. "I try to trust him, Dionne. But when he acts suspicious, what am I supposed to think?"

Suzette grabbed a remote off her stone-topped coffee table and flicked the family's wide-screen TV to life. We had a few minutes left before the Stellar Awards broadcast started, and probably less than that before the other wives of Men with a Message arrived to watch our husbands' performance. Like Suzette, those who had children—which was everyone except me—had put the kids with babysitters or family for the night. This was our time to bond and support our men in their ministry.

"You know," Suzette finally said as we sat listening for the front doorbell, "if I was married to Jesse, I wouldn't have to even worry about rumors of him being sweet, know what I mean? One thing's for sure, girl, your man never had any gay rumors to contend with."

"Oh, please," I said, stifling just how much her dig irked me. "Don't even act like you'd rather change places with me and Jesse." Not only was life with a reformed playboy full of unpredictable bimbo eruptions—Jesse had successfully fought off five different paternity suits since we'd been married, all of them dating back to the years before we met—but my husband and I had barely survived blows that had most couples filing papers, rushing into the arms of adulterous lovers, or setting a date with Judge Mablean Ephraim. For reasons I struggled to accept as His own, God had so far denied us the ability to become parents, through natural or adoptive means. There had been so much confusion, disappointment, humiliation, and frustration, that my parents, Suzette and Coleman, and two other good friends had each talked us away from the cliff of divorce at various points. In each case the only reason we hadn't jumped was that one of us—never the same one from one time to the next—was always looking for one more way to move forward.

"You-all have always made me so proud," Suzette said, tugging me out of my momentary wallow. "Do you know you're the only person I've shared my suspicions of Coleman with?"

"Oh, that's just 'cause you can swear a reverend to secrecy," I replied, chuckling.

"You couldn't have it more wrong," Suzette said, rubbing my hand tenderly. "I'm telling you, Dionne, because you're the only person who can credibly counsel me about sticking it out in a troubled marriage. Most of the folks I know who've faced infertility are on their second or third spouse right about now."

"I appreciate that," I said, unable to look at my friend as my eyes brimmed with tears.

The doorbell chimed suddenly, and Suzette hugged me close before rising from her couch. "Enough with the sad talk," she said, smiling and thumbing the wetness away from my eyes, then her own. "You-all's trials are coming to an end, anyway. I'm claiming right now that God is steering things to a happy conclusion with this adoption. And think," she said, winking, "this is just the first child of however many more God has in store!"

As my friend hustled to her front door, I stared at the large TV screen, where an earnest group of chunky sisters stood belting out the opening number of the Stellar ceremony. "Lay aside every weight," I whispered to myself, eager to unload the unease creeping through me. For some reason, while I was still worried about Suzette and her distrust of Coleman, something told me my run-in with Carly that evening hadn't been as random as it seemed. Was God trying to tell me something, placing me in the path of someone I'd once blamed for my inability to raise a child as if it were my own? Even after two years of prayer and confession, was there still some reason I was unfit for motherhood, some reason our adoption of Vanessa's baby was as doomed as the others?

3

Jesse

ngulfed by manufactured billows of smoke, the massive stage of Maryland's First Baptist Church of Glenarden sprang to life with fluorescent strobe lights. On cue, a piercing spotlight first hit Micah, Frank, and Isaac as they formed a line at midstage. Dressed in identical black blazers, white silk shirts, and carefully rumpled Levi's, they kicked into a meticulously choreographed routine. As organs, piano, guitar, and synthesizers filled the air, Coleman and I took our places at opposite ends of the stage, sending up a trademark harmony that sent the audience into a spiritual frenzy.

As I launched into Men with a Message's newly released single, surrounded by my faithful brothers in ministry, my mind was backstage, down the street, and around the corner. Even with the flash of the lights, with the thousand-plus worshippers thanking God for our inspiration, and despite the focus our new dance moves required, I couldn't shake the sound of footsteps. Micah's footsteps.

When we'd arrived earlier at Glenarden, the megachurch hosting tonight's area-wide youth benefit, everything had been cool. Two weeks after winning three Stellar Awards and becoming Grammy nominees for the first time, very little divided us. Since returning from Nashville, we had followed a productive but reasonable schedule, perfecting CD tracks in the studio by day and devoting evenings to our families. Home lives were running more smoothly than ever, meaning the devil had less room to play with our group dynamics. Each morning everyone had shown up for work with fewer insecurities, anxieties, and proverbial chips on the shoulder.

Shortly before the show began, we had huddled in the church nursery, which they provided as a dressing-room space, and joined hands with our band for prayer. Micah piped up just as I cleared my throat to kick things off. "Hey, I know we go on in a few minutes," he said, his voice low, but his tone urgent, as he swept his eyes around the circle, "but I don't want to waste time on this after the show, since we all need the freedom to head home as soon as the show's over. Whatever happened to that big article on us, Jesse? You know, the interview you were supposed to do with that Angie sister?"

My friend couldn't have chosen a worse moment to bring Angie up. In the two weeks since I had abruptly ended our conversation— the two weeks since she'd hit me with the bomb that she was plugged into the sins of someone *besides* me in our group—I had convinced myself the whole thing was a nightmare. To be honest, I had spent my plane rides to and from Nashville thinking of how to handle Angie's inevitable next call. I figured between the fact she had actual dirt on somebody and the fact that I'd revealed I had my own mess to hide, her interest in us wouldn't die anytime soon.

For whatever reason, though, she'd been AWOL since that night. I'd received no voice message, e-mail, or letter from the sister. There were a number of ways to read this development, of course, but I had gone with the most convenient one—given the many demands on my time. The fact was, Men with a Message was never going to captivate mainstream America; we were a gospel group whose biggest star was a has-been in the eyes of the MTV and BET crowds. Angie had access to R&B, rock, and hip-hop acts with much larger fan bases, and odds were that a story had broken around Beyoncé, Kanye West, or Maroon 5. We were probably on her back burner again; I was happy to stay there as long as possible.

"Yo, Jess, make it quick." Coleman had sprayed himself with one too many spritzes of his Polo cologne, and the high-powered scent nearly made me sneeze as he squeezed my hand and his words reminded me to answer Micah's question.

"Well, like I told you-all in Nashville," I replied, thanking God I didn't have to lie as long as I didn't say too much, "our interview was cut short, so she owes me a call to close the loop. I'll let you know when I hear something."

Micah's thick eyebrows rose in time with the skeptical frown on his face, and his double chin jiggled a bit. "One minute she couldn't speak to you fast enough—then the next you're an afterthought? That don't quite compute."

"Welcome to what used to be my world, brother," I said, sweeping my eyes around the circle while dredging up a convincing chuckle. "The media machine builds you up just long enough to tear you back down. Sometimes they jump right to the tearing down, know what I mean?"

"They can't tear us down before we get more press," Micah said, his somber gaze trained on me from less than a foot away. As the most active producer in the group, and the one most deeply rooted in scriptural knowledge, Micah was our true leader. Coleman was the star entertainer onstage, and the group looked to my opinion on all business matters, but when it came time to make the final decisions, Micah had a way of naturally guiding things. Right now, he was guiding me in a tutorial of the big picture for Men with a Message. "We came together five years ago, J. Law, because we wanted to reach more of the unchurched than most gospel groups. We want to grab up the young fans of urban radio and get them hooked on this Jesus thing. We can't do that if we don't get on the world's radar screen—this Angie sister *can* get us onto the screen, right?"

Meeting Micah's gaze, I wondered momentarily if he was the one Angie had the goods on. What secret could Micah Harris, who'd been a married father since eighteen and had never had a drop of alcohol in his life, have possibly done to embarrass the group and its mission? "Just keep in mind, there's no point pushing it," I said finally. "We don't want to get on the radar screen for the wrong reasons. Let's chill a few and see how things play out."

"If I may be the voice of reason, brothers, we don't have time to solve this right now." Coleman's tone was brisk and his voice rose as if to say his was the final word for now. "Call her, Jess, and update us next week. Let's pray."

We were still breaking from the prayer circle when Micah stepped over to me. "So, regardless of what Coleman's trying to say, we have an understanding, right?"

The dressing room was already a frenzy of activity again, with everyone checking their looks in the mirrors and flipping through their Bibles for inspiration, but Micah and I stood toe to toe whispering like two library patrons. "I told you I'd handle it. Got it covered."

"What did you mean," he said, shifting his weight between his stubby, chunky legs and checking the fit of his sport coat in the mirror, "when you said we don't want coverage for the wrong reasons?"

I had said too much while trying to get Micah off my back earlier; it was too late to run from it now. "I should have shared this before," I said, lowering my voice again, as if this were a major revelation. "Angie and I have a bit of history, know what I mean?"

The edges of Micah's frown turned up, but his eyes were not smiling. "You dog, you. So what, she's trying to trash the whole group 'cause you didn't stick around for breakfast after a one-night stand?"

"It's complicated, man," I said, patting him on the shoulder. "Let me smooth things over. It may take some time, but I probably have to make restitution for the past."

"That's all well and good, that's what the Spirit wants you to do," Micah replied, giving me a sudden, vigorous handshake. "But once you do what *God* tells you to do and make peace with the lady, I need you to do what *I* tell you to, for the sake of this group's mission. Did I mention that my cousin found out about that story your, uh, ex is writing?"

"Yes, Micah." Micah's wife's second cousin, or something like that, was an assistant editor at *Essence* and had apparently shared that Angie was shopping a big feature story on the gospel industry. Thus, his asexual hard-on anytime her name came up. "We will be in her story," he said, shaking a finger in mock self-righteousness, "or you will answer to me." Squeezing my shoulder, he bolted out the door as I mouthed a "whatever" in response.

Out there on the stage, the cavernous sanctuary filled to the brim with the faithful as well as those who simply enjoyed playing church, I fought the dialogue playing out inside my head as Coleman and I stepped to the edge of the stage, trading riffs and runs to the delight of the audience, his powerful bass countering my smooth, supple tenor. Poised there with our microphones aloft, we sang of Jesus' presence, His grace, and His faithfulness. For a few moments I remembered God was actually in control.

Twirling and pivoting between each line, pointing confidently toward teens and twenty-somethings overcome by the Spirit, I even caught Dionne's eye as the song wound down. I'd been hoping she could come, but hadn't been certain she'd make it because she had a big job interview for a ministerial position at Rising Son, a white nondenominational megachurch in Columbia. She had made it, though, even taking a seat two rows back from the stage. Still dressed in the olive double-breasted jacket and black slacks she'd worn for her interview, my beloved was a tall, voluptuous, and striking figure, youthful-looking but clearly wise beyond her years. Not to mention sexy. I blew a kiss toward Dionne, spurring a wide smile and a wink from my beloved.

The mental image of my wife motivated my quick movements when I returned to the dressing room with the group. In a flash I grabbed up my leather travel bag, my Bible, cell phone, and car keys and hustled out the door. I was halfway down the hall when I heard the dressing-room door open behind me. "Jesse!" Coleman's booming voice rang out, its echoes lunging after my heels.

What did he want? I'd been more worried about Micah trying to hem me up than Coleman, my best friend in the group. "Hey," I said, pivoting back to face him, but still moving toward the door. "Call me. I got to get home to my baby."

Standing there at the dressing-room door, Coleman looked away suddenly, his broad shoulders slouching. "Hey, man, I need to—well, go on, then."

Something in his tone slowed me down. "What's up?"

"Go home to your wife, man." One hand clawing at his short, tapered fro, he waved me away with the other as if I'd been pestering him. "I'll get at you later. God bless, brother."

"God bless you too, man. I'll holler." Turning back around, I heard the dressing-room door slam. Standing there, for reasons I was yet to understand, I was overcome with a brief, unexplainable shudder of guilt.

4

Dionne

I had just pulled into our garage when Jesse sped into the drive-way behind me. He met me at the door of the Volvo, taking my leather work satchel and in a swift motion planting a kiss on me with his smooth, cherry-tasting lips. "Well, Minister Law," I said, smirking as we separated for air, "you know how to take a sister by surprise. How'd you get away from the concert so fast? Don't you guys normally stick around for prayer?"

"They're fine without me for one evening," he replied, smiling as I played with his slick, curly hair. "What do you want for dinner? I thought I'd make Cornish hen."

"You're going to spoil me, boy," I said, pecking another kiss on him. "Don't think I'm not onto you. You've been making like Rachael Ray the past couple weeks, but as soon as the next CD drops, I'll be back to carrying the load in the kitchen. Guess I'll have to strap the baby to my back and pull out the pots and pans once he's here, huh?" Jesse assured me we'd figure out the best way to find the right balance;

after all, we had waited for years to become parents. We weren't going to let day-to-day routines spoil the blessing.

Once Jesse pulled his car into the garage and had dinner going, I joined my husband at the kitchen island and we took turns reading aloud from *What to Expect When You're Expecting*, a pregnancy book we had bought in order to track Vanessa's experiences as the day of our baby's birth grew closer. Now that she was nearing the third trimester, it was sobering to think of the myriad ways in which Vanessa's body was changing, the way that pregnancy dictated so much of an expecting mother's day. I could tell it affected Jesse too.

"It amazes me," he said, his chin tucked toward his chest, a grave look in his eyes, "that any mother can give her child up for adoption. It's no wonder so many of these women have flipped on us at the last minute, is it?"

A faint ringing invaded the recesses of my mind, and I fought off the sense of panic Jesse's innocent words had started. "God is giving us this baby," I said, my lips drawn tight, though I struggled to smile with my eyes. "He'll give Vanessa the peace she needs to hold firm with her decision."

As we sat down to our meal of the hen, a vegetable casserole, and monkey bread, Jesse raised a glass of chilled apple cider to mine. After he had blessed the meal, he smiled over at me. "In case I wasn't clear enough earlier, baby, I'm as confident as you are. This is the right birth mother, and the right baby. This is meant to be."

Emotion overwhelmed me and I reached for my husband's hand. "Jesse, I just want to thank you so much."

"Thank me?" Jesse looked like my words had knocked the wind out of him, as if the idea he'd done anything worthy of thanks were unthinkable.

"It's no accident we've made it this far," I said, feeling my forehead crease as my eyes welled with tears. "I haven't forgotten how evil I acted when I was at my worst." I had made peace with just how far gone I was when it hit me that I would probably never get pregnant. It hadn't been easy, hadn't been the type of pain I could pray or fast away, or banish by quoting Scripture.

After months of trying to get pregnant, the disappointment had first crystallized a little more than a year ago, when my eight-year-old niece, Allison—my *younger* sister Lisa's oldest child—asked me a simple question. *When will you and Uncle Jesse make a baby?*

I loved Allison to the core of her soul, always will, but for some reason her innocent question made me see my life through an entirely new prism. *How is that?* The question came. Despite constant effort, I still couldn't accept that after spending my entire life protecting my sexual purity, serving God, and praying for others, I was carrying a burden few women had to bear. Especially given that unlike many an "accidental mom," I truly wanted motherhood as part of my life.

I was in my parents' bathroom crying, minutes after Allison's question, when my father knocked quickly, then opened the door before I could request privacy. "I knew you weren't in here doing any business," he said, grinning in that outlandish way of his. Daddy had run his own lumber company for years, building a modest fortune on the strength of his blunt determination, but he enjoyed playing the clown at home.

I don't remember what I said in response, but I'll never forget his next words. "Just realize this isn't about you," he said, drawing me close and rubbing the back of my freshly permed head. "This is about that man I told you not to marry. The hustler."

This much I remember: telling Daddy to never use that term about Jesse again, then storming past him and out the front door.

If I didn't know any better, I'd think Jesse was reading my mind as we sat there, reliving the flashback with me. "There were a lot of outside influences pressuring you then, Dionne," he said. "None of that happened in a vacuum."

"Maybe so," I said, meeting his reverent gaze, "but that doesn't excuse anything I did or said. And while God ultimately repaired our breach, if you hadn't stuck it out when I tried to run you off, we'd have never seen this day."

5

Jesse

As guilty as Dionne's impassioned words made me feel as we sat there across the dinner table, I knew exactly what she meant. Nearly a year earlier, she and I had lain tensely in each other's arms, arguing whether to make another seemingly futile attempt at conception. Although my optimistic faith had been chafed and grated to the size of a mustard seed, I reached dutifully for the hem of my wife's slip, ready to merge again and give my seed another chance. That's when Dionne stopped me short, enclosing my left wrist in her soft, dewy palm. "Jesse," she had said, a flat expression in her eyes, "I think you should get checked out."

"What do you mean?" I froze in position, then leaned against the mattress on one elbow.

"I mean, I've been tested and poked like some guinea pig, and I know I'm part of the problem, but maybe you are too." Dionne's tone was clinical, her rich alto voice hollowed out by scars I could feel. Her eyes disregarded me, focusing instead on one of the paintings behind my head. "If you're as infertile as I am, we may as well know. Then we could just call this whole thing off."

"Oh . . . okay." Shifting in place, I reminded myself that I had initially planned to get my little guys tested to confirm their potency. Dionne and I had tried to get pregnant for nearly a year before she submitted to the testing that revealed her complications. Because her gynecologist counseled that without extreme measures it could easily take another year to achieve success, we had continued on for the past several months, confident that with God's wonder-working power, it was just a matter of time. Now she was concerned about me being part of the problem.

The possibility had crossed my mind. I didn't know of too many other childless thirty-year-old guys who had been with as many women as I had. I mean, it wasn't unheard of, but it couldn't be common by any stretch of the imagination. "If it will make you feel better, I'll go see Dr. Norton next week," I said, without covering the sigh creeping just beneath my words. If anything, the Spirit seemed to be hinting that Dionne and I prepare for the possibility we might never succeed at this precious mission. Digging further into which of us was less fertile felt like the wrong focus, but the anguish on my wife's face pressed me to honor her request. A part of me almost hoped the docs found something wrong with me—maybe that way I could more effectively share and ease the pain emanating from Dionne's pores.

My wife, however, had reacted to my offer by abruptly turning her back and burrowing into the covers. "Just forget it, Jesse."

"Baby, I said I'd go."

"You don't think there's any point. I hear it in your voice." She still wasn't facing me, content to show me her back. "Just remember that God works in mysterious ways, okay? Sometimes I think he's punishing us both for your lifestyle."

Actively concerned now, I hopped over Dionne and stood at her side of the bed, staring into her glowering expression. "Dionne, what are you saying?"

"Maybe you wasted your seed on all those sluts," she replied, sniffing and turning away again. "Dumping your sperm into all those condoms, forcing girls onto patches and pills, letting others abort children you helped create."

I told myself not to get defensive, but next thing I knew, I had folded my arms across my naked chest. "You don't think we serve a God capable of forgiving me, is that it?"

"He can forgive," she said, turning to me finally with tearstained cheeks, "but maybe he doesn't forget, Jesse. Maybe that's what explains why we've been cursed with this . . . this barren marriage. Maybe God would have struck any woman you married with fertility problems, something to make you pay for misusing women all those years."

"Do you hear yourself?" I demanded, reaching deep for a calm tone. "We've talked about everything I went through, Dionne, about all the wounds from losing my mom at two, to being called a 'bastard' by my own family. You know my womanizing didn't just happen, there were causes."

"Just get out!" Dionne's shriek hung in the air for what felt like minutes before I responded.

"You're hurting," I said through clenched teeth, my voice a whisper. "I'm not going to fight you, baby. I'm going downstairs and pray God fills you with his peace, okay?"

"I said, get out!" My calm exterior had made no impact whatsoever. Dionne sat up in the bed, pointed emphatically in my direction. "I'm through carrying all this guilt, Jesse! I see how you look at me every time we make love, and I see your face every month when the pregnancy test shows we failed—or maybe you think it's me who's the failure! You'd really like to be with someone else at this point, wouldn't you?"

"Baby, no—"

"Get out!"

Trying to understand how God had let things get this far—leaving this unanswered prayer to fester so long that it was literally turning my loving wife into someone else—I grabbed a pair of jeans, a sweat jacket, socks, briefs, and a pair of shoes. Five minutes later, I charged out of the house.

The following week I met Vanessa.

"Dionne, this is about what God has done," I replied to my wife now, tapping her hands and then kissing each lovingly. "We're each filthy rags. God's grace got us this far—"

From the kitchen island my cell phone emitted a shrill ring. Ignoring it, I finished my soothing words to Dionne and asked about her job interview, which she began to recount until the phone rang again. "May as well get it," she said, interrupting herself but staring toward the phone with a dart-sharp gaze. "Sounds like somebody's pretty impatient."

"I'll just shut it off," I replied, rising and moving toward the island. Grabbing the phone, I glanced at the caller ID screen and it stopped me cold: Angie. "Unbelievable," I said, hoping it was under my breath.

Dionne frowned. "Who is it?"

"A journalist who's been trying to set up an interview with the group." I did not want to get into the habit of lying to Dionne about anything besides the obvious. "Let me get rid of her."

"Hello, Angie," I said, straining to sound at ease as I walked past Dionne out into our foyer. "I'm gonna have to call you back. My wife and I are eating dinner."

"I'm waiting" was Angie's chipper-sounding reply.

"For what?"

"My apology, brother."

"Yeah, about that," I said, the nasty ending to our previous meeting replaying in my mind. "I get a lot of disrespect from the mainstream press, Angie, you know that. No one wants to believe that people like me accept Christ for serious reasons. They always chalk it up to the fact we couldn't cut it as real stars."

Angie sighed. "Okay, so I hear the violin strings now. Your point?"

God forgive me, I quickly recalled why I'd kicked this sister to the curb years earlier. "I overreacted with you. I'm sorry."

"Good," she said. "I'm not going to take up your time right now, don't want to intrude on your family time."

"Thank you."

"Don't thank me yet," Angie replied. "We're going to need another face-to-face, Jesse, and this time you may want to bring a friend with a thick checkbook."

6

Jesse

Sitting across the table from Dionne, I reached forward and gripped her left hand, raising a glass of our favorite sparkling cider in my right. "To the best mommy-to-be in the world."

My wife raised her glass to meet my toast, her freshly done bangs shaking softly as she grinned. "I think you've crossed into the land of exaggeration, Jesse Law. I'm not doing the hard work yet, remember. That's on poor Vanessa."

Poor Vanessa. I couldn't imagine that she knew it, but the words left a sour, accusing taste in my mouth. I gripped Dionne's hand more tightly, wishing to God above that I could take back the week during which I'd most likely conceived this child with Vanessa. But then, hadn't I convinced myself that was part of God's plan all along, his way of bringing Dionne the baby she so dearly craved?

"Hey, Brother Law." Dionne was smirking, but her words slapped me back into reality. "You trying to show off your muscles or something? Ease up, babe."

I released my grip on her hand and cleared my throat before sampling the cider. "My bad, I guess I'm finally feeling the impact of all that shopping." We had dedicated this entire Tuesday to baby preparations—three hours setting up our registry at Babies "R" Us, four hours visiting furniture shops spread between Baltimore and northern Virginia, and another hour at Home Depot picking out paint and wallpaper for the nursery. Now we were closing the day with a night in DC's popular Adams Morgan district, enjoying a steak dinner at one of our favorite restaurants before hitting a nearby jazz club.

Dionne set aside her house salad and winked at me. As sensual as she looked in her suede bolero jacket, silk blouse, and matching skirt, the look in her eyes would have gotten her in trouble if we were at home. "You know we still need to figure out the issue of child care, right?"

We had discussed Samuel's day-care arrangements daily as far as I could recall, but were still struggling with the best approach. Complicating things, oddly enough, was that we each had family members available to watch him during the day. Dionne's parents, who were retired entrepreneurs, had watched each of her sister's three children while they were infants, and were eager to go back into service with this little guy on the way. On the other side of the ring stood Mrs. Frankie Law, my stepmother—my mama, in every way that mattered. Mama had a few more obligations than my in-laws, including the hulking, aging house where she had raised me and my seven Law half siblings, a recent diagnosis of diabetes, and a bad back that could betray her at a moment's notice.

Bottom line, there were issues on both sides. Despite my mother's success raising eight children and her ongoing babysitting of dozens of grandchildren, Dionne was concerned about her health and her ability to reliably safeguard Samuel. And while Dionne's parents were perfectly capable and boasted a newly built, sprawling dream home, her father looked down on me with as much vigor as I disliked him.

"What if we just had them trade off days watching him, and suggest they each just keep him half of each day?" Dionne had clearly thought this through in detail. An index finger at her chin, she peered at me. "See, I could drop him at the day-care center where Suzette takes her kids each morning, then the grandparents could pick him up at noon each day. Does that sound reasonable?"

"Oh, my goodness! DC is getting to be too small." The woman's words clipped through the hearty conversation and smooth jazz filling the restaurant, and I grabbed the sides of my chair when I recognized Vanessa's voice. I didn't even have to turn my head; she had already stepped from behind me to the middle of the table, right between Dionne and me. "What brings you guys all the way into DC?" A black Gucci bag slung over her shoulder, Vanessa's lace-and-chiffon blouse, pin-striped trousers, and black pumps were those of a hot college student, not an expecting mom. Short and petite, she didn't appear "pregnant," until you caught sight of what looked like a monstrous beach ball just above her waist.

I sat still, calculating my reaction as Dionne's face slowly spread into a pleasant smile. Shaking Vanessa's hand, she nodded gleefully toward the birth mother's belly. "It has been weeks since we saw you," she said. "How are you feeling?"

"Oh," she replied, shifting her weight and patting at her stomach, "I'm getting by. I sleep a lot, eat a lot, and, believe me, pray a lot." When she winked at Dionne—playfully and convincingly—I wondered at her acting ability. She made the experience sound pretty trite, but in truth Vanessa was calling me daily with grueling progress reports I could never share with my wife.

"Well, trust me, you are in our prayers several times a day," Dionne said, placing a hand on Vanessa's stomach. My wife trained a lighthearted but curious gaze on me now. "Jesse, you're being rude, aren't you? Cat got your tongue?"

"Naw, come on," I said, chuckling and patting Vanessa's left arm. "I was just letting you girls get your digs in with each other." In my worldly days I had faced plenty of these incidents—caught between two of the many women in my life—and I was disturbed by how easily my flesh could reach back and draw on that experience. Refusing to show weakness or surprise, I looked up at Vanessa. "What are the odds we'd all wind up in the same place tonight? I didn't know any better, Vanessa, I'd think you were stalking us or something."

Vanessa started a bit, her eye contact breaking down before she recovered and smiled at Dionne while crooking a finger toward me. "Your husband is a mess." *And how*, I imagined she wanted to add.

"Hey, I'm just saying," I said, stretching back in my seat. "It looks bad, sister. Didn't you read all the regulations from the adoption agency? We're not supposed to have any contact without the agency's supervision."

Dionne sighed and aimed a scolding expression in my direction. "Stop being silly, Jesse. Who are you here with, Vanessa? Do you and your company want to join us?"

"Oh, uh, no." Vanessa's head dipped again, and I stifled a grin at how easily Dionne's well-meaning invitation had thrown her off. "I came here with a colleague from the hospital. She already went up front to pay, so I better go catch her."

"Okay." Dionne stood and brought Vanessa into a close hug, driving a stake of guilt through me in one motion. "God bless you. We can't thank you enough."

Vanessa pulled slowly from my wife's embrace, waving toward us both. "I'll see you guys at the agency in a couple of weeks, right?"

"Yes," Dionne said. She looked at me again. "Jesse, are you going to give her a good-bye hug?"

I wondered for a second if we were all on *Cheaters* or some other

Jerry Springer–inspired programming. Sucking my teeth, I stood and brought Vanessa close, the smell of her perfume reminding me too vividly of how we'd all come to be here. My back to Dionne, I whispered just loud enough to be sure Vanessa heard me, "Wait outside."

7

Jesse

Ten minutes later I was out on the street, after excusing myself to use the men's room. Vanessa stood under the front awning, awkwardly suffering the flirtations of a Hispanic valet. Gently taking her by the arm, I maneuvered her past the resentful-looking teen and we walked one door over, into a designer furniture boutique.

"Is this supposed to be a threat?" I said once we were inside, feigning interest in the merchandise, the sounds of aggressive traffic and energetic conversations seeping into my ears from the street. "You still think you're gonna raise this baby yourself, don't you?" Vanessa had backed off all the talk of keeping Samuel for weeks now, but this stunt contradicted that message.

"I'm trying to make a life-altering decision," Vanessa replied, her eyes looking both wounded and hard. "I need to observe you and Dionne together as much as I can, to see if you're really appropriate parents for my baby."

I didn't even speak the other part of the truth. *Our* baby. "We've talked about all this," I said, fondling a glass figurine on the shelf of a stainless-steel entertainment center. "It's settled, Vanessa."

"You settled everything," she replied, eyes glistening now, "with the old Vanessa. I'm not some *Fatal Attraction* tramp, Jesse, out for revenge. I'm a more thoughtful person, a more *spiritual* one, than the girl you met at your sister's house."

Vanessa's statement both impressed and jarred me at once, and the memories of those ill-thought-out, impulsive days came rushing back.

For six years I had defied Chris Rock's famous declaration that when it comes to fidelity, a man is as faithful as his options. Despite already being a has-been when I married Dionne, would-be Delilahs had lurked around every corner, hoping to feast on the fumes of my fame or maybe to simply prove that my spiritual transformation was a hoax. Time and again I battled temptation and my naturally flirtatious nature by calling on two strengths: a Holy Spirit–inspired ability to finally see women as more than body parts, and true devotion to Dionne and all she meant to me.

On the day I met Vanessa, though, the latter part of this equation had been battered to shreds. A week had passed since Dionne had suddenly and vengefully kicked me out of the house, and while we had talked some about the despair she felt about our inability to have a child, my shock and betrayal were still fresh.

In the week since my wife had so inexplicably turned on me, I had tried to keep moving forward, holing up in a Motel 6 and sharing our separation with just two people—Coleman, whom I'd asked to keep it confidential from the rest of the group, and Mama. I'd first stopped by to see her on a late Saturday morning, dropping my usual defensive, manly front and letting my anger, disappointment, and despair dribble out.

"You know your mama doesn't do psychotherapy, Jesse," she had said, dropping her vegetable peeler and steadying one of my little nephews in the center of her lap. She reached both hands toward me. "Let's pray." She delivered a stirring exhortation, a motivational plea of faith as intense as if she were in front of a congregation of hundreds.

When she was finished and I had sat back in my seat, she stood with the baby's chubby arms wrapped around her neck. "You said you were through recording for the day, right?"

"Well, yeah."

"Good. Then instead of sulking for the rest of the day, you can go do some good with your time." She whispered now, nodding her head toward the sleeping toddler. "On the fridge over there is your sister's latest phone number," she said matter-of-factly.

"She called today?"

"She first called me 'bout a week ago," Mama said, crooking an eyebrow as if offended that I might expect her to have returned Carol's call. Carol was not related to Mama or to my late father; she was my natural mother's 100 percent Caucasian daughter, an alcoholic with a gambling addiction to boot. In short, Mama was getting too old to "save" anybody beside her own children and grandchildren. Taking Carol's number off the fridge, I reached her and learned my sister was being evicted from her rented duplex and needed help getting her stuff out.

I followed Carol's directions to a block of ragged, one-story wood homes. Climbing out of my car, I nearly tripped over the remnants of a metal chair that had been haphazardly tossed into the middle of the street. As I regained my balance and shut my car door, a short, petite sister across the street climbed from a sparkling Lexus SUV. She had on a pink-and-green nylon sweat suit, which perfectly matched the Alpha Kappa Alpha sorority sticker on her car's back window, and had what looked like a nice grade of black hair tied back in a silken band. On such a gray, overcast afternoon in a pretty crappy neighborhood, she lit up the place.

Quite simply, neither of us—her in the classy ride and the saddity sorority colors, me in a freshly waxed BMW and a designer sport coat and jeans—fit in that neighborhood, and it made sense that we each froze in place at the sight of the other.

"Hello," she said, nodding with something that was neither a smile nor a frown. Her black-framed glasses made her look scholarly, but between her spotless auburn-brown complexion and the magnetism of her dewy brown eyes, I couldn't deny an immediate sense of attraction.

"Good afternoon," I replied, pausing in place as she crossed the street. As she stepped past both me and my car, I found myself guessing at how she had wound up living in a hood like this. Just as quick, though, I dismissed the curiosity; the more I dwelled on it, the sooner I'd have to pull up alongside her and get my questions answered. And that could only lead to trouble. . .

My eyes narrowed as I realized she was headed for the same address Carol had quoted me over the phone. Instead of watching the sister's graceful glide from behind, I stepped onto the sidewalk and grabbed the slip of paper I'd used from my pocket. We were headed toward the same address.

I arrived at the door just as the sister pressed the doorbell, impatiently clearing her throat as she did so. When she realized I was at her side, she placed a hand on her hip and scooted a step away. "May I help you?"

"I don't think so," I said slowly, wondering if Carol had just been too out of it to give me the correct address. "I'm here to see my sister."

The woman's pert little nose turned up with what felt like amusement. "Oh right. Sure." She put her hands on her slim but curvy hips, shaking her head as if dazed. "Carol really goes all out, concocting these stories about her various visitors."

So I did have the right place. "Hi, I'm Jesse," I said, extending a hand. "Carol's half brother—no surprise, our mother was all about integration."

"Oh, I'm sorry," she replied, chuckling softly. "You'll have to excuse me. My nerves are a little shot these days." She held onto my hand, an increasingly warm smile trickling into her gaze. "I'm Dr. Vanessa Bright, Carol's landlord."

"Go ahead, sister," I said, impressed. The girl didn't look thirty years old and not only was she healing folks' physical vessels, she was renting out properties?

Vanessa suddenly released my hand, as if she realized she had a bigger purpose than making nice with me. "Owning real estate is not glorious, Jesse," she said. "Case in point, I don't suppose you're here to help your sister finally move her lazy butt?"

Before I could answer, Carol swung the door open. Staying in the doorway, her left hand grasping the doorknob as if ready to slam it shut on us, she kept chewing hard on a stick of gum. "Thought you'd just use your key and come on in, boss lady," she said, aimless contempt in her voice. The contempt shifted to indifference as she glanced at me and pulled at her stringy blond hair. "What's up, Jesse? Gone bald, huh?"

"No, just experimenting," I replied, chuckling and pulling her into a stiff hug. I hadn't seen my sister in so long because the last time we'd had her over—at Dionne's insistence—she had complained the whole night that I never sent her checks like I had in my "superstar" days. "I can still grow a full head of hair," I said as Vanessa and I stepped into the small foyer, "but most of the guys in the group lost their hair at twenty-five, so I thought I'd try to fit in for a while."

"Oh, the problems some people have," Carol replied dryly. "Let's get to work." She jammed a finger in Vanessa's direction. "*You* can wait outside." I knew just enough about Carol's pattern to imagine the events that had prompted the hate emanating between these two: bounced checks, drug raids, and probably some damaged property. I had no doubt that Carol had tested young Vanessa's patience, and the landlord's reaction showed it.

Vanessa's small nostrils flared like a bull's when focusing on a red cape. "I'll wait wherever I please, Carol. You're already in violation by still being here. Don't make me call the police into this again—"

"Carol, let it go," I said, grabbing my sister's pudgy left arm and moving down the hallway. "Just show me everything that needs to go."

"Oh, please." Carol slapped my arm away and reached back for the door, clearly intent on slamming it. "I'm not letting this uppity witch tell me—"

"Take your hands off my property!" Vanessa's pupils flashed as she caught the door before Carol could shut it. Before I knew it, she had kicked the door back, knocking Carol over as she lit across the threshold. "You are such white trash!" Her eyes were trained on my sister, daggers poised for the kill.

"Hey, hey," I said, the gruffness in my voice telling me I actually feared for my wayward sister's health now. "I was on your side until this, Doctor," I said, backing her up against the door without touching her. "Gonna have to ask you to wait outside." I rested a palm on her shoulder, relieved to see her eyes cool and the pace of her breathing slow. "I'll have her out of your hair as quickly as possible."

The next minutes were a whirlwind. Vanessa wiped her eyes and nose and returned to her car. I wrestled a knife away from Carol and convinced her Vanessa's racial slur wasn't worth another trip to jail. I helped my sister carry a chewed-up cloth love seat smelling of orange soda, several plastic chairs, which looked older than me, and a flea-bitten twin mattress to her rusting pickup truck. More than a few times, Carol would finish dumping a trash bag of her miscellaneous junk into her truck or my car and then charge Vanessa's Lexus before I brought her down.

Once the cars were loaded, Carol complained of a stomachache and excused herself, apparently intent on inflicting a departing blow to the bathroom. As she bounced back inside, Vanessa climbed from her SUV, literally licking her lips for a fight.

I met her at the curb. "She'll be out in a minute, just chill."

"You need to get her some help," Vanessa replied, jamming a finger into my chest. "Your sister is seriously messed up."

"Is that your professional diagnosis?" I cocked my head at this beautiful but clearly conflicted woman. "I'm making a wild guess that your med school didn't train you to treat people the way you just handled my sister."

Vanessa frowned, looking around suddenly as if concerned her behavior was being filmed. "You don't know the history there, brother. You don't know the history."

"No doubt," I said. "What if we just said a prayer, Vanessa, right now? I'm sensing these types of outbursts aren't the norm for you. There's other stuff happening in your life, right?"

Vanessa broke eye contact for a second, hugging herself against the nippy early-spring air. "It's a long story, stuff going on with an old boyfriend." She had a funny look in her eyes now, but somehow I knew instantly what it was. "Oh, my God," she said. "The more you talk, the more I see it. Are you Jesse Law, the singer?"

Here's proof my heart was in the right place—I really wanted to say no. "That's beside the point, frankly. I'm offering you prayer, a source of peace through Jesus Christ—"

Vanessa pressed a warm hand to my chest, and this time the defensive anger was gone. A sure-footed look in her eyes, she smiled. "I know exactly what you're trying to tell me, brother, heard it all before. And I certainly don't need to hear it from you."

I crossed my arms, but prayed for patience. "How's that?"

She looked away for a moment before reestablishing eye contact. "I never owned any of your CDs exactly, but most of my girlfriends did back in the day, and none of them believe you've really found God. They think it's just another gig, since the pop scene dropped you like a hot potato." She frowned good-naturedly. "But then, what else would explain you making the time to come help your junkie sister?"

"I don't deserve any medals for this," I replied, laughing. "We're not here to talk about me right now, Vanessa. I'm not the one who just lost her cool. You should have been the bigger person back there."

Vanessa held out a hand. "Can you save me some time, I'm due back at the hospital in half an hour. Just give me one of those silly little gospel tracts and I'll be on my way."

I felt the Spirit leading me to combat this sister's cynical vibe, so I slapped her open hand playfully. "You've clearly been blessed, sister, with a gift to heal others, to treat the body. To do that, you need to be healthy yourself, and a relationship with Jesus Christ can help you—"

The front door of Carol's unit swung open and she breezed into view, still zipping up her ratty denim jeans. "All right, let's go, baby brother." I was proud of her; she didn't even acknowledge Vanessa's existence.

My eyes were still on Carol, who was hurtling toward her truck, when I felt Vanessa's hand slip over one of mine. "I shouldn't front, Jesse," she said, her voice low as if worried Carol would hear. "You probably saved my career today. If I'd done to your sister what I wanted to do, I might be getting booked at the local jail, for all I know."

Or you could be six feet under, I thought, keeping it to myself. Carol had sent more than a few abusive boyfriends to the ER over the years.

A mixture of spiritual concern and sexual heat stirred within me as I stared at this attractive little woman, and I once again felt the spirit of other entertainers who'd wrestled with the secular and the sacred— Marvin Gaye, Sam Cooke, and Al Green, for starters—resting on me. Converting her caress into a platonic handshake, I smiled into Vanessa's gracious eyes. "I just hope you can give God another chance in your life, that's all. I'm not trying to judge you. I just pray you can see God in the way I've been blessed to." I used this closing line at most every Men with a Message concert, but between my separation from Dionne and the sight of Vanessa at this moment, it left an artificial aftertaste in my mouth.

Vanessa smiled back, turned toward her Lexus, then glanced back in my direction. "I'm at Valley Hospital every day," she said, her tone respectful, but her intent clear. "Don't pray for me, call me."

Full of wary intrigue, I had smiled weakly, but said nothing as Vanessa walked to her car. *Let someone else save her,* a voice said. *Just let it go.*

As I now stood opposite Vanessa in the furniture boutique, the irony of her new claim—that she was a newly energized, spiritually mature woman—hit home. I knew I should be happy for her in an odd way, respectful of the distance she'd covered as a result of our shared trial, but the base truth of the day we'd met overwhelmed me. "I was going to mind my own business, just so you know," I said, regret and anger warring within me. "Don't tell me you didn't see my wedding ring. You should have just let me walk away, Vanessa."

"I know, I know," she said, grabbing my shoulder as I turned to leave the store. "I fanned the flames, Jesse. I'm trying to make up for it now by letting you two have this baby." She sniffed as her eyes began to fill anew with tears. "But I have to do it my way."

8

My alarm clock hummed to life, forcing me to finally get off my back and hop out of bed. Taking a final lingering look at my sleeping husband, I dashed to the dresser and tapped the clock back into silence.

I had been awake for ten minutes, stealing precious glances at Jesse and thanking God for minting gold out of the rotten ore resting inside each of us. We were still seeing a Christian therapist every couple of months, still healing from the wounds of our recent past, but with our upcoming adoption, everything had fallen back into place. I lived every day for the opportunity to raise a child with Jesse, and I was excited about the unique ways in which God would use us as parents.

As I padded into our master bathroom, I wondered how much longer Jesse would sleep before coming in to "visit" me. While there were other aspects of our strengthened bond that I enjoyed more—long walks in Rock Creek Park, weekend trips to spa resorts, and songs Jesse was writing specifically for me again—his heightened sex drive was the most persistent.

As newlyweds we had fulfilled his early promise to help me make up for "lost time," as he lovingly referred to it. For the entire first three years of our marriage, my girlfriends' jaws would drop when I answered their queries about how often, where, and how long my husband and I expressed our love for each other. "Uh, that ain't natural" was my sister Lisa's reply when I first told her. My hairdresser, Louquisha, who had three teenagers by the age of thirty, swore I needed counseling. "You sounding like a nympho to me, girl."

Everyone's reactions were entertaining in those heady days, but once I went off the pill and we prayed about becoming parents, everything changed. First I became more self-conscious every time we lay down, obsessing over positioning, rhythm, ovulation cycles, room tempera-tures, you name it. By the time I looked up nine months later, not only was there no baby, but our record-setting lovemaking frenzy had dribbled into a pattern that my eighty-year-old grandparents could have put to shame.

"And how may I help you this morning?" The sudden rush of Jesse's breath on my neck and the scratchy sound of his voice reminded me that happy days were here again. Now that we had survived last year's short separation and were finally growing our family, both my husband and I had relaxed, our natural chemistry again flowing as it had in those early years. I turned and kissed him deeply, our loving bond melting away the vagaries of morning breath.

Once we were finished fondling each other, I turned my attention to my side of the vanity, first washing my face, then brushing my teeth as Jesse took a seat between the two sinks. "So you know I'll be hot if you don't come back home with a job offer today, right?"

Now that a week and two follow-ups had passed since my first in-terview for youth minister at Rising Son, my protective husband had grown increasingly suspicious of the church. Men with a Message had performed at Rising Son several times in the early days of their career, the first contemporary R&B gospel act to do so. Jesse's friend Micah had attended Bible college with the younger brother of Pastor Norm, Rising Son's senior pastor, and Jesse had even attended a few Bible studies with Pastor Norm and other church leaders. All that said, he still didn't quite trust their motives in interviewing me.

"I know you think they're just stringing me along," I said, stepping over to our shower and reaching in to start the water. "I don't see that, honey. Everyone I talked to says Pastor Norm always takes candidates through multiple interviews like this." So far, I had survived intense interviews with the pastor and his associates, as well as a panel of ministry leaders and the board of trustees.

"Maybe they'll prove me wrong and come correct," Jesse said, winking. "Truth told, I'm probably scared they'll make you an offer, because you just might accept."

"Jesse, please," I replied, sighing as I tied up my hair. "Don't start with the black-power stuff again. You're talking to a proud Howardite here." I had yet to figure out how my half-white husband, who had spent his childhood on the chitlin' gospel circuit and his twenties in drug-filled concert halls and New York studios, saw fit to lecture me on the racial implications of working for a white ministry. "Don't forget," I said, looking over my shoulder as he lusted after my now-naked figure, "I'm the one who heard Kwame Ture, Steve Cokely, and Louis Farrakhan speak live, every year I was in college. I know the dangers of ministering with the 'enemy.' So get off my back!" I flicked my tongue at him playfully.

As I showered, Jesse and I continued the conversation over the rush of the water. We didn't really view our "fair-skinned" brothers in Christ as the enemy, even if we liked to joke about it every now and then. The simple truth was, not even the blood of Jesus completely elimi-nated the natural cultural differences and charged history that some-times separated white Americans and those of color. As a child I had faced my share of racism at the private Christian school where my parents enrolled me and my sisters, and even in my years of adult ministry, I had seen the sins of our fathers rise up to shatter well-meaning attempts to live in Christ-centered, color-blind harmony.

Jesse knew I was fully aware of that reality, and that's why he stopped hassling me a few minutes before I left the house, after we'd shared a light breakfast of intentionally burnt toast, juice, and scrambled eggs. "Knock 'em dead," he said, kissing me after we had prayed that God's will be done.

I wasn't miserable with my present job, organizing teen evangelism and educational programs for a Missionary Baptist community development corporation, but there were times I felt like I had done all I could do at Mt. Calvary. I was ready for a new challenge, a way to "expand my territory," in the words of Jabez.

Pastor Norm himself greeted me at the main entrance of Rising Son's sprawling Columbia campus. A tall, lumbering man with an unusually thick brown moustache and a matching mass of carefully combed hair atop his long, oval head, he was dressed this morning in a freshly starched olive oxford shirt and a pair of efficiently ironed navy Levi's. "Good morning, Dionne," he said, his smile a little tight, but his eyes pleasant and warm. "You really didn't have to go all out," he continued, holding the door open and nodding toward my teal pants suit and black pumps. "We're all friends around here now."

Determined to be myself, I crossed my arms and cocked my head as if annoyed. "Oh, I don't have to dress because you're already impressed?"

"There is no doubt about that, Dionne, trust me," the pastor said, tapping my shoulder playfully, then pointing toward a nearby staircase. "Let's go to my office, shall we?"

We walked up one flight of steps, then took an elevator to a third floor I hadn't realized existed. As he swung heavy oak doors shut behind us, Pastor Norm quickly dumped the pleasant small talk we'd made going up the stairs. "Have a seat, please. I don't know that you'll like what's coming, but I'd be irresponsible not to ask you some important questions."

I settled into a thick leather chair across from the pastor's tall, wide, expensive-looking desk. "Okay," I said, crossing my legs. "Let's hear them."

Taking a seat in the chair next to me, he didn't mince words. "You're about to become a mother, praise God, and I couldn't be happier for you and Jesse. Question is, can you promise me that won't distract you from the duties we'd need you to handle here?"

"You can't ask me that," I said, the words snapping out before I could be sure they were true. It was easy to forget that nonprofit and religious employers often got away with stuff the usual corporations couldn't pull, but this would never hold up in court. "With all due respect, if you want to hold motherhood against me, that's between you and God."

Pastor Norm crossed his legs now, but kept his eyes on mine. "I see," he said, tapping his chin. "Well, let's lay that aside for the moment. You know I have another concern about you. I hear rumors you're not a fan of our commander in chief."

"Excuse me?" *This is not happening*, I thought. Jesse and I had joked for years about the fact that while Pastor Norm preached a good sermon for a white boy, he couldn't help slipping in a plug for the Bush administration whenever he got a chance.

"I feel duty-bound to speak out on political issues when the Lord leads me," the pastor continued. "Now, I know that my first duty is to teach Scripture, but if I can illustrate certain points by linking them to current events, I think that's the responsible thing to do. Do you agree?"

"Actually, I do," I replied, feeling quite freed by the very fact he had raised the subject. Just to make sure I was clear, though, I made it a point to sharpen my answer. "You see, if I were in your shoes, I would feel obligated to point out the many ways in which *your* commander in chief has violated tenets of Scripture." I just barely fought the temptation to do a laundry list—the war in Iraq, neglecting Hurricane Katrina's evacuees, slashing programs to help the poor while cutting taxes for the wealthy, to name a few—because if I'd gone there, we'd have argued all afternoon long.

"Mmm-hmm," Pastor said, tapping a cheek in response with his mouth closed. "So I've just asked you one sexist question, and another that could indicate I'm some right-wing bully. How does that square with what your friends in the Black Church community think of me? Or more important, how they think of this church?"

Shrugging, I replied, "There's no easy way to say it, Pastor. From the kids I'm ministering to now, to the black pastors throughout DC and Maryland that I work with, they all think I'm nuts for having the slightest interest in working here. They think by coming here, I'd be abandoning the very people I've spent years helping, to be window dressing for a church serving middle-class white folks with no real problems." I was on quite a roll, but I stopped myself there before revealing that my own husband was among these very critics. After all, this was about me, not Jesse and his group.

Pastor Norm smiled, stood, and snapped his fingers. "That's why I'm offering you the job, Dionne," he said. His tone grew increasingly fervent, preacherlike, as he walked to his desk and grabbed up a manila envelope. "All details of the offer are there. I told you that God has laid on my heart a call to take this church to a new level. We're not going to get there without new blood, Dionne, people with different experiences, new insights, and, most important, the courage to share them. Rising Son needs you."

I resisted the temptation to open the envelope, resting it instead on my lap and smiling in barely contained enthusiasm. I had really applied for this position as Rising Son's youth minister on a whim, after Micah called us about the opening. I had been vaguely curious at first, but with the offer now a reality, I realized that it presented an unbelievable opportunity, at least as long as Pastor and his team hadn't been pulling my leg. Raising the envelope in my left hand and pointing to it with my right, I gave him another chance to dim my growing excitement. "Does this offer package lay out details on the youth ministry's expanded budget?"

Pastor took a seat on the edge of his desk, a few feet in front of me now. "Dionne, I hope that at least you don't doubt *my* sincerity about this ministry's growth." He had been candid all along that some of his well-heeled members were uncomfortable with his plan to establish youth evangelism centers in the poorest sections of DC and Maryland. Pastor Norm had a revolutionary vision: In his dreams Rising Son would use the centers to provide first-class tutoring, basic health care, and Bible-study resources to children in these low-income neighborhoods. Once they had shown these children's parents how sincere they were about improving their lots in life, they would start a shuttle service to bring these families out to the church's sprawling campus for the most popular of Rising Son's four Sunday-morning worship services. If the man had his way, God would use him to build the most radical example of racial reconciliation the country had ever seen.

Now he wanted me to be the foot soldier who would make it happen.

Walking out to my car a couple of minutes later, after telling Pastor I needed a couple of days to discuss the offer with Jesse and seek the Lord on it, my ears rang with revelation. After spending seven years laboring in relative obscurity while my husband moved through numerous stages of fame, I felt something shift in my world order. With such a remarkable opportunity in front of me, it wasn't impossible to picture a future where Jesse and I would be equals in the eyes of the public, he the big-time gospel singer, me the much-noted "mainstream" youth minister.

Sliding and snapping my seat belt into place, I took a breath and resisted the temptation to mentally fast-forward through all the things I could accomplish if I accepted this job. I had a sensation that I had already moved beyond a sense of how God wanted to use me, into very fleshly, prideful territory. When had I ever had a problem with taking a public backseat to Jesse's career? When we walked the aisle together, my two goals had been simple and united: to love and honor him unconditionally while glorifying God. Matching his income, public profile, or reputation had never been part of the deal.

Before starting my ignition, I shut my eyes and sought my God in prayer, quoting from James 4:6 and its promise to give grace to the humble. "Lord, still my pride," I said, "fill me with your Spirit right now so that I don't lose sight of your will and what that means for this offer—"

My cell phone, which I had set into one of the cup holders to my right, began pulsing at just the wrong time, its subtle movements sending it bouncing against the plastic surrounding it. I instinctively grabbed the phone to make sure it wasn't an emergency involving Jesse, my family, or one of the troubled youth under my wing.

When I recognized the number as Suzette's, I almost put it back down, but something told me to go ahead and answer. "Hey, girl."

"Dionne." The voice was muffled, struggling to get my name past its lips.

Momentarily pulling the phone back from my ear, I wondered if I'd interpreted the number incorrectly. This person's thin, uncertain tone sounded nothing like my girl. "Who is this?"

"I—it's me." She was just loud enough now that I knew it was

Suzette, but she didn't sound right. "Dionne, can you help—can you help me out?"

I started my engine, shifted my car into reverse. "What's going on, Suzette?" I said while fishing for my phone's earpiece.

"Girl, I've gone and done it now." Her strength seemed to be returning, but she still sounded wiped out.

"Suzette, honey, I can just barely hear you. What happened? Were you in a car accident or something?"

A hoarse, whiny chuckle escaped; then she said, "Or something. Something only you can know about."

"Oh no." My stomach churned, an unsettling sensation spiking its way from the pit and working its way into my throat as the realization spread: Coleman. "Are you okay?"

"I c-caught him red-handed, girl," Suzette said, hacking and coughing violently. "Followed that Adrian boy whose apartment we staked out a couple of weeks ago—you'll see, Rev, I was right all along." She paused suddenly, then screamed, "Oh God, it hurts!"

"Suzette, do you need me to call 911?" The fear in the pit of my stomach had nearly turned to panic. I had to know where she was.

The other end of the line was quiet now; my friend's breathing was all I could hear, and even that sounded increasingly shallow.

"Suzette!" I was the one screaming now. "Don't make me come through that phone! Tell me where you are, right now."

Again, silence.

Listening intently, praying desperately, I sped through Rising Son's campus toward the exit driveway. I had no idea where to go, but I had to get Suzette to tell me while she still had time.

9

Jesse

I was stuck in the midst of traffic on the George Washington Parkway, the wrong woman seated next to me. Moaning every couple of minutes, her eyes shut in search of a nap, Vanessa lay in the passenger seat. I braked when traffic in my lane suddenly slowed again, stealing a sideways glance at the woman carrying my child.

"Hey," I whispered, not wanting to completely disturb her sleep. "Can I get off at any of these upcoming exits?" We were in danger of being late for her biweekly visit to the gynecologist. I had never driven Vanessa to these appointments before—since learning of her pregnancy, I had made it a point not to be alone with her—but I had called that morning after seeking God about how to deal with the deception she and I were inflicting on Dionne. As angry as I was about her latest "stalking" act, her increasing sense of peace about letting Dionne and me raise Samuel had me questioning my own assumptions.

I had always ruled out the possibility of telling Dionne about my betrayal, but lately I had been thinking more about my stepmother's love for me. After my natural parents' death, Mama had grafted me into her large, religious family tree, despite knowing I'd been the product of her own husband's affair. How could I come through all that and not think Dionne was capable of eventually showing little Samuel—and eventually me—the same type of love?

In talking with Vanessa the day before, I had confessed to some of these misgivings, and she in turn had apologized for her surprise visit in Adams Morgan. It had been the least confrontational conversation we'd had in weeks, but near the close of it, she'd admitted to feeling extremely wiped out and needing someone to drive her to this appointment. She was so beat, she'd even taken her first days of sick leave in her two years at the hospital.

I had taken pity on her, and now we were trapped on a parkway that felt more like a parking lot. "I've never seen it this bad before," she said, shielding her eyes against the beam of sunlight as she opened them. Surveying the sea of cars stretched before us, she sighed. "Hopefully, it'll clear up."

I felt my teeth gritting as I asked, "Remind me again why you aren't seeing one of your colleagues at Valley, instead of driving forty minutes out of your way?"

"There's the anger, I was waiting for it." Turning toward her window, Vanessa ran a hand through her hair, which was styled in a lush bob. "Don't act stupid, Jesse. You know I don't want the hospital staff all up in my business. As it is, they're placing bets on who fathered this baby."

A lump in my throat, I nodded in recognition of her common sense. It amazed me sometimes how my joy over little Samuel's pending arrival—and my fear at being found out as a lying adulterer—had made me blind to the very real trials that Vanessa faced. As a professional black woman who had done everything right careerwise, it couldn't have been easy for her to have to waddle around her workplace with everyone knowing she hadn't been in a real relationship when she got pregnant. There were plenty of "liberated," humanistic women who would have had no shame in their game in this day and age, but Vanessa was no longer one of them. While she was a "lapsed" Christian when we first met, she was old-fashioned enough to be initially devastated at the thought of being unmarried and pregnant.

"I know you didn't want to waste your time with me today," she said now. "So I do appreciate the sacrifice you're making in getting me over here. I mean that."

"I'm just doing what any responsible father should do for his baby's mother," I said, my chin tucked toward my chest.

From the corner of my eye, I saw Vanessa shift carefully in her seat, like a trainer preparing to wake a sleeping lion. "Jesse?"

"What's up?"

"I meant what I said earlier, I think I'm okay about you guys raising the baby. I can go through with the adoption. Dionne deserves this baby, if no one else."

Clearing my throat and accelerating the car as the road began to clear in front of us, I glanced over toward Vanessa. "You can't know how true that is."

"One thing. Why can't we just tell her the truth?"

We had come to the right exit finally; clearing my throat again, I hopped onto the ramp and wished I could rewind that question right back into Vanessa's mouth.

"It shouldn't be an unthinkable idea." She placed a hand to my shoulder as we came to a stop at the bottom of the ramp, where a red stoplight awaited us. "I think it's what God's asking of all of us. Like I said, my connection to Jesus has been rekindled, Jesse."

I couldn't answer her. At first blush at least, her words felt too convicting.

"I want to be forgiven," Vanessa said. "It's best for me, for my ability to really accept God's salvation, and, more important, it's the best way to make sure Samuel is born under a blessing and not a curse."

"Vanessa, I can't—" I cut myself off, the imagined sight of Dionne's horrified expression, her crumpled soul, boring a hole right through the middle of me.

"I want to be forgiven," she repeated as I turned into the lot of her doctor's office. "I want my baby—your son—born under as much of God's favor as possible."

In that instant, as I pulled into a space near the door, my soul cried out within me. *Lord Jesus.* Was this what it had come to? Momentarily forgetting Vanessa was there, I shut my eyes and asked God's forgiveness for what felt like the hundredth time. How had I gotten here again?

"Can we just tell her, Jesse?" she asked. "Please?"

I climbed out of the car and walked around to the passenger side door. Opening it for her, I said, "You better get in there, no sense in missing your appointment. Have to keep that baby healthy."

Once I had helped her struggle to her feet, Vanessa ran a hand over my cheek. "I promise, nothing else would change. Matter of fact, if you agree to tell her everything, I'll sign papers tomorrow to make the adoption official." She patted my arm and began waddling toward the door. "I'll be back as soon as I can."

I checked my watch. I had scheduled a late lunch with Angie Barker about her article on Men with a Message; if we hit another bad patch of traffic on the way back to Vanessa's, I'd have to scoot that back. At the moment I had bigger worries. Walking back to my driver's side door, I waved Vanessa to go inside. "I'll be out here." Collapsing into my seat, I shut the door and gripped my steering wheel as the Holy Spirit embedded a painful truth deep into my soul.

I wasn't making the best of a bad situation.

I wasn't protecting Dionne.

I wasn't saving Vanessa from the trials of single motherhood.

I was living up to the doubts Dionne's own father once expressed to me. "I know all about your father's reputation, God rest his soul," he had said the day I asked him for his daughter's hand. "I have to be honest with you, son, I'm not so sure you're any different from the old man." He had gripped my hand as if intent on crushing it, and though I'd tightened my own grip and practically cracked a couple of his bones, he struggled not to show it. "You better prove me wrong."

My shoulders shaking suddenly with laughter, my eyes tearing up, I sat in my car, no longer caring who saw or heard me. The irony was, the only way I could ultimately prove my father-in-law wrong was to first prove him right.

10

Jesse

My head still reeling from my budding decision to tell Dionne the entire ugly truth, I just barely managed to walk tall as I stepped into the lobby of the Landover Starbucks, where I'd agreed to meet Angie. She was already seated at a table near the back, and I steeled my spine and cracked my knuckles as we made wary eye contact. The sister was dressed to the nines— a sharp maroon-and-navy dress that could have been picked out by Oprah's personal shopper—and had her hair styled in an intricate layer of French twists. When I had seen her last, Angie had been in low-key chill mood; I took her overt "fly girl" act as a sign that she meant business today.

I had never really addressed her wisecrack from the other night, when she'd all but hinted at expecting a payoff to keep whatever secret she was sitting on quiet. No, I wasn't going to let her throw me anymore than she already had that night in the alley. Instead, I had smiled calmly on my end of the phone and suggested she meet me here today. She'd sounded surprised initially, suggesting I might want to meet her someplace completely private—like her house—but I had stuck to my guns, insisting if we were going to talk, it was this suburban coffee shop or nowhere. The truth was, I wanted as many folks as possible around when I met Angie.

That whole "safety in numbers" thing.

"You always leave your women waiting, Jesse?" Her shapely legs crossed, Angie kept her eyes on the BlackBerry in her lap as I removed my suit jacket. "I mean, you always kept me waiting back in the day, but you were in demand then." She looked up as I eased into the chair across the way. "These days, not so much."

"Love you too." Huffing good-naturedly at her little crack, I shifted in my seat, trying to get comfortable while playing with the cuff links on my silk shirt.

"I had a memory about us the other day," she said, reaching over and resting both of her hands on mine as I tried to figure what drink to order. When I nonchalantly began to ease out of her grasp, she raised her eyebrows as if offended. "I'm not making you uncomfortable, am I?" She looked over my shoulder, smirking. "I do believe a couple of ladies in here have already recognized you. You afraid this little lunch will start some rumors?"

Chuckling, I said, "Like you said the last time I was concerned about that, ain't nobody thinking about me." I still slid my hands free, though, taking the opportunity to rap her knuckles playfully. "Now let's finish that conversation we were having."

Angie sat back in her seat, crossing her legs again and rolling her shoulders confidently. "Oh, we're going to do that."

"All right, then," I replied, scooting forward in my seat and shutting my eyes. "Join me in prayer first?" *Lord,* I prayed in advance, *I'm not playing games. Please step in here and save Angie and me both from ourselves. I have enough sin to repent for as it is.*

She scooted her chair back from the table, nearly popping out of her seat in the process. "What do you think you're doing?"

My hands locked together, my tented elbows on the table, I opened my eyes slowly and innocently. "I'm thanking God for the food we're about to receive," I replied, shrugging and trying to ignore the eyes of a young white guy at the next table. "I'm asking Him to guide our discussion. You have a problem with that?"

"Well, I mean—" Angie wouldn't look me in the eye; her gaze wandered about the store like an aimless child. "How would I have a problem with prayer, Jesse? You do know I'm saved too, right? Have been since the year my son was born."

I finished my prayer, let Angie say one too; then we went up and ordered our drinks. Once we returned to our table with hot beverages in hand, I nodded in her direction, trying to sound patient. "So, with God watching over us, why don't we start from scratch, home slice. Just what type of story are you writing about Men with a Message?"

Angie took a sip from her caffè mocha before answering. "I suppose I'm still deciding how you-all will fit into the narrative," she said. "You may as well know, the possibilities are endless."

We worked on our drinks as Angie gave me the lowdown on her article. It turned out Micah's expectation that it was something for *Essence* was only partially right. Angie was crafting a no-holds-barred, "tell-all" exposé of the gospel culture's underbelly, under the premise that the music of the Black Church was a window to its soul.

As disillusioned as I'd been with the church as a teen, Angie put me to shame. She seemed intent on leaving no skeleton unexploited, determined to blow all attempts at public relations and image management to shreds. She had used contacts at every level of the church culture—secretaries, ministers nursing grudges, gospel producers, road managers, security guards, and background singers—to craft a living, breathing portrayal of abnormally flawed humans holding themselves out as God's purified vessels. Without naming names, she nearly salivated as she ran down the list of "sins" she'd be unveiling: gambling addictions, incest, serial adultery, embezzlement, prostitution, manslaughter, and, of course, down-low homosexuality.

"I still have some time before I choose which magazine to go with," she said after going back to the counter for a blueberry muffin. Cutting into her first slice, she spoke of the interest she had from editors at several publications, including *Essence*, but she planned to hold out for *Rolling Stone*. "This is big news to white folks." She was laughing now, holding a hand over her mouth to keep bits of muffin from escaping. "I mean, black folks already know how dysfunctional our church culture is."

Absorbing the depth of her hit piece, knowing my group was squarely in her sights, I stewed in silence for what felt like minutes before Angie spoke again. "Truth be told, Jesse," she said, peering at me with a tinge of sympathy, "Men with a Message could either be the saviors of the piece—you know, inspiring examples living up to their public image, with the extra dramatic kicker of *your* personal transformation—or you-all can be, well, part of the problem."

I finished the last swallow of my tea, my insides churning for reasons unrelated to the chai seasoning in my drink. I had just prayed about coming clean with Dionne about Vanessa and the baby. A part of me wanted to do just that, but now I was staring into the eyes of someone who'd unquestionably make it her business to publicize my sin beyond the four walls of my home. *Who gave her the right?*

Knowing my flesh was at war with the Holy Spirit, I lowered my voice and scooted closer to Angie. "The cute and cryptic act is already tired," I said. "Get to the point, okay?"

Angie hesitated a moment, seemingly recognizing the defensive anger I felt boiling just behind my eyes. "Before we go any further, you may as well know this much. There's a part of me, Jesse—a petty, immature part—that still kind of hates your guts for never taking me seriously back when we dated."

Yeah, well, I thought, *not sure how much I've improved in that department, even a decade-plus later.* I had nothing to say.

"The easy thing to do," she continued after another swig of her mocha coffee, "would be to just drop this bomb on you and your boys in print. I could leave you scrambling, out of your mind right at the moment your group's career is taking off."

When she went quiet suddenly, I decided to go with humor. "But," I said, rolling my eyes playfully, "you won't take that route because . . . why?"

"The other way I could get you," Angie said as if she hadn't heard me, "is blackmail. And it's not like I don't need the money, honey. This journalism gig doesn't pay that well, especially when my baby's headed for college in a few years."

"You're saved, Angie," I said matter-of-factly. "You don't make a habit of blackmailing your subjects."

"Never done it before," she said before shoving the last bite of her muffin into her mouth, "but there's a first time for everything."

As irritated and edgy as I was, she actually had me amused now. "You realize my take-home pay is roughly equal to the average bureaucrat's, right? And my wife works for a street ministry."

"Oh, please, sexy," Angie said, her tongue playfully flitting between her teeth. "You and I both know I'm not interested in your money. I'd be interested in the dollars you can access through your friends on the 'worldly' side of the business."

"Angie," I said, pushing my chair back slowly, "you actually think you're going to sit here and shake me down?" Not wanting a scene, I stood but resisted the urge to lean over the table and stare her down. "I'm going to the bathroom. While I do that, why don't you say a prayer and realize you're not making any sense? You've already told me you don't have anything on me." I knew those words had gone too far, could feel the rebellious, hotheaded spirit that Christ had helped me control coming back to run things. I had a figuratively loaded gun pointed at my head, but I had to call Angie out on this. At least I would know what I was up against.

She looked up at me with a smile loaded with false innocence. "Oh, did I say I had no dirt on you? I may have misspoken."

Every muscle in my back coiled, tightening in preparation for what could come next.

"Oh, Jesse," Angie said, waving lightheartedly and reaching beneath her chair and retrieving her purse. "Far as I know, you're a model husband—this isn't about you. You're still a household name in some communities. If I had dirt on you, honey, I wouldn't have a choice but to print it."

Registering the candid ease with which Angie had said those words, a shiver danced up my spine as she reached the long fingers of her left hand into her purse. Refusing to break eye contact, I set my jaw, slid back into my seat, and realized she was still talking.

". . . So maybe this is about you—I think you want Men with a Message to succeed, that you sincerely believe God is using all of you to spread the Gospel. I get that, I really do, and that's why I'm going to leave money out of this." She let a beat pass as she retrieved a slim stack of photos from her purse. "We have enough history, I just figure you deserve to see these first." Like a victorious poker player, she gently laid the stack flat in front of me. "Go ahead and relieve yourself, don't tarry on my account. You'll want to be alone when you see those, anyway," she continued, flicking her tongue with a familiar flourish. "I have more at home."

The store's background music—a special Ray Charles collection—as well as people's surrounding voices and the whinny of the barista's equipment dimmed slowly in my ears as I walked to the men's room, the photos resting in the sweaty palm of my right hand. By the time I reached the door of the restroom, all sound had been sucked away; only my own breathing and footsteps accompanied me inside. My senses remained—the pungent smell of incense wormed its way up my nostrils—but my mind felt nearly vacuumed of all substance.

Feeling like Angie's personal marionette, I plodded into the nearest bathroom stall and latched its door shut behind me. I still couldn't quite fathom what was coming; days later, I would laugh at my innocent hope that all Angie had handed me were old shots from the handful of dates we'd had as kids.

In the first photo—which had the words "April '96" scrawled on the back—two young brothers were embraced in a passionate kiss. Dispelling any doubt, the taller, bulkier brother had one hand wrapped around his lover's waist.

In the next photo the two men were separated, but still holding hands, and the wider-lens shot indicated they were posing in front of a statue in Dupont Circle, one of DC's historic bastions of upwardly mobile homosexuals. I had driven through Dupont Circle enough— even shopped in the area through the years, always with a young lady at my side, of course—to recognize the guys' surroundings. Still, the width and breadth of the shot made it impossible to get a clear view of the two young men's faces.

The third photo closed the loop for any inquiring mind. The lovers were seated on a bench, and this shot was close up, enough that you could recognize the clothing from the earlier pictures while determining whether these were folk you knew. The smaller man, a high-yellow brother with a head of dreadlocks, looked like any number of guys I'd passed on the street. The other man was exactly who I'd feared, despite the fact we'd squashed the question of his sexual preference years before. At the sight of Coleman's face, I hit my knees, right there in the stall, and began praying for my brother in Christ. I didn't know what to say, or what to do, but I had to start somewhere.

11

Dionne

You'll have to pardon my French, but my fool friend Suzette was all the way in downtown DC, not far from the Logan Circle apartment where she'd spied on Adrian, Coleman's supposed boyfriend, earlier in the month. As Suzette directed me to the address of a bar on Massachusetts Avenue, I had to grit my teeth to keep from scolding her for continuing this ridiculous surveillance. Although she sounded a little better, her speech was halting and uncertain, enough so that I held my tongue and just told her to be patient until I got there.

Suzette's Buick was parked in a tiny lot just off the alleyway abutting the bar, a place called Therapy Café, which looked nicer than your average watering hole. When I found my friend, she was slumped against the Buick's steering wheel, her face turned so that she could see me as I approached. Once I was a few steps away, she slowly extended her left arm and opened the door. "Hey" was all that escaped from her mouth, and she didn't move another inch.

Leaning inside the car, I peeled back the shoulders of Suzette's white cotton jacket and ran my hands over her neck and chest, making sure there were no serious wounds. Her labored breathing filling my ears, I stepped back but carefully placed a hand beneath my friend's neck, refusing to gasp when I saw the puffy, darkening skin around her left eye. "What happened, honey? Where do you hurt?"

"We should just go," Zette replied weakly, the look of a frightened child in her eyes as she drew into a ball. "He might come back," she said, eyes darting to and fro as she balled the hem of her spaghetti strap dress between both fists.

I instinctively looked over each shoulder, scanning the lot and the alleyway to find we still had no company. I didn't know if I was dealing with a serious threat or paranoid delusions. I pinned my gaze back to Suzette's. "Zette, I need to know if I can move you or not. What happened?"

"I t-took a blow to my head. It was that monster's fault . . . Oh God, Dionne," she continued, weeping softly, "I can't let Coleman find out about this."

"We have bigger worries right now," I replied, leaning into the car and sliding my hands underneath her arms. Suzette had two inches of height and thirty pounds on me, but I was determined to get her into my car. "I'm taking you to Howard's emergency room." The idea of a blow to the head was scary stuff—my mind raced with fears of internal bleeding or other damage.

"No!" She flailed at me suddenly, knocking me back. "I don't want this reported. Just take me home!"

I'd be lying if I didn't tell you that was enough to stir up this sister's flesh. "Just take you home?" I pointed a finger toward her face, then retracted it. "Zette, you are not getting my help on your terms. I said you're going to the hospital, and that's where—"

"Dionne, please," Suzette said, grasping my hands as if she were hanging off a cliff. "I don't want to subject my kids, maybe not even

Coleman, to what happened here. I—I should have stayed away from all this, minded my own business like you said."

The thought of Suzette and Coleman's precious little ones—Coleman Jr., Joseph, and Edith—amidst this developing soap opera brought tears to my eyes, and my righteous anger dimmed.

"One more thing," Suzette said, still hanging on for dear life. "Can we please take my car home? You can leave yours here, no one will recognize it. I can't have that man finding my Buick and running the plates. He might track me and Coleman down at home."

I don't think I could have been much more confused than my friend had me at that moment, but something told me it was time to make a deal and get going. "It's a good thing for you I already took the day off work," I said, trying to affect a light tone. "Let's get you into the passenger seat."

Once I had Suzette situated, I kept her talking as I strapped myself into her driver's seat and quickly got comfortable with everything. As we first pulled out of the lot and into traffic, she was still tight-lipped, but as I drove in the direction of Howard Hospital—a cousin of mine was an ER nurse there and could help get Zette seen with as little fuss as possible—I got her talking about what had happened. As the story progressed, I understood more and more why she'd been so desperate to escape Therapy Café.

Suzette had grown weary of trying to catch Coleman in the act with this mysterious Adrian. The few times she had successfully followed him to Adrian's apartment, she had emerged with suspicious behavior, but no hard evidence. While she'd used her charm and humor to pump the apartment staff for information on Adrian's background and marital status, she'd never managed to get inside his place or actually see him interact with Coleman.

She decided that morning that it was time to stop dancing around the corners of her husband's possible other life and confront this Adrian directly. What did she have to be ashamed or afraid of? Between Oprah's many shows on the subject, the continued success of J.L. King's books, and the few personal stories she'd heard from friends, she wasn't the first wife placed in this painful situation. And if Coleman was guilty of what she suspected, he was the one who had to answer to God, not her.

Bolstered by this reasoning, Zette drove to Adrian's building early that afternoon, then followed him when he walked over to Therapy about an hour later. Once she saw him enter through the front door, she pulled into the parking lot, checked her makeup and hair, and set out in hot pursuit.

Inside the café, which was just opening and taking on the first stirrings of lunch traffic, she took a seat at the bar, a couple of stools down from Adrian and two other men. Adrian, a tall, youthful brother with a willowy build and a short fade haircut, wore a conservative gray wool suit, much more traditional-looking than his more streetwise-looking companions, each of whom sported a sweat suit.

Sitting there within earshot of their conversation, Suzette nursed a vodka with orange juice—a violation of the promise she'd made Coleman to abstain from alcohol, but who cared when he was probably guilty of far worse—and noted that they sounded like three men having the usual surface-level, meaningless banter. The poor performance of the Washington Wizards, conflicting opinions of Marion Barry's latest reincarnation, and arguments over which of several new movies was really worth checking out—nothing "gay" about the topics. That said, she noticed a palpable difference between Adrian's tenor and his friends'—a softer vibe emanated from him, just enough to set off her "effeminate" monitor.

Suzette realized with surprise that she was disappointed—in her heart of hearts, she had still held out hope for Coleman, praying that Adrian would turn out to be so masculine, so undeniably manly, that she could drop this campaign of surveillance and suspicion. While she knew there were plenty of "undercover" brothers with hard-core shells, she had been prepared to grant Adrian the benefit of the doubt. However, the way the brother held his drink, the way he enunciated his words, and the way he habitually tossed off a high-pitched titter after every joke seemed to signal the worst. Ready to strike, Suzette moved over one seat, landing right next to her suspect.

As Suzette recounted the details of her dialogue with Adrian and his friends, she got more and more upset, but from what I picked up, she started by engaging the guys in harmless small talk. She asked for directions to a nearby clothing boutique and posed as if she were unfamiliar with downtown. After a few minutes, she got them talking about their favorite music, dropping hints about how much she was personally into gospel music. The other two men, one of whom wore an expensive-looking leather Nike sweat suit and towered over everyone else in the bar, laughed off her questions about when they had last been to a gospel concert, not to mention church.

Adrian, however, engaged her. "I like Yolanda Adams and Vickie Winans," he said, turning over his shoulder and shrugging. "I'm pretty picky about gospel, though. I like artists who are really about ministry, you know? Music is just a racket for some of those jokers, they just front like they're all pristine and pure, but their personal lives make yours and mine look like monks, you know?" He winked at Suzette, seemingly confident they were sharing a common joke.

It was easy to picture my girl's reaction, though. She apparently took Adrian's innocuous comment as a dare. "Well, you need to check out my favorite group," she replied. "You heard of Men with a Message? They're a hometown group, matter of fact. Most of them are from DC or PG County."

"Hmm." Adrian had rolled his eyes, drawing raised eyebrows and amused glances from his bigger friend, whom the others in the bar had referred to as "Earl." Adrian turned all the way toward Suzette, opened his mouth to speak, then stopped himself. "Men with a Message, huh? I've heard of them, sort of a New Age version of the Winans or Commissioned?"

"That's right." Suzette's right hand was balling into a fist; Adrian's amused reaction felt like it had already confirmed her worst fears. She poured as much sugar as she could into her brittle smile. "They have some real talent in that group. I mean, Jesse Law used to be the man out there on the worldly stage, but now he's serving the Lord."

Suzette didn't go into detail, but apparently Earl and the other brother had burst into laughter at the sound of my husband's name, making the predictable jokes about my baby being yesterday's news. Adrian, however, had looked at Zette with sincere curiosity. "Okay, maybe they got talent, but just about anyone with a contract has that. What really makes them so special?"

Suzette let it fly, gushing as blindly as she could. "Coleman Hill's voice is just heaven-sent. When he sings, I feel God's hand on me," she said, slapping away the fact that these words were gospel truth before the emotional distance that had cropped up between her and Coleman in recent months. "That brother is going places."

"Oh, he goes places all right, hmm." As his trademark titter punctuated the smart remark, Adrian shifted in his seat. "Honey, you can trust me on this one. Mr. Coleman can sang his butt off, but there's a lot of layers to that onion."

It was really difficult to trust Suzette's account after this point, which she went into once we were seated in a far corner of Howard Hospital's ER. Adrian's last remark had left her mind blank and rendered her deaf. She shoved him from his bar stool, kicked him in the groin more than once, and let loose a barrage of shouts and threats that she couldn't quite recall. It wasn't clear how long this lasted, but it sounded like everyone else around them was too shocked to step in.

At first.

At some point Earl in the leather sweat suit got involved. Suzette spoke of him coming at her swiftly and forcefully, the veins in his neck popping out and drops of spittle flying from his mouth. A fist cuffed her good in the eye, then she was aloft in the air, the muscular figure taking her into a bear hug and lifting her in one swift motion. She swung her purse violently, landing it against his temple. The impact forced him to drop her and she dashed outside, the clapping of his footsteps loud in her ears as he chased her toward her car. She had reached her door before he grabbed the back of her weave and yanked her toward him, at which point she swung hard toward his chest, lost her balance, and banged her head hard against the side of the Buick.

"Oh, Zette," I said as she collapsed into my arms. Her black eye was covered with a pair of sunglasses, but it seemed a vain touch—given that her sobs were drawing more and more eyes to us. Rubbing her back and her arms, I quieted her slowly with a prayer, asking God to give her His peace that passeth understanding, to counsel her on the error of her ways, and asking He help her take this opportunity to confront Coleman directly instead of unpredictable, volatile strangers.

It looked, praise God, like I'd get to counsel her more deeply later.

Once my cousin Rita got us through an expedited registration process and placed Zette into an ER room, I explained again that we needed to keep her "underground." Rita was understanding and said she could keep Suzette in the ER for a couple of hours at least; they would need that much time to do a CAT scan and a couple of other tests to assure she hadn't sustained any internal bleeding or other damage.

With my girl in good hands, I waited until she was asleep comfortably in her bed and prayed anew as I walked to my car. Turning over the ignition of Suzette's car, I toyed with calling Jesse, but decided to

wait. Bringing my husband into this right now would only complicate matters further, and my Bible told me that as much as I trusted
my husband to protect me *when he was around*, my ultimate hope for
safeguarding lay in He to whom I could always appeal.

Stepping across the threshold into Therapy Café, I crossed my arms
and scanned the bar as urgent steps propelled me forward. By now,
the mingling afternoon crowd was at full blast. There were so many
people around—most of them twenty- and thirty-something professional types—that trying to scan the place for someone fitting Suzette's descriptions of Adrian or her attacker felt pointless. Instead, I
took the sole free bar stool. When the bartender gestured for my order, I raised my voice to compensate for the crowd. "Where's Earl?"

"Somebody say my name?" From a few stools down, a peanut-
brown brother matching Suzette's description sizewise leaned forward,
his large, catlike eyes narrowing as they stared me down.

I slid off my stool and walked over to the brother, who was in fact
wearing a leather sweat suit. "My name is Reverend Dionne Law," I
said, extending a hand that Earl may as well have crushed between
boulders, his grip was so ridiculous. "I thought I should get your side
of the story, before I go to the police."

The truth of Suzette's story radiated from Earl's reaction. Taking a
moment to register the concern on the face of the college-age girl
seated next to him, who'd been happily flirting with him until my
arrival, Earl flicked me an annoyed gaze. "I work here, all right." It
was a statement and a warning. "Let's take this to the back office."

"I'm not comfortable with that," I said, crossing my arms again.
"If what my friend says is true, you don't hesitate to put your hands
on women."

"Okay, okay," Earl replied, laughing falsely and patting the girl on
the shoulder. "I, uh, had a misunderstanding earlier today, Deidre."

He nodded to me. "I'll clear us a table in the corner over there, come on."

It was pretty clear that Earl had some official role at the café; four tough-looking young men were enjoying their meals at a corner table until he rolled up on them, snapping his fingers. "I'm taking this one over, fellas," he said matter-of-factly.

The youngbloods glared at Earl sideways but were gone before I could protest on their behalf. "Okay," he said while motioning for me to take a seat, "whatever she told you, most of it's probably true."

"Did you hit her, chase her to her car even?"

Earl sat ramrod straight, like a banker negotiating a deal, but he couldn't quite meet my stare. "Look, I'm not into begging, sister, but I'm asking you up front to hear me out before you involve the police. I've got what some might call an unfortunate past."

"Let me guess," I said, my tone still blank and official. "A rap sheet?"

"A 'rap sheet,' yeah," Earl said, clearly amused by my term. "Guess that's what they call it in the movies, huh? Doesn't matter. All I'm saying is, I may have reacted too instinctively with your friend— what's her name?"

"You don't need to know that," I replied. "Look, she already told me she started it, attacking this guy, uh," I said, stammering with shame about my prior knowledge of Suzette's stalking. "Um, I think she said his name is Adrian?"

"Yeah," Earl replied, "that's my baby brother you talking about." He lowered his voice, but his tone grew steely. "That's who she bum-rushed, kicked in the nuts, and called a 'faggot.' And that was only the beginning—the stuff she was saying, my big mama would have needed a gallon of soapy water to cleanse that mouth."

I dropped my eyes this time, knowing in the depths of my soul that this stranger was not exaggerating.

Earl wasn't ashamed of what he'd done, I could see that, but he was respectful enough to look away every few words. "I had to get her away from him," he said, measuring his tone and speaking with deliberation. "Things got out of control real fast, and I know from experience that Adrian can't handle that type of stress."

I wiped a tear from my left eye. "You couldn't have just escorted her outside? Why did you hit her, chase her?"

"Ma'am," Earl said, surprising me with the term—given that he looked at least five years older than me, "my main goal was to get her away from Adrian before he started reliving the beating he took last year. While my brother was still on the floor, curled up in a ball, I took your friend by both hands and picked her up so I could get her outdoors. She fought me the whole way, though. And let me tell you, when you have a woman that strong and big swinging fists and sharp nails at you, you have to protect yourself. If I landed a blow to her while trying to keep from getting my eyes scratched out, well, may your God forgive me."

I fought the shaky sensation welling up inside me, the tragedy of what had happened closing in. "So why did you leave her there at her car, after she'd banged her head so violently?"

"Ma'am," Earl replied, spreading his hands in supplication, "she went down hard, I'll admit, but she got back to her feet pretty quickly, opened her car door, then told me to go have sex with myself, if you know what I mean." He held both hands up. "Something told me if I took another step toward her, I'd be back in lockup before I knew it."

"You weren't afraid she'd come back and press charges?"

His mouth shut, Earl rolled his tongue around his gums and eyed me with what almost felt like sympathy. "I do have witnesses, Reverend, remember, beyond my brother. The bartender," he said, pointing, "and four other patrons were in here when it went down, along with the owner who was sitting with us. That said, don't think the cops wouldn't see my 'rap sheet' and have a good time makin' me sweat before finally letting me go."

I shook my head, accepting finally that Suzette's desire to keep this nightmare quiet was the right instinct. "Let me at least speak to the bartender and owner," I said, my voice shaking. "If they vouch for you, you won't hear from us again."

"All right, sister." Earl pulled a cigarette from the pack he'd been holding during our conversation, lit it, and took his first pull before looking me over with stern eyes. "Legal or not in here, there's just times a man needs a smoke," he said. "You tell your friend everything's cool so long as she just forgets Adrian even exists," he continued. "That woman's problem is with her two-faced husband, not my brother. At least Adrian's honest about who he is."

I nodded weakly, robbed of the appetite for a scriptural argument over homosexuality.

"I mean," Earl continued as I reached for my purse, "I'm the first to understand how upset women get about gay brothers. For years I didn't even *talk* to Adrian; couldn't believe he was *sweet*. Our parents ain't raise us to be like that, know what I mean?"

"No, I completely understand," I said, easing back into my seat and sensing Earl needed this moment to vent. I may have been more sensitive than the usual audience in his life. "Whatever you think about the acceptability of the gay lifestyle, our people have been the slowest to acknowledge it."

"That's for sure." Earl blew out a plume of smoke, confirming I wouldn't be able to stick around for long; the acrid smell could quickly make me sick. "Yeah, after he first 'came out' to the family when he was in college, I pretty much avoided him. Even when he came to visit me in prison, I was embarrassed, you know, scared my fellow inmates would see him and think I was the same way. And *you know* that was the last place you'd want folk getting the wrong impression." We shared a laugh before he continued.

"Anyway, when I saw him in the hospital last year, after some punks attacked him and a boyfriend at a club in Virginia, I about lost my mind. I mean, if you're not down with what those dudes do, it's all good, but to beat 'em until they're black-and-blue . . ." He stopped speaking and strategically broke eye contact. "Never again, sister," he said, "never again."

I sat there silently with Earl for a few seconds as his emotions hung in the air between us. Just as I opened my mouth to share a word of spiritual counsel, my cell phone sounded off from within my purse. "Earl," I said, placing a hand on his elbow, "if you'll excuse me, I may need to take this call."

"Not a problem, Reverend," he said, slapping a hand against the table and rising to his feet. "When you're off the phone, I'll send Charlie and Murray over. They can put you at ease about what went down."

I mouthed "thank you" to Earl as he turned away, then opened the phone to answer Jesse's call. "Hey, handsome," I said, struggling to level out the anxiety in my tone.

Jesse didn't sound too much happier than I felt. "You okay, babe?" I hadn't done a very good job, apparently.

"I'm all right," I said. "I—I have good news about my interview today. I'll give you the details when we get home, but Pastor Norm just might make a believer out of you."

"That sounds great," Jesse said, though his tone didn't match the enthusiasm in his message. "Look, I'm not gonna be home on schedule for our workout." With me off for the day, we had planned on going to the gym early before showering and making it a date night.

"Okay," I said, confused. "You guys going back into the studio for the afternoon or something?"

Jesse paused, then sighed, as if struggling with what to say. "I'm over at Coleman and Zette's," he said. "I'll fill you in tonight, but in the meantime they need some serious prayer."

I looked up to see Earl still hovering over me, a concerned look in his eyes as I spoke. "Baby," I said, "you'll be filling me in sooner than that. I better go pick Zette up now."

12

Jesse

Suzette!" Coleman's face lit up in pained shock when our wives walked into his kitchen, where we'd been praying and paging through a well-worn Bible his grandfather had purchased the year he was born. Even though I had shared the little bit about Suzette's adventures that Dionne had relayed over the phone, the sight of Suzette's face—the swollen, blackened eye only partially concealed by a large bandage—caught Coleman off guard.

He bolted from his seat, rushing to her as she recoiled in what felt more like shame than rejection. "I didn't know it was this bad," he said with righteous, wounded anger.

"I'm okay, Coleman," Suzette mumbled before craning her neck and turning her eyes upward. "The kids home?"

"Yes," Coleman said, pressing his hands lovingly into her arms as he helped her out of her jacket. "I mean, I hadn't expected Jesse to come over when he did—"

"They're fine, Zette," I said. "Coleman let them set up their video games on the TV in your master suite. They're in their own little world up there."

"Good," Suzette said, her voice still weak, even though a flicker of the usual fire had returned to her eyes. "Just so long as they haven't heard a thing you two been talking about."

I looked away from Suzette toward Dionne, who was now leaning against one of the counters and tapping a foot softly. "Hey," I mouthed, knowing my eyes were asking the real question on my mind: *Should we get out of here and let these two work this out? Or are we all that's standing between them and the type of fights that end marriages?*

An uneasy, murky silence filled the kitchen. It felt like everyone was waiting for someone else to speak. "Coleman and I have spent the last two hours praying and studying the Word," I said finally. "God has moved in a mighty way, and Coleman would like all of us to hear him explain how."

"This is private, Coleman." Suzette hadn't moved one inch from the spot where she'd landed when she first entered the kitchen, and she showed no interest in taking a seat or even leaning like Dionne against a counter. "I love these two, but you are *my* husband. Whatever sins you have to fess up to, I'm the one who should hear about them first."

"Really?" A hand at his chin, stroking his beard, Coleman had wandered over to the sliding glass door near the kitchen's island. "When do I hear about *your* sins?"

Suzette's eyes flashed and she started so fast, I was surprised that she didn't actually move. "What did you say to me?"

"Jesse told me you went into DC trying to play detective," Coleman said, "but, Suzette, what were you doing that got you into a physical fight? No lady, least of all a Christian lady, should—"

"Coleman." Dionne raised a hand calmly, shutting Coleman down with love in her eyes. "Suzette went overboard, but what she did today was motivated by her love for you." It felt like the bottom of my stomach dropped out when my wife shuddered and tears sprouted from her eyes. "She just doesn't want to have to *share* you, Coleman, that's all."

Coleman seemed intent on avoiding Suzette's deadly glare; instead, he crossed his arms and stared back at Dionne. "You're putting a nice wrapper on the ugly truth, Dionne," he said. "My wife is a homophobe. All these years she told me she believed me, trusted my word over the slanders of people trying to tear me down and question my sexual morality." Coleman's voice had risen now and the volume intensified as he continued. "Now I learn she's been tracing my every step like I'm some criminal she can't trust, some animal she can't just come to with her suspicions or concerns!"

"How would I come at you, Coleman?" Suzette shrieked at the top of her lungs, loud even for her. She finally took a step forward now, her right arm leading the way as she pointed vengefully toward her husband. "Just what is the right way to ask my *man* if he's less than a man, Coleman? Huh? Should I have just brought a naked brother up in this house, seen how long it would take you to chase him around?"

Coleman took three steps, until he stood toe to toe with his wife. "Woman, you're out of line!"

The thunderous quality of Coleman's yell did what everyone had feared; in seconds the sound of little feet on the staircase filled the house. "Mommy, Daddy," Coleman Jr. said, panting as he rounded the corner with little Joseph on his heels. "Wha-what's wrong?"

Coleman nearly fell onto his backside, he pulled away from Suzette so quick. Clamping a hand to the side of his short Afro, he struggled to catch his breath. "Boys, go back upstairs. Make sure all this noise hasn't woken your sister up."

The boys backed away toward the stairs, but the looks in their eyes confirmed that at three and five they were old enough to know all was not right in their world. Thinking he was whispering, Joseph leaned over to his big brother as they backed out. "Mommy's crying."

Once they were back upstairs, Dionne cleared her throat. "They shouldn't be here, not right now. Let me call my parents." The Favors lived a few miles up the expressway from the Hills. "If they're available, Zette and I can take the kids over there for the evening."

When the women returned to the house forty-five minutes later, Coleman and I were still sitting in the family room, staring blankly at the DVD of the movie *The Gospel* he had thrown in to pass the time. To be honest, we weren't sure how much more to say in prayer about the photos Angie had handed me, and Coleman had refused to respond to the images in them until Suzette returned. While he wanted company in this dark hour, he still wanted his wife to hear his confession the first time it fell from his mouth.

Both wives filed into the family room with their heads down and their faces ashen. Dionne practically fled to my side, leaning heavily into me as she burrowed in next to me on the Hills' love seat. Suzette, for her part, left Coleman to himself on the large couch facing us, choosing instead to take a seat in front of the television set. Hugging her knees to her chest, she threw her head back with what felt like resignation. "Okay, Dionne convinced me that I should let you talk first, Coleman. You have the floor."

Coleman gestured toward his wife. "You should be here at my side, Suzette," he said, his voice just above a whisper.

"Why don't I make that call," she said, still unable to meet his gaze, "once you've said your piece?"

"So be it." Coleman clasped his hands together and perched forward on the couch, peering across the room in a way that begged Suzette to acknowledge him. "Zette, you may not like what I'm about to say, but

I hope you can respect it." He inhaled deeply and shut his eyes before exhaling loudly, the words rushing out as if Coleman hoped to fling them as far from him as possible.

"I was born gay," he said, eyes still shut, his hands now gripping at the edges of the cushions beneath him. "There's no point dressing it up, nothing gained by excusing it or trying to explain it away. I wasn't abused by anyone, I loved my father dearly, and I definitely never thought the idea of kissing another boy was cool. It was just something I always wanted to do, from the time I was around seven or eight, I guess, when my other friends were getting all bothered by the sight of little girls." Coleman bit his lower lip and began to moan softly. "I think I was eight when my father first took up the issue of homosexuality in his sermons—no need to tell you it just confirmed my knowledge that my feelings were unnatural, unclean. You-all can't imagine—well, maybe you can if you've ever struggled with a drug or alcohol addiction—the hellish path that set me on.

"Suzette," he continued, waving a pleading arm in her direction, "you need to know, I fought these feelings I was born with from day one. I resisted all sexual activity throughout my teens, specifically to make sure I never crossed the line that really mattered. I was convinced that if I ever indulged my sexual urges, not only would God strike me down, He'd expose me to all the people I loved—my parents, my father's congregation, my friends—and my life would be as good as over."

Dionne furtively grabbed for my hand then, and I grasped her hand gratefully as I processed Coleman's confessions. I had known plenty of gay people in my life—from the poorly closeted choir members, singers, and musicians I'd encountered in my family's gospel industry circles to the comparatively proud producers, managers, and bodyguards I'd traveled with while touring the world. I knew that the Bible's condemnation of homosexuality clashed with the very real fact that these people didn't seem like they'd had a choice of sexual orientation. Truth told, I had gradually taken to ignoring the entire issue. It wasn't that I didn't care—it was that I didn't know how to reconcile reality to the Holy Word to which I had surrendered my life.

Coleman told us about his college years, the period during which he had experienced a couple of trials—including his father's death—that had left him open to Satan's attack and led him to experiment with his long-repressed feelings. Adrian Wilkes had apparently been his guide on that journey of discovery.

"Maybe I lost my mind with my father's death, with the feeling that I no longer had to stand up to the image of being his son," Coleman was saying, his chin in his upturned hands. Suzette was still sitting in front of the TV, her eyes riveted on him, her mouth closed probably longer than it ever had been while she was awake. "I never 'came out,' or any of that nonsense, but I was reckless enough to bring Adrian home with me that summer and hang out all over DC with him in tow. We didn't just hang in Dupont Circle—which is where we were in the photos Jesse got hold of—we went down to the harbor in Baltimore, to Georgetown, even to some wineries in Virginia."

Suzette shook her head. "Oh, Coleman, how could you?"

His head swung up suddenly as if he were offended. "Zette, let's remember that I hadn't even met you at this time, okay?" He softened his tone as he continued. "I spent a lot of time with Adrian that summer, but by the time I returned to school in Tennessee that fall, I was fully convicted of my sin. God put an increasing burden on me, until one night I broke down in my dorm room and prayed for His forgiveness. I promised God that night that I would honor my father's memory, and honor my Heavenly Father's glory by living life according to the Scripture's dictates." He sniffed away a single tear and looked at Suzette. "By the time we met, baby, all that felt like the distant past."

Suzette looked first toward Dionne and me, as if expecting us to jump in, but we sat with our hands clasped and simply smiled weakly in her direction. "We're just here to observe, honey," Dionne whispered. "Whatever's on your mind, say it, ask it."

"You're gonna have to spell it out for me, Coleman," Suzette said, her eyes weary and filling anew with tears. "How many men have you slept with since we've been together? And how long have you been back with Adrian?"

Coleman stood and shuffled over to the television, then took a careful seat next to his wife. "You need to understand, Suzettte, that God has put His hand on me. I may have been born gay, but that doesn't change the fact that I haven't touched *anyone,* male or female, except you, since the day we met. I have renounced my homosexuality. Do you understand?"

Suzette blinked back her newest tears, shaking her head with what I guessed was the same confusion coursing through me. "You're gay, but you're abstaining? Is that it?"

Coleman took her hands in his. "Yes."

"D-do you actually find me attractive? I mean, how do you lay down with me the way you do?"

Coleman glanced at me and Dionne, and for the first time I wanted to disappear from the room. "It took some prayer at first, but, baby, every time we tried to conceive a baby, and every time now that we lay down to show our love for each other, I just pray for God to take control." He pulled her chin to his and kissed her. "And He always does, doesn't He?"

"Oh God." Suzette sat back and ran her hands through her hair. "Please tell me this is all a big hoax, Coleman."

"I should have leveled with you years ago," he replied, pulling her close again and stroking her cheek. "God has forced the issue, though, and I guess we have to face it together now. Please forgive me."

Suzette placed a hand on Coleman's wrist. "You still haven't explained what you were doing in that man's apartment the past few weeks."

"He got back in touch with me about six months ago," Coleman said, his eyes flecked with tendrils of shame. "Apparently, this journalist friend of Jesse's had started snooping around and tracked Adrian down, trying to confirm things about our history. Adrian was inclined to give her a tell-all, unless I consented to take the time to explain myself." He rolled his eyes with regret. "I did the right thing to break things off with him that summer, but I didn't do it in a mature way. I basically stopped returning his calls and even avoided him when we passed each other in public. He was carrying a grudge, insisting I meet him at one of his rental properties to talk things through. I think he figured he might seduce me again, but you have to believe me when I say nothing ever happened."

Suzette bent her head low for a moment, but didn't let go of Coleman's hand. When she looked back up, she shifted her gaze between me and Dionne. "I love you two, but you can go now."

"Are you sure?" I asked.

"Yes," she replied, patting Coleman's hand. "None of this seems real, I'm not gonna lie to y'all, but I promise not to kill him in the time it takes to go pick up the kids and bring them back."

Dionne went to Suzette and embraced her in a silent hug as Coleman stood and met me at the middle of the room with a firm handshake. "I'm in your debt, brother," he said, his eyes both rueful and relieved. "I know this is only the beginning. I'm not sure whether this should just stay between the four of us or not. I mean, when I woke up this morning, I had no idea—"

"I feel you," I said, my head dropping for a second. "We'll figure out whether to tell the rest of the group. There'll be time for that later," I said, hoping in all honesty Coleman would choose to keep his secret to himself. Right now, the most important thing was for him to secure his wife's trust and safeguard his children. Not to mention, if Coleman set some new standard for self-disclosure, my personal mess—one that I'd promised myself I'd at least confess to Dionne—might eventually have to go before the group as well.

A sudden memory of how this had all come out seized me and my voice dropped to a hushed tone. "We are agreed," I whispered, "that you don't want this ever getting into the public record?" I had no idea how to convince Angie to keep a lid on her photos and the back story—especially while trying to save my own marriage, once I revealed my own sins to Dionne—but if there was any way to do it, Coleman couldn't afford sharing his testimony with anyone else.

With our wives trailing behind us, Coleman looked over at me as we headed toward their foyer. "It's ultimately in God's hand, brother, but I definitely don't want my kids learning of this now. It would be too painful, too confusing while they're so young."

We shook hands again and I smiled wryly. "For the record, I'm taking that as a yes. I got your back."

Outside on the front porch, alone for the first time since our world had tilted so unexpectedly, Dionne and I erupted into a feverish kiss, nearly attacking each other. As I stepped back and wiped tears from her eyes, I offered her one arm for support as we headed down the walkway toward my car. "I love you so much, baby. I thank God for you."

Rubbing my hand affirmatively, Dionne looked back at the Hills' house with longing. "Jesse," she asked, her voice catching, "can God bring them through this?"

"Nothing is impossible with Him."

Dionne stopped me in my tracks and drew me back to her for another kiss, then patted my cheeks and looked into my eyes through more tears. "God, Jesse, look how fragile the most treasured relationships can be. Suzette and Coleman are two of the best people we know, and look at what God has placed on them. Baby, I thought we had it bad, but now He's brought us so far. We have to be strong for them, Jesse. You know?"

"I know, baby, I know." I massaged Dionne's arms through her jacket. "They were there for us, and we'll step up for them now."

"Lord Jesus," Dionne said aloud, praying in the moment and gripping my hands as I bowed my head with her. "I won't lie. I could never deal with what you've asked Zette to bear. How can she trust a husband who never revealed such a scandalous past? I know you can do everything, Lord, but this feels so scary for both Coleman and Suzette. Please prosper them, Lord, as you promise in Jeremiah 29, but as you do that, Lord, use Jesse and me as vessels for their recovery. Fill us and empower us, O God. . . ."

And it was then, as my wife's prayer made every hair on my body stand at attention, that I decided to delay confessing my own horrible truth. Dionne and I were on the same page about the Hills. As contradictory as my dear friend's confession seemed—being a gay man determined to live a straight life—the conviction in his voice and on his face had sold me. His marriage and his family would need our support now more than ever, and to do that, not only would I have to postpone coming clean about the baby, I'd have to use any means necessary to keep Angie from publishing those photos.

13

Dionne

Two steps from the ballroom door, Coleman paused suddenly and pivoted back to face me. "He's gonna lose it when he sees you, Dionne."

A playfully wicked smile flickered across my face as I stepped past Coleman and flung back the nearest door. "He'll get over it," I insisted as the chatter of six hundred Republican fat cats and true believers beckoned us inside. "He'll know I'm not your woman, at least. I don't think he'll forget Suzette anytime soon." Jesse, Zette, and I had taken several days to convince Coleman not to warn Adrian that he would have company this morning. If there were any hope of talking him out of cooperating with the nasty article Angie Barker was preparing for *Rolling Stone*—the one in which she planned to splash pictures of young Adrian and Coleman making out like two kids on lovers' lane— we needed the element of surprise on our side.

"We're in your hands, O God," Coleman said under his breath as we crossed the threshold into the deafening swarm of congressmen, White House staffers, ministers, and activists. As a successful political consultant for the Republican National Committee, Adrian regularly bought an entire table at these types of prayer breakfasts. As part of his running attempt to humiliate and blackmail Coleman, he'd summoned him to today's festivities at the Watergate Hotel. Adrian had covered Coleman's ticket, of course, but Coleman had sprung for mine, as well as the tailored pin-striped suit Suzette had helped me pick out. Because I was still more accustomed to rubbing shoulders with homeless teens than with "holy" high rollers, my wardrobe was light on the type of business attire Adrian and his clients expected.

After a few minutes of sliding uneasily through one crowd after another—almost all which smelled of a combination of musky cologne and hair gel—we finally found Adrian standing near one of the buffet tables. I had to admire the physical metamorphosis the brother had achieved since the days of his youthful affair with Coleman. The dreadlocks and goatee were gone, his lanky physique had filled out some, and he was dressed in an expensive-looking navy pin-striped suit with a flashy two-tone dress shirt and bold maroon power tie. The apparently free-spirited, openly gay boy had transformed into a well-heeled member of the "Establishment."

Somehow, though, Adrian had pulled this off without totally stifling his sexuality. It nearly oozed out of his pores as he entertained two tubby, white-haired men in blazers. I realized quickly that Suzette had been in serious denial the day of their confrontation. She'd claimed she wasn't certain about him at first, but one look and it seemed unlikely Adrian Wilkes had spent one second in anybody's closet.

Adrian somehow sensed our arrival before Coleman had even cleared his throat. Interrupting his own story—something about his recent role in a closely contested House race—he locked eyes with Coleman. This sister would be lying if I didn't admit that at that moment I felt like I was interrupting something.

"Well, he's finally here," Adrian said, gently resting a hand on

Coleman's massive left shoulder. "Jerry, Phil," he continued, nodding toward his elderly colleagues, "this is my close friend, Coleman Hill. Coleman is a very successful gospel singer." He and Coleman spent a few seconds throwing out household names to help the old guys understand Coleman's style of music, finally settling on, believe it or not, Sam Cooke.

Adrian allowed himself a distracted glance in my direction. "I don't mean to be rude, dear, but you would be . . . ?"

"This, uh," Coleman said, clearing phlegm from his throat, "is my friend Reverend Dionne Law. Dionne is an associate minister at Rising Son Church, out in Columbia, Maryland." Not surprisingly, everyone had heard of it. Pastor Norm, whom I still hadn't talked much political sense into, was a regional champion of the religious right—although he stopped short of the hateful language of many of his peers.

"See?" Adrian said, smiling anew as he shook my hand with what felt like relief. "I told Coleman that if he accepted my invitation, he'd not only be blessed to hear some great speeches on faith in politics, he'd see how many of his friends in ministry have awakened to the things our party can offer them."

"Well, personally," I replied, sweeping my eyes over the room quickly, "this is my first time at one of these breakfasts too. I'm impressed with the diversity here." Before the Bush administration convinced me the GOP had lost its natural mind, I was a registered Republican. The main reason had been abortion, which I believed was a mortal sin, followed by the fact that Republicans at least talked a good game about respecting the Christian Church and its role in society. From what I could see today, though, the Bushies hadn't scared everyone away quite yet.

Adrian let me make nice with Coleman and his friends, plus another dozen or so folks who passed through our midst in the next few minutes, and then it was clear he was ready to handle business. "If you-all can excuse me, Coleman and I need to run a quick errand out to my car, so we're back in time for Senator Brownback's keynote. I've got a few boxes of party literature out there."

Backing away in time with Adrian's steps, Coleman hesitated before finally saying, "Dionne should come along as reinforcement, Adrian. She can hold doors open for us on the way back."

Adrian twitched, but let that be it. "Let's go, then."

Once the elevator doors opened and we emptied into the Watergate's front hotel lobby, Adrian's friendly, warm exterior soured and he nodded toward a far corner where a couch and chairs sat near a window. "Real cute, Coleman," he said, glancing between us. "Real cute, bringing her. I'm tired of these games."

Coleman waited until he and I had taken a seat on the couch to respond. "Adrian, look," he said as his ex paced back and forth before us, arms crossed. "I came this morning because I respect the pain you feel, okay? I'm not here to play games. Fact is, I'm here to get you to stop playing them with me, man. Life is too short for all this—me having to look over my shoulder dreading your next call, and you wasting precious time trying to make me miserable. I won't preach at you or quote any Scripture this time. I'll keep it simple: there has to be a better way."

Adrian came to a stop. "Why is she here?"

"I'll handle it," I replied, patting Coleman's hand before he could speak. "I'm here, Adrian, not just because I'm Coleman's friend, but because I'm also cool with your brother, Earl."

That brought Adrian up short. Frowning, he ticked his head in my direction. "What, you another one of Earl's babymamas? You sort of look the part—long-legged, cute face, plenty of meat on you, but just short of being fat."

Confused as to whether I should be flattered, I shook my head. "Guess again," I replied, my tone betraying my annoyance. I tried to get a good look into Adrian's eyes, to open the door to some soul sharing. "I met Earl the day Suzette attacked you at Therapy Café."

Adrian shut his eyes for a second, and a sigh escaped him that made me feel like I'd knocked the wind out of him. "Therapy, huh?" He recovered, snapping his fingers as he met my gaze. "Earl told me about you," he said, smiling now. "Sounded like he got a few laughs out of you. He said you went in there ready to charge him for beating on that cow, until you realized she committed a hate crime on me."

Coleman stood so fast, he startled me. "She was wrong, Adrian, we've talked about that." He took a glance around, seemingly ensuring that we hadn't drawn any spectators, then tapped Adrian's chest, nearly knocking his ex down in the process. "Regardless, that's the mother of my children. Show some respect."

"I thought it might help," I said, guiding Coleman back to his seat with a gentle hand to the shoulder, "if a neutral party shared how sorry Suzette is for what she did to you. I think there are a lot of hurt feelings here, Adrian, but if everybody settles down and gets hold of themselves, we can avoid a lot of worse pain and suffering."

"Reverend," Adrian replied, rooting his feet to the carpet and crossing his arms again, "you're not a neutral party, for two reasons. One, you're not *my* friend, and two, if you work at that Rising Son Church—which, for the record, is a great supporter and friend of my political party—you also hate what I represent. So thank you for your time, and get to steppin'. Coleman has a decision to make."

Lord, guide my tongue, I prayed as I searched out a reply. I didn't want to lie. "Yes, I'm a friend of Coleman and Suzette's, Adrian, and, yes, my church's doctrine says that homosexuality is an abomination against God. We follow the strict interpretation of Scripture, and I'm sorry to say, I haven't seen anything in the Bible to contradict that view. From all I see in the Word, God's ideal is the married sexual union of man and woman."

I held up a hand to silence him as his back coiled defensively. "I can believe that and still love you, Adrian. I believe you're just following what comes naturally, and no one can hate you for making that choice."

"It's not a choice!"

Coleman, who had calmed down, chimed in with a whisper into my ear. "You're not really helping, Sister D."

Afraid I'd lose my chance to reach him, I grasped hold of Adrian's nearest wrist. "Can we lay aside the issue of choice, or, more important, your ability to read my mind and my heart? Without proof, can you take me at my word that the problem is not your being gay, it's that you're trying to take Coleman away from his family?"

Adrian's eyes flashed angrily, but he didn't exactly slap my hand away. "Who says I'm trying to take him away from his family? I just want him to own up and be honest about who he is."

Coleman, who had clearly conducted this conversation with Adrian more times than he cared to count, shook his head and looked away. Looking back up at Adrian, I smiled. "So that's all you want? You'd be happy if he went on CNN and TBN tomorrow, told the world he was born gay, but then chose to stay with Suzette and the kids? If he did all that and never saw you again?"

Adrian could barely hide the sneer lurking behind his forced smile. "Like that would end the story." He jammed a finger toward Coleman's nose. "He'd be perpetrating a fraud still, with that nonsense about being 'healed' of his homosexuality."

"Are you sure," I asked, my tone tender, but my gaze narrow and forceful, "that this talk about Coleman's honesty isn't just a cover for the simple fact you want him back? That, like many single straight people, you're just another lonely thirty-year-old who's fixated on a past love?"

Adrian's eyes bugged so wide, I was sure he'd raise his voice, but he was clearly skilled at discussing sensitive matters in public. He kept his voice low and steady as he said, "She's saying what you ain't man enough to say, isn't she, Coleman?"

"You think I'm afraid of you?" Coleman was back on his feet now. Unlike Adrian, his volume was out of control. "It's nothing but the grace of God that's kept me from putting you in your place before now—"

"This conversation is over." Adrian dusted off his suit jacket, as if cleansing himself of our presence. "You had it right earlier, Coleman," he said. "The games are old, and they're over."

Coleman leaned over, his flaring nostrils now within an inch of Adrian's own flat nose. "That's what I've been trying to tell you."

"Yeah, the games are definitely over," Adrian said, holding Coleman's gaze with the care of a killer sizing up his victim. "You've convinced me all right, boy. I'm through with this, especially if it means you dragging one friend after another out to question my character. I'll show you *character*. Better yet, I'll teach you a big lesson in it." He looked from Coleman to me, and the confidence swelling his chest filled the room. "A few more interviews with Ms. Angela Barker, of *Rolling Stone*, and I'm through with you, Coleman Hill."

Caught off guard by how quickly things had gone from bad to worse, Coleman and I were still processing Adrian's threat—no, his promise—when he jammed a finger toward Coleman. "It's all on you now, boy, Mr. Hard-Core Hetero. Better hope that 'healing' of yours ain't an act."

14

The security guard, who was dressed like a Secret Service agent—nondescript business suit and tie, the wiring of a listening device hanging from one ear—flicked my Styrofoam container judgmentally. "What you got there, sir?"

I was backstage at downtown DC's Verizon Center, clearing the last hurdle standing between me and an old friend, Max Soul. Max and I had first met nearly a decade earlier, just as my worldly career peaked and he was the opening act of my North American tour. In the years since, Max had pulled off a rare transformation, slowly changing his style and growing his fan base from a conventional bunch of hip-hop–loving teens to a diverse mix of rock and pop fans aged twenty to forty. In four hours he'd be performing, for the third consecutive night, to a full house.

Having surveyed the contents of my Styrofoam dish, the guard waved me into Max's cavernous dressing room. Crossing the threshold, I noted Max was alone, his back to me as he sat before a mirror playing with his long braids and talking on a nearly invisible Bluetooth device.

He winked at me in the mirror, waved me into a nearby chair, and was through with his conversation in a couple of minutes.

"What up, mate?" Pivoting to face me, he eyed the container in my hand. "That can't possibly be what I think it is?"

"Still piping hot, thanks to how quickly you had your people wave me through," I said, setting the Styrofoam in front of him and laughing as he ripped the lid off. "A hot breakfast fresh from Florida Avenue Grill, just as delicious as you recall." On several tour stops in DC, back in the day—including the early morning when I first met Dionne in that Howard University shower—Max and I had cut out to hit bars and clubs through the night before wrapping up with breakfast at the Florida Avenue landmark. That was a seriously long time ago. These days Max didn't even keep a home in the States—his brand of soulful rock had won him so many fans in Europe, he spent two-thirds of every year in the UK.

By the time I had removed my jacket and gloves, Max had his chin embedded into the mass of scrambled eggs, grits, hot apples, and hotcakes before him. It was a pretty scary sight, one that would have taken him down a few pegs in the eyes of the editors who voted him onto *People*'s "Most Beautiful" list.

I let him inhale his meal and make small talk before raising what I knew was an ugly request. "How is business these days?" Against my will, I felt my old self returning again, inflecting each word of the question with the underlying message: *you're loaded, and I want a piece.*

"My accountants and those other buggers in suits handle all that, Jesse, you remember how 'tis," Max replied, wiping fried potato grease from his mouth with a silk napkin. "Those were some fine eats, but my trainer will kick my bum good, she ever catches me with such a toxic combo."

"With each passing year," I said, chuckling, "you sound less and less like a boy from the hood of Minneapolis." Max had actually registered as a British citizen last year, formalizing his disdain for African-American culture and "life in the States" in general, as he liked to say.

Ignoring me, he tossed the container into the trash and crossed his legs without taking his eyes off me. "Why you got your hand in me pocket, Jesse Law?"

"Why you got to take that tone with a brother?" I replied. "You are still a brother, at least in the spirit of being an international black man, right?" With his reddish yellow complexion and naturally straight hair, Max had always made me look fully African by comparison; as fellow brothers of biracial heritage, we enjoyed arguing over who looked the least black.

"Jess," Max said, standing now and eyeing a portable oaken wardrobe in the far corner of the room, "I got to be dressed for final rehearsals in an hour, mate. Get on with it."

"Look," I said, scooting forward in my chair, but keeping my tone nonthreatening. "I don't believe in calling in IOUs anymore—especially not since accepting Christ, you know that."

"Trust me," Max said, taking a seat on a couch along the nearest wall. He rolled his eyes as he continued. "I recall quite well your pious promises from those glory days of your 'salvation.' So what's changed, old pal?"

"I've got a little situation," I said, suddenly conscious of how this all must look to Max, whom I'd spent the past five years trying to convert to the faith. "A friend of mine needs a cash infusion, enough to get rid of a troublesome ex. Someone trying to make his life hell."

Max had pulled out a set of nail clippers and was going to town on his fingernails, an act that would terrify his handlers. "This friend is in show business, of course, eager to make an embarrassing person go away."

"You know how it works." I wasn't the only one who had endured my share of paternity suits.

Max sized me up with a peripheral glare. "Don't lie to me, boy. This 'friend,' real or not?"

I had already discussed my next step with Coleman, Suzette, and Dionne, who had reluctantly agreed to my having this conversation with Max as a Plan B. "This is about someone you could hardly care less about," I said. "My friend Coleman Hill."

"Oh, you have an actual name for me now," Max replied, cracking a sly smile. "And one I recognize. Have to confess, kid, I've actually spun a couple of those CDs you sent me. You're my chap and all, but that Coleman, what a set of pipes on that one! I believe you wanna save his bum from the fire."

"Out of respect for him," I said, "I'd rather not go into further detail. Trust that it's something deep in his past, for which he's long since repented and been forgiven."

Max's forehead wrinkled as his mind teased out possibilities. "Fathered a bastard or two? Drove drunk, hurt somebody? Sold drugs? Used 'em?"

"Grow up," I said. "You of all people should know better."

"I wasn't done yet. Hiding the sausage with Harry? Armed robbery? Helped with a gangland slaying?"

"I figure over our two tours," I said, sighing, "that I probably bought you twenty-five thousand worth of blow, girls, liquor, and assorted toys. Agreed?"

"For the record, I didn't ask for any of that stuff—"

"I'm not asking for payback," I said. "Just asking you to consider that twenty-five K is a drop in your bucket these days." I stood, not wanting to wear out my welcome. In an age of online banking, it's not like I needed to leave with a check right then. "For Coleman, it could save his career and his family."

"I'm taking next week off after this leg," Max said, bringing me in for a brisk hug and handshake. "Call my cell again when I'm in Palm

Springs. I'll have all the time in the world to hook you up with me chartered accountant, CPA, whatever they call him here. Whatever Coleman needs, he's got."

"Appreciate it, brother." I turned back toward Max as I stepped toward the dressing-room door. "My invitation for you to join me and Dionne for dinner before you break town still stands, man. Better get us while you can—a few more weeks and we'll be bringing our baby home."

"Send pics of the crumb snatcher," Max replied, his voice in my ear as he followed behind. "For the record, mate, I couldn't be happier for you about this little one you've got coming." He leaned over my shoulder as he said, "Might actually make an honest husband out of you now, eh? A lot of my married mates stopped screwing around when the first baby came, at least for a little while."

I had the door halfway open, but my friend's carefree words left me rooted where I stood. I let the door swing back shut as I swung around to face him. "We've had this conversation, Max. When I married Dionne, I was serious about being faithful from jump. I don't cheat on my wife." *Or more truthfully, as my boy Bill Clinton might say, I am not presently cheating on my wife.*

Max rolled his eyes—a gesture I was accustomed to, but one that filled me with embarrassed rage for some reason. "What's so funny?" The question burst from me with unexpected force, but that didn't stop me from stepping toward my smaller friend with a speed that made him stumble.

"Calm down, old pal," Max replied, laughing as he caught his balance. "You know all secrets are safe with me. You just revealed that your boy Coleman's hiding some earth-shattering secret, for Pete's sake."

There was no choice but to spell out the battle raging within. "Max, you need to understand that I work hard at being faithful to Dionne. Do you understand why? Do you think I've been lying to you all these years I've testified about the impact Christ has made on my life? Is that why you always blow me off?"

Max met my stern gaze, but his eyes were full of sympathy. "You know what? I may not buy the Christian act as a choice for me, but I at least believe you're sincere, unlike most people. You *want* to be faithful to Dionne, at least. You *want* to be like this myth of Christ. That beats most of your hypocritical brethren, I say."

"What makes you think I cheat on Dionne?" I wasn't asking so much out of confusion anymore; given the unfortunate truth, I was in detective mode now.

Max could barely hide his amusement at the irony. "Don't drop dead on me, mate, but a word of caution. If you cheat on your wife in my city, even while I'm away on tour, I just may hear about it. Especially if you're at the Conrad. . . ."

The Conrad. London. The five-star hotel where Samuel had most likely been conceived. An ocean and a continent away, Vanessa and I had been spotted by someone in Max's circle, and as a result, I'd probably turned the brother off Christianity for good.

Who else had seen us?

15

Jesse

Vanessa emerged from the operating room in her scrubs, glasses slightly crooked as she retied her hair into a ponytail. "You have real nerve," she said, eyeing me impatiently as she half-waddled past. "We agreed a long time ago that you weren't to come here."

Silence was our companion until we entered the interns' locker room, which reeked of Pine Sol. Vanessa darted around a corner to ensure we had no company; then she turned toward me with her hands on her hips, a frown on her face. "What?"

"You should sit down," I said.

"Don't tell me what to do," she replied. The hands didn't leave the hips.

"No, I mean you're obviously worn down, Vanessa. You don't have to stand while we do this."

"What are we *doing*? I'm due in another OR in ten minutes, Jesse."

"Have it your way," I said, pacing back and forth near the door.

"Has anyone contacted you recently, asking questions about me? Or about the baby's father?"

Vanessa grudgingly eased herself down onto the wooden bench, sighing. "My mother calls weekly trying to solve the mystery of the 'phantom babydaddy,' if that's what you mean."

"No, I mean strangers. People who figure there's a story to be had."

"I don't know what you're talking about."

"Vanessa," I said, my lips pursing, "I promised you I'd tell Dionne the truth, didn't I?"

"Yeah, about that—"

"I know, I know. When, right?"

She shrugged. "The thought had occurred to me." She reached down and rubbed her wide, round girth. "Baby will be here in a couple months, Jesse, and you promised you'd tell Dionne over a month ago."

"I will keep my word," I replied. *Don't know when, but I will.* "I just need some time. And without your help, Dionne's going to find out from someone other than me." I told her about my exchange with Max, about the fact we'd clearly been spotted during our week in London. Max had too many details—he'd not only known we stayed at the Conrad, he had an exact description of Vanessa's hairstyle, height, build, and the flattering dress she had worn during one of our nights on the town.

"We weren't very careful, were we?" Vanessa said after a few moments of silence. Not that she'd been the one with everything to lose, but she was right. Our weeks-long affair had been a whirlwind; a phone call, an impulsive rendezvous at her place, followed by more of both. The first night of adultery left me in a virtual daze, simultaneously drunk with the thrill of the illicit chase and convinced I'd committed an unforgivable sin. In a very real way, I had convinced myself that I no longer deserved to have Dionne back, so I might as well enjoy myself before the bottom dropped out.

I stared at Vanessa across the musty little locker room. "I take responsibility for the fact we were seen." Inviting her to London was my idea—the trip had been scheduled for months before my separation from Dionne, a combination of business and pleasure. With Dionne at least temporarily out of the picture, I decided I needed some company in the evenings after spending each day recording tracks with a major British gospel choir that had recruited me as a guest vocalist. For all the dirt I had done in my Before Christ days, the double life I lived that week—singing of God's sufficiency and holiness by day and inventing new ways to sex Vanessa at night—stood alone in my personal Hall of Shame.

Vanessa had wobbled back to her feet now. "What do you want from me, then? We're down to four minutes, for the record."

"Just promise me that you'll let me handle things with Dionne. I'll do it soon, trust me."

Vanessa put a hand to her back, sighing with a force clearly against her will. "Why are you worrying about me, Jesse? You're not keeping a promise to me." She fixed me with a stern stare as she said, "Your promise was before God."

16

Dionne

Suzette and I stood near the back of the crowd of gospel DJs, journalists, and church folk crowded into Nashville's Opryland Resort and Convention Center, where Men with a Message's record label had reserved a ballroom for their new CD launch and press conference. With everything going on in our respective lives—Suzette's struggle to salvage her marriage and let Coleman keep their troubles quiet; my fevered anticipation of baby Samuel's arrival and the demands of my new job at Rising Son Church—a two-day trip to Music City was the last thing either of us felt like bothering with.

On the small platform stage, Jesse, Coleman, Micah, Frank, and Isaac sat behind a draped table fielding questions between short performances of some of the CD's most catchy tracks. The music was as beautiful as always, but to be honest, Suzette and I were so consumed by the pressures bubbling underneath the guys—troubles Jesse and Coleman alone knew of—that it was tough to give it the proper appreciation.

"You know that little fool hasn't even returned Coleman's calls,"

Suzette whispered out of the side of her mouth. I kept my gaze aimed toward the front of the ballroom, where Jesse entertained the media with wisecracks about how low-rent gospel tours were compared with his days playing in packed stadiums, but my ears jumped at Zette's little broadcast. Because I had failed so miserably to quell the firestorm swirling around her, Adrian, and Coleman, she had asked me to keep my nose out of things and not question her about Coleman's attempts to calm Adrian down again. She had even refused Jesse's offer of the money from his friend Max Soul, insisting that it was clear Adrian didn't need the money and was in this for payback, not paychecks.

Now that my girl had opened up the subject, I leaned closer to her to keep it on the table. "So, do you think Adrian's already given the journalist everything she wanted? Even the pictures?"

"God only knows, and I mean that literally." Suzette's eyes were hooded and weary, and though her complexion was still radiant, I noticed she had developed her first frown lines. "He's completely shutting Coleman out, letting us fear the worst. I just pray every night, girl, that for my kids' sake, God strikes the little lightweight down."

"Zette," I said, patting my dear friend's hand, "Adrian is God's child too. We all are." Recent events had reminded me all the more of that occasionally inconvenient fact. Less than a week ago, I had run into Carol, Jesse's estranged sister, at the local Safeway. I hadn't seen Carol in nearly three years, since we had last had her over for dinner. She'd ended that evening by hitting Jesse up for an unexplained loan, effectively killing the goodwill I had labored to build between my husband and his half sister.

I had barely recognized Carol in that Safeway aisle—the girl cleaned up pretty well. Her usually stringy blond hair had been stylishly trimmed, her normally pale skin had a bronze hue, and she looked twenty pounds lighter. A few minutes of conversation revealed that

Carol had accepted Christ at a small neighborhood church, which helped explain the absence of the calculating cunning I usually spotted in her watery blue eyes. Our conversation was so pleasant, I had decided to collaborate with her on a surprise for her little brother: Carol had agreed to come to the hospital within hours of little Samuel's birth. Jesse would be shocked, I figured, but grateful. Because he had no "full" siblings, it seemed my husband's relationships with all his brothers and sisters were strained to some degree. That didn't keep him from admitting often that he longed to see that change.

Reminded now of the way Coleman had defended Suzette against Adrian's mean-spirited reference to her weight, I reprimanded my friend for the homophobic slur she'd applied to Adrian.

"Oh, please," she said, giving me an aw-shucks grin. "A sister has to vent, Rev. He's trying to take my man."

I assured her that while Adrian's attraction to Coleman had felt like a fourth member of our confrontation that day at the Watergate, the heat had felt one-sided. "Whatever Coleman's sexual instincts once were, Zette, I really don't think he feels anything for men anymore. At least not Adrian."

"That's only 'cause Adrian's trying to blackmail him," Suzette said, her arms folded. She nodded toward the back door. "I need some air. Tired of whispering, besides."

We went outside to a pool area. Late March in Nashville meant that it was still a little too nippy for actual swimming, but the sun was strong and it was nearly 60 degrees. As a result, a few dozen people lay in the chairs surrounding the massive pool, some engaged in conversation while others read or engaged in lazy naps.

Settling into chairs near the deep end's diving board, I tried to keep Suzette talking about her ability to trust Coleman, which seemed surprisingly shaky. "How can I know my husband really wants me," she asked, her chin dipping toward her chest, "and not just me as part of the package, with the kids being what really matter to him? How do I know Coleman's not fantasizing about a man every time we make love? Dionne, if that's what it takes for my man to sex me, I'd rather he not touch me at all."

"Zette, Zette," I said, reaching over to wipe her eyes with a tissue from my purse, "you're jumping to one conclusion after another. Don't go there, girl, not until you two get that therapy you've been talking about."

"Who has time for therapy? I'm too busy with the kids to see a shrink weekly, and Coleman keeps promising he'll make time *after*. After the guys finish the new CD, after they do the launch tour, after he gives them a heads-up about Adrian possibly going public and embarrassing all of them by extension." She shut her eyes and shook her head. "When does *after* become *now*?"

I was about to suggest she get Coleman to commit to a timetable when a hippy sister in a pair of tight red shorts, stockings, and a matching long-sleeved blouse waltzed by. "What's up, sisters?" She adjusted her sunglasses, sliding them down the bridge of her nose until she could make eye contact with each of us. "Not many of us ebony beauties out here. You enjoying this sun or wishing you had loaded up on sunscreen?"

"Ah, we just out here killin' time, sister," Suzette replied, a smile breaking wide across her face. I could relate to her sense of relief, the appreciation for a small-talk break from the heaviness. "We're here against our will, just showing some respect for our hubbies. What business brings you out to Opryland? You don't look like you're in the gospel industry."

"Oh no," the sister replied, smiling good-naturedly. "I'm not in the industry. I do report on it, though."

I felt my eyes narrowing as I spoke. "Report on it?" Suspicion rising within, I extended a hand. "I'm Reverend Dionne Law, and this is my dear friend Suzette Hill. I'm guessing you already know that, though."

The woman smiled unflappably, then reached for a nearby chair and pulled it between me and Zette. "Holy Spirit intuition," she said, tapping her temple while smiling at me again. "You were onto me right away, huh, Reverend?" She reached into her purse and handed us each a business card. "Angela Barker. I'm pretty sure you've heard of me lately."

"Hmm." Zette took her card, placed it in her lap, then flicked it toward the covered pool. "Gotta be a pretty unhappy person, spending so much time ruining the lives of God-fearing folk." She snapped her fingers dismissively. "You can be gone now."

I knew my girl was bluffing like nobody's business, and given the stakes, I couldn't let her play such games with her family's happiness. I looked at Angie's card with care before looking her in the eyes. "You're a legend in your own time, Ms. Barker, at least around our households. You seem to be taking your time with this article—am I off base to think you're conflicted about whether to publish it?"

Angie shifted her weight and crossed her legs, showing off a snazzy pair of black pumps. "No conflict about the story in general, no," she said. "The things in this article are going to set some heads afire. Who knows—the Black Church, the gospel industry, this entire town we're sitting in, may be embarrassed enough to finally clean their own house. Did you know there is evidence that black clergy and church leaders molest children at the same rate as Catholic priests?"

Suzette had opened up a paperback copy of a Victoria Christopher Murray novel, so I took the bait. "You're bluffing," I said, frowning at Angie's poor taste to even go there without proof. "You're talking to someone who reads and researches enough to know there's no study backing up a claim like that."

"Well, the statistics will bear me out someday," Angie said, drawing her back straight and tightening the fit of her sunglasses. "In the meantime I have plenty of anecdotal evidence that will—"

"I know," I said, rolling my eyes with exaggeration. "Set folks' hair on fire."

"No offense, but what you-all think of me is really beside the point. I'm here on pretty important business. There's a lot of disturbing rumors I need to validate for my story, and most of 'em don't involve your husbands. But with you-all here, I'm looking for more honest responses than I'll get from Coleman or Jesse."

"I'll see you inside, Dionne," Zette said, rising slowly as if she had not a care in the world, as if Angie were both invisible and mute. "The press conference should be wrapping soon. I need a nap before dinner." I was proud of my girl; I knew every fleshly impulse inside her itched to pitch Angie headfirst into the empty pool.

"Sit down, Mrs. Hill."

My mouth gaped at Angie's instructive tone. This girl did not value her life.

Suzette's right fist balled involuntarily and she flashed a deranged, toothy smile. "Excuse me, what did you say?"

Angie wasn't stupid enough to get in Zette's face, but from the safety of her seat, she answered the rhetorical question. "Where is Adrian Wilkes, Mrs. Hill? He's the only source of mine who's dropped off the face of the earth."

The fist dropped to Suzette's hip, but stayed balled up. "How would I know where Larry Lightfoot is?"

"I haven't been able to reach him for a week and a half," Angie said, "so last night, just before catching my flight out here, I went to his apartment and ran across his brother—big guy named Earl? He tells me he reported Adrian missing a week ago. He was last seen at his office, headed out for the night, then poof." She looked between the two of us. "Mighty convenient for Men with a Message, huh?"

The speed of Suzette's reply surprised me. "You already have everything you need from homeboy, right? Pictures? Quotes? What do his whereabouts matter to you? It ain't like you're writing this story out of a love for mankind, and certainly not for Jesus."

Angie's lower lip dropped involuntarily and she turned to me. "Is this really all you have to say when a man's life could be in danger? Reverend, are you on the same page as your friend here?"

"Let's be clear," I said, turning to face Angie and conveniently blocking Zette's access to her. "You come here out of the blue, roll up on us with claims about Adrian being in danger, and just expect us to make nice with you? Sister, if you know Jesus, you should realize your style is nothing like His.

"Now," I continued, "with that said, I can speak for Jesse and for the Hills when I tell you no one wants to see Adrian hurt. If he's missing and there's information any of us can give to set his family's mind at ease, we'll give it." I took a beat. "You, however, are not the right messenger." I scribbled my e-mail and phone numbers onto her business card and thrust it back toward her. "If Earl or anyone else in Adrian's family wants to talk to me or my husband, or send the police our way, we can be contacted via any of these numbers. We'll be back home tomorrow."

"I appreciate the gesture." Angie pocketed the card and I could tell she was struggling to ignore Suzette, who still stood with one hand on her hip and a foot tapping impatiently. "Reverend, I know this was an uncomfortable exchange for all of us, but I was in the area and I knew you were here, and I just thought you might know something helpful." She stood and began straightening out her slightly too-tight shorts. "I'm concerned about all this for two reasons. One, as much as I understand sisters who resent gay men because of the 'down low' phenomenon, nothing changes the fact that these brothers are still *our brothers*. Our sons, our nephews, our uncles. We can't just act like they don't exist. Their health, as well as the health of the sisters they may also sleep with, is at stake."

"You make it sound noble and all," Suzette said, rolling her eyes. Still standing, she took another step toward Angie. "Your cause ain't noble, sister. You're just playing in the gutter of our people's shame—making a spectacle of our confused boys and the stupid sisters who sleep with them. You want to do something noble, put your pen down and raise money for AIDS prevention."

"We all have a role to play, sister," Angie replied, arching her back so she could make eye contact with Zette. "The only way some sisters will start evaluating the men they sleep with is if they get hit over the head with examples of celebrities who are going both ways.

"We're getting off track here," Angie continued, slowly rising and standing nose to nose with Suzette now. "The most immediate issue, for both of your families, is that if Adrian doesn't quickly turn up safe and sound, his story will become yours."

"Yeah, we know," Suzette shot back, her neck working overtime as she tossed in the female equivalent of the "N" word. "You'll personally see to that, won't you?"

"You don't understand." Angie looked from me to Zette. "This ain't about me anymore. It's about my own story getting away from me." Angie began chopping the air with her right hand, her tone increasingly fervent like a preacher's. "For the past three months, I've talked with disaffected members from every corner of the Black Church, and in every nook and cranny of the gospel music industry. There's a lot of hypocrisy, greed, pain, and suffering out there. But nothing has tripped me out more than how disaffected the homosexuals in the church are today. Too much has changed—celebrities coming out of the closet, liberal churches appointing openly gay clergy, increasing support for civil unions and gay marriage. A lot of our gay black brethren are tired of being shoved in the back of the closet and the congregation, while they get demonized from the pulpit. There's a sea of change out there, girls, and it's coming fast."

I nodded, annoyed at how naïve Angie must think we were, but appreciating the earnest nature of her message. "I've ministered to urban kids for ten years," I said, "and you're not telling me anything I don't already know. I've seen some of my gay kids accept God's healing power and turn from the homosexual lifestyle, but I've noticed many of them stay in it, even if they technically try to hide it from me. The sense of shame is fading."

"You better believe it," Angie said. "People better start recognizing that they're going to stop having it both ways, knowing their church is five percent gay, but singling those members out as if they're uniquely evil. These folk are gearing up to stage some major activism. It took interviewing some of Adrian's friends to open my eyes to what they have in store. And if they suspect Adrian's the victim of foul play, at the hands of one—or two—of gospel's fastest-rising stars?" Angie looked past me this time, and I knew that her words had again seized Suzette's attention. "It's on."

17

Jesse

Coleman's eyes darted to mine the second I opened the passenger door to his Lincoln. "Shut your door and lock it," he said. "I'm expecting the call any second."

Sliding into the car and ducking out of the way of a misting rain, I nearly sneezed at the fruity, familiar scent of Nerds, Coleman's kids' favorite candy. Checking my watch impatiently, I asked, "What's the name of this organization again?" It wouldn't be long before the rest of the group started wondering where we were. Men with a Message was due onstage in forty minutes, where we were opening for Yolanda Adams.

Coleman began to answer my question, but stopped when his cell hummed to life with a call, filling the car with a Deitrick Haddon ring tone. "This is Coleman," he said, his tone cautiously defiant as he punched the speakerphone button.

"Mr. Hill," said the female voice on the other end. The sister's tones had the rich, smooth sound of a radio DJ. "This is Rachel, of

Gays for an Enlightened and Truly United People, also known as GET UP. Thank you again for taking our call today."

Coleman glanced at me while mouthing, "Like I had a choice."

"Mr. Hill," Rachel was saying, "we wanted to thank you personally for cooperating with the ongoing investigation into Adrian Wilkes's disappearance. We just spoke with Mr. Wilkes's mother and she was very grateful. She, at least, seems convinced that your hands are clean in this matter."

Coleman's brow was tightly knit, a hand resting against his forehead. "I appreciate that."

"What the family's not convinced about—Adrian's brother, Earl, especially—is your wife's level of cooperation. Are you aware, sir, that while you had made no apparent calls to Adrian for several days before his disappearance, your wife had called him several times a day for that last week?"

Coleman shook his head. "My wife," he said, "did what most any wife would do when fearing the loss of her husband to another, whether man or woman. She got a little out of control, okay? Wanted to tell Adrian how much I meant to her and, especially, to our kids. She was just asking him to back off. She already told me she kept calling back because he wouldn't return her messages."

"So why won't she explain that to the police? Why did she insist on having legal counsel before cooperating?"

"You know what," Coleman said, his chest heaving with an aggravated sigh, "it's beside the point. Once I vouched for her whereabouts on the night Adrian disappeared, the police said they didn't need to grill her anymore. We've both been cleared, Rachel." Coleman glanced at me, asking wordlessly whether it was time to launch the offensive we'd discussed earlier today. It was the only reason I was here, to provide him moral support as he took a possibly hazardous step.

"Rachel," he continued, "I've done some research into your organization." Actually, Dionne had conducted the research over the past few nights, utilizing Google, Wikipedia, and her extensive network of Christian ministers and activists. It was her way of occupying herself while I worked feverishly in the baby's nursery, painting and assembling furniture.

"I understand," Coleman said, "that your group's mission is to force honest conversations in the Christian Church—Black, white, and yellow—about homosexuality. I want you to know I respect that. Frankly, I'm aware that many of the gospel music legends who inspired me to become a singer shared my struggle. Some, like me, were born gay; others were drawn into it as a result of incest, molestation, or a search for validation they couldn't find anywhere else. And every one of them, like me, had to decide how to deal with this seed placed in them.

"Where your organization differs with me, Rachel, is that I think every man or woman who's attracted to the same sex should deal with that reality in his or her own way. Can you respect that?"

Rachel coughed, but her voice had a smile in it as she answered. "Mr. Hill, trust me, as a rule we definitely agree that every Christian's working out of his sexuality should be a private matter. GET UP advocates monogamous, safe sex and we pray for the day when the entire Church views gay marriage as a right, but we understand no one's perfect. In the same way heterosexuals shack up, sleep around, and commit adultery, we understand that our gay brothers and sisters engage in the same behaviors at some point or another. The sexual journey is something worked out between every man or woman and God, one on one."

Coleman smiled, nodding. "So you aren't like ACT UP and those other hysterical heathen groups, trying to 'out' folks and fight hate with more hate?"

"Mr. Hill," Rachel said. "Watch it. I really don't think you can question the motives of any gay activist unless you've spent time in the struggle."

"Oh, I've struggled, believe that. Like I said, my struggles were private, and I need you to respect that."

"As a rule, I agree with you," Rachel replied, "but, sir, there is a life on the line right now. Worse yet, it appears your wife's homophobia may have put Adrian's life in harm's way. GET UP will not sit idly by. There's too much at stake, and, frankly, you're just high-profile enough to bring important light to the issues that all homosexuals—you included, Mr. Hill—face."

Coleman's nostrils flared as he suddenly punched his phone's mute button. With the pitter-patter of raindrops against his windshield in the background, he looked at me with an urgent plea in his eyes. "You hear that? She's trying to bait me, Jesse. I am *not* one of them!"

I sympathized with Coleman's frustration, but could only tap my watch in response. "We have ten minutes."

"Lord, give me strength!" Coleman's eyes were still raised toward Heaven as he deactivated his mute function. "I have to go, Rachel. I don't know if you have any children, ma'am—I mean, I know there's a lot of ways a lady can get herself pregnant these days—but if you do, think of them before you drag me and my family through the mud. I swear to you that I, my wife, and everyone we know have clean hands. We're praying for Adrian's safe return right along with everyone in his life."

"Well, keep praying," Rachel said. "Because if we find out anything calling your innocence into question, we're prepared to go 'nuclear.' Between Adrian's connections to the national Republican Party and your status in the gospel industry, we could get major press coverage. Add in the controversy, sexual tension, and your proximity to power and fame, and we can force a meaningful conversation among Christians about homosexuality."

"If you wanna do that," Coleman said, his tone increasingly surly, "you can do it without me. You telling me you don't have enough press contacts to stir up media coverage of these issues? Please."

"Like it or not, you're in the middle of this." Rachel's statement rang with finality. "Your wife is a homophobe who may have harmed a prominent member of our community, and on top of that, sir, you're perpetrating a lie when you claim to no longer be gay."

Rachel's words had sucked the figurative oxygen from Coleman's car. Struck by the sight of my friend's cloudy, wounded eyes, I could only hover anxiously as he whipped his face from my view. I considered grabbing the phone and telling Rachel the call was over, but he recovered before that was necessary.

"I see," he said, his voice shimmering with emotion, "that Adrian had a chance to share his theories about me with you before he disappeared." He gripped the phone as if ready to crush it with one hand, then lifted it gently back toward his mouth. "Thank you for this call, ma'am. It's been very informative and I now know what I need to do. You take care—"

"What you need to do is help find Adrian—" Rachel's warning was clipped short as Coleman abruptly closed his phone.

I waited until we'd climbed from his car to speak. "You plan on explaining yourself?"

As my friend stared back at me, a wary glint in his eyes, I realized I wasn't sure I wanted Coleman to explain himself. The honest truth, so help me God, was that I still hadn't fully reconciled the existence of homosexuality with my Christ-centered worldview.

Things were so simple in my worldly days. As a kid I'd been among the most crude tormentors of classmates who gave off the slightest whiff of being "sweet." And frankly, if I hadn't spent my late teens and early twenties traveling the world, I could easily have been on the perpetrating end of a gay hate crime, for all I knew. By the time I accepted Christ, though, my time in the entertainment industry had familiarized me with enough gay culture that I'd come to just see them as people doing what came naturally.

Once I committed to living out God's Word, however, I felt compelled to view homosexuals through a more discerning lens. There were too many scriptural references—from the Old Testament's use of Sodom as the epitome of a city opposed to God's will to the instructive, grace-covered writings of the apostle Paul—to deny that God had some issues with the homosexual lifestyle.

I was still working through the particulars of my views as recently as three years ago, when Dionne and I gathered at my mother's home for Christmas dinner with all of my Law brothers, sisters, nephews, and nieces. Late in the evening, as everyone sat burping over second helpings of peach cobbler and sweet potato pie, the conversation—which was always heavily animated when you got all the Law kids in the same room—got especially heated when the name of a certain colleague of mine, a gospel singer with an audience twice the size of Men with a Message's, came up.

The artist in question had stirred up a mini-firestorm by admitting, somewhat like Coleman, to a gay past. The difference was that he explained his activities in light of an abusive childhood, not to being born homosexual. My second oldest sister, Mary, who had been the lead singer and key producer for the Law Sisters group, was not impressed. "Some things are just better left unsaid," she had stated flatly.

"Why would you say that, sis?" Larry, Harry's twin and the older brother by two minutes, had nearly dropped his fork in disappointment. "The brother's just being real about dirty laundry that fans of gospel need to see aired. I applaud him for opening up. I may not be performing anymore, but God's definitely taught me as a

pastor that when you let your congregants—or fans—see you leaning on God for strength and healing, it helps them trust Him that
much more."

My sister Darla, who may or may not have spent all evening nip-
ping from a bottle of scotch out in the garage, shook her head in response. "Hmmph. Folk don't want all that drama from us. They just
want to hear good sangin', Larry."

Opinions flew around the table as voices rose in volume, and Mama
predictably began to referee. "You-all are getting out of control," she
cautioned a few minutes later. "Lord have mercy. One at a time."

Taking in my family's antics with a hint of amusement, I looked
over my brother Harry's bald head to see my oldest nephew, Larry Jr.,
standing in the dining room's doorway. A senior in high school, the
tall, thin boy had his mother's good looks—my sister-in-law Anna was
Miss Alabama the year she and Larry met. Dressed in a pair of ratty
jeans and a plaid pullover sweater, Larry Jr. watched us with his arms
crossed and his lips pursed. "Uncle Jesse," he asked, his raspy voice
penetrating the clatter suddenly, "what you think about these old singers going on about homeboy's testimony? You the only one here who's
still recording music."

"Boy," I replied, chuckling, "didn't anybody tell you that you
don't qualify for the 'grown folk' conversation until you turn eighteen?" He knew I was playing. Even though I only saw Larry Jr. and
his family a few times a year, we had retained a special bond. I was
his "cool uncle."

The room erupted in laughter, but my nephew would not be moved.
His smile tightened a bit as he said, "Naw, for real. Everyone else has
said where they stand. I wanna hear what you think."

"Well, Neph Number One," I said, referencing the nickname I'd
tagged him with since he'd been four months old, "since you're the first
to ask, I personally think folks need to leave the brother alone. I'm with

your dad. I think any testimony that shows a gospel artist or minister leaning on God to overcome the flesh is a good thing."

"Okay, I hear you," Larry Jr. replied, straightening his stance, but keeping his eyes trained on me. "Let's say that the brother wasn't just saying he *used* to do gay stuff. What if he just said, 'Hey, Church, I'm gay.' Would you be down with that?" For a second it seemed time stood still—the room grew so silent—and my nephew caught it too. "I already know what they'll say, Uncle Jesse," he said. "I've been hearing gay jokes and slurs at every family gathering since I was two years old. What about you, though?"

Mary looked over her shoulder, right into Larry Jr.'s face. "Boy, stop being silly and go back downstairs with the kids."

My brother Larry had an increasingly pained look on his face, but he looked up at his son with stern eyes. "Not right now, son" was all he said.

"Take a seat, youngblood." I stood, patting my chair. "It's past time we started treating the teens in the family as growing adults." As Larry Jr. made his way toward my chair, I leaned against the wall, one hand on my mother's shoulder. "And I'll answer your question. If this brother had said he was actually living the gay lifestyle now, he'd be admitting to a sin. No worse, but no different from admitting that he was committing adultery or fornication with a woman. Sin is sin. As long as he's trusting God to overcome it, though, he's on the right track."

"What if he's born gay, though?" Larry Jr. looked up at me, then let his gaze hop from one face to another. "What if being with someone of the same sex is the only way he'll ever have a fulfilling sex life, the only way he'll ever have a family of his own?"

"I hate to open your eyes to a biological fact, virgin," Harry said, elbowing Larry Jr. suddenly, "but no man ever gonna make a baby with another man. Hello!"

"It's not natural," Mary said. "That's why it's best kept quiet. Let those folks do what they do—I just don't want to hear about it."

"So you don't want to hear about me, then." Larry Jr. was out of his seat now, his back coiled and his eyes piercing his aunt Mary in a manner I personally found disrespectful. Though my heart heaved with sympathy, I quickly moved to my nephew's side.

"L.J.," Mary said, her eyes growing wide at the anger in the eyes of a child she loved dearly. "I know you're not saying that you're—"

"Gay." Larry Jr. leaned over the table, hands on his hips. "Say it, Aunt Mary. 'I have a gay nephew.' Wake up! This stuff is in the Law family blood too, as much as it's somewhere in every family tree! We ain't *that* special."

"Oh no," Darla replied, leaping to her feet and grabbing at Larry Jr.'s elbow. "You just confused, baby! Don't say you gay! Oh, Lord Jesus!"

"I'm out of here," Larry Jr. muttered, pushing past his own father, then stopping when I placed a hand on his shoulder. "What you want?"

Yanking my nephew out of the room and into Mama's foyer, I pressed my nose close to his. "You don't just drop a bomb like that and step," I said. "Show some respect, L.J."

Larry Jr. looked at me, genuine shock in his eyes. "Why I owe you that, of all people?"

"What are you talkin' about?"

"If nobody else understood," he said, his eyes tearing as he pulled away, "I thought you might have."

I halted him in place, simultaneously shooting a nasty look toward Mary and Darla, who had begun to inch in our direction. "You thought I would understand because I used to be out in the world, is that it?"

"Yeah," he replied. "You know how the world works, and you know people aren't born like this unless it's God's will."

"Larry," I said, lowering my voice, "I don't think we know that God willed anyone to be gay."

"Oh man," Larry said, shaking his head almost violently now, "you've drank the Kool-Aid just like the rest of them. Get off me!" The emotion animating my nephew's eyes now sent a clear message: either I let him go, or I'd have to take him out with my fists.

He was still my "Neph Number One," still the loving little boy who'd idolized me as a preteen. I dropped my hands from him, and he bolted out the front door.

I'd had three years since that afternoon to put everything together, but to be honest, it felt like I had erased the rest of that evening from my memory. All I can say for sure is that from the moment Larry Jr.'s revelation set in, the room erupted in tears, recriminations, and a solemn appeal for unconditional love from my brother Larry. That's about it. One thing I knew: Larry Jr. went away to college and hadn't graced a family gathering since.

Coleman never chose to explain himself, but his words pulled me back into the moment. "Four and a half minutes," he said, one eye on his watch as he picked up a brisk jog that I quickly matched. Peering straight toward the backstage door flanked by two security guards, he addressed my question. "I meant what I said, brother. God spoke to me during that call." He came to a dead stop about fifty yards from the door as we both stood vainly trying to shield our hair from the intensifying rain. "You don't need to know much more than that. No time to explain it now, and once I kick things off, it'll be between me, Adrian, these kooks in GET UP, and God. I want you and Dionne clear of all this, man—you've done plenty for us."

"Just don't forget to give the group a heads-up, whatever you've got in mind," I said as I took a step toward the door, which one of the guards had already opened upon seeing us headed his way. As much as we'd prayed we could cool things out before Coleman's past became public, I took his grave tone as confirmation of what my gut had long told me: if we stayed quiet much longer, Micah and the rest of the group would hear about everything from someone else. With a control freak like Micah, that was the last thing any of us needed.

18

Jesse

I don't know about Coleman, but the only way I got through the next forty minutes—our return to the dressing room, the final primping from hair and makeup, the group prayer, and our emergence onto a stage towering above thousands of screaming fans—was to release the players in our respective dramas to God's divine will. As we walked the backstage corridor with Rachel's threats fresh in our heads, I prayed for Adrian's safe return, for Suzette's ability to get over Coleman's past and Adrian's role in it, for Vanessa and the baby's health and strength, and, finally, for Dionne's ability to forgive me whenever I got around to delivering the terrible truth. It made for a mouthful of a prayer, but if I'd carried those burdens onstage, I'd have never gotten a single note out.

From the minute we launched into "Rubber Meets the Road," our new single, I felt God's anointing on the entire band. The one nice thing about opening spots, which were usually limited to four or five tracks, was that you could pour everything out in one fell swoop, often upstaging the main act in the process. We had no desire to disrespect

Ms. Yolanda like that, of course, but by the same token this was a chance to expand our audience, to pick up more unchurched folk, so we had to go for it and we did. The crowd exploded with what felt like pleasant surprise as Coleman and I alternated lead vocals on "Rubber," an up-tempo funky cut evoking the sound of the Neptunes; swooned in spiritual meditation as I held court with "Perfect in Weakness," my newest ballad; hopped in the aisles with "Up in Here," Micah's old-school, organ-heavy but fast-paced number; then finally swayed reverently as all three lead singers harmonized on "Fill Me," the classic soul-styled ballad that first put us on the map.

As was always the case, I brought "Fill Me" to a close, ad-libbing praises to God and stretching out falsetto notes as the audience wept and moaned a few feet beneath me. My eyes closed, a hand raised heavenward, I can honestly say that for those moments my sins with Vanessa and the coming storm around Coleman were as good as vacuumed from my mind. The personal journey I'd overcome was foremost on my mind: the idea that this little biracial bastard child, who spent years scorning Christians and seriously questioning God's existence, had come to feel His embrace so warmly, so viscerally.

"We want to take the time now," I said finally, my voice reverberating through the concert hall, "to bring up any of you who haven't accepted the Lord Jesus as your Savior. I know that Sister Yolanda will make the same offer when she's up here, but neither tomorrow nor the next few minutes are promised to us, y'all. If you need to get right, now's the time. Won't you accept the nudging of the Holy Spirit and come on down?" I stepped back and swept an arm toward Coleman, whose hardened expression made me doubt that he'd been mentally transported in the way I had. "My brother Coleman Hill, the ordained minister among us, stands ready to pray with you. Please come!"

The band's music swelling behind us, Micah, Coleman, and I continued with our meditations and harmonies as a few dozen people trailed their way down front. Not surprisingly, a high percentage were young, scantily clad sisters, the type who tended to be more interested in laying their hands on us than vice versa. "You know their hearts, O Lord," I whispered, trying again to dismiss years of evidence that our music's message didn't always hit home.

Once a good mass of folks had congregated at the edge of the stage, I hopped down among the crowd with Coleman and Micah, reveling in what could be one of our last times doing this. Joe, our manager, had been after us for years, insisting we start conducting our invitations from the security of the stage. "You don't see Kirk, Fred, Donnie, or any Winans walk the aisles at their shows, do ya?" Never mind that none of us had attended every concert by every major gospel star—no one knew for sure how often anybody got down with the masses. That said, with our audience expanding and with increased warnings about possible lawsuits if we accidentally landed on top of anyone or had to defend ourselves from an irate fan, we'd accepted that pretty soon we'd have to take Joe's advice.

Flanked by Micah and me, Coleman made his way down the line of penitents, placing a hand on each one's head and personally praying the salvation prayer with them as the hall filled with grateful shouts of "Hallelujah!" As Coleman completed each prayer, we hugged the women (having to work harder in some cases to end the hugs than in others) and exchanged vigorous handshakes with the brothers, breaking policy only with the kids under eighteen, whom we bear-hugged without restraint.

We were two-thirds of the way through the line when we reached the physical outlier of the group, a lanky but massive thirty-something brother standing well over six feet. As we had worked our way through the line, he had kept his eyes closed and his fists clenched, seemingly lost in his own world. Based on his gear—a shiny, expensive-looking leather sweat suit—and the blazing intensity in his eyes, I figured this was probably his first salvation experience. This didn't seem to be a brother interested in "playing church."

"Jesus is real, brother," Coleman said, smiling, as he stood toe to toe with him. Coleman's eyes had a new light now, a sign that his prayers over the others had lifted the burdens on his shoulders as well. "May I pray with you now, uh—what is your name?"

"Name's Earl." The brother held on to Coleman's offered hand and trained his eyes onto my boy's as if they were deadly weapons. "Earl Wilkes, 'brother.' Funny you should greet me with that phony term, 'cause God only gave me one biological brother—Adrian Wilkes."

Here's the difference between me and my good friend Coleman Hill: he froze, while I jumped into action. I instinctively ran interference by signaling offstage security with my pager, then taking Micah by the shoulder. "Dude's talking gibberish," I whispered into his left ear as if sharing a state secret. "Best to let Coleman keep him talking while the bodyguards get over here. Help me see to this next lady's needs."

What did I say about the difference between me and Coleman? He stood mute and immobilized as I navigated Micah around both him and Earl. By the time Micah and I had placed our hands around the shoulders of the middle-aged woman to Earl's left, Coleman finally rediscovered his voice.

"Earl," he said, voice barely above a whisper, "I don't know where your brother is. You and your family are in my prayers, though."

"I don't want 'em," Earl replied. I looked over just long enough to see him shove Coleman, a move sudden enough that even though Coleman was nearly the same size as Earl, it sent him stumbling back up against the stage.

"I'm here to save *you*, Coleman Hill," Earl said, his voice loud enough that everyone within the first several rows could hear.

"Look now," I said, turning on a dime from Micah and Ms. Kathy, with whom we'd been praying. I faced Earl head-on, and as I grabbed his arm, I was reminded of my mother's favorite saying about my father: she would say that *the reason that man never lost a fight was because he made people think he was crazy enough to do* anything *to win.* Co-opting that same vibe had saved my butt more times than I could count as a worldly man, and I tried to project the same attitude now. When Earl predictably shoved me off him, I got right back in his face. "Don't make me bring my flesh out to play," I said, snaring his shoulder again. "Now security's on the way—"

Earl and I were wrestling now, jostling each other as he insistently tried to shove his way toward Coleman. "Get out of the way, partner," he said, spitting the words through clenched teeth.

"My wife talked to you the day Suzette Hill attacked Adrian," I said, nodding over my shoulder toward Coleman. "I know about the way your brother has suffered, and I know how much you love him. I respect your pain, man, I really do."

Earl didn't let up, but neither did I. One hand on my neck, he leaned toward me while eking out another step toward the stage. "You take up for him, you're feeding the same jacked-up mind-set that led to my brother's disappearance, to the hell he's suffered at the hands of you colored Christians." He stopped moving and yanked me closer. "You and the KKK—just the same in my book."

"You g-got this all wrong," I protested, clawing Earl's hands from my neck. "Coleman didn't hurt Adrian, and he wouldn't let Suzette do that either."

"Last chance, Law," Earl said, his voice raspy now. "Move."

I responded by jamming an elbow into his gut. The big guy recoiled in pain, but no sooner had he lost hold of me than he reared back with a right hook, which caught me on the chin. I didn't quite go down, but I lost enough balance for him to shove past me and grab Coleman by the shirt collar.

"Give me that microphone!" Earl had an arm around Coleman's neck now, and when Micah and I lunged toward them, he jabbed his free arm in our direction. "Another step and I break this fool's neck!" He held out a free hand and a clearly weakened Coleman dropped his microphone into it. Earl looked at the mic as if shocked he finally had an audience, then spoke into it with an urgent, powerful tone. "Coleman Hill is gay, and I couldn't care less about that," he said to the now-hushed audience. "The problem is, he hates that reality so much, he's silenced my brother so he can hide that from you hypocrites. Gotta sell those CDs, right?"

He paused, now realizing that a very late group of four bodyguards was pushing its way through the crowd. "They gonna shut me up in a sec, but this ain't over." He released Coleman, then shoved him again. "You help the police find my brother!" The first guard to reach Earl tackled him, and the air filled with a screech as the men knocked him around and wrenched the microphone from his hands.

Micah was at my side again, along with Frank and Isaac, who had dropped their instruments the minute Earl first shoved Coleman. Micah's question sounded like a series of one-word statements. "Jesse! What—Is—He—Talking—About?"

Possessing no good answer, I glanced over to Coleman, who leaned against the stage praying as the bodyguards spirited an irate Earl through a side door. The hall buzzed with a mixture of confused chatter, wagging tongues, irreverent chuckles, and plainly audible sobs.

As if he could feel my gaze, Coleman raised his head and slowly walked toward the four of us. His chin raised high, his lips shut tight, he had a tear in his right eye, but even Micah could sense this was not a man to mess with. "Coleman, where'd this kook come from?" He even slapped Coleman's back, an admirable attempt to lighten the mood as the people we'd just prayed with melted away, their attempts to connect with God shattered.

It wasn't until then that I realized Coleman still had the microphone in his hand. Leaving it limp at his side, he ran a hand over each of our shoulders. "Forgive me" was all he said before turning away and facing the audience. Raising the microphone to his lips, he cleared his throat.

"God bless, God bless," he said rapidly. "God bless, everybody. I want to apologize for the spectacle you just witnessed. We're about to say a prayer for that brother who just left, and for his missing loved one, but I realize some of you may be disturbed by the accusations he made about me. God laid on my heart, just earlier today, that I need to be transparent with you-all. So it's like this.

"I'm a living witness that God can heal *anybody* of *anything*. For anyone out there tonight who like me was born gay, know that you can be brought out of it. . . ."

19

Dionne

I was in my office at Rising Son, putting the finishing touches on the agenda for an upcoming "Youth Explosion" we were planning with a consortium of local churches, when Vanessa waddled past my doorway.

"There you are!" she said, smiling brightly as she caught herself and paused at the threshold. "Good afternoon, *Reverend*." Placing her hands on her hips, she looked toward my ceiling with eyes of skeptical wonder. "Very nice digs," she said, a hand shielding her eyes from a ray of sunlight streaming through the large window over my shoulder. "I guess working for God doesn't mean total sacrifice, at least not at a megachurch."

I sat back in my seat, crossed my legs, and hugged myself. Vanessa had thrown me with this visit—based on the call we'd received from the adoption agency two nights earlier, she was unexpectedly friendly. "Excuse me, but I thought you were upset with us, Vanessa."

She took a few steps into the office and gently placed a hand on my door, as if requesting permission before starting to shut it. "I hope the agency didn't give you the wrong idea," she said. "I mean, I was upset when I first heard about everything, but I told them—I just need some assurance you can still provide well for my baby."

Rubbing my arms anxiously, I searched for an appropriately respectful but calm tone. "Vanessa, Jesse and I don't make a lot of money, but we have saved well through the years precisely because we know how risky a career in music is. Trust me, we won't be homeless even if Men with a Message breaks up."

Removing her roomy trench coat, Vanessa slid onto the couch in front of my window. "So you're admitting there's a chance Jesse winds up unemployed behind all of this." Within days of Earl's attack on Coleman, and Coleman's emotional testimony about his sexual past and proclaimed healing, articles predicting the end of Men with a Message had popped up online and had been corroborated by gossips on black radio. Considering Jesse's residual fame and the fact that the group's new single was already getting secular radio play, the fuss had gotten attention in a few mainstream media sources as well.

"It sounds like the guys have some tough decisions to make," Vanessa said as I joined her on the couch. "I mean, personally, I have sympathy with what Coleman says—as a person of science, I'm convinced that chemical reactions drive sexual attraction, so I don't see how you can't be born gay. But a lot of Christians prefer to ignore science when it doesn't suit them, and they don't want to hear their favorite singer say he was born liking men." She shook her head sympathetically. "Coleman is going to cost them some sales. Is Jesse comfortable with that, especially as one about to become a new daddy?"

"Jesse performs to glorify God," I said, my hands clasped as I whispered another prayer for my husband, for Coleman, for the entire group. Except for a testy exchange following that fateful concert, Men with a Message hadn't met formally to discuss where to go next. Jesse, of course, wanted everyone to take Coleman's confession as far as it went—he was no longer gay, no longer acting on it, anyway, so let it be—but we had a strong sense that wouldn't satisfy Micah, who considered himself the group's leader.

"Vanessa," I said, moving closer to her and tentatively feeling her belly for a kick from little Samuel, "is there anything else we can do to put you at ease?" In truth, I needed her to put me at ease. From the moment I'd learned of Coleman's public confession, I had barely slept a wink, and while I was concerned about him and Suzette, the real driver had been fear about Vanessa and the baby.

Legally, she had up to thirty days after the baby's birth to change her mind and raise little Samuel on her own. What scared me was the fact that despite my daily reliance on the Holy Spirit and all he had brought Jesse and me through, I knew I'd never let Vanessa rob me of the gift of motherhood. Now her surprise visit, at a time when I had enough uncertainty in my life given the trials Jesse and the group were facing, felt like an attack that I had to fend off.

Vanessa considered my question for a minute before shrugging and smiling. "I just wanted to say that I overreacted, kind of panicked, I guess," she said. "You see, Dionne, I've been on edge about this whole process—having the baby, giving him to you and Jesse—because of unconfessed sin in my life. And I was just thinking, maybe it would help if I could talk through some things with you."

"That would be great, honey," I said, standing even though guilt riddled me as I did so. "Now's not a good time, unfortunately. I have my weekly meeting with my boss—Pastor Norm—in five minutes. And I'm not completely prepared, unfortunately."

"Oh, uh, okay." Vanessa accepted my hand so she could rise, then patted my arm. "Call me tonight, then? I'd really like us to do lunch before the baby comes. I think, honestly, it would be good for both of us."

As a minister I should have focused on the plea riding underneath her words; unfortunately, as a woman desperate to become a mother, I heard a challenge. "I can't promise a call tonight," I said, unwilling to show weakness to the mother of *my* child. "But tomorrow's better. Just call me—*call* me—at the office tomorrow, okay, Vanessa?"

Once we had exchanged a wary hug, I helped Vanessa back into her coat before letting her out of my office. Shutting the door after her, I collapsed against it. "Forgive me, Lord," I prayed. My meeting with Pastor Norm wasn't due to start for another hour.

That made the knock against my door all the more surprising, an emotion extended when I found Pastor standing out in the hallway. "I'm early, I know," he said, bounding past me with his hands raised in apology. "Got a minor emergency at home, Jeannie needs help disciplining our oldest. Kid's fifteen going on twenty-five." He blocked my way back to my desk and motioned to the couch. "Why don't we park here for a second, keep it informal. We can talk detailed plans and metrics and all that good stuff next week. I just had to cover one urgent matter with you before I scoot."

"Okay," I said, taking a seat as Pastor faced me from the adjacent easy chair. "What's up?"

"I need to get you and Jesse over to the house, and time's of the essence now that the baby's almost here, right?"

I nodded, overcome momentarily by the tinge of doubt pricking me.

"So let's say Saturday night, okay? Jeannie's got a great menu planned. You guys just bring a salad and we'll have everything else covered."

"Jesse should be free, but I'll make sure tonight."

"Great." Pastor smiled and began rubbing his palms together. "One other thing. I finally got you the spotlight sermon appointment you've been agitating for. Two weeks from Sunday, all three services, you are delivering the day's Word."

I couldn't have felt more honored. I had only been at Rising Son for three months, and I knew assistant ministers who hadn't preached a main morning worship service in years. "Is the theme around youth?"

"Yes and no," Pastor replied, leaning forward with his elbows on his knees. "I do want you to bracket your message with talk about the struggles of our youth, but the focus should really be on the way society is shifting underneath our feet, how we have to more than ever anchor ourselves in the Word's teaching. For instance," he said, his tone almost blithe, "this will be a great time for you to take a public stand about the issues facing Men with a Message."

"Okay," I replied, stretching out the word lightheartedly. I had been waiting for Pastor to respond to the voice mail I'd left him the morning after Coleman's public confession. Between Pastor Norm's personal friendship with Micah, and the number of Baltimore-DC black pastors who counted him a friend, I knew he would get wind of everything. The odd thing was, he hadn't followed up with me about the controversy yet.

"So tell me," I said, "what sort of stand are you looking for me to take?"

Pastor smiled and rubbed his hands together again. "Dionne, we both know your friend Coleman's put a pretty contradictory message into the marketplace of ideas. Let me sum it up, and you tell me if you agree with it. Coleman says he *chose* to seek treatment for his homosexuality, so that he could be healed of it, right?"

"Yes."

"But then he traces his homosexual behaviors as a youth back to being born that way, correct?"

"Well, yes."

Pastor flicked my knee playfully. "So, while God was in the divine process of creating Coleman Hill—a great man of God, from all I can see—He 'slipped up' and slid the gay gene into his DNA?"

I felt my neck tilt to the right as I stared into Pastor's eyes. "I think that's stating it too literally. Coleman's not blaming God for anything, he's just stating as a fact that he was naturally attracted to other males, that it was an impulse he had to overcome. And he did just that." I crossed my legs and drew up my back. "I think it's a very inspirational story, frankly."

"Dionne, you're not that naïve. Coleman's doing what so many of us do when caught in our sin—he's embellishing to make himself more sympathetic. I mean, if he admitted that he had sex with men just because he felt like it or wanted a thrill, would he get the same reaction as when he claims he didn't have a choice?"

"But he's admitting that he ultimately did have a choice," I replied, my voice louder in my own ears. "He's saying that regardless of what led to his gay lifestyle, he chose to turn from it and build a traditional family."

Pastor stood and walked toward my desk, hands in his pockets. "He's your friend, I get that, okay? You, and I imagine Jesse as well, are too focused on the fact that your friend is committed to doing right now, but you're overlooking his endorsement of the *foundational* argument of the gay rights movement: that they're born that way." Pastor turned back to face me, and I saw that the usual smile in his eyes was gone. "This story is already spreading like wildfire through the Christian community. Men with a Message is an important group, not just in gospel, but in contemporary Christian circles, and young teens and twenty-somethings are learning from Coleman's example. Do you want them to take away the message that homosexuality is really okay, because God makes people that way?"

I exhaled and fanned myself with a sheet of loose notebook paper. "Pastor, we were getting along so well." Three months, and despite our differences on many political issues, I'd found Pastor Norm true to his word when it came to politics. While he still liked to slip a pro-

Bush blurb into every other sermon or so, he had respected my disdain for the "commander in chief."

"I've been happy to keep you out of the loop about our occasional partisan activity, Dionne," Pastor said. "But eventually you've got to show you're willing to stand with the Church and the Bible against worldly messages. And don't misunderstand—as much as the parents like the work you're doing so far with the kids, and as much as the board admires your results, everyone is looking at you with renewed curiosity right about now. We need to see you standing on the right side." He crossed his arms, and I suddenly felt like I was being interrogated. "You *do* believe homosexuality is a sin, don't you?"

"Certainly," I replied. "But once again, so does Coleman."

"This isn't really about Coleman," Pastor said, taking a seat against my desk, but not uncrossing his arms. "It's about the sin of homosexuality, and the fact that we need to correct the message Coleman has communicated about it. At next week's services I'll have a number of journalists in the audience. When you criticize Coleman's remarks, your words will travel far beyond Rising Son's sanctuary."

I raised a pair of defiant eyes to my boss. "You see, this is precisely the type of game I'm not a fan of. I've ministered to more than a few gay teens in my years on the streets, Pastor. The ones who have turned away from their natural desires did so because of one-on-one attention, not some fire-and-brimstone sermon."

"And nobody's stopping you from ministering to the same type of kid directly here," Pastor replied. "There's another audience besides the kids, however—the adults who know better, and that's who Rising Son also needs to reach."

When I silently returned his stare, he continued. "Dionne, you know that you're being used by God in this ministry, in ways you've never been before. You've already played a role in adding two hundred urban African-Americans to our church rolls. You've convinced us to contribute thousands of dollars per month to struggling churches in Southeast DC. You've been good for us, and we've been good for you. But nothing," he said, approaching me again, "is free."

I shut my eyes as I heard Pastor Norm come to a stop a few feet from me. It was hard to argue with his logic about the duty I owed the church, especially when I did believe that, at the end of the day, homosexuality was a sin. If my pastor felt that Coleman's claim of being born gay contradicted that simple truth, maybe it did need to be knocked down.

"I took the liberty of outlining a framework for your remarks about all this," he said. "They're over in my office. I can grab them quickly and we can review, if you want."

"Respectfully, Pastor," I replied, rising and shaking his hand, "I don't need your notes. If you don't mind, I'll honor your request, but I'm going to do it my way."

"You're going to show Coleman what you write first, aren't you?" Pastor shrugged. "That's your right. You probably don't want to ambush a good friend." He playfully bopped me on the shoulder, then grabbed for the door. "Do as God leads," he said as he opened it and filled the doorway with his big-boned frame. "Just e-mail me a first draft by next Wednesday. I'm very curious to see what you come up with, Reverend."

Truth be told, I was in more suspense than Pastor Norm was.

20

Jesse

Coleman insisted the meeting be at his home. A week had passed since Earl had attacked him and dragged his business into the street, and the entire group had spent the past seven days on an agreed program of individual fasting, prayer, and meditation. To his credit, that had been Micah's suggestion. "You don't make the best decisions while the bullets are hittin' you," he'd told me the night of Earl's attack when I reached him at home. "Best to let everyone cool off and get Spirit-filled before we sort this out."

When Micah and I pulled into the driveway, the new Ford Taurus and late-1990s Cadillac told us that Frank and Isaac had already arrived. "Hope they didn't start without us," Micah said, his voice an irritated growl. I had offered him a ride to Coleman's because we only lived five minutes apart, and because I hoped to apply some Law charm, score enough points to keep him from taking over this meeting entirely. Given that he'd done nothing but mutter and nod as I stressed the need for patience and tolerance, the odds of my success weren't looking too good.

"You-all missed out, man," Coleman said, his voice booming with laughter as he answered the door with an apron tied around his waist. "Frank and Isaac were not good stewards of their bodies. Brothers been here ten minutes and already polished off all the griddle cakes!"

"Stop it, man, just stop!" Isaac, the pip-squeak of the group whose slight frame belied a deep, leaden belly, yelled from his perch on the family room couch. "You know good and well your greedy butt—and those chunky babies of yours—ate up most of them flapjacks!"

"Link up, brothers, link up," Micah said, breezing past Coleman with barely a glance and moving briskly to the center of the family room. He extended both hands and shut his eyes as Coleman warily shut his door and frowned at me.

Once we had formed a circle, we each offered up sincere prayers requesting God's providential insight and wisdom. "Let your Spirit, Father, and your Word," I prayed finally, "guide our words and our decisions, nothing else. You brought us together nearly five years ago, God, and your Word says what you have joined together, let no man tear asunder. Keep that before us, O God. In Christ your son's name, we pray, amen."

Coleman remained standing as the rest of us took seats on his couch, love seat, and easy chair. "As I've tried to individually tell each of you over the phone this past week," he said, his arms at his sides and his hands flexing, "I owe the entire group an apology for not sharing this unfortunate business with you sooner. I want two things clear, once and for all, and then I'll hear you out about how we move forward. First, I've committed no sin of any nature with Adrian Wilkes in the time I've been in Men with a Message. Any meetings I've had with him recently were responses to his attempts to blackmail me with my past. Second, and most important, I have nothing to do with the poor brother's disappearance. As hurtful as his attacks on me and my family were, I never meant the man any harm, and I trust he'll turn up safe and sound. The one sin around this episode I committed is that I didn't disclose a painful, shameful element of my past to you-all. I left you uncovered, and for that, I ask your forgiveness."

Frank stroked his beard and looked around the room. "Okay, I'll bite first. I forgave you the night of the concert, Cole, I told you that."

Isaac looked at me as if requesting permission, and leaned forward in the easy chair when I nodded wordlessly. "I'd be lying to say you didn't take me by surprise with this one, though," he said. "Coleman, I forgive you for holding this back from us, because who can blame you? I mean, not that I could ever see touching some hairy dude in the way I touch my wife, but if I *did* and it got caught on camera? Brother, it's a testimony that you haven't folded out of embarrassment by now."

With Isaac's backhanded support permeating the air, Micah settled back into the couch and nodded toward me coolly. "Would our star attraction like to share his views now? And maybe share exactly when he learned of Coleman's news?"

"We all know what we know," I said, staring back at Micah stubbornly, the scratchy sound of my voice evidence of the anxiety deep within. "Nothing's gained by rehashing history. As we sit here, Coleman's told all of you everything he's told me, and the question is, how Christlike will our reaction be?"

Micah chuckled. "Interesting take." He looked toward Coleman as if about to speak, then stopped himself suddenly and swung back my way. "Clarify your last statement, Jesse."

"Don't make me say it." I sighed, stood, and crossed my arms. "What would Jesus do in a situation like this? We already know. In John 8, when he came upon the crowd preparing to stone the woman caught in adultery?"

"*Let he who is without sin, cast the first stone.*" Micah dutifully recited the Scripture, but his lower lip was curled and his right eye twitched. "What are you alleging, brother? You think everyone in this room is harboring a secret that could bring Men with a Message down?" He crossed his legs, but his gaze hardened. "Are *you* harboring a secret that could get us kicked off the biggest tour we've ever been placed on?"

Coleman's eyes hopped straight over to Micah's, and though his chin dipped, he stood straighter and taller. "I am sorry about what happened," he said, "but I can't control what others do." Micah had raised the first of a few elephants in the room—our painful expulsion from an all-star international gospel tour featuring just about anybody who was anybody. That had proven to be only the first of several blows—blows that seemed to be coming by the hour now. Concerts, church appearances, even guest appearances on other stars' CDs, were being yanked from our reach at an alarming rate.

"Don't get it twisted, Coleman," Micah replied, standing himself and stepping past me to grab Coleman by the shoulder. "I forgive you, brother. I feel like I know your heart, and I can believe that everything you say is the truth. Unfortunately," he said, clapping Coleman's shoulder while looking away, "you need forgiveness from more people than us."

"This will all settle down," I said, praying I was right. "People always panic a little bit when they learn something unexpected about an artist they like, gospel or secular. Give them a few weeks. You'll see."

"I'm not the first gospel star to admit my demons," Coleman said, his eyes landing on each of us in sequence. "The past couple of years alone, we've seen major vessels of God admit to pornography addiction, adultery, drug use, and homosexual pasts. Almost all of their careers survived." Coleman's facial expression was stoic, but his tone was urgent now, pained. "We sing for a very forgiving people, you-all. I don't believe in exploiting that, God knows, but this storm can blow over."

"You've cost us money, but that scar can quickly pass and heal," Micah said, placing a hand on Coleman's shoulder again. "I get you on that, man." He looked over his shoulder, past me, to Frank and Isaac.

"You make an impassioned, reasonable plea, Coleman, but you're ignoring one thing."

"Which is?"

Micah turned away again, but faced me this time. "Jesse Law, after all the filthy sin you engaged in when you were worldly—all the groupies, the hookers, the coke—what's your take on how homosexuality stacks up?"

I pushed aside the arguments Dionne and I had pursued the past couple of days as she prepared her "antigay" sermon for Rising Son. I had known Micah would press this issue today, and there was no space for equivocation in this instance. "It's sin," I said, "and the Bible says it's an abominable one. You don't have any conflict here, Micah." I pointed in Coleman's direction. "He believes the same thing."

Micah smiled broadly in response. "So I'll ask him this next. First you: is God in the business of manufacturing gay folk?"

"What?"

Micah sucked his teeth with annoyance and swung toward his true audience. "Coleman, this stuff about you being born that way is nonsense. I'll say it flat out: I can't share a stage with a man pushing that line of homosexual, gay-marriage-supporting propaganda."

Coleman's lips parted. "You can't . . ." His response caught in his throat. He locked his knees and put his hands on his hips. "Micah, you know I'm not one of *them*," he finally said. "I don't believe in gay rights, or marriage, or whatever—"

"You may as well." Micah looked toward what I realized was his peanut gallery, and Frank piped up for the first time in a while. "Isaac and I discussed this with Micah," he said, remaining seated and smiling anxiously. "Cole, you gonna have to take back what you said about being born gay. You can't risk sounding like you support sin, man. And the group sure can't risk it. Please, Cole, just clean that up."

"We, uh, already talked with Joe," Isaac said. Joe, our manager, had weighed in with all of us individually, but agreed to let us hash things out as a group before he got involved. "He says there's all sorts of ways you can publicly clean things up, clarify that you weren't born like that and that you're living proof that people who first choose to be gay can be healed of that addiction and build a normal family life." Isaac began ticking off possibilities on his hands. "Tom Joyner, Russ Parr, Steve Harvey, probably even NPR, will all take you on radio. And you may not believe it, but he thinks we could get on *Oprah* behind this! You know she loves these down-low stories about brothers. You could snare her interest based on all the rumors and talk, then knock her over the head with a Christlike message on air, you know?"

Coleman, who had paced his family room's floor during Isaac's well-intentioned explanation, crossed his arms and looked up. "Jess, are you on the same page?"

"This," I replied, pacing the floor behind the couch myself, "is my first time hearing any of this game plan, Coleman. Apparently, the agreement to process things individually was followed more by some folk than by others."

"Your loyalties," Micah replied without rising to match my combative tone, "were clear from the start, Jesse. You had every opportunity to share all this with us before it exploded in our faces." He turned back toward me now. "You may as well know," he said, "that if Coleman can't see clear to respect our wishes, we want the both of you out."

Any instinctive response of mine was stifled, for it was at that exact minute that my cell phone sprang to life with my most recently purchased ring tone, Marvin Sapp's "Do You Know Him?" The number: Vanessa's.

I was still fiddling with the phone, sending her call through to voice mail, when Coleman erupted in belligerent laughter. "Trashing the group," he said between breaths, and I caught his meaning right away.

"You're trashing the group, getting rid of your two main draws, all to prove some point?"

Micah stared first at Coleman, then at me again. "I'm the main producer," he said defiantly. "You two are vocalists more than anything else, and there's always more where you came from."

"Get out of my house." Coleman waved a hand through the air, his tone burdened with finality.

"Coleman, everyone just needs more time to cool out," I said, sliding my phone back onto my belt. "Let's all connect again tomorrow, maybe get Pastor Willis to come in and mediate." Willis, the leader of the church that Coleman and Frank shared, had served as our spiritual adviser since the group's founding.

"Let's take some time to pray on things," Coleman said, his tone cold.

Distracted now with my own problems, I grabbed my phone again and started for the door. "Later, then."

Coleman didn't stop me as I hustled past him, but did lay a quick hand on my shoulder. His eyes, however, were on the others. "You-all can follow him, please."

I continued on my way through Coleman's foyer, tuning out Micah's insistence that Coleman only had a few days to consider their offer. When I reached my car, I hopped in and began dialing Vanessa's number while putting in my phone's earpiece. Micah got the point; he trailed Frank to his Cadillac, clearly understanding he'd talked his way out of a ride home from me.

Backing out of the Hills' driveway, waiting for my chilled leather seat to warm, I felt the world shifting beneath my feet. Worse yet was the shame about who it was I was calling at the moment my professional world was crumbling around me: Vanessa, not Dionne.

"Took you long enough."

"I was in a meeting. What did you want?"

"Are you taking me to my appointment tomorrow?" Things had gotten so tense between us since I'd delayed confessing the truth to Dionne, I had missed three weeks of taking Vanessa to the doctor, sometimes by her choice and sometimes by mine.

"I'll take you," I said, "if you promise not to make any more surprise visits to my wife's office. For someone interested in her well-being, Vanessa, you caused her nothing but pain and uncertainty with that little move."

Her response was laced with acid. "When are you going to tell her?"

"I understand," I said as I screeched to a halt at a red light, "that you got a nice-sized check the other day."

"Yeah, fancy that," she replied. "A fat check arrived from some accounting firm, asking me to apply it to pay off my med school bills. Why am I not surprised you know about it?"

I swallowed the lump trying to rise in my throat. The money, funneled through several sources, had initially been the funds my boy Max Soul contributed to help Coleman buy Adrian's silence. With that situation having gone off the rails, and Vanessa itching to take ours off the same cliff, I'd decided not to let my friend's dollars go to waste. "Three months, Vanessa," I said. "That's all I need before I can tell Dionne. Time for you and the baby to have a safe delivery, time for Men with a Message to get our drama straightened out, time for Dionne to bond with Samuel before she knows the humiliating truth. Can you honor that?" The sudden silence on the other end of the line emboldened me. I could nearly feel Vanessa's breath on my cheek as she calculated life without a slew of loans hanging overhead. Flesh emboldened, I repeated myself: "Can you honor that?"

21

arl sat nursing a deep mug of hot tea, the knees of his long legs nearly lifting his table at the back of Therapy Café. Recognizing me as I approached, he smiled with bold amusement. "Well, well, the lovely reverend walking into the lion's den." He slid out from behind the table as I took a seat. "Didn't think you'd actually show."

"I'm only here because you agreed to it," I replied. After giving Jesse and Coleman a heads-up, I had called Earl the day before. My spirit was convinced that it wasn't good for anyone—Earl, Coleman, Suzette, or, bless his heart, Adrian—to leave the emotions swirling among them in their current raw state. Now that Earl and Coleman's confrontation was over two weeks in the past, I hoped Earl might be ready to hear me out.

"I'll shut up with the smart remarks," Earl replied after he'd slid back into his seat. "After the grace your boy showed, if this is the price, I'll pay it." After delivering his stunning confession following Earl's attack, Coleman had put his faith on display by marching backstage and insisting that security release Earl without contacting the police or bringing charges. His only requirement had been that Earl hear him out. According to Jesse, Coleman had spent fifteen minutes insisting that he and Suzette had nothing to do with Adrian's continuing disappearance.

"I see a glimmer of God at work in you, Earl," I finally said after some small talk and an update on his search for his brother. "To be honest, as a 'fisher of men' called by God, I'd be irresponsible not to press you on it. Do you think God is using this turmoil in your life to bring you into a relationship with Him?"

Earl shook his head. "God's not gotten very good representation in my life, sister." He turned his tea mug up, swallowed what sounded like the last few drops. "If you preachers keep batting averages on possible converts, you might want to keep steppin'. I'll bring your stats way down."

"All messengers are flawed," I replied. "But don't fault God for that. You do understand that He gives us all free will in how we live our lives, right? That He doesn't want robots, and that's why the salvation process, and our walk with Him, gets messy sometimes?"

"Oh yeah," Earl said, "I've heard that line of reasoning from some of my boys who do church on Sunday, clubs on Saturday. Real convenient logic for them, you know?"

"Earl," I said, my voice dropping in volume, "why don't you stop with the flippant act." The more I talked to this man, the more I felt I knew him, without a lot of detailed conversation even. He emitted a vibe, a mixture of calm recklessness and patient playfulness familiar not only from kids I had counseled in recent years, but in the couple of "bad boys" I had dated back in the day. Jesse was the only one I had ever tamed, but there were some before him who, if they'd just respected my need to keep my legs closed, could have been my first loves. Earl just felt real familiar to me.

"You think I'm being flippant, huh?" The hunch of his neck and the intensity of Earl's stare told me he took offense. "How flippant would you feel if one of your loved ones, maybe that pretty boy husband of yours, was missing right now?"

"I'm sorry," I said. "I just want you to understand that God stands ready to comfort you in this time, and you can appeal to Him for help in finding Adrian. You don't have to wait until your brother is back to consider the Gospel message—"

Earl smiled suddenly, but there was a slyness that set off a flurry of butterflies in my stomach. "Oh, you trying to save my soul, Reverend?"

I wasn't yet ready to face my feelings, so I ducked my head like a nervous schoolgirl. "My calling is to save souls, Earl. I'm here as a minister."

He smirked, in a way that I could tell was beyond his control. "I've embarrassed you, beautiful. I'm sorry."

Beautiful? I guess I'd been so focused on ministering to teens and now white folk, the idea of a client finding me attractive was a little jarring. That didn't keep me from giving as good as I'd got. "Now you're just being cruel, playing with a mousy church girl's ego."

"Okay," Earl replied, chuckling but not backing off his eye contact. "If that's how you wanna laugh a brother off. You may as well know, Reverend Law, you won't be gettin' me to walk no aisles with you until we get to know each other better."

A grin leapt across my face—though I suspected Jesse wouldn't be laughing if he overheard this exchange. "My husband should probably be witnessing to you—is that what you're saying?"

"Let's not go there," Earl said. "We're already playing with fire as it is—a mutual attraction, plus the fact your hubby's boy probably knows where my brother is."

It was time to pull this car over. "You're focusing on the wrong suspects," I said, ashamed at my inability to convincingly deny his comment about our shared attraction. "You can't keep harboring ill will toward Coleman when he's already told you—"

"Well, that's what I intend to do," Earl said, slamming his mug against the table suddenly. When he saw me jump reflexively, he slapped the side of his head. "I'm sorry, I'm a fool. I know you mean well, Rev." He composed himself, eyed me more closely. "You got a legal document for me to sign or something? Something to keep me far away from your crazy girlfriend and her confused hubby?"

I bit. I shouldn't have, but I went for it. "What are you talking about? Suzette's not the same out-of-control woman who attacked Adrian, Earl. She's grown these past few weeks."

"Yeah, well, you can keep preaching at me, but you better believe I'll be keeping my eyes on her," he replied. "You tell her that too. Maybe it'll encourage her to clean up her act in the meantime."

I sighed. "I'm not prodding you for gossip," I said, gathering my purse and keys. "Call me if you want prayer, or if there's anything I can do to help find Adrian, okay?"

"I'm just saying," Earl said, a wicked chortle in his throat, "I can't prove your girl did anything to Adrian yet, but she's definitely doing something to someone besides her confused hubby, probably to a brother who *knows* he likes women. People talk, you know."

The imagery that raised—Suzette laying up under some mystery man—nearly made me nauseous, but had the ring of truth. I knew based on my girl's confession that she was heartbroken with suspicion about Coleman's ability to truly love, or at least lust after her, but I didn't want to believe she was already cheating on her husband. I certainly knew she hadn't played a role in Adrian's disappearance.

"You're lashing out, I understand," I replied slowly. "We all probably deserve that. Look, you know how to find me—"

Earl nodded toward my purse and I suddenly recognized the purring. "That ain't my phone sounding off."

Sighing and realizing I'd have to fight another day for Earl's soul, I answered the phone without checking caller ID. "Hello?"

"Dionne!" Jesse was yelling, the sound of rushing wind engulfing his voice. "Hey, baby, it's time!"

I turned away from Earl, who still eyed me like a conflicted predator. "What?"

"The agency just called," he said. "Vanessa's water just broke! Samuel's on the way, baby, and Vanessa wants us there."

"But," I stammered, my life's greatest desire rushing at me unexpectedly, "she's n-not due for another couple of weeks."

Jesse just laughed, as if he'd known all along the exact moment Vanessa would deliver. "Just meet me at the hospital, '*Mommy.*' I love you so much."

22

Dionne

I couldn't stop crying. My baby son, Samuel Emmanuel Law, was nearly twelve hours old, but I still couldn't believe he was actually here in my arms, and so absolutely, unquestionably perfect. "Thank you, Vanessa," I said for what had to be the twentieth time as I cradled him from the comfort of a rocking chair near the foot of her hospital bed. My vision blurred from streaming tears, I managed an embarrassed glance toward Samuel's birth mother. "I really mean it."

Vanessa, who had just returned from a trip to the bathroom with the nurse's help, eased back against her inclined mattress and smiled narrowly. "Dionne, I should be thanking you. I'm not equipped at this phase in my life to raise that beautiful boy." Her voice caught in her throat for a minute, but she quickly pressed forward. "I'm sorry for expressing doubt about you guys when the controversy over Jesse's group broke. I'm confident you two will give Samuel all the love and care he needs."

"Okay," I sighed, my gaze dropping back to Samuel's bald, circular head and keen, arresting chocolate-brown eyes. "I was afraid I was overdoing it saying thank you so much, but now you have me beat. You know we're not perfect beings, but trust me," I said, leaning down and planting a long kiss on my son's satin-soft cheek, "we'll lean on God every day to give him the best possible life."

"I know you're not perfect," Vanessa replied, chuckling. She rose up slightly in the bed. "Speaking of that, where is Jesse, anyway?"

"He went downstairs to get some breakfast," I said. I checked the clock on the wall, realizing my husband had been gone for almost an hour. "He should have been back by now, though. He probably started calling more family and friends with the news. Our cells seem to get better reception downstairs. He probably got carried away with conversation."

Vanessa frowned and reached for the hospital phone on her night-stand. "What's his cell number?"

I ticked it off for her as I held Samuel closer and sniffed his sweet, Similac-soaked scent with the fervor of a drug addict. In the back of my mind, it felt a little odd to have another woman calling my man to task—but with my hands tied, who was I to argue?

"Hey," Vanessa said into the phone when Jesse had apparently answered. "You get tired of your son that fast? People are looking for you." She paused as he responded, her expression darkening a little for some reason. "Dionne was wondering where you are too," she said defensively. "Wait any longer and Samuel will be wondering where his daddy went to."

"I'm sorry if I'm acting impatient," she said to me as she set the phone back into its cradle. "It's just, I've pressured the nurses and my OB to fast-track my checkups and clearance so I can get home as soon as possible. So there's only so much time for me to tell you both some things that have been on my mind."

"Vanessa," I said, slowing the pace of my rocking as Samuel's eyes shut and he began to snore, "I told you we're not leaving until you're officially cleared to go home as well."

Vanessa looked like she was struggling to keep the game look on her face. "No, Dionne, I already said you guys can leave as soon as the baby's cleared."

"I'll tell you what, let's wait until Sharon gets back," I said, referring to our social worker, who was due back before noon to ensure the adoption process moved forward smoothly.

"Fine," Vanessa replied. "I just need to say my piece while this is on my mind, though."

"I won't stop you from that much. What is it you want to share?"

"It's about Samuel's birth father. There are some things you deserve to know, Dionne."

"What type of things?" The rush of his words, the urgency in his tone, startled me, and I turned to see Jesse standing in the doorway, his narrowed eyes dancing from me and Samuel to Vanessa. His cell phone hanging loosely from his right hand, he marched over to me and held his arms out. Taking his signal, I leaned forward and slid the baby into his arms. Standing back to his full height, Jesse put Samuel over his shoulder and ambled toward the room's large window. His words coming from over his shoulder, he repeated his question: "What things are you sharing with us, Vanessa?"

Vanessa's eyes turned toward the ceiling. "Things about the man who got me pregnant with Samuel."

The silence emanating from Jesse was heavy with indifference, and I resisted the urge to get up and slap him in the back of the head. I was pretty sure of the emotions filling Vanessa right now. Here she had signed away rights to the beautiful baby Jesse now held in his arms, and if she wasn't tormented over that decision, she wasn't human. Talking out loud about the loser who had helped make Samuel, and then fled the scene, was probably therapeutic, a way of validating her decision to give away that man's child.

"Take a good look at the baby's features," she said. "I mean, a close look. Most newborns, from what I've seen, come out looking pretty bland, pretty indistinct. Maybe some day they'll be fine as Denzel or as fly as Halle, but it's usually hard to guess at that during their first few days of life. Then we have this baby, who already has raised little cheekbones, a perfectly proportioned little nose, and eyes that you know will someday make one woman after another act a complete fool." Vanessa's tone had nearly turned mirthful, but now it darkened again. "His father had all those qualities and more. To be honest, he looked an awful lot like you, Jesse."

With Samuel's blissful, sleeping face staring at us over his shoulder, Jesse kept his back to us. "Why do we care what the man looked like, Vanessa?"

"Jesse!" I resisted the urge to hop from my chair and confront my husband for his tone, choosing instead to calm the increasingly tense atmosphere from where I sat. I was having a hard time recognizing the increasingly callous man sharing this room with Vanessa, Samuel, and me.

Less than twenty-four hours before Sharon had called with word of Vanessa's labor, Jesse and I had enjoyed one of our most enriching spiritual conversations in months. I had finally completed a tough-talking draft of the "antigay" sermon Pastor Norm had commissioned from me, and as usual I'd asked Jesse to help me edit it. Before we'd known it, we had not only cracked open our Bibles in order to compare the Scriptures that seemed to speak most clearly to the issue of homosexuality, we'd gotten to sharing the misgivings we had about how to minister on such a personal, controversial issue. Jesse had helped me moderate some of my message's application points, while agreeing with me that this was not an issue from which the Church could shrink. We'd even come away convicted enough to each vow to check in on friends or loved ones we knew who were struggling with their sexuality, including our nephew Larry Jr.

This man in the hospital room, though, was nothing like the man with whom I'd had that edifying conversation. Staring at Jesse with irritated wonderment, I chastised him for disrespecting Vanessa. "She's sharing from her heart, and it certainly doesn't hurt for us to know something about Samuel's biological roots. Someday he may insist on meeting his blood relatives. We should have some facts ready for him, some insights." I turned back to her. "Go ahead, Vanessa."

"My point about what he looked like," Vanessa said, "is that he was one of those biracial, mixed, pretty-boy types accustomed to women throwing themselves at him. And as you know, it takes a man of strong character not to take that as license to treat women as disposable, interchangeable goods."

I stood and moved to Vanessa's side, placing a hand on her left shoulder. "Was it a loving relationship?"

"I thought it was headed that way," she said, and her eyes flitted past me toward Jesse and Samuel. "He was technically in a long-term relationship with another woman, but things were rocky. He pretty much convinced me after a few weeks that he was about to move out and get serious with me."

"Let me guess," Jesse said, finally turning around and facing both of us as he switched Samuel from one shoulder to the other. "He wound up staying with the girlfriend."

"Yes," Vanessa replied, "even before he knew that I was pregnant. I guess that's why I knew better than to hold out hope that me having the baby would change anything. As soon as my doctor confirmed I was expecting, I knew abortion or adoption were my only realistic options."

I stroked Vanessa's shoulder lovingly. "Did you ever give him the chance to help with the baby?"

"I finally told him, once I was about two months along," she replied, wiping tears away with one hand while accepting a tissue I offered from my purse with the other. "Can you believe he had the nerve—the disgusting nerve—to suggest I let him raise Samuel with his girlfriend?"

"Oh Lord," I said. The cruelty of men who let flesh take rule never ceased to amaze me. "What a heartless . . ." I let my silence communicate what a four-letter word might have otherwise accomplished.

Jesse had walked to the other side of the bed now, a hand massaging Samuel's back as the baby began to coo. "I'm sorry, Vanessa," he said, his voice increasingly husky and hoarse. I was surprised to see tears glistening in his eyes. "Dionne and I are both sorry you had to endure such a humiliating request. We'll make sure Samuel grows up to be a better man than his birth father."

Vanessa sniffed back tears and glared at Jesse. "You make sure of that."

23

Jesse

ess than an hour after Vanessa had nearly lifted the veil of our deception, I was back in the hospital cafeteria. In the hours since the baby's safe delivery I had shared the happy news directly with my mother, four of my siblings, dozens of friends, and Joe, Men with a Message's manager. That conversation, however, had short-circuited my desire to speak with anyone else in the group, especially Coleman or Micah.

"Jesse, you got to level with me, son," Joe had said around midnight when I'd first reached him with the happy news. "I couldn't be more overjoyed for you and Ms. Dionne, but my phone's been blowing up with calls all night. Cable news is going crazy with this story."

"What story?"

"Oh, just a little yarn starring that gay group—GET UP, whatever—and Men with a Message!"

I had slid into a seat at the nearest cafeteria table, my mind rushing to insist Joe was exaggerating. "Calm down—what's the story, exactly?"

"Apparently, these activists circulated press releases alleging that DC police have made an arrest in the disappearance of Coleman's boyfriend."

"Joe, stop it."

"Whatever you wanna call the boy," Joe said, "the issue of his disappearance is not going away. The gays claim the cops arrested a well-known gangbanger from PG County. Brother's name is Dante 'D-Boy' Holmes. Apparently, they ran DNA testing on Adrian's home, found evidence that ole D-Boy was there recently. Supposedly, a search of his car found blood consistent with Adrian's DNA."

"What?" My brain was too battered by the sudden emotional shift—from the euphoria of seeing my son born to learning Adrian may have been killed—to process all this, but I held the phone.

"You waitin' for it?" Joe inhaled. "The gays say—"

"Joe, you mean GET UP, right?"

"So, like I said, the gays say that D-Boy just so happens to be a high-school classmate of Coleman's, and that other witnesses claim they saw Coleman hanging out with the banger a couple of weeks before Adrian's disappearance."

It sounded bad, and a quick trip to my car later that morning, to catch some cable news on my satellite radio, confirmed my fears. Numerous press outlets ran quick hits on it as a developing scandal, and it didn't take a genius to do the math: politics, sex, "down-low" allegations, celebrity, and now potentially murder. News hounds found the story irresistible.

The knowledge of the brewing storm had clamped itself to my shoulders, but I refused to let it steal my joy over Samuel. I was determined not to tell Dionne about it until we were settled at home with the little guy, but I couldn't let everything fester without my involvement. That sense was confirmed the minute I caught Micah on the phone. "He's going to take us all down with him," he said as soon as he heard my voice.

"Coleman's not doing this," I said. "He's at the mercy of these activists, and a media that loves to catch Christians in hypocrisy. You and I both know he would never harm anyone—"

"Jesse, stop." Micah's tone was a tank, rushing insistently over the phone line. "You're a *father* now, man, so I shouldn't have to spell this out for you. Coleman has put Men with a Message in an impossible position. This story is officially out there now, and he's never accepted our offer to clear the air."

I can't explain why, but at that moment something deep inside me snapped. I found myself speaking feelings that had knocked around inside for weeks. "You mean your insistence that Coleman take back his claim to being born gay? As a man who was definitely born straight, Micah, I can tell you that was no 'offer.' You're asking the man to lie and say he chose being that way. Why, in our Lord's name, would a man born straight look at how society treats homosexuals, and *choose* that attraction?"

"Okay, I see God has major work to do on you too." Micah paused, then charged forward. "I pray you and Dionne raise that child well, Jesse, but it's clear you're not a real father yet. I perform to glorify God and earn a good living for my wife and babies. And I can't do that when two of my members mock my attempt to honor God's Word."

"You don't have the contractual say over who's in or out of the group," I said, bubbling with rage that I had to even call out a fact Micah had long forgotten. "We let you lead the way a lot, but you're not judge and jury, brother."

Micah's tone was nearly venomous now. "You're protecting a possibly murderous fag—do you realize that, Jesse? What's that say about you?"

I held the phone away from me for a second, inhaling before replying, "Before I had Christ in my heart, Micah, any dude who came at me like that got his teeth busted." I stood and walked to the nearest corner of the cafeteria, burning for privacy. "Why don't you come on down to the hospital and repeat that slur about a brother in Christ one more time. You better pray the Spirit hasn't fled me by then."

I hung up before he could reply.

I dialed Coleman's cell number this time, predictably getting his voice mail. "I'm not playing some game of calling all your numbers," I said. "I know you keep this phone on you all the time, and I know you recognize my number. You can hide from the others, Coleman, but if you're innocent of what they're starting to accuse you of, I've earned a callback." I punched the call to a close and stood against the wall, smoldering with righteous anger. *If you and Suzette lied to me and Dionne about all this,* I thought, *God help your souls.*

The phone rang, and seeing Coleman's number, I answered on the third ring. "Yeah."

"I'm on my way to the hospital," he said, his voice weaker than usual, his tone confessional. "Just be patient with me, Jesse. Please."

24

Jesse

e had me terrified, man," Coleman said as we trudged down a hallway leading to the hospital chapel. "All I did was ask D-Boy to get me back on even ground by striking some fear into Adrian. Hurting him was never part of the deal."

I looked my friend in the eye without breaking stride. "And how, preacher man, do you ask a gangbanger to just put a *scare* into someone?" I shook my head, using the motion as an outlet for my frustration with a brother I'd trusted. "I mean, where's the fine line between letting the air out of his tires and leaving a horse head in his bed?"

"I don't appreciate your tone," Coleman said, stopping suddenly and staring me down. "Don't judge me until you've been in these shoes. He was threatening my family's safety, security, and peace of mind. I had to protect them!"

Reaching the doorway of the chapel, I swung a door back, peeked inside to verify we'd be alone, then held it open for Coleman. "After you."

"I won't ask the predictable questions," I said, taking a seat in the pew in front of the one into which Coleman had collapsed. The past hours' news had injected me with new doubts about my friend's innocence, but either way I was hardly surprised he had suppressed his links to D-Boy. "Obviously, you were hoping Adrian would turn up okay, that you'd never have to reveal your attempt to quiet him down. Just tell me, though, as the friend who tried to help you squash this from the start—what'd you authorize D-Boy to do?"

Coleman gripped the pew bench and stared toward the chapel's marble floor. "Adrian didn't want that money you set aside for him, Jesse," he said slowly. "He wanted me back in his life and when he couldn't get that, he wanted revenge. Those gay activists—GET UP—their crusade against the Church just gave him the perfect way to make me pay."

I nodded, acknowledging the tough fact that had always made this a nearly impossible situation.

"I'm not calling Adrian and those activists terrorists," Coleman said, "but the similarity is that there's no negotiating with them. They want it their way—the Church admits that homosexuals are born that way and are no worse sinners than straight folks—or the highway. I appreciated all that you and Dionne had done to try and find a way out for everybody, but it wasn't working.

"So I approached D-Boy, seeing as how I've known him since we were both four years old. Told him the honest truth about what Adrian was holding over me—he could relate 'cause he's got a gay uncle and a couple cousins too. I just asked him what types of things he could do to convince Adrian to find another target instead of me, you know? Things that wouldn't hurt him."

It turned out, of course, that D-Boy had been too savvy to give Coleman any details about how he'd deliver the threat to Adrian. The less his naïve friend knew, the less he could be pressured to reveal to the authorities.

"He promised me no harm would come to him," Coleman said, standing and eyeing the wooden cross at the front of the chapel. "I would have never gone through with it otherwise."

I placed a hand to my forehead, slowly kneading the flesh there. "Adrian seems like a cocky little customer. Wouldn't surprise me if he told D-Boy and company where to go stick it. How you think they'd respond to that?"

"Oh God." Coleman's voice crumpled in on itself and I started in alarm as he bolted toward the chapel's altar, his sobs permeating the small room.

He was on his knees before the cross, his cries erupting jaggedly when I reached him. Staying on my feet, but placing a hand to his shoulder, I let him cry it out as I prayed for God's provision on my brother in ministry. *He's a good man, Lord, and he loves you.* The force of Coleman's guilt frightened me—were these the cries of a man who'd been an accessory to manslaughter?—but I knew good and well the intensity of the emotions pummeling him.

In all the years I had known Coleman Hill, the most shameful acts in his life involved loving another man, and then, in recent days, possibly placing the same man's life in danger. By comparison, my greatest hits collection was considerably lengthier—cocaine and heroin use and trafficking, funding two girlfriends' abortions, committing adultery as a single and a married man, and direct and indirect participation in numerous beat-downs of rival singers, dancers, and druggies through the years. As Scripture says, though, Christ's salvation had removed me far from that corrupt history, placing me as far from those sins as the east was from the west. Coleman had that same grace for whatever he had done, and I sensed that he needed to be reminded of that.

"I should just end this," he said a minute later, the words coming out choked and hushed. "That's the only reason I came to tell you this, personally, Jess. So I could stop myself."

"What are you saying, man?" I got onto my knees so I could look him in the eye. "You're not thinking about hurting yourself, are you?"

"Jesse," he said, wiping furiously at the countless tears still sliding around his face. "I've worked so hard at this, for years. I've done what the Bible, what everyone in the Church, told me I should do. So why is my family being put through all this? Why does *my* sin get dragged out of the closet?"

I ran a hand over my mouth, searched the cross for an answer. "You know all the rationale, man." Harsh truth tumbled from my lips. "You have the wrong sin in your past, Coleman. Seems like no matter how much society progresses on other fronts, people are still pretty touchy about the gay issue."

"Yeah, my wife included." Coleman bit his lower lip. "We've been keeping this from you guys the last few days, but so you hear it from us first, I'm putting Suzette out of the house."

"What?"

"God has forgiven my past," he said, his eyes flashing with defiance for the first time, "but my own wife can't. She says she tries, but then she goes off and starts seeing another man—sleeping with him! Says she's lookin' back on all our years together, that she's not convinced I have the passion for her that a wife should expect from her husband."

"Coleman, man," I said, inhaling with shock, "I'm sorry, brother." I was hardly surprised; I loved Suzette like a sister, but that didn't change the fact she was an impulsive hothead. "I don't want to know who she's seeing," I said, holding up a hand, "but the important question is, can you guys get past this? Maybe she just needed to get this out of her system."

"I don't know where we're headed," Coleman said, shaking his head as new tears sprang from his eyes. "All I know is I can't count on Zette, not when she questions my honesty. She's as bad as Adrian, saying she's not sure I can be healed of homosexuality!"

The question had haunted me for a while, so I asked it. "What do you think? Are you healed?"

Coleman trained his eyes on the cross again, his stare so intent it seemed he was willing Christ to materialize there in the flesh. "During the last conversation we had before I sent D-Boy to see him, I told Adrian about the process I went through to deny my urges for him and other men. I think I always had just enough sexual attraction to women to go that way, but the intensity was never like it was with other men."

I nodded as if I understood, focused on being respectful. "So you chose to focus on your attraction to women and ignore men?"

"Something like that. Again, I never had a choice about being attracted to men, but I had a choice about whether to act on it. And except for Adrian, I never did. So with Suzette, the challenge was to convert the emotions I felt for him and place them on her.

"Praise God, it worked! And the attraction grew through the years, to the point where I don't even have to think of men anymore when she and I make love."

"Hmm" was the best reply I could give as my eyes focused hard on the worn carpet below. Between you and me, my friend was treading on "too much information" territory now. I'd had many openly gay friends in my worldly days—not to mention quite a few we all knew in the gospel industry—but to hear what I'd always viewed as a "straight" friend talking this way left me feeling a little dizzy. "So, uh, what did Adrian think of your process?"

"You know good and well what he thought," Coleman said, his chin turning rigid. "If Adrian's lying in a ditch somewhere, it's only my fault if D-Boy played a role in it. May God forgive me if that's true, but if so, I'll pay the penalty." He took another long look at the cross, then surprisingly punched me in the shoulder. "Help me up."

I knew he was emotionally drained to put that on me; the brother had two inches and fifty pounds on me. I pulled him to his feet, though, and steadied him. "I don't want you talking crazy anymore," I said. "Are you sure I can trust you to drive home safely?" When he waved me off with a shrug, I kept an arm around his shoulder. "So we're clear, Coleman, whether you're gay, straight, or asexual, you have too much to live for, man. Your children, your ministry, your friends—"

"Yeah, friends like Men with a Message?" He gave a wry grin. "You don't have to worry about me taking care of myself, man, because I'm doing two things before this night's through. First I'm calling the police before they call me, so a detective can come interview me in full about D-Boy, Adrian, everything, and I'm not bothering with a lawyer. Then I'm calling Joe so he can deliver the news to the rest of the group. I'm out."

I had begun to smile with assurance at his first promise, but his second just enraged me. "Coleman, don't let them scare you off. As men of God, we need to fully hash this thing out."

"No," he said, patting my shoulder and turning toward the chapel door. "There's enough drama in everyone's lives as it is—my marriage possibly ending, you and Dionne welcoming baby Sammy into the family, and me doing what I can to help Earl and the rest of Adrian's family find him. The last thing any of us needs is a knock-down-drag-out over who's in and who's out of the group."

"How will you support your family?" I asked. When we first formed the group, we'd all had day jobs as ministers and counselors, but with our most recent contract, we'd come to rely on our music money, first and foremost. "Your music minister gig is only a part-time salary, right?"

Coleman shrugged. "I'm in this situation—more important, Adrian is in whatever situation he's in—because I put my trust in man, not in God. I'm not making that mistake again. If I have to take out a second mortgage to get through a patch, I'll do it. God will provide."

"You recruited me into Men with a Message, Coleman," I said, embarrassed at the pleading nature of my tone. "Now especially, I'm not sure I can picture being in it without you."

"The group is changing lives, man." Coleman smiled for the first time of our entire exchange, and he waved me to match his stride toward the chapel door. "I may not be able to take part anymore, but don't stop letting God use you just because I've messed up my part in all this. The group needs you, Jesse," he said. "Frankly, you're the member I most admire—not only were you the least judgmental of me, you're the one out of all of us facing the most temptation to backslide. You're my role model, man."

As I followed Coleman into the hallway, the anvils of guilt my friend's praise created burrowed into my shoulder blades. "I'm no role model." As the door swung shut behind me, I ran a hand through my hair in shame. "God, if my sin was exposed in the way yours was, you can't imagine how sickened you'd be."

"That was the old you," Coleman said, turning away from me and toward the hospital's main lobby.

I only wish, I thought as I nodded a good-bye to my friend. As Coleman faded into the distance, merging into the stream of blue scrubs, white coats, wheelchairs, and rolling beds, I realized that I had left Vanessa and Dionne alone for nearly an hour. That thought, fresh from Vanessa's earlier emotional striptease, first filled me with fear, but instead of rushing upstairs impulsively, I followed a still, small voice and turned back into the chapel.

Coleman had stopped running from the tough issues in his past and present. I found myself longing for the freedom and peace that had permeated his parting smile tonight. My fists balled, but my heart opening, I moved intently toward the cross, determined to emerge with the strength to finally tell Dionne the truth about Samuel.

25

Jesse

When I returned to Vanessa's hospital room, newly prayed up and determined to confess everything, my spirit was warmed by the sound of my mother's voice. From four doors away, I heard the boom of her raspy belly laugh and smiled wide. I had been too consumed by the competing dramas of the moment to remember her promise to come over as soon as she could to see Samuel. My son was no blood relation to Mama, and was in fact her twenty-fifth grandchild, but apparently the thrill was new with each birth. Arriving at the room, I flung the door open, eyes roving for the three most important people in my world—Dionne, Samuel, and Mama.

Mama was there, but she had brought company.

"Hey, baby brother!" My sister Carol's back was to me as I strode in, but she eyed me over her shoulder. She held Samuel while Mama leaned over the both of them protectively and Dionne and Vanessa carried on with small talk. Rising from the bed and holding Samuel out toward me, Carol flashed an oddly friendly smile. "He is beautiful, ain't he? Congratulations, new Pa-pa!"

Accepting my son from Carol and cradling him with my right arm, I felt the earth shift beneath my feet, but resisted panic. "Thank you," I replied, kissing her cheek and then Mama's. "I'm glad to have family here to share this moment." Because of the complexities involving Vanessa and our need to respect her final chance to commit to the adoption, Dionne had asked her family to wait and see the baby once we brought him home. I had asked the same of most family and friends, but knew with Mama that it was a futile request. What I hadn't counted on, by any stretch of the imagination, was Carol's presence.

Holding Samuel close, I leaned down and planted a quick kiss to Carol's forehead. "What you been doing?" I asked. "Hanging out at Glamour Shots or something?"

"Doesn't she look beautiful?" Mama said as she came alongside me and hugged me around the shoulders. "Amazing what having a little talk with Jesus does for the soul."

I kissed my mother on the cheek before turning back to Carol. "You really do look great. How long have you two been here?" Did I still have time to keep Carol from asking the obvious, devastating question?

"I gotta say, Jesse," Carol said, her eyes growing wider, "I about had a heart attack when I saw who the birth mom was! What are the odds, huh?"

From her perch in the bed, Vanessa cleared her throat and aimed a pained smile toward us. "Carol, I guess I should be grateful that you didn't pick up where we left off. I might have your hands wrapped around my throat about now!"

"Naw," my sister replied, waving blithely toward Vanessa. "That was ages ago for me, Vanessa. I've moved on. Now, that doesn't change the fact you was a lousy landlord, but it ain't my place to harp on it or hold it against you."

Standing there between the hospital bed and the door, my son in my arms as my eyes anxiously searched Dionne's face for even a hint of betrayal, rage, or suspicion, I knew deep down I was toast. Years of following Christ had left me without the necessary skills of deception to clear the hurdles before me.

Dionne was on her feet now, and her expression—arched eyebrows, tight mouth, penetrating stare—said it all. She didn't raise her voice, didn't show out, just asked a single question as our eyes locked. "Jesse, what are they talking about?"

My time was up.

26

I was literally dizzy as I climbed into the passenger seat of our BMW. Against all odds, my tone was even, my words carefully chosen as I looked over at my husband. "You really want to lie right now, don't you?"

His eyes nearly glowing in the darkened car, Jesse seemed to be staring a laser beam right through the dashboard. "What I want, baby," he said, "is a different set of facts. A different truth."

Blood drained from my face, but I refused to be silent at my husband's ominous setup. "It looks bad," I said, sighing as if I were merely frustrated at the signs that life as I knew it was coming to an abrupt halt. "But it's looked bad before, and you've always proved that I could trust you."

He had. As a natural flirt who spent years overriding spiritual and psychological struggles with sex, Jesse had been chased by other women as long as I had known him. Worse yet, because most people still thought he had money from his days as a secular star, some of the same women saw deep pockets and tried to tie him up with paternity suits, betting he'd pay them to just go away. For seven years I had stood by my man, enduring court dates and lawsuits that always dissolved when DNA tests vindicated Jesse or the plaintiff got a sudden conscience. Every time Jesse's fidelity was challenged, he showed himself to have been faithful.

It took a while for everyone else to catch up to me, though. The first three years of our marriage, my father said the same thing every time he caught wind of a new accusation against Jesse: "Sweetie, where there's smoke, there's fire." Though he was the most blunt, my sisters and many girlfriends tried to hint as much. Only my mother, who was smitten with Jesse the first time they met, had refused to ever believe the worst of my husband.

"Dionne, I love you," Jesse said now, reaching for my hand, which I let him cover with his own. He held eye contact with me, his gaze wounded yet strong. "I told you my last lie back there in the hospital room. Vanessa and I couldn't honestly explain ourselves in front of Mama and Carol."

I stared back at my husband, pushing past the catch—and the rising taste of vomit—in my throat. "Just say it, Jesse."

"The reason we never mentioned that we first met through Carol," he said, "is because Vanessa is the lady I was seeing during our separation."

Tears were spilling down my cheeks, but I dredged up a chuckle as I wiped my eyes. "Oh, she's a *lady*, is she?" I was hit suddenly with a flashback of Samuel's beautiful little face, from just twenty minutes earlier when we had delivered him to the maternity ward's nursery, where he was undergoing routine testing. Emotions finally got the best of me and I asked, "You're Samuel's father, right?"

"Yes," Jesse replied, his eyes holding to mine with unswerving strength despite the tears forming there. "Baby, you have to give me time to explain everything—"

"I don't *have* to give you anything!" I raised a fist, ready to swing, and Jesse grabbed it.

"No," he said. "God knows I deserve it, Dionne, but not here. What if someone walks by, sees us going at it? Samuel could wind up in a foster home!"

"Get off me!" I swung again, tore away from my husband, and nearly kicked the passenger side door open. Brisk April air swooped down the corridor of the parking garage, buffeting me, but I felt no relief. One arm gripping the nearest armrest, I leaned my head out over the pavement, a stream of vomit violently erupting from me.

When Jesse pulled me back inside the car and reached over me to shut the door again, he lay his head against mine. "Please, baby," he said, tears flowing from his eyes onto my nose, "don't show out, not here."

"You are unbelievable." It was a simple, factual statement, nearly chilled of emotion as I wiped my mouth with a shaky hand. "You may be right, Jesse, but for you of all people to lecture me about how to protect Samuel's interests? Are you kidding me?" I rammed an index finger into his chest. "Samuel's going to grow up and hate you as much as you hated Phillip," I said, spitting out his father's name with the same rage Jesse displayed before the Spirit helped him forgive.

"Dionne," Jesse replied, his eyes staring limply at the finger I'd tried to implant into his chest, "if you don't think I've already been tormented by that reality, you don't know me like you should.

"Right now," he said, his voice so hoarse it sounded like a whisper, "this is about you. I need to tell you the whole truth, Dionne. I need you to understand how it got to this point—"

"No doubt about that," I interjected, popping my door open. "You'll explain it all to me, but not here, not where you can invent facts and make it all sound more sympathetic than it should be."

Jesse hopped out of the driver's side as I shut my door. His hands on the top of the car, he stared across at me as if I'd lost my mind. "What are you doing?"

"I'm going back upstairs," I replied. "And so are you. I want to hear the 'truth' from the both of you, at the same time. Harder for either of you to lie when you're in the same room."

Jesse hesitated, stroking his chin. "I don't think it's a good idea, you being in the same room with her right now. She's scared about your reaction, and remember, she still hasn't officially signed all the adoption papers."

"Oh, this is a great idea, believe you me," I said, striding past Jesse as if I didn't care whether he followed. My heart was breaking, but I forced a crooked smile as I said, "Besides, you just settled this whole adoption business. You may never play a role in raising him, Jesse, but thanks to you, Samuel is my son now, more than ever."

27

hree months to the day they had met at Carol's house, Jesse was summoned to Vanessa's condominium. Driving down the BW Parkway, chewing his lower lip in half, he had prayed the same phrase over and over. *Give me the right words, Father.*

Six weeks had passed since Jesse had officially reconciled with Dionne, six weeks since Vanessa had accepted his decision with a respect and maturity he'd known better than to expect. Now, after forty solid days with no contact—no dead bunny rabbit stuffed into a pot on his stove, no incriminating messages left on Dionne's voice mail—Vanessa had called, insisting he come by, and she'd been neither respectful nor mature.

"Clean up your language," he had snapped when she reached him at the recording studio, where he took the call on an outdoor patio. "We agreed to end this with class, Vanessa."

"You get your high-yella butt over here now, or I'm calling precious Reverend Dionne."

"She knows I was seeing someone during the separation. You have nothing to hold over me."

"Oh really? You think she wants to hear the play-by-play of every time we made love?"

He was in his car five minutes later.

Vanessa lay sprawled at the top of her steps when Jesse let himself in; he didn't have a key or anything, she had just left the door half-cracked as if Hyattsville were a crime-free zone. Peering up at her from the landing, Jesse squinted at his former lover. Vanessa's sweat-pants and shirt were wrinkled, her hair was askew, and based on the smell in the air, he wasn't certain how recently she had bathed.

"I'm here," he said cautiously as he leaned against the wall a couple of steps beneath her. "Are you ill? What's going on?"

"You came." Vanessa's eyes, barely open now, glimmered with a lazy hope. "I-I didn't think you'd—"

"You've been drinking," he said, reaching up and steadying her chin. "Oh, Vanessa. You haven't gone into the hospital in this condition, have you?"

"Oh, thank you for your concern, Jesse," she replied, patting his cheek with mock appreciation. "Such a sensitive man, always looking out for my unsuspecting patients. Dionne's a lucky woman." When Jesse simply stared back sternly, she answered his question. "I called in sick yesterday, if that makes you feel better."

Jesse took the last two steps and sat down beside her. "What's this all about?" It wasn't like he didn't think he knew—he'd left women in worse condition in his Before Christ days—or like there was anything he could necessarily do about it. Unlike in the old days, however, it didn't mean that he didn't care.

"I was thinking," Vanessa said, her chin now in her palm, "of exactly how to hurl myself down this flight of steps." She nodded over her shoulder, toward a bathroom. "A few emptied bottles of Tanqueray and Guinness in there were supposed to give me the courage to do it." She slumped forward, and Jesse wrapped an arm around her to keep her stable. "Why can't I just do it?"

"Why would you even think that way?" Jesse felt his forehead crease with concern—well, guilt—and hugged the woman at his side. "You have so much to give this world, so much to give the right man when God brings him into your life. You don't need me."

They had already agreed to this. The day Jesse told Vanessa he was reconciling with Dionne, they agreed that their affair had not been a merging of soul mates. Rather, it had been a pleasant indulgence in one of those "what-if" affairs, a simple case of two mutually attracted consenting adults pausing to experience each other.

What other conclusion could they have reached?

Their first night together had occurred a week after their first meeting. Jesse, trying in vain to fall asleep on the lumpy double bed in his hotel room, had indulged in a few minutes of a guilty pleasure, *Def Comedy Jam*. *Def Jam* was admittedly trifling stuff, completely lacking in any edifying ingredients, but with his marriage crumbling, he'd enjoyed a few good laughs before his eyes shut and his snores filled the air.

One problem: Jesse hadn't accounted for the soft-porn movie that apparently followed the comedy hour. When he involuntarily stirred around two in the morning, he awoke to the still-running television and the fevered thrashing of an overheated, physically fit young couple. Although he had worked hard—not always successfully, but very hard—at fleeing all forms of pornography since marrying Dionne, the half-asleep Jesse was no match for the heat the movie scene stirred in him. Before he knew it, he had spent half an hour viewing the remainder of the film, his body humming with passion as the couple pleasured each other.

He couldn't sleep. Ninety minutes after the movie had faded from the screen, Jesse had feverishly hopped beneath a chilling shower, said two lengthy prayers, and read aloud to himself from several of Paul's

New Testament books. His body prickled with the hunger, the thirst to make love. Over the course of his marriage, he had heightened Dionne's enjoyment of sex to the point that they'd been intimate several times a week for the majority of their marriage. Now here he sat, struck celibate for what was going on five weeks, with little hope of when or if Dionne would get her act together and take him back. . .

He took another shower.

He rifled off dozens of push-ups.

Then he called Vanessa, and the rest was history.

"You're right, Jesse, I don't need you," Vanessa replied as he lifted her up and away from the steps. "A-at least I didn't think I did, not before this."

Despite himself, Jesse felt his eyes swell in horror as she recounted the three positive pregnancy tests, the seven weeks she'd gone without a period. When that reaction brought on Vanessa's ragged fit of tears, he sat her down on her bed and hugged her close. "Oh God, forgive us. Forgive me," he said, his voice booming in his own ears as he rocked Vanessa into a calmer state.

He drew her chin up toward him, rested his gaze on hers. "Do you want to be a mother?"

"W-why do you think I tried to throw myself down the steps? This isn't part of my plan, Jesse, especially not without the baby's father at my side. I have a career to build."

"You can't be thinking of abortion," Jesse replied. "Maybe I'm not the one to deliver the message, since it's my sin that put you in this condition, but I can't back off that." He rubbed her stomach, swore he could already sense a faint bulge. "This is a precious life growing here." He inhaled suddenly before continuing. "Would you let Dionne and me raise it?"

Vanessa buried her face in her hands suddenly, sobbing again.

Jesse waited respectfully.

"This doesn't change anything, does it?" Vanessa asked, her eyes aimed at her off-white carpet. "I mean, your first instinct isn't to raise the baby with *me*, is it?"

"I love Dionne," Jesse said, his tone just shy of sounding apologetic. It wasn't like they hadn't talked this out before. Their heady affair hadn't been limited to sexual acrobatics. Jesse admired Vanessa's medical intellect and the servant's heart she brought to her calling, her bubbly sense of humor, and her determination to independently establish herself before relying on any man. She, on the other hand, saw Jesse as a perfect embodiment of what so many women wanted—a tamed bad boy equipped to hang tough in the hood, but who could show a softer, sensitive side after sex and during emotional conversations.

That was why Vanessa had toyed, five weeks in, with trying to compete with Jesse's determination to reconcile with Dionne. She still couldn't believe she had offered to let him move in with her, that she had suggested he could divorce Dionne whenever he found it convenient—he obviously had an image to manage—and that if things stayed on track with them, they could get married in two years when she entered private practice. All that, of course, had just been the appetizer.

"We weren't equally yoked," Jesse reminded her now. "We don't see eye to eye about how to best live out the Christian faith, you remember that. On issue after issue we were on different pages."

"I know, I know," Vanessa replied, looking away and placing a hand over her mouth when a rush of nausea hit her. "You're being kind, though." She stared over the cliff momentarily, weighing whether to admit that she had skipped taking her YAZ contraceptives for the week they'd spent in London. She would eventually break and tell him, but that afternoon she lacked the courage. "The bottom line is, I'm not Dionne."

Jesse let his silence confirm her assessment. As she began sobbing again, he pulled her to his side. "I'm here for you, Vanessa. I mean it. Will you at least consider my offer?"

28

Jesse

can't believe how much he's changed in two weeks." Vanessa
fought vainly to hide the proud smile tweaking her lips as she
fondled the photos I'd laid before her. "These are mine?"

"Yes," I replied, nervously drumming the tabletop between us.
"Dionne specifically wanted you to have those."

Vanessa reclined slightly in her satin-backed kitchen chair, her eyes
on the photos even as her words sliced through me. "I can feel your
anxiety, you know. You haven't been in my condo since I told you we
were expecting." When enough time had passed that she decided I
wasn't taking the bait, she took another shot. "I guess Dionne was
okay having you alone with me for now. After all, I'm no sexual threat
for at least another four weeks, right?"

Despite myself, I was still drumming the tabletop. "How long do
I need to stay here?"

"What?"

"I said, how long do I need to stay, so you don't feel slighted when
I cut out?"

"Well, thank you for asking," she replied, a demure smile crossing her face as she set the baby photos down. "We haven't talked since you guys left the hospital with Samuel. Now that the air's been cleared, why can't we just make innocent small talk?"

I felt my eyes flash with irritation, and tried to compensate by leveling my tone. "The air's not clear yet," I said.

Vanessa cocked her head as if confused, her gaze shooting past me and her eyes narrowing. "Jesse, we confessed everything to her, and unless I missed something, Dionne's moving forward with the adoption process. She even let us leave the hospital alive!"

"Yeah, well," I replied, my eyes dropping to the table, "a lot has happened since the day we checked Samuel out of the hospital."

Vanessa set her batch of photos down. "Anything you can share?" When I flashed a slit-eyed stare, she shrugged. "Just trying to make sure my baby's not in the middle of some *War of the Roses* situation. You two are going to stay together, aren't you?"

"Sure. I mean, all I did was slip and fall into your bed, then try to hide the fact we were adopting a child that was already mine." I had promised myself I would be more careful than this—the last thing I needed was to get Vanessa riled up and thinking of trying to get Samuel back.

After promising to pray for us—a sincere but frankly comical gesture—Vanessa ushered me toward her front door. As she swung the door closed behind me, her parting words stirred fresh unrest into me. "You tell Dionne, I don't want Samuel raised in a broken home."

Vanessa's implicit threat was still working on me an hour later as I stood in the home of Wylie Willis, Coleman's pastor. Pastor Willis, Coleman, and I stood in the center of the pastor's massive family room, which had a brick fireplace and an eye-catching view of the wide deck and forested backyard outside. Arrayed around us were the major players in the battle to decide Men with a Message's future: Micah, Frank, and Isaac, along with our manager, Joe, and Sylvia Bronson, the senior A and R executive from our record label.

Pastor Willis led us in a rousing prayer, then stepped forward as Coleman and I hung back. "Brother Hill has asked me," the pastor said with a preacher's drawl, "to set the context of this afternoon's discussion. He knows there are legal considerations behind all decisions made here today—Sister Bronson and Brother Joe, I believe, are the attorneys in the room—but as his senior pastor, Coleman has asked me to help you understand his mind-set." The pastor, a short, compact brother in his early forties, clasped his hands and peered toward the fine, immaculate carpet beneath his leather wingtip shoes. "I have counseled Coleman at several points over the years about his battle with homosexual impulses, and I have always told him that by resisting urges whose *existence* he cannot control, he is doing the Lord's work. God's Word tells us, understand, that homosexual *behavior* is an abomination. I find no evidence in Scripture where a man *tempted* to sleep with another man is any different from a man tempted to commit adultery with a woman. The issue is not the impulse—it is the act. And on that score, I am here to tell you that Coleman Hill is a hero. Cast him out of this group at your own peril."

"Pastor," Micah replied, standing from his seat upon one of several beige leather couches. "With all due respect, I didn't come here today to litigate the specifics of Coleman's sex life or his 'urges.' We've had that conversation, and I take my brother at his word. I believe he hasn't touched another man since the days those horrifying snapshots were taken of him and the brother that went missing. The question," Micah said, turning and nodding toward Frank, Isaac, and Sylvia, "is whether he's ready to stand up for what's right. He's got to denounce the idea that God would implant a 'gay chip' into an innocent child."

Coleman stepped forward, a hand resting now against Willis's shoulder. "Thank you, Pastor," he said. "Micah," Coleman continued, stepping closer to his old friend with a deliberate pace, "where do you get the right to dictate my theology?"

"Coleman, Coleman," Frank said, springing suddenly to his feet. "Stay cool," he pleaded, glancing toward Micah as if that would shut him up. "Nobody's dictating anything, okay? We just want you to help calm this storm, that's all."

"Calm the storm?" Coleman crossed his arms, licked his lips. "I've done all I can to calm the storm, Frank. First," he said, ticking off reasons with extended fingers, "I've done interviews in every media venue that would let me, reassuring people that I've rejected the gay lifestyle and that it's not God's ideal for his people. Second, I've confessed everything to the authorities about my involvement in Adrian's disappearance."

"CNN, MSNBC, FOX," Micah said, his voice a growl as he defiantly crossed his arms. "They're still running stories on that mess every day. People think we're coddling a murderer by keeping you in the group."

"Forgive my French, but that's a load of bull," Coleman replied. "Last week I told Joe everything I told the police. And while the media's not reporting it, you may as well know, the police are now convinced that Adrian survived his run-in with D-Boy and his crew. It looks like he got smart with them, they roughed him up, and then they dropped him off somewhere near the Capitol. He was humiliated, yeah, but they swear he walked off, cursing them and promising revenge."

Micah frowned. "The police bought that?"

Coleman spread his hands and shrugged. "If there was evidence to contradict that, don't you think somebody would be in police custody by now? Don't get it twisted. No one—not me, not Suzette, and not one member of D-Boy's crew—has been charged behind all this." He took a second to collect himself before saying "Personally, I think the whole thing is being stirred up by that crazy group of gay activists. You-all are playing into their hands."

"I've heard enough," Micah said, shaking his head and turning toward the front door. He paused, turning back toward Sylvia and Joe. "Either he's gone, or I am. And for the record," he said, now flashing an outstretched finger in my direction, "I'm not so sure about that one either."

"Micah." Isaac's voice caught everyone off guard. The quiet one of the group, a brother who usually voiced his opinions through Micah, Isaac stayed seated, but let the passion in his tone command our attention. "You can't act like this is some easy decision. I'm with you spiritually, brother, but I can't expel Jesse or Coleman without asking how Men with a Message survives after they're gone."

Sylvia chuckled and rolled her eyes. "Finally someone speaks the truth." Everyone had awaited her weigh-in, and the room now filled with hushed silence. "Boys, like it or not, you've got a newly released, expensive CD that just shipped to stores. While the group's moral reputation is taking a hit—and don't think that doesn't worry me on some level—your sales are doing A-OK. People who usually don't think twice about gospel are snapping this release up. Some of them, because they're just curious about Coleman—some of them, frankly, because they've just realized that Jesse Law is still recording music. Without these two as your lead vocal draws, I'm not sure how marketable the rest of you are." Sylvia cleared her throat and stood. "There," she said, "the elephant is no longer in the corner." Trading glances with a wounded Micah, she reached into her purse. "Pastor, I hate to stink up your lovely home. Mind if I step out back for a smoke?" When the pastor nodded and slid open the glass door leading to his deck, she flashed her hazel eyes toward Joe. "You're the manager," she said as she ambled past him, "fix this. The label has too much at stake."

Hands on his knees, Joe cleared his throat as Sylvia slid the glass door behind her. "We can work this out, fellas," he said. "Let's go around the room, okay? I want each of you to state what you need in order to continue forward with the group. I'll take notes, and figure out the right compromise—"

"No." Micah's word rang through the pastor's home like the report of a rifle. "James 4 says if we put God first, we are not to enjoy the world." He stabbed a finger toward the deck, where Sylvia had her back to us as she enjoyed a cancer stick. "She's just put us on notice, brothers. Either we enjoy the group and its worldly success, or we stand by the principles God has laid out in His Word."

"Oh man." Two simple words escaped me before I knew it, but my tone—somewhere between a strangled chuckle and a chortle filled with contempt—caught Micah on the chin.

"You laughin' at me, Jesse?"

"I guess so, Brother Micah," I said, the corners of my mouth tightening with each word. "If you're trying to make some famous last stand over homosexuality, partner, you got the wrong target in Coleman. The man's told us that's in his past, that he denounces it." I jabbed a finger despite myself. "Beyond that, any extra demonizing you wanna do of gays is between you and God, not Coleman."

Micah shifted his stance, clearly wishing he could get up in my face. "So now I'm 'demonizing,' huh? You sound like those secular liberals right about now, partner."

"Are we comparing notes on past sins, is that it?" I asked, crossing my arms. "We've all committed wrongs of some type in the past twenty-four hours, but as long as we didn't kiss a dude, none of that matters?"

Standing and moving so that he was between Micah and me, Isaac nodded soberly in my direction. "I hear what you sayin', Jesse, but let's not forget what Scripture itself says about the sin in question here. It gets called out as especially unnatural in more than one book, in both Testaments."

I reached out for Isaac, grabbed him by the shoulder, and pulled him close. "You have a degree from seminary, brother?"

I had clearly violated my friend's personal space, if the tightness of his brow and his mumbled reply were any indication. "You know I don't, man. I'm a musician."

"And I'm a singer," I replied. "So let's not get into fights over scriptural interpretations." I took a breath, looked around the room, and came to a rest on Micah's hardened stare. "Micah, let's play a game. I call it, Gay Folk. The way we play is, we go back and forth naming people we know that are gay or might be.

"Okay, I'll start. There's Ricky, the label's accountant. Brother shoots me flirtatious looks every time I go pick up my royalty check, though he's never gone beyond that." I looked at Micah again. "Your turn." When he responded by shutting his eyes in annoyance, I continued. "Okay, I'll keep going and you jump in whenever you choose. The keyboardist girl we hired to play on most of this CD's tracks, her name's Dana, right? Cute sister, but she told me during a studio break one night about her girlfriend. It was a passing comment, caught me off guard, but I figured the label knew it when they hired her."

Frank chuckled. "I coulda told you that the first time I laid eyes on the girl." He squared his shoulders playfully. "Sister's *buff*."

Micah found his voice all of a sudden. "Frank, shut up."

"Yeah, Frank, this game is for me and Micah, though he's not very good at it. I got number three, man. Your older cousin, the one who comes out to most of our concerts? Runs with several other dudes, all of 'em single with no kids, even though they're in their forties? You know, the one who gives evasive answers when we ask why he never brings a date. What's his name?"

Micah had been pacing toward the pastor's foyer, but he wheeled back toward me now. "You keep my family out of this," he said, teeth clenched as his hands balled up.

"Okay, never mind that, then." I pointed a finger outside, straight at Sylvia's back. "There's talk about our fearless leader out there. Divorced for ten years now, no evidence she's dated a man since, and she's known for constantly hiring the finest young female secretaries. Now, I don't know that there's truth—"

"Jesse, please, for God's sake, and I say that sincerely." Joe was at my side now, his stubby fingers pressing into my shoulder. "Of all the roads, let's not go down that one. It's disrespectful, and it could end this group's career, like that," he said, snapping his fingers.

My point had been made. I took a deep breath and shut my eyes as I felt the words worm their way up my throat. "I've been unfaithful to my wife," I said, my insides shaking. "With another woman. Dionne has known for a couple of weeks now."

A hush fell over the room until Coleman extinguished it with a whispery, "Jesse, no."

"Don't get me wrong," I said to no one in particular, my eyes inclined toward the pastor's vaulted white ceiling. "I doubt that I'm the first in this group to stray from his wife, but that's why it's really not controversial, isn't it? It'd only be a problem if I'd cheated with a brother, right?"

Frank slapped a hand against the side of his head, his eyes not able to meet mine. "Lord, Jesse—you're messing with us, right?"

"I wish," I replied. "Let me force you brothers now to do what you should, if you're going to be consistent about all this. I'm withdrawing from the group. If Coleman's not morally fit for Men with a Message, I'm surely not."

"Uh, have a seat, youngblood," Joe said, his tone falsely playful, like a father trying to talk a son out of foolishness without being caught in the act. "Emotions are flying around right now. You're probably exaggerating—"

I rolled my shoulders and raised my hands, knocking Joe's hands from me. "Is Coleman in the group or not?" When no one except Joe would meet my stare, I filled the void of stony, cold silence.

"Pastor," I said, nodding toward Willis as he sat stoically at Coleman's side. "Thank you for opening your home. There's one thing you didn't share with everyone earlier. You-all need to know that Coleman has considered taking his own life behind all of this."

Coleman rose from his chair. "Jess, that was between you and me, man."

I flipped up a hand to ward off my friend, determined to fight the tears welling up. "Forgive me, Coleman, but I care too much about you to let you suffer in silence. All of you need to understand, this man is more conflicted about his past than you will ever be. The idea that he needs to prove his sincerity by denying he was born gay, that's madness."

From behind us, the sliding glass doors by the deck slid open suddenly. "So?" Sylvia stood in the doorway, with hands on her hips. "Did you work this out like good grown Christian folk?"

Micah met Sylvia's gaze first, his face hardening with the intensity of a fist. "Don't think you'll like the answer."

"Micah, chill." Coleman crossed the room and brought Sylvia into a quick but firm hug. "I'm resigning from the group, effective today," he said. "Men with a Message isn't the group I thought it was."

Sylvia patted Coleman's shoulder, applying the touch of a loving aunt, if not a mother. "Baby, let's not be impulsive. I know they're being judgmental, but they'll get over it." She glanced over her shoulder before patting Coleman's cheek. "Some people like to make a show over certain issues, but they know what time it really is."

"It's more than a show now," Coleman said, his stern eyes finding me. "It's a matter of trust—trust I no longer have in anyone in Men with a Message. *Anyone.*"

29

Dionne

For the fourteenth day in a row, Samuel served as my reliable little alarm clock. I awoke and turned to see him screeching from the comfort of the bassinet that lay inches from my bed. In the glow of the night-light just behind him, I could see the adorable features of his little face, all of which were scrunched tight as he screamed for his next bottle.

By the time I had picked him up, soothed him with kisses, and pulled on my robe, my mother was at our bedroom door. "That little booger's like clockwork," she said, smiling and handing me a freshly warmed bottle as she swung the door open. "We'll see how long that holds up." She leaned past me to plant a sloppy kiss on Samuel's forehead. "You were just up at four. Sure you don't want me to feed him?"

"Mom," I said, my eyes widening to bolster my point, "he's my son, my responsibility. I've got it."

"Excuse me, young mama," my mother replied, huffing. Her voice trailed down the hallway after her as I turned back toward the rocking chair my parents had purchased the day of our arrival. "The feeding you don't need me for," she said, "but you're happy to move into my house. . ."

Holding Samuel in the crook of my arm and angling the bottle's nipple into his quivering little mouth, I made a mental note to set Mom straight when I had a free second. *I'll be out of you-all's hair ASAP*, I would say.

I peered down at the wondrous little creature feverishly sucking back the precious formula. Though he was at the center of the most devastating betrayal I had ever suffered—God willing, please, the worst I would ever have to suffer—my grip on this bundle of joy had not weakened one bit. If anything, as the stench of Jesse and Vanessa's confession permeated my spirit, I held Samuel closer to my breast. Smudging his face with tears as I leaned down to kiss him again, I whispered, "Nothing can change my love for you."

That simple statement was the only thing I was certain of anymore. In the space of sixty seconds, Carol's innocent unmasking of the truth had ripped away the foundation of my daily life and my very hopes for the future. The moment I realized Jesse and Vanessa had hidden the history of their acquaintance—especially after the combative exchange they'd had when Vanessa first raised the subject of Samuel's absentee father—everything had pretty much fallen into place.

I had always known that Jesse had seen another woman during our separation. I hate saying it, but—bottom line—I knew he was a man, and given how suddenly I'd severed things between us, I knew some Jezebel would quickly pull him back into his old, fornicating ways. The thought, though, that he could keep a secret about his child—*our* child—from me was beyond the pale, well outside the box of anything I could have ever feared.

Thank the Lord that I had already been cleared for six weeks of maternity leave—I was in no condition to minister to anyone with the fool's choices of options coursing through my mind. Pastor Norm had even decided to go ahead and preach the antigay sermon he'd first assigned to me.

What was I supposed to do with this man I'd pledged my life and loyalty to, a man capable of such a cruel fraud? Hour by hour I pinged and bounced from thoughts of divorce, to reconciliation, to just showing my you-know-what by shaming Jesse through a tell-all sit-down with Oprah.

Right now, my real focus was on keeping our claim—no, *my* claim—to Samuel. If the adoption agency got wind of my husband's psychopathic behavior, they were sure to try and keep the baby with Vanessa or place him with another family. Short of losing my salvation, there was no way I'd let either option become reality.

Pondering everything, I could see that my heart had already broken free of its moorings, that a familiar sense of betrayal had dulled my ability to sense God's spirit in my life. In this moment, the sense of shock had left me too numb to acknowledge the war raging within.

A pair of knuckles rapped hard at the bedroom door, and I looked down to realize that Samuel had not only drained his bottle, he had drifted right back to sleep.

My father gingerly turned the doorknob as I sat there massaging the baby's back, my ear to his mouth in search of a telltale burp. "Hey, sweetie," he said, using the whisper he reserved for the presence of his infant grandchildren. "You two doing okay in here?"

"Why wouldn't we be?" I accepted Daddy's kiss to my cheek, but dodged his attempt at lingering eye contact. I had managed for this long to conceal exactly what Jesse and I had fallen out over, and wasn't ready to crack yet.

"Your mother said you were short with her just now," Daddy said, a hand on my shoulder. "Now, I know she can be a bit presumptuous when babies are around—after three children and five grands of her own, she seems to fancy herself an expert—but if you're going to be under our roof, Dionne, you need to show her proper respect."

"Daddy," I replied, resisting the urge to speak in my most adult tones, "I'm working on two hours of sleep here. Can you save the lecture for, say, this afternoon?"

"I'll see what I can do about that," he said, chuckling. "I'm headed to the store in a few—the little one need another round of diapers or wipes? More of that awful-smelling formula?"

"The proper name is Similac Advance," I replied, referring to the formula my father insisted was poisonous. I was tiring of his insistence that I should have moved heaven and earth to have Samuel breast-fed.

"Couldn't you have made a deal with the birth mom?" he'd actually asked a few nights back. "You know, paid her extra to pump the milk and ship it over weekly or something?"

"For the record," I said now, "we have plenty of everything on hand. What you can do is bring your daughter a couple of her favorite bagels on your way back."

He gave me a mock salute and turned back toward me as he reached the doorway. "Bagel Café, one blueberry and one Dutch apple?"

"I can always count on you, Daddy." Smiling as Samuel delivered a hearty burp, I stood and moved toward the bassinet.

"Absolutely, sweetie." Daddy turned over his shoulder at the sound of the front doorbell. "What the?" He stepped back across the doorway, passing me and Samuel to peek out the guest room's window, which looked out over the front lawn. As I collapsed onto the bed, I caught the rise in Daddy's shoulders, sensed the hardening of his spine.

"What is it?"

Daddy shook his head, eyes still penetrating the darkness. "Oh, he's out of line." He turned suddenly, his footsteps morphing into stomps as he exited the room. "Excuse me while I go teach your husband a lesson. Fool should know to call before popping over."

30

Jesse

Harold Favors whipped open his front door so fast, he caught me off guard. It wasn't yet seven in the morning, but my father-in-law's bulging neck muscles and keen stare were evidence he'd had plenty of time to work himself up.

"I owe you some thanks," he said, bolting across the threshold toward me. Six foot three, wiry, and potbellied, Harold had a couple of inches on me and clearly fancied that was all the insurance he needed. "You and Dionne have adopted a beautiful little boy there," he continued, his arms crossed. "Marcia and I couldn't be happier to see Dionne growing into motherhood. She will never be the same, praise God, and Samuel will add new richness to our lives." He paused for effect. "And now that Dionne has Sammy, she can finally be freed of her playboy husband." He slapped my shoulder, clearly reining in his desire to slap my face, instead. "Bye now, Jesse."

The smell of fresh cedar and brick filling my nostrils, I stared back at Harold with eyes that felt dead, vacuumed of emotion. I knew from Mama, who was in daily contact with Dionne, that she hadn't yet shared the sordid truth with her parents. An observant seven-year-old could tell something was seriously wrong with our marriage, of course, but my wife had apparently chosen to minimize drama by keeping the nature of our problem private. Given my contentious history with Harold—and the fact that the revelations of my deception would validate his every long-held suspicion of me—I had every reason to crumple before him now in abject shame.

There was only one problem with that logic: I had sinned before God, not before Harold Favors.

I shrugged his hand off my shoulder. "Will you tell Dionne I'm here? If she's feeding Samuel right now, that's cool, I can wait. I haven't seen the baby in nearly a week."

My father-in-law frowned. "And?"

"Harold," I said, fists balling, "this really isn't your business."

"What did you do, hustler?" He took a step toward me, placing himself firmly into my personal space. "She catch you giving it to some teenage fan? Or let me guess, you wouldn't be in the same club as your buddy Coleman?"

This man had no idea how much he was testing my spiritual walk. Between being newly unemployed, and in serious risk of losing my wife and child, it took every ounce of Holy Spirit power in me to hold my peace. "I'm going to go sit in my car," I said, nodding as Dionne's mother stepped into the foyer behind Harold. "Mom Favors, will you at least let Dionne know I'm out here? I just want to see the baby."

"Harold. Move." Mom Favors used the strength of her stare to telepathically shove my father-in-law out of the way. Embracing me in a hug, she placed a hand to the back of my head and whispered, "I'm rooting for you two, Jesse. Remember Matthew 5:32. Divorce is never the answer."

Respecting her obvious desire not to get into an argument with the old man, I whispered a quick "Love you" and released her. Looking back over her shoulder as she stepped past Harold and back into the foyer, she warmed me with eyes full of concern. "I'll go tell her you're here."

"I'll be in my car," I said, my hands in the air as if Harold were holding a gun on me. When she had disappeared, I looked back at my father-in-law. "You know, regardless of what happens with me and Dionne, your new grandson will always be my son. You may as well find some way to treat me like you've got good sense. You know, lean on some of that Christlike love you taught Dionne about from childhood."

Harold took a few paces farther down the porch, taking a second to hawk up a glob of spit before responding. "Two weeks now I've had my grown daughter, the minister, the most self-sufficient of the bunch, living under my roof and looking like the walking wounded." He snapped off another stream of spit, letting this one land atop my right Timberland shoe. "It's the strangest thing, Jesse. Dionne beams every time she looks at the baby, but any other time, I swear, she's a shell of herself. So don't try to tell me you aren't the cause of that, and don't try to tell me this doesn't prove my conviction, from day one, that my princess kissed a frog the day she chose you."

Walk away, Jesse, the Spirit-filled voice said. *Go to your car, and wait.*

I turned on my heels, determined to go deaf until I was safely encased inside the BMW.

"Of course you're walking away, hustler," Harold said, his volume rising as I proceeded farther into the cool morning's air. "Every word I've said stings because it's true. The apple doesn't fall far from the tree."

"Shut up," I said, the words shooting forth as I pivoted. "My father was a weak man—a drug addict, a whoremonger, and a liar. But not even he gets credit for the sins I've committed against Dionne. That's on me."

Hands folded across his chest, Harold smiled smugly. "So you admit your sin—"

"Not to you," I replied. "You don't deserve to sit in judgment of a thing, Harold Favors. I've never seen a man so consumed with envy."

"What are you talking about?"

"You may have known a little bit about my father—probably lost a few dates to him, if I had to guess. But Dionne's told me enough about you to fill in the picture. I succeeded where you failed."

"You've been hitting that crack pipe too hard, son." Harold waved a hand in the air and began to head for his front door.

"You followed all the rules," I said, my voice now loud enough to wake the neighbors. "I know the drill, Harold. You spent your teens and twenties working from sunup to sundown, forsaking all manners of fun—women, liquor, drugs, cigarettes—and a part of you regrets it. Not that things haven't paid off in their own way, but I know what you hate about me is that I had my chance to live worldly, footloose and fancy-free."

"You show respect, boy." Harold stormed back into my path now, a fist raised. "Take it back right now, or so help me, I'll set you straight while I'm still young enough."

I spat the words out through clenched teeth. "Try it. Please."

"Daddy!" A motion light clicked on behind us, Dionne's yell cut a clean path through the morning's crisp air, and Harold and I froze where we stood. "Get away from him! I mean it!"

My father-in-law pulled back his raised fist, clearly embarrassed at losing his temper in front of his "baby." Backing away, but still delivering a look poised to kill, he whispered his parting line: "Later."

"Your call, Harold," I said loud enough for Dionne's benefit. "Your call."

"I'm sitting here for two minutes," Dionne said once she'd read me the riot act for coaxing her father toward a sucker punch. Seated in the BMW now, we stared at each other across a gulf filled by betrayal, shame, and mistrust. "When we finish this conversation, Jesse, Mom will bring Samuel down. You can spend half an hour with him in the living room. When the time's up, you'll hand him back to Mom and leave. For now, that's it. If I'm up to it, maybe you'll get the same access next week."

I had no grounds on which to argue, and nodded in agreement. "I don't know if you'll ever care to really hear it, but I am so sorry." I let silence weight my words before saying, "This doesn't have to be the end."

"That will be my decision, thank you very much," she replied, her eyes staring out the passenger side window. "Tell me one thing. You told me right away, while we were still separated, that you had seen someone. I mean, Jesse, why didn't you just tell me the entire ugly truth all at once?"

"Baby, we explained that," I said, referring to our encounter with Vanessa in the hospital. "I had no idea Vanessa was pregnant when you and I agreed to reconcile; I told you everything I knew—that another woman and I had been intimate for several weeks. That was the truth. You didn't want any other details at the time—her age, her job, her height, nothing."

Dionne frowned. "I was there, it's not like I've forgotten." She crossed her arms. "You were afraid I wouldn't take you back simply over having seen someone else. Do you remember that?" Dionne's stare lacerated me from head to toe. "I forgave you that, Jesse. I decided to take you back into our home, into my bed, knowing that you'd be exposing me to every person that your mystery lover had slept with. Wasn't that evidence that I could make the next step and forgive the fact that you got her pregnant?"

"Are you kidding?" I gained control of my tone, slowed the pace of my words. "Baby, you nearly ended our marriage because of your infertility. How could I come back after one confession and say, *Oh, by the way, it turns out I'm* not *infertile, and another woman's having the child we always wanted*?" My eyes welled with tears that my masculinity wouldn't let me shed, but I heard a catch in my voice as I battled a stew of shame, anger, and despair. "I think, honestly, that I blacked everything out. I had to find a way for everything to make sense, and the fact that Vanessa didn't want Samuel gave me the opportunity. Viewing this as a chance for us to raise a baby together, well, that may be the only thing that stood between me and a straitjacket."

The car filled with silence for several seconds, and Dionne's downcast gaze had me wondering if I had reached her. I had no fitting excuse for what I had done, but this had really been the first time she had let me fully explain myself. I bit my lower lip and waited patiently, praying for an undeserved breakthrough.

"I just realized we're well past two minutes," Dionne finally said, sighing. She opened her door without even glancing toward me. "Call my cell in five minutes, then come to the door so Mom can meet you with Samuel." She placed a hand atop the car as she leaned back in to lash me with another stare. "And if Daddy comes at you wrong again, Jesse, keep your distance. If you hit him, trust me, I'll see to it you go to jail."

31

Dionne

There, now, doesn't this feel *good*?" Suzette had come by my parents', intent on getting me out of the house without the baby. After wearing Mom and Daddy out with a string of stories and local gossip, she'd convinced me to leave Samuel with them and go out for a drive.

As she spurred her Buick up an entry ramp onto the BW Parkway, I grimaced but answered her question honestly. "This is a nice change of pace, Zette."

"Lessons learned after surviving three newborns," she replied, glancing over and flashing a toothy smile. "No matter how much you love that little one, you will always need 'me' time, even if it's just a drop in the bucket." I was definitely feeling her; it didn't hurt that it was a beautiful day for a drive—summer was nearing, evidenced by blossoming flowers and blue skies beaming with sunlight.

Before we knew it, Zette and I had spent so much time immersing ourselves in small talk that we'd arrived in DC. As she came to a stop at the intersection of Florida and New York Avenues, we decided impulsively to drive over to my old stomping grounds at Howard. We found a new coffee shop near the campus, and spent nearly an hour there as my girl caught me up on the goings-on in the lives of others with, well, normal problems. As cleansing as it probably was for both of us to sit there academically discussing others' issues, the shattering truths hanging over our respective marriages really never left the table.

By the time we climbed back into Zette's Buick and rolled past Howard Hospital, I couldn't help myself. Nodding toward the emergency room, I admit I wasn't as subtle as I probably should have been. "Feels like just yesterday I drove you over here in a panic," I said, unable to make eye contact.

"Please," Zette replied, her right eyebrow twitching so quickly I almost missed it. "Ancient history."

I patted my friend's knee as she stared at the red light, willing it to turn green so she could distract herself with driving. "It's okay," I said. "We can talk about it." Pretty hypocritical coming from a woman who had yet to share the betrayals my own husband had committed.

Suzette's eyes clouded defensively as she gently patted my hand, then slid it off her knee. "I have come a long way from the hysterical shrew who attacked Adrian that day," she said. "I respect you too much to go into it, Dionne, but believe me when I say, I have a much more healthy way of dealing with Coleman nowadays."

It wasn't even my friend's words so much as her tone that brought memories rushing back. Memories of snippets of rumors I had heard almost since the day that Coleman revealed his past to all of us. Because all of my colleagues in ministry knew that Suzette was my best friend, no one had said anything to me directly, but I had heard enough inadvertent suggestions to get the point. People were placing bets on exactly who was involved, but they seemed convinced that my girl was committing adultery.

"Suzette," I said finally, after an uncomfortably pregnant pause during which my friend had locked her eyes on the road and kept her hands gripped to the steering wheel, "what is this new way of dealing? It doesn't involve another man or anything, does it?"

"Dionne," Zette replied, while otherwise ignoring me, "lay back in your seat, and enjoy the ride home."

"This is me, girl," I said, turning to face her as she made the U-turn back onto New York Avenue. "I'm not here to judge you. Just talk to me."

"Oh, please," Suzette replied. "You're a virgin-plus-one, Dionne. You ain't ready for this topic."

She didn't know it, but there were two people in the car with Mrs. Suzette Hill at that moment—the long-suffering friend hoping to protect her from the consequences of sexual sin, and the new mom struggling with an unthinkable betrayal. The second one spoke now. "You know too much Holy Word," I said, speaking in a near-monotone, "to be out there whoring just because Coleman's embarrassed you."

Her mouth slammed shut, Suzette pursed her lips, still refusing to make eye contact. "Just shut up now, okay?"

Something new, something largely foreign, rumbled in my stomach. "What did you say?"

Suzette bit her lower lip, but flashed an impatient gaze toward me this time. "I said *shut up*, Dionne. I take you out as a favor, and in return I get interrogated? I don't have time for this. By the time I get you home, I'll almost be late to pick up the kids from my mother's."

"This is not an interrogation," I replied. "This is me trying to see if you need help figuring out how to process your understandable pain about Coleman's past."

Suzette mumbled a string of curses, her tone just low enough that I couldn't verify exactly what she was saying about me. "Will you feel better if I confirm your suspicions? You don't need to know the details, but if it'll help you sleep at night, there is one fine gentleman I've been spending time with. And for the record, he's not a man of the cloth, not one of Coleman's colleagues or anyone connected to my church. Happy now, Miss High-and-Mighty Reverend?"

I could feel Suzette's eyes on me like lasers as I absorbed her confession. I was wishing I had just left well enough alone, because for some reason it felt like this confirmed that Coleman had been the one betrayed, assuming his claims of marital fidelity were based on truth.

"Dionne," Zette said, fully engaged with me now, "you may as well know I'm not seeing the guy anymore. It was more of an emotional affair than anything physical, though it did go there once or twice."

"So," I said, "how can you be sure it's over? Or that you won't be tempted by the next brother like him?"

Sighing, Suzette shook her head. "I don't know, how's that? Maybe you've forgotten, Dionne, but some of us are fighting for our lives right now. We aren't all blessed with a new baby and a loving, *straight* husband."

Dear God, I thought, *if only she knew*. "Zette, Coleman loves you," I said, the words tasting clammy in my mouth despite their truth. "You need to show some appreciation for that. I mean, seriously, the last thing he needs, with people questioning his sexuality, is you stepping out on him."

"See, now we're drilling down into unknown territory," she replied. "There's a lot of issues here, girl. Part of me wants to leave Coleman, but what about the kids? I don't want to do that to them. Of course, now that his foolish butt actually quit Men with a Message, maybe I need to find a new provider, anyway. I still can't believe Jesse followed my idiot husband out the door."

I sighed, wishing I had the strength to at least tell my best friend the whole sordid truth. "Jesse has his own reasons, trust me."

"The one thing that man and I still have in common is that Coleman's every bit as stubborn as I am. I'm still trying to talk him into making peace with Micah and them fools, but his mind is made up. So now he's unemployed, except for his minister of music role at the church, but that ain't gonna cover all the bills we got. I'm starting to wonder why I should stay with him. Why should I live the rest of my life with a broke, gay husband who has to play like he's in love with me?"

I started to speak, then decided to keep it simple as impatient anger swelled within my chest. "Suzette."

"And that disgusting *Rolling Stone* article hits the stands tomorrow, full of pictures of Coleman and Adrian as boy lovers. People are already talking about us behind our backs. Now I have to figure out how to keep the kids from having some stupid playmate wave those photos around!"

"I'll help you get through it," I said, coughing nervously as Suzette pulled off at a parkway exit and rolled into a gas station. The Spirit whispered in my ear, telling me I needed to talk some things out before I could fully minister to my friend in her precarious situation. The problem was, I was really disappointed in my friend for even temporarily cheating on Coleman, who I felt, in my heart, had been faithful to her even while hiding his gay past.

As Suzette reached for her driver's side door, I touched her shoulder. "Jesse and I are still here for each of you," I said. "And trust me, the first step to getting through this is for you and Coleman to hold fast to each other."

"You know what, girl," Suzette replied, "save your prayers, okay? You two focus on raising that beautiful baby, don't burden yourselves worrying over us. Because, frankly, there's a lot of factors at play here. Not the least of which," she said, leaning toward me and lowering her voice, "is the fact that once a girl's been loved by a real man—one who knows how to tear it up without any acting—it's not easy to go back."

"God can do anything." I reached out for my friend even as she pulled away and opened her door. "Suzette, you're not that shallow. You never complained about Coleman's ability to romance you before."

Halfway out of the car, Suzette turned over her shoulder, her eyes cutting at me wickedly. "That was before I knew he liked boys at least as much as he likes me."

My girlfriend had always been a "wiseacre," as my grandmother used to say, and I knew Suzette's crack was meant to lighten a heavy conversation. With the clouds over my own marriage, though, the attack on Coleman hit me in the heart and I burst into tears. Ragged sobs racked me, causing Suzette to inhale suddenly and dive back into the car.

"Dionne, hey, what's wrong?" She held me close, then held me at arm's length, looking me over. "I was cracking wise about my husband, not yours, girl." Thumbing tears from my eyes, her voice dropped to a whisper. "Oh, good Lord," she said, "don't tell me Coleman's turned Jesse sweet too!"

This is why I love Suzette Hill. For a good twenty seconds, the clouds parted as I enjoyed a belly laugh at her poor powers of perception. "I'm sorry," I said, my voice slowly steadying as the laughter subsided. Hugging my friend again, I spoke into her left ear. "You're off base in one respect, girl, but it's not your fault. Just let me talk."

32

Dionne

Earl's hand was on my knee, but for all the right reasons.

As the pastor's baritone boomed with another invitation for the unsaved to come forward and accept Christ, Earl balled up his right fist angrily. It was as if he could only express his internal struggle that way, given that his left hand had flopped almost lifelessly onto my knee as his eyes welled with tears.

When I leaned over and placed an arm around his shoulders—or as far around them as I could get—he sniffed and whispered, "I can't."

"Jesus loves you, you heard the message today," I counseled in a low whisper. "You don't have to do anything else before you accept that love, Earl."

"The anger . . . the bitterness." Earl shook his head, though he was clearly already at a spiritual tipping point. "How can I accept Christ now? Rev, He still ain't help me find my brother. Adrian could be dead!"

"This is about trust," I whispered, patting his shoulder. "You don't have to understand everything perfectly or know all the answers to accept God's simple gift of salvation. You just have to believe that Jesus died for your sins, and that He provides a Holy Spirit to help us walk according to God's will. Do you believe that?"

Earl shuddered with recognition. "Yes."

I took my hands off him, wanting to make sure the decision was his. "If you need me to walk with you, I'm here."

Before Earl's phone call, it had been a Sunday morning no different from the first three Samuel and I had spent at my parents'. I awoke bleary-eyed, around six, to feed the baby, who was still too young to be diagnosed with colic, although by now I didn't need it spelled out for me. Most nights, no one in the Favors household got much sleep because Samuel, gassy and anguished, could howl for up to an hour at a time.

The timing of Jesse's confession robbed us of the special joys most first-time parents experience during a baby's first weeks, but the one blessing was that because Samuel and I were sharing a bedroom, it was no hardship to be there for him around the clock. My schedule consisted of feeding my little man, calming him, playing his music, and catnapping alongside him whenever possible.

The pressure cooker of life with a colicky infant, combined with my constantly sleep-deprived state, helped me keep my family at bay. Daily they would try to pull the full truth out of me regarding Jesse's betrayal. In addition to Mom and Daddy, my sisters made a habit of stopping by to watch the baby and simultaneously pump me for information. I had insisted so far that it was too painful to go into, and further shooed them away by promising to reveal all my marital secrets when they revealed all of theirs. Amazing how quickly that backed folks off.

Everyone except my younger sister, Lisa, that is. I guess she was still too young—and too dumb?—to have any secrets of which to be ashamed. She had come by the house that morning with a huge box of Panera Bread bagels and muffins and a quart of hot coffee.

Although wearing her Sunday best, Lisa had thrown on a housecoat and taken Samuel into her arms. She rocked him and smiled placidly across the table as I polished off a cup of coffee and a Dutch apple bagel. "So I hear Jesse will be at church this morning," she said.

I leaned back in my chair and raised my eyes to hers with a dispassionate gaze. "That's nice." Lisa and her family had joined our DC church, Metropolitan Baptist, about eighteen months earlier, so I wasn't surprised that she was tapping into my husband's whereabouts. Shame on me and Jesse, for that matter: I could never regret convincing my sister to bring her family to a church that had ignited their spiritual growth, but given Lisa's penchant for gossip, I had no business directing her to my own place of worship. My commitments at Rising Son meant I rarely attended Metropolitan these days, but Jesse hadn't yet transferred his membership.

"Now don't act funny with me, girl," Lisa continued, "but the boy is my *brother*-in-law. So, if he does show up, don't think I won't go up and continue the conversation Daddy started with him."

I stood and headed toward the garbage can with my paper plate in hand. "Leave it alone, Lisa."

"Whatever. So, can I at least ask him about these rumors that Men with a Message have split up?"

I sighed, wearily massaging my forehead and praying for patience. "They have split, okay? Tell whoever you want, I don't think Jesse cares at this point." There was a time I'd have been really torn up to see Men with a Message, whom I'd seen do mighty things for God, disintegrate so quickly. Frankly, Jesse had given me much bigger disappointments to focus on.

"Dionne?" When I met my sister's gaze, I was moved by the sight of real tears on her face. "What happened? I don't understand, really. How does a couple go from being such strong witnesses for God, to . . . this?"

"I'll explain things once I get my legs under me, Lisa," I replied. "P-Please, can't you give me some time?"

"Why?" She ran a hand over Samuel's fast-growing head of spiky hair. "We all love you, girl, and it's clear Jesse's put you in a world of hurt. How can we help if we don't know exactly what went down?"

I couldn't fight the frown spreading across my face. "You don't need to know 'what went down' just to show your sister and nephew love, do you?"

Shifting Samuel more securely into the crook of her left arm, Lisa leaned forward and reached her right hand toward me. "Sis, I'm not going to tell a soul outside of this house. I swear."

I held my breath, considering whether to cross the void before me. To date, Suzette was the only person with whom I'd shared the ugly truth, but given my fresh shock at the fact she had cheated on Coleman, our rapport was a little strained. Between that and the biblical exhortation to not forsake the fellowship or supporting prayers of the righteous, opening up to my own flesh and blood was starting to look tempting.

"Is that your phone or mine?" Lisa checked her purse and sighed. "It's not me, good. I was afraid it was James calling to bug me about getting to church on time."

I grabbed my cell from the table, curious who could be calling at this early hour. With a little trepidation, I opened it and said, "Hello?"

"Hey, Rev," the male voice replied. "How's motherhood?"

"Who is this?"

"Okay, I think you froze the phone with that tone. This is Earl, but I'll let you go for now."

"No, no," I replied, my words coming faster than usual. "I'm sorry, Earl. I didn't catch your voice." I remembered very well the promise I had made to be spiritually available for him, although a queasy sensation in my stomach told me there was more to my eagerness than that.

"Well, hey, I'm sorry for bugging you, but I had a rough night.

Long story short, I can't shake this anger. I want to go out and bust heads until I find someone who can help me locate Adrian."

"But you know there's no point to that, right? That you'll just put yourself in danger of landing in jail again?"

"Well, that fear hasn't stopped me from turning these streets upside down the past few weeks," he replied. "Between you and me, I didn't just beat on Coleman to get my point across. I made a visit to that D-Boy character and his boys as well. I rattled 'em, but they didn't cop to nothing new."

Ignoring Lisa's furtive stare, I stood and walked into my parents' living room. "So where does all this leave you?"

"It leaves me . . . I don't know, it's like I'm suffocating, Rev. I just feel like if I sit home today, I'll lose my mind with rage. And the good bars don't open till late afternoon, know what I mean?"

"Why don't you go to church?" An internal voice threw my question back at me: *why aren't* you *going to church these days?*

To my surprise, Earl already had a house of worship in mind. "There's my great uncle's church," he said. "He's a deacon or trustee or something up there. I was thinking, maybe I should go and see if some singing and preaching will help calm me down. But I don't wanna go by myself."

I shook my head, turning over my shoulder to make sure my sister wasn't there with the baby, watching me grin like a schoolgirl. "So you're trying to drag a new mama away from her baby to help you, a grown man, have the courage to step up in God's house?"

"You can bring the baby."

After a few more minutes of conversation, I learned that the church was a Southeast DC storefront, one I had never heard of. Better yet, Earl was considering the early service, which I could attend and still return home before my parents left for their own morning worship service.

Time blurred, and the next thing I knew, I was freshly dressed and showered, my hair pinned into a ponytail as I drove to the address Earl had given me. He was outside the storefront's main entrance as I walked up the block, and the sight of him in a relatively conservative beige double-breasted suit nearly stopped me in my tracks. Maybe it was something about being on the verge of divorce, or maybe I was just losing my mind, but I couldn't deny that Earl Wilkes was one handsome man.

He tipped his leather hat in my direction. "Where's the baby?"

"Sleeping contentedly in his grandmother's arms," I replied. "I should thank you for this invitation. I'm not just here for you—I needed some exposure to God's house today myself." This was true, and it wasn't like Metropolitan, or anyplace where I'd be recognized, was an option at the moment. "It's been too long."

Earl frowned. "So the grapevine's right, huh? Not only did your hubby quit his group along with Coleman, he quit your marriage?"

"Let's not go down that road, okay?" I placed a hand to Earl's wrist, smiling for reasons I couldn't fully explain. "Jesse and I are human, but our marital struggles aren't nearly as important as what you're battling with right now. Let's go hear some Word."

By the time service ended and I had helped the pastor test Earl's certainty about the blessed salvation decision he had made, I was emotionally exhausted. I nearly collapsed against Earl as he walked me down the block toward my car. Acting as if he'd actually had to catch me, he pulled me alongside him with a playful hug. "Baby's got Mama worn out, eh?"

"Yeah, kind of." The thought of Samuel—that precious bundle of blessings with unlimited potential, the one I might now have to raise in a broken home—jarred me suddenly and I was overcome with emotion. Before I knew it, my face was wet with tears and I was clinging to Earl, my head buried against his chest.

"Hey, hey," he said in soft reply. In an instant I felt his hand on my chin and knew that newly sanctified or not, he was going just where I wanted him to. Our eyes lingered on each other wordlessly; then our lips merged, our tongues began to fly and float, and he pulled me into an embrace that took me back to my earliest days with Jesse.

"That's classy, real classy." The man's shout caught me and Earl by surprise, and while we were still locked together, we whipped our heads toward the voice. At the sight of Jesse—he stood across the street, leaning against his BMW, hands in his pockets—I instinctively shoved Earl away.

"Don't stop on my account," Jesse shouted, staying right where he was.

With my voice caught in my throat, I felt my stare turn deadly as it pierced my husband.

For a second the three of us hovered there on the street, unsure of what might come next. I can't speak for Jesse or Earl, but I had nightmare visions of us winding up on the eleven o'clock news.

Earl dove into the void first. "Hey, yo, brother," he said, shrugging and then raising his hands innocently. "I just accepted Christ, okay, but I don't really want to die today. If you two are still together, I'm happy to stay out of this picture." He turned in my direction, his eyes tentatively daring me. "All Rev has to do is say the word."

Jesse stepped toward the middle of the street, his stare meeting Earl's and his tongue stuck between his teeth. After a few beats he swung his eyes back to me. "Is this how it goes, baby?" he asked. "I guess it would serve me right. Just understand," he said, jamming a finger in my direction, "you've lost the moral high ground now."

I was still shaking with shock when the BMW peeled away.

33

Jesse

I started to regret my decision to come to Nashville before my butt hit the cab's seat.

"Men with a Message!" The driver, a twenty-something blond-haired white guy with a crew cut, pointed and snapped his finger as I climbed in. "I knew as soon I pulled up that I recognized you. You're Jesse, right? You guys are awesome!" He turned around fully, apparently needing to face me head-on with his look of sympathy. "You guys aren't breaking up, are you?"

Drawing on the mustard seed's worth of Holy Spirit left within me, I worked up a smile and good-naturedly shook the driver's hand. Satan wanted me to be annoyed at the fact I'd been stuck with a fan at the lowest point in my career—for that matter, in my life—but I'd recovered enough since my run-in with Dionne and Earl to resist the devil and his lies.

I was not proud of my behavior the previous Sunday. There were so many catalysts, but possibly the final straw had been my phone conversation with Coleman the night before as I lay on the king-sized bed I had shared with Dionne for nearly eight years.

"Why are you calling me?" Coleman's tone was edgy, challenging.

"I need someone to talk to," I had replied with understated honesty. "Dionne and I are estranged, my mother is frustrated with me, and I'm learning that most of my friends were basically fair-weathers. I just need to hear a fellow believer's voice, brother."

"What, you think we're still homeboys? You think I still owe you, since you stood up for me? Please, Jesse. All that time I was being real with you about my struggles, you were hiding sins too scandalous for me to imagine."

"So we're comparing sins now?" I replied. "Coleman, have you forgotten one of the reasons I took up for you, was that people were trying to magnify homosexuality as a unique abomination?" I heard fire entering my tone, but I couldn't believe this ingrate was judging me. "If you're worried that I'm deceived about the depths to which I sank spiritually, don't be. I know I'm a filthy rag."

"I need time before I can trust you." Coleman paused before continuing. "I thought you were a better friend, to be honest."

"Take your time, then," I said, my stomach knotting with resentment. "God's blessings on you and the family."

Hanging up, I can honestly say I had never felt more alone. Staring out the bedroom window at the dusky night sky, I drifted off to a depressed sleep before waking around five o'clock in the morning. My heart full of yearning, I did the only thing I could think of when sleep continued to evade me. I drove to the Favors' house, intent on drawing comfort from the close presence of the woman I loved and the son I had brought into the world. That was why I was parked half a block from the Favors' beautiful dream home, tears in my eyes and a Bible in my lap, when Dionne's car roared out of the driveway and passed me in a blink. With nothing else to do and a head full of curiosity, I had followed her, never guessing I would get an eyeful of her and Earl Wilkes.

When the cab pulled onto my brother Larry's block, a street of historic-looking homes in the West End neighborhood of Vanderbilt University, I was still trapped in genial small talk with my worshipful cabby. Easing the conversation to a close as respectfully as I could, I handed him his fare and tip and stepped onto the sidewalk, a small duffel bag over my shoulder.

"Get in here, boy," my brother said when he opened the door. Wrapping me in a bear hug once I'd set my bag down in the foyer, he laughed. "You melting away already? I know you said you were going to start fasting, but goodness."

"I haven't eaten right since the day I began all this deception," I replied. I had fasted since the day of Samuel's birth, but my antics a week ago with Dionne had pushed me to raise my game spiritually. The time I would ordinarily spend eating or preparing a meal, I was now devoting to additional prayer and meditation, delving deep into the remaining emotional scars and deficiencies that had led to my disastrous decision to deceive Dionne. In addition, I had entered into a program of daily counseling sessions with Pastor Hicks from Metropolitan, who was gracious enough to see me in his office, since I was too ashamed to show my face at morning worship. I had a long road ahead, but I at least felt confident that I wouldn't slide deeper into the near-stalking behavior I'd exhibited toward Dionne and Earl.

"Do you really think she loves him?" Larry looked at me over the top of his freshly cooked burger, which his wife, Anna, had grilled on their kitchen range. He had apologized for tempting me before handing over my delicious glass of ice water.

"I figure it's not my place to ask what she feels for Earl," I said, fingering my water glass. "I've kept my distance since the day outside that church. I don't want Dionne to feel threatened by me, Larry. If she wants to take up with the guy—if she wants to raise Samuel with him—who am I to complain?"

"We both know it's not that simple," my brother replied. "But there will be time to sort all that out. My guess, baby brother, is that Dionne still wants to spend the rest of her life with you. She may need time to reach that conclusion, but I'll be surprised if she doesn't get there." My big brother had already made clear his disappointment in me and scolded me for repeating a twisted version of our father's sins, so now he was ready to counsel me in the loving way he did daily with his church members. "Well, fasting man, if you have the energy, I'd like to take you out tonight for our social justice ministry's monthly prison revival service. This group of guys is pretty young—twenties and thirties mostly. Most of them grew up on your music, Jesse."

I cut my eyes at Larry, shrugging. "And?"

"Some of these young dudes are on the verge of accepting Christ," Larry replied. "The impact of seeing you there, even if all you do is sing a song or two, it could really make a difference."

My eyes were on the marble face of my brother's kitchen table. "These cats being locked away, they haven't caught wind of my personal 'issues,' eh?"

Larry chuckled. "Well, to borrow from Rick James's phrasing, the prison grapevine is a powerful thing, but it probably isn't tracking the particulars of your marital problems, no."

"Tell me what songs you want sung," I said, sighing. "And if God moves on my heart, I'll try to throw in a testimony based on past trials He's brought me through."

Larry clapped me on the shoulder. "Thank you, brother."

"And here I thought you invited me out here for my charming company."

The front doorbell chimed, and Larry glanced over his shoulder as Anna yelled that she would get it. "Well, there was another reason, but I'll let that take care of itself."

"My baby!" I heard Anna's exclamation out in the foyer as clearly as if she were still in the kitchen. I heard hugging and kissing, and then she appeared in the kitchen doorway with Larry Jr., who was now several inches taller and maybe a dozen pounds heavier than when I'd last seen him that fateful Christmas. He smiled at me, stroking what was to me a new goatee, as his mother played with the brim of his NYU baseball cap.

"Look who we have here," I said, grinning in genuine surprise and rising to match his brisk handshake. In the past we'd always hugged upon greeting, but given that our last parting was so tense, I wasn't surprised that we each retreated into our own personal space. "You come home just to see your has-been uncle?"

"Don't flatter yourself," Larry Jr. replied, smiling wide. "I came home for a hot date. My pops invited you out here so you'd coincide with me, not the other way around."

I returned to my seat, motioned for my nephew to join his father and me, with whom he'd already exchanged backslaps. "Really."

"I've been seeing you in the news for a while," Larry Jr. said, settling into a chair. "And not for anything about your own life. I'm talking about your boy Coleman Hill."

My lips closed and I raised my eyebrows, letting them ask the question.

"I wanted to see you, Uncle Jesse," my nephew said, "because I think you can do the Church a great service."

34

Dionne

It is a real joy to have you back, Dionne," Pastor Norm said as he unlocked my office door for me. "Good, this one actually works." He turned to me and plopped the key into my hand. "We changed the locks while you were getting up to speed at the mommy thing. It's a recommended annual practice, to minimize the risks of sabotage by former employees and such."

He stood in the doorway, hands in his pockets, as I walked slowly toward my desk, which was awash in the same batch of books, documents, and CDs that I'd left behind the day before Samuel was born. "I'll check on you in a couple of hours," he said. "Don't jump back into things too quickly. Remember, half days for another six weeks until the baby's a full three months. Then I get you back full-time."

My back to him, I smiled despite myself. "If you don't know me well enough to realize I don't do half days, Pastor, you haven't been paying attention."

"Oh, I've got your number. Dionne, as a father who sees the toll each baby takes on my wife for the first few months, I can't let you walk around here with dueling priorities. Keep Samuel first, okay? Brian Collins and his wife have done a beautiful job running the urban outreach in your absence, and they're not going anywhere. Use them. They're ready and able."

"Yes, sir."

"And, uh, when are we having that counseling session we discussed?" Between Suzette and my mother, to whom I'd also finally revealed the sordid act separating me and Jesse, I had been convinced to open up to my boss and spiritual shepherd as well. Pastor Norm was visibly shaken to hear of Jesse's deception, but the sympathy that flooded him felt totally genuine. I was convinced that he wanted to shepherd Jesse and me through this spiritual valley, and he was clear about how he expected the story to end. "I won't see an assistant minister of mine get a divorce, at least not before all other options are fully explored. You and Jesse owe God that much."

I scheduled some counseling time with Pastor for Thursday, then pulled out the one thing he had asked me to place at the top of my list: the "antigay" sermon he had convinced me to preach shortly before Samuel's birth, in reaction to Coleman's public statements about his homosexuality. Pastor Norm had taken the initiative in my absence to craft and preach a sermon of his own on the topic, but he felt that our growing urban and minority congregants needed to hear a similar message from me.

The problem was, I wasn't sure I was still the same Dionne Favors-Law who drafted the sermon outline now sitting in my lap. So much had changed in my life in the intervening weeks, and on top of that, my husband's stance on the underlying issue was drawing new heat and light.

For reasons I still didn't fully understand, Jesse was popping up everywhere in the media. From Tom Joyner, Doug Banks, and Russ Parr on the radio, to *Larry King*, *Ellen*, and *Tyra* on television, friends were telling me they couldn't get away from my estranged husband's pretty face or at least his scratchy voice, and that wasn't even counting his appearances on BET and TBN programming. With Adrian still unaccounted for and the police investigation apparently gone cold, Jesse was preaching a message of concerned tolerance. "You enjoy having me on," he told Joe Scarborough on MSNBC, "to fuel this spectacle of 'gospel gays,' but I'm just here to say there are real lives affected by all this. First of all, Adrian Wilkes and his family, but that's only the beginning. The truth is, Christians of all colors are walking around with willfully blind eyes when it comes to homosexuality, and there's a lot at stake here, from the rising rates of HIV/AIDS among black women to a level of paranoia that's getting out of control. I'm just trying to get an honest conversation going."

Whenever reporters pressed him for a "solution" to the issues of hypocrisy and denial in the Church, Jesse used the same tease of a response. "For now, all I can do is suggest that every Christian watching take time to engage their gay brethren openly about these issues of whether people are born gay and whether they have a choice about living that way. My thing is, can't we find a healthy middle ground between those who want to condemn gays and those who fully endorse their lifestyle? How can people make healthier choices if no one's talking to them?"

Scanning through my sermon text's bulleted points and scriptural references, my thoughts kept drifting back to heated conversations I'd had with Jesse, Suzette, Coleman, and Adrian the past few months. There was so much pain, uncertainty, fear, and discomfort clouding the issues, there were times I wondered where God's hand lay in all this. I couldn't say that in a sermon preached from Rising Son's pulpit, could I?

My desk phone rang, and when I answered, it was Earl. "Hey, just seeing how your first day back is going."

"I'm just getting settled in, thank you very much." A vision of tapped phones in my head, I said, "Did you really have to call me here? I have a cell phone, you know."

"Excuse me," he replied. "Just trying to make sure my shepherd is staying on the path."

"I'm not your shepherd, boy, you better stop." My face flushed at the mutually flirtatious tones of our voices. With Jesse keeping his distance except for a weekly visit to sit with Samuel in my parents' living room, I had little reason to avoid Earl's continued advances. We hadn't gone past first base by any means—a little hand holding here, a highly charged kiss there, had been it for our displays of affection—but to be honest, I came away from each interaction feeling more soiled. And for the record, I was well aware that Earl was not the guilty party in the room, not by a long shot.

"Okay, I'll behave," Earl said, his tone hardening. "Listen, I just got some news about Adrian."

"What?"

"Apparently, he had some extra credit cards, ones he didn't leave records of, so I didn't know to cancel them. Can you believe some fool just got rolled up in Baltimore for trying to use two of them?"

"That's good, right?" I asked. "I mean, maybe a trail can be constructed from this thief back to someone who can help locate Adrian?"

"We'll see," Earl replied. "You'll love this, though—the fool is tied to D-Boy's gang." I could hear an ominous tension building in his throat. "The police have pulled D-Boy and company back in for deeper questioning. I told them they better haul Coleman back in too."

"I really don't think Coleman knows anything more than he's already shared," I said. "But maybe I can talk to him. Would that be okay?"

I was pleasantly surprised when Earl calmed down enough to agree to that. "You're really stretching this brother's spiritual muscles, Rev," he said.

"Stop calling me that. It doesn't feel right anymore."

"Why? 'Cause you don't want me calling you that when things go to the next level?"

"I'm hanging up now," I said, hot and bothered all over again.

"Bye. Call me when you talk to Coleman."

By one-thirty, half an hour after I was supposed to be off for the day, I headed outside to my car with a feeling of refreshed satisfaction. As much as I had missed Samuel from the moment I set foot out the door, I couldn't deny that at heart I was meant to be a working mom. I enjoyed spending my days and nights with the little man about 80 percent of the time, but there were definitely stretches where my sanity teetered and tottered at the demands of a dependent infant. At work, by comparison, I had the undeniable freedom to exercise my God-given spiritual gifts in the ways that best accomplished God-glorifying results. That said, don't think I didn't call my parents, who were keeping Samuel during the day, every hour on the hour.

I had one more stop to make on the way home, and as I neared Vanessa's house, I gathered strength by gritting my teeth. Without the power of the Holy Spirit flowing through me, my flesh would have literally been happy to decapitate Dr. Vanessa Bright. Take her apart. Dismantle her. Roll her over. Pick your violent metaphor.

I thank God, though, that He had planted in me an odd little seed of appreciation toward this woman. The bottom line was, no one forced her to give birth to Samuel Law, the beautiful little man I would spend the rest of my life with. She could have so easily done what millions of women did every year with inconvenient pregnancies. Instead, she had heeded the appeal of a husband intent on giving his wife the child she—I—had always craved.

Vanessa opened her door and quickly stood aside, eager to usher me in. "You didn't have to go through this trouble," she said. "I told you to just drop the photos in the mail, Dionne."

Passing her the envelope, I took a pass on Vanessa's invite, my feet staying rooted to the welcome mat on her small front patio. "I figured I could go out of my way once. I wanted to thank you in person for signing the adoption papers." Against my will, I felt a trickle of tears sting my cheeks. "I can't tell you what this means to me. Jesse, too, in his own way."

Vanessa held the door open, still standing in the hallway. "Jesse and I haven't talked in a month," she said. "He told me to get all my information from you—said we needed a clean break so we can both get right with God."

"I respect that."

"So I don't know exactly what the status of you two's marriage is, but I hope you guys can work things out."

"We're okay financially, if you're worried about that. Jesse accepted a full-time adjunct role at Howard's Division of Fine Arts. And though he's not returning their calls yet, several gospel labels are interested in him."

"I could eventually provide Samuel with financial stability," Vanessa replied, her eyes cutting at me in exasperation. "I'm talking about your ability to become again the strong, beautiful couple I came to know during my pregnancy—the ones who wanted to raise this child."

"Vanessa, just trust that we'll see to it Samuel has an enriching home environment either way—"

"What bothers you more, Dionne?" Vanessa nodded down the hallway, clearly hoping again to coax me inside. "The fact Jesse slept with me, or the fact he fathered a child with someone other than you?"

As if she had a right to know the answer. "Good-bye, Vanessa," I said, turning to go.

When the good doctor shot a hand out and ensnared my shoulder, I instinctively whipped around with my back coiled and a frown on my face. "What are you doing?"

"Don't go yet. Please." Vanessa didn't let go of me, but it was her face—her quivering, crumbling features—that kept me from shoving her away. "Just give him a chance," she said, her voice breaking into what sounded like a hiccup. "He really loves you, Dionne. No one knows that more than me."

I still wanted to shove her away, but as the Holy Spirit descended on me, I chose instead to slip from her grasp. "It's in God's hands now, Vanessa, no one else's. Good-bye."

35

As Coleman climbed into my car, I turned up the volume on my stereo. "Shut your door, I want to hear this," I said without bothering to make eye contact.

"Good morning to you, too," Coleman replied as he locked the passenger door and settled back. As I pulled out of his driveway and into the street, our ears filled with the dulcet tones of the DJ, a host on one of the satellite radio gospel shows.

"So, y'all, it looks like some pieces of the puzzle are falling into place with everybody's favorite hit makers, Men with a Message. Word is that although their original label chose not to re-sign the group without leads Jesse Law and Coleman Hill, group founder Micah Harris and the remaining members have signed a new deal with Verity, and they've recruited a new young lead whose voice is smokin'! I hear the cat sounds like a young Marvin Sapp." Coleman and I had already heard this news, and it hadn't come as too much of a surprise. While we liked to think of ourselves as irreplaceable, the truth was there was always a richer baritone or a smoother tenor lurking in the choir stand.

The DJ wasn't finished with his rundown, though. "More of a trip, though, is the news that Coleman Hill—you know, the brother whose 'issues' caused the breakup—has also signed a deal of his own with an independent label, At His Word Records. Yeah, you never heard of them either? Don't sleep, 'cause word is this label is funded by some major evangelical leaders, you know, people makin' that Pat Robertson and Frederick K. C. Price type of money! Sounds like brother Coleman will be getting *paid*! So the question is, who planted those embarrassing photos of him—an enemy or an ally, know what I mean?"

When I turned to glance his way, Coleman was peering intently out the window, his lips pursed in a silent whistle. I held my tongue long enough to let the DJ finish.

"And, ladies, just so you don't keep burning up my phone lines all morning—no, we still ain't heard nothing about Jesse Law's career. Hey, the brother did sell a couple of million records in his day—could be he doesn't need the work!"

We had driven another three miles before Coleman said, "I was going to tell you this morning, man."

"You would have been too late," I replied. "I heard this exact same report last night, while driving home after my evening visit with Samuel. This was after hearing rumors from any number of people for the last week-plus." I turned to face him while braking at a red light. "Just so I'm clear, is our friendship officially over, or what?"

Coleman sighed, tugging on the brim of his Orioles ball cap. "There was a time I'd have called you before signing any deal, Jess. Don't act like things haven't changed radically since then."

"Are those changes my fault?"

"Well, let's think about that," Coleman replied, his words gaining sudden force. "You and Dionne stood before me and Suzette and swore you'd help us through the revelations about me and Adrian. Where you guys been lately, old friend? Oh wait, that's right, you pretty much ended your marriage by cheating on your wife, then lying about your own child's identity!"

Love your neighbor as yourself. Jesus' words from Matthew 22:39 kept my hands on the steering wheel and my voice calm as I responded. "So you see two friends drowning, and your first thought is to blame us for not saving you first?"

"That's not what I mean, come on." Coleman sighed again, this time sounding impatient with himself. "I just didn't expect to have my two strongest pillars of support pulled during my and Suzette's greatest hour of need, that's all. Don't think we weren't praying for you guys, though."

"I hear you," I said.

"Bottom line, when you revealed your own sin, I figured I had to look out for me and my family and rely on God only. So I've been seeking Him in the Word and through prayer, plus counsel from Pastor Willis, while making some very tough decisions."

"Coleman," I said, "I only have two questions. Are you and Suzette going to make it, and why have you been so secretive about this new record deal?" I had it on good authority that he hadn't told anyone in our circle—not Joe, our manager, not one of our attorneys, not even any of the many fellow artists who had called offering prayer and encouragement—about this mysterious new label to which he'd signed his life.

"First, the record deal," Coleman replied as we cruised toward our breakfast destination, a Shoney's near College Park. "They made me an offer I couldn't refuse, man. They're independent, but the investors have deep pockets. What they said on the radio, about ties to folks in league with Robertson, Falwell, and Price, it's true. None of those cats are actually investors, but these are their former mentees, their bankers, their lawyers."

I didn't even ask the question, just raised an eyebrow.

"Some would call them right-wingers, if that's what you're thinking, but they're not kooks. It's not like I had my choice of gigs, Jesse. Most of the black gospel labels wouldn't return my calls, or when they did, all they talked about was waiting to see if things would 'blow over,' they kept saying. I told them all, thank you very much, but my kids gotta eat and my wife has to stay kept, and they can't afford to wait."

Coleman took a minute to further justify his decision by detailing the terms of his contract. At His Word had decided to make him its flagship artist. They'd signed on the dotted line with him, committing not only to four CD projects guaranteed for release over a six-year period, but they were also guaranteeing two professionally produced, nationally distributed videos to accompany each CD, along with a twenty-city tour, in addition to executive producer status on every CD, ongoing use of a luxury company car, and a royalty rate that was twice the industry standard. As long as he didn't lose his voice anytime soon, Coleman and his family would be living a very comfortable lifestyle.

As we pulled into the lot of the Shoney's, I took a measure of the contented look on my friend's face. "Well, the more you talk about the deal, the harder it is to take issue with. You sure there's no catch?"

Coleman's expression darkened slightly as he opened his door. "No catches, Jesse. I'm going into this with open eyes."

Once I had climbed out, I stared at him over the top of my car. "What does that mean, exactly?"

Coleman shook his head and tugged on his ball cap again. "You're gonna hear about it eventually, anyway," he said, more to himself than to me. "There's a public relations clause included in the agreement. I get paid for each one, but I have to do a certain number of media appearances for the first year of the contract."

"Oh." I heard the laughter in my voice, wishing I could take it back—given that this was really no laughing matter. "Let me guess, you have to go around correcting that little thing about your having been born gay."

"No," Coleman shot back, rearing up and balling his fists. "All they want me to do, Brother Know-It-All, is say what I've always said: that I overcame the desire to act on my homosexual nature through reorientation training, prayer, and Scripture."

Too embarrassed for my friend to look him in the eye, I toed the ground with my shoe. "So they want you to be the poster child for 'healed' gays?"

"Those are your words," Coleman replied. He drummed his fingers on the roof of my car. "Are we going inside or not, man?"

"Just one question," I said, walking around to Coleman's side of the car. "Have you seen any of my recent media appearances? You have any opinion about them?"

Coleman rolled his eyes. "Aside from the fact that it's my fault you're in the middle of that whole media circus, no. Frankly, I don't know why you're wasting time trying to play Jesse Jackson between the gays and the gay-haters. It's not worth the effort."

"I don't get it," I said, frowning. "How is your little PR arrangement with your label any different? You're wading into the same waters by preaching this sexual reorientation message."

"The difference," Coleman replied, "is that I'm offering a solid truth. God heals. What are you offering, besides a bunch of mumbo jumbo, 'can't we all just get along' emotion with no foundation?"

I could see I wasn't going to win this argument, and a glance at my watch told me we were late for our brunch date. "Never mind," I said as I headed toward the restaurant's entrance. "You want to tell me on the ride back whether you and Suzette are going to make it?"

"All I know," Coleman said as he fell into step beside me, "is that At His Word expects me to have a loyal wife at my side. I've offered that role to Suzette, if she'll have it."

"How long are you giving her to make up her mind?" Between the "gospel grapevine" and a few cryptic comments from Dionne, I knew that Suzette was still struggling to trust Coleman's ability to "live straight" and that she had probably committed adultery at some point. As jacked-up as my marriage was, I still gave us better odds than the Hills.

"She has however long she needs," Coleman replied.

"You think that's wise?" I asked. "I mean, from both a personal and professional standpoint, doesn't that leave you exposed to her whims? You could wake up any day and find she's taken up with the milk-man."

Coleman yanked on the front door and stood aside, holding it open for me. "I've worked too hard to get here," he said, the look in his eyes both strained and defensive. "I'm not starting over."

36

Jesse

ngie Barker sat at a table along the back wall of the Shoney's, a Washington Wizards cap drawing attention to her piercing eyes. She nodded casually as Coleman and I took our seats. "Good morning, boys." She peered over her menu at us. "I see Coleman had the good sense to go bummy today like me, sweat suit and all. What's your excuse, Mr. Law?"

Chuckling, I surveyed my slacks and silk shirt. "What, you think I should have a hat with a long brim so no one can see my face? Unlike you two, I don't have a high-profile career to protect anymore. I can just be me."

"Don't believe that," Angie said, flicking a finger toward my shoulder. "Three tables behind you to the left, there's a table of thirty-something white girls who followed you from the door all the way over here—with their leering eyes, that is. They look ready to sop you up with a biscuit. Some of them probably lost their virginity to your early music, cutie."

I elbowed Coleman lazily. "And to think that you questioned the wisdom of meeting with Ms. Barker after all she's put us through. I told you she was all class, all the time."

"I'm glad you schooled him," Angie said, a whiff of good-humored defiance in her tone. She snapped her fingers in the direction of a young Asian-looking waiter before turning back to us. "I appreciate you-all agreeing to meet me. Jesse, after you reached out, I wasn't sure how far to press my luck."

I had contacted Angie a few days after my Nashville reunion with my nephew Larry Jr. Little Larry insisted that my celebrity, combined with my position in the midst of the scandal surrounding Coleman, gave me a unique platform from which to call for tolerance and honesty in the Christian community. In the three years since he had largely walled himself off from me and the rest of the Law family, my nephew had drifted back into many of the Christian convictions of his childhood. "I wanted to get away from all religion," he told me, "or better yet, do one of those really liberal deals like the Unitarian Church, something New Age maybe. Like it or not, though, it felt like my father's preaching, our grandparents' teaching, and all those memory verses were just too embedded. I always knew I needed Christ in my life."

As a result, Larry Jr. had actually joined a Progressive Baptist congregation in Manhattan a few months ago, and had asked his parents to stand by him as he tried to reconcile his sexual orientation—he was convinced God had made him gay and approved of him living accordingly—with the traditional teachings of the faith. "I'm not the first to do this," he told me the weekend I was in Nashville. "There's thousands, probably tens of thousands of us out there, equally committed to following Jesus while being true to how God made us."

Larry Jr. had weighed heavily on my mind as I reached out to Angie. "The damage to Coleman, to me, has been done," I said when we first spoke. By now, not only had all of her stories featuring Coleman's past run their course, but she had caught wind of my separation from Dionne.

Angie, however, had promised not to pursue that story, indicating that she already knew it involved fertility problems, which she considered too serious a matter to play with. "I still stand by the story I ran on Coleman, though," she had said.

"There's no point rehashing that," I replied. "What I need from you now is to take all this titillation you raised—and the big-time bylines you got—and turn it into a vehicle for good. We can't do that until you help me understand how you initially found Adrian."

"Just so we're clear," Angie said now, looking more directly at Coleman than at me, "I'm not giving up any of my actual sources. I'll talk in general about what I know about the people surrounding Adrian if you think that'll help, but I won't say who gave me what evidence."

"We're not asking for all that," Coleman said. "What we need is closure. A lot of people are giving me the benefit of the doubt, but I know some tongues are still wagging. I need to silence them for my family's sake. My children deserve better than to have kids calling their daddy a murderer."

We spent nearly an hour deconstructing the individuals in Adrian's world, including the entire leadership of GET UP, the activist group that had driven the media coverage. It was not a simple exercise; Adrian had a complex life, full of demanding political consulting clients who stood against everything he and GET UP were fighting for, along with a diverse roster of past boyfriends. We started to sympathize with the police: honing in on a short list of suspects in his disappearance had seemed plausible, but the deeper we dug, the less likely it seemed.

Just about the time our efforts started to feel completely futile, Coleman pushed his latest breakfast buffet plate away and shoved his chair back. "I'll be back in a few," he said. "When I am, please tell me we'll have some way of bringing Adrian home safely."

"Pray," I said, my eyes focused on my cooling cup of hot tea. "Pray hard."

As Coleman walked off, Angie forked another bite of scrambled eggs before looking up at me cautiously. "Jesse, I did want to say one thing to you while we're alone."

My heartbeat fluttered a second, wary of a last-minute come-on. It wasn't like I didn't still find her physically attractive, and to be honest, our banter had remained flirtatious even in the most contentious times. The last thing I needed right now—as I waited for Dionne to possibly forgive me—was an offer to relieve all the sexual tension that had built in me since the day I'd been revealed as a lying cheat.

Angie persistently chased my eyes with hers before saying, "Thank you."

"For what?"

"For helping me believe that God can actually change people." She reached over to tap my tented hands, then quickly pulled back. "The old you would have reacted nothing like the man I confronted with those photos of Coleman. I don't know what I was expecting, but you didn't give it to me. I was ready to have you threaten my life, offer me hoards of cash, or frankly . . ." Her voice dropped to a whisper. "Well, if you'd offered to work off your debt in my bedroom, I wouldn't have exactly laughed you off."

I resisted the urge to frown at Angie's characterization. "I'm no saint, trust me. You don't owe me any thanks."

"You don't understand," she said, her voice still low to the ground and furtive. She looked over her shoulder, then back at me. "I've been all over the map about whether to share this, but between you and me—okay?—there are things about Adrian's disappearance, and about this GET UP group, that would have made me think twice about publishing the story if they'd happened earlier."

"What do you mean?"

"I'm saying," Angie replied, "that Adrian's disappearance was pretty inconvenient for Coleman, wasn't it? Didn't really make his life easier, exactly."

"Mine either."

"Uh-huh," she said, leaning closer as Coleman emerged from the bathroom. "On the other hand, his disappearance was right on time for other folks, perfectly in tune with their agendas." Her eyes flashed righteously as she said, "I don't like being had, Jesse, and I've put a private investigator on retainer. Do you want in? It'll cost you, but I think we agree it's a worthy cause."

37

Dionne

"I'm sorry, Rev, but to be honest, I don't get it." Earl was seated on the carpet of his family room, where we had spent the past hour outlining a program for Adrian's memorial service. We had made pretty good progress, but the recent change of subject had Earl sidetracked. "Spell it out for me," he said, nearly shoving my laptop computer to the side.

"Regardless of anything else," I said, my chin rising in defiance at his tone, "my husband deserves to see his own son."

"Yeah, okay," Earl said, his back resting against his love seat, "but why the sudden change of venue? For weeks now, you've been making him come up in your folks' house while you leave them be. Now you're going over to his house—or is it still *your* house?"

"I can't hide from him!" I hadn't meant to shout, but as I stood and began pacing the floor in front of Earl, I realized that I was way out of my depth in this conversation. Here I was, just now ready to interact with Jesse again, if only to prove I could be civil toward him, and Earl was acting like the jealous boyfriend I'd never had as a single woman.

He kept his back to the love seat, tracking me with his observant eyes. "You already told me Pastor Norm wants you to reconcile with hubby," he said. "Are you really gonna tell him—or anyone, for that matter—about us?"

"Tell them *what* about us?" I peered down at Earl, my hands on my hips. "You think I'm ashamed of anything about our relationship?" I ticked my points off, finger by finger. "We haven't been intimate yet, I haven't spent one night away from my baby, and my husband knows all about us and has agreed not to make it an issue."

"Don't go throwing that goody-two-shoes mess about sex at me," Earl replied, his eyes flashing. "I told you I'm too new in Christ to know anything different than getting down with women I love, but I haven't pushed you in that area. But you're gonna tell me you're not embarrassed about being emotionally intimate with me?"

I bit my lip and instinctively turned my back, coming face-to-face with a family portrait of Earl, Adrian, and their parents from earlier, simpler years. My trip to Earl's house today to work on a potential memorial program—Adrian still hadn't been found, but nearly three months into his disappearance Earl wanted to be prepared—had just been the latest of the private lunches, late-night calls, and movie dates that had built an emotional bond between me and Mr. Earl Wilkes. He had been a patient, soothing shoulder on which I could cry, and I had been the one person with whom he could transparently share the sorrow and helplessness engulfing him as each day passed without word of Adrian's fate. To the outside world, Earl was a rock, one of those street-smart brothers you messed with at your peril, but when we were alone, he was a puppy dog.

So, yes, he was right that while I hadn't let him do anything more than kiss me in the same way he had the day Jesse "caught" us, we had definitely crossed a line into intimate territory. "What I decide to do," I said now in a low voice, slowly swinging back around to face him, "is between me, God, you, and Jesse. I respect Pastor Norm and am attending individual counseling with him, but that man hasn't walked a mile in my pumps."

"Okay." Earl leaned forward, springing to his feet. "So I am in the mix," he said, taking my shoulders in his hands. "So where's this train headed, Dionne?"

I looked away. "Don't, Earl."

He stared at me wordlessly, his expression blank. "After a few weeks, I may not know much about walking with Christ," he said finally, "but even I know that if you still consider yourself Jesse's wife, you got no business being here with me."

Earl's words carried with them the weight of God's truth, and my stomach nearly turned over as I realized that my flesh had no interest in hearing it. Looking up into his eyes, I finally faced up to a very real fact: Earl was right to feel threatened, but maybe not for the reasons he thought. On the one hand, see, he was absolutely right that a part of me hadn't completely shut the door on returning to Jesse to raise the child God had brought into our lives. On the other hand, the accompanying truth was that before I did that, I wanted to claim a little piece of what most of my brothers and sisters in Christ seemingly had. Male or female, African-American, Hispanic, Caucasian or Asian, gay or straight, young or old, nearly every saint had a laundry list of "fun" they'd experienced before joining the fold. As one of the few sheep who'd galloped into "sainthood" before experiencing anything else, my flesh was screaming loud for the opportunity to grab some fun. And as Earl used his soulful stare to ask just what I wanted, it felt like he was reading my mind.

When Jesse opened the front door to our home, he stared at Samuel and me with tangible longing. "You have the keys still, right?" he asked.

"It's been a while since I've been back," I said, handing the baby to Jesse and sliding out of my jacket as I surveyed the foyer's wallpaper, which I had chosen and put up two years earlier. "We took the front door, Jesse, so we didn't surprise you."

"It's pretty rare for me to have company of any type," he replied. By now, he had taken Samuel around to the great room, laid him on the couch, and taken him out of his car seat. "It does turn out I have visitors today, though."

"Who?"

"Larry and his boy, Larry Jr., are here. Do you remember I went to visit them last month?"

"That's right," I said. "You-all must have had a good visit, I take it."

"Yeah, I'd say so." Jesse held Samuel, gently moving him up and down and chuckling along with each of the baby's giggles. "I've actually been meaning to fill you in on some of the things we talked about. You may recall the last time Larry Jr. came out to a family gathering, it didn't go so well."

"I remember." The thought of my gay nephew and his spiritual condition had haunted me off and on since Larry had first come out to the family. As a minister who counseled teens and had seen several successfully renounce their homosexuality, I had always wished for the opportunity to at least talk with Larry Jr. and understand his decision to live a gay lifestyle.

Jesse spent a few minutes filling me in on the details of his conversation with the "Larrys" a few weeks earlier, mentioning that Larry Jr. had rededicated his life to Christ, but was determined to help more Christians understand that some homosexuals were acting out an inborn, God-blessed desire that was no less moral than the heterosexual impulse. "I have to tell you," Jesse said, "neither my brother nor I are quite on the same page with Junior, but we at least agree there needs to be more open conversation about these issues. That's why I've been running my mouth on all those talk shows."

"What type of responses are you getting?" I asked.

"Do you really have to ask?" he said, a hoarse chuckle underneath his tone. "Maybe a fourth of folks say 'thank you for speaking up,' another fourth say 'you're right, we need to talk about this 'cause I've got gay family members and I'm uncomfortable with how to come at all this.' Everybody else tells me I'm going to hell for even raising the topic."

"Although I think I know where everyone else is coming from," I said, laughing at the sight of Samuel pulling at Jesse's nose, "some people really need to ask themselves 'What Would Jesus Do?' before expressing their thoughts."

"There's an interesting concept," Jesse replied while rubbing noses with Samuel.

"What's the interesting concept?" I had to ask because Samuel's quick fingers had snared Jesse's lower lip for a moment, rendering him mute.

"What would Jesus do, and say, about homosexuality?" Jesse looked past Samuel's fidgety little figure to lock eyes with me. "How'd you factor that into the sermon Pastor Norm made you preach? I've, uh, obviously been out of the loop."

"Well, now that you mention it," I said, "I'm still struggling to wrap up a draft of it." We talked for a few minutes about the ways in which we'd both struggled with the issues, going back through the years and up through our recent, disappointing attempt to shield Coleman and Suzette from his past.

"Food for thought," Jesse said, nodding toward the stairs. "Larry and Junior should be getting up any minute now. Their flight got in late last night, so I've let them get some shut-eye, but I told them to be ready to meet Samuel by ten o'clock."

"I hear you," I replied. Our separation hadn't yet severed the telepathic link that lets couples read one another's minds. "Yeah, I'd be happy to talk with them both about the sermon too. I can use a diversity of opinions, as long as they're Word-centered."

"Cool," Jesse said, kissing Samuel on the cheek and placing him on his right shoulder. "Let me go ahead and get them up," he said, standing. Bouncing Samuel playfully, Jesse took a few steps, then stopped as he neared the foyer.

Still seated, I shifted uncomfortably when I realized he was staring at me wordlessly. "What's wrong?"

"Nothing's wrong," he replied, stabilizing Samuel's position atop his shoulders without letting his eyes wander from mine. "That's the point, Dionne. Isn't this a nice moment?"

Yes, and I want more of them. I felt a trickle of shame burn my chest when I heard what felt like my soul's answer. Something deep down wouldn't let me share it, though, so I replied by clearing my throat and reaching for my purse.

When I looked up, Jesse and Samuel were gone.

38

Jesse

arry Jr., Angie, and I arrived at the Georgetown area headquarters of GET UP just as the press conference began. The
building's small lobby was crammed with journalists wield-
ing PDAs, cameramen swinging all sorts of equipment, and assorted
usual suspects for events of this nature. I saw two nationally known
minister-politicians, who shall remain nameless, several behind-the-
scenes gospel industry players, and a handful of young folks in suits
who struck me either as Capitol Hill aides or church activists.

A lean, attractive white woman with a brunette buzz cut stood at a
lectern jammed into the far left corner of the room. "My name is
Rachel Hughes, president of GET UP DC," she said, immediately
confirming my impression that she was the same activist I'd heard
Coleman speak to before he was outed. "We're here, regretfully, to
announce our sad conviction that based on the investigation to date
and the constant run of dead ends, our brother, Adrian Wilkes, has
likely met with foul play."

Righteous despair fueling her words, Rachel continued. "GET UP believes the best way to honor Adrian's probable death is to step up our campaign against homosexual bigotry in God's Christian Church. As a gay Christian organization, we are dedicated to freeing our brothers and sisters from their figurative entrapment at the back of the Church's bus. . ."

Rachel went on this way for a while as cameras flashed, video cameras hummed, and journalists taped, scribbled, and typed. She got further attention going when she was joined at the podium by the two minister-politicians, who flanked her with somber expressions and nodded humbly when she referenced their valuable counsel.

"Adrian was most likely killed," Rachel said now, "because his former lover was so frightened at the thought of being outed in front of the Christian community, that he chose to jeopardize the life of this man he once loved. We're not here to prosecute Coleman Hill, though, or even the possible assailants who actually took Adrian's life. As God's children we take our Lord at His Word in Scripture and will leave that side of justice to the authorities. We will, however, focus on prosecuting the culture that put Adrian, Coleman, and the other players in this sad story into jeopardy in the first place. We will . . ."

Standing between me and Angie, who had her arms crossed and her lips twisted, Larry Jr. nearly glowed with admiration. "She is powerful," he whispered, smiling. "You have to give her that much."

"No doubt," I replied, nodding. "That's why I wanted you to at least see this much. This group just might be on the right track, kid."

My nephew shook his head and bit his lower lip. "Too bad they'll be shut down in a few days."

"You can still learn from them," I whispered back, catching Angie's impatient stare. "Maybe pick up where they leave off. Just don't make the same mistakes."

• • •

The three of us were still clustered into a corner of the lobby an hour later, after Rachel had finished her screed, the minister-politicians had rhymed the audience into submission, and the majority of the crowd had dispersed. By now, there were only a dozen of us left, clumped about the room in groups of two or three, including Rachel, who was a few feet from us wrapping up an interview with a brother whose press ID indicated he was with the *Village Voice*.

The *Voice* reporter was still shaking Rachel's hand good-bye when she recognized us. "Angie?" she said first, before taking me in. Her eyes widening a little more than she'd probably intended, she nodded. "Jesse Law, correct?"

"What's up, Rachel?" Angie reached a hand forward, smiling placidly as they exchanged a brisk shake. "Looks like you stirred everyone up, well done."

"Well," Rachel replied, her eyes glancing my way almost shyly, "you know more than most how long we've fought a good fight to get this far."

"Mmm," Angie replied. "It's just a shame that it took a personal tragedy to help you get some real press coverage."

"Listen," Rachel said, now turning to face me, "you should all know that GET UP feels partially responsible for Adrian's getting caught up in all this. Mr. Law, you may as well know, our group did not initially advise him to provide those photos to Angie. I wonder sometimes, if we had really pushed back on him, kept Angie's story from being so explosive, would things have taken such a nasty turn?"

"Rachel," I replied, "I want you to meet my nephew Larry Law Jr." I ushered the kid forward, continuing as they dutifully shook hands. "He's an, uh, a member of your constituency and a fine young man. I couldn't be more proud of him. I want you to know, I specifically brought him along to help me hold my peace in front of you."

Rachel didn't shrink from the heat of my stare, her gaze respectful but direct. "I understand. GET UP realizes that there is always collateral damage when we take stands for important causes. I'm sorry if all this busted up your group."

I shrugged. "Don't forget about the children involved here, least of all Coleman Hill's little ones."

"Mr. Law, I understand you'll never be a fan of GET UP," Rachel replied, "but after hearing my presentation today, I hope you understand our greater cause at least."

"I do," I said as Angie zipped her shoulder satchel open. "That's why I wish you could have just been more patient."

"I'm a journalist, Rachel," Angie said, shoving a ream of photos into the activist's hands. As half of them scattered to the ground, Angie's tone darkened. "I write *nonfiction*, do you understand me? You tried to put me on front street, and I don't play that."

"What are you talking about?" Rachel's brow wrinkled, but she stooped to her knees to gather up the loose photos. She hadn't looked at any of them yet.

"Adrian Wilkes is alive and well," Angie said. "You need to understand, I'm not new, girl. I cut my teeth in journalism working for the *Baltimore Sun*, doing police reporting, so I know about suspicious Missing Person reports. With each passing week, I smelled a rat about Adrian's disappearance. I finally got concerned enough to hire a private investigator to sit on GET UP—this building, your apartment, and the homes of your entire board." She looked hard at Rachel's face as the activist scanned the photos. "Now tell me, how did he get four different shots, digital time-stamped shots, mind you, of Adrian entering or leaving this building as well as your apartment over the past month?"

Rachel's tone was calm and her expression unchanged as she said, "Not here." She turned on the heels of her shoes and we trailed behind her, passing the handful of remaining folks, most of whom seemed to

270 • *Xavier Knight*

recognize me. Ignoring their quizzical looks, we hustled up the stairs to Rachel's office.

Once Larry Jr. had shut her door behind us, Rachel let the photos fall to her desk. Her shoulders high and tight, her tone now erased of all humility, she said, "Let's make a deal."

39

Dionne

I was almost finished with my sermon, and to be honest, I don't think I had ever been more anxious about the reaction. Salty drops of sweat trickling into my mouth—my forehead was dry, but not the area above my upper lip—I pressed home my concluding lines. "I'm not here this morning to counsel that we abandon God's principles," I said. "I'm here to say, people of God, that we're called to stand by those principles with a loving spirit, not a judgmental one that drives our brothers and sisters away." A light wave of approving murmurs and claps rippling through the sanctuary, I reiterated the message's key points before thanking God and turning the microphone over to Pastor Norm.

"Thank you, Reverend Dionne," Pastor said, taking the mic and strolling down to the floor in front of the pulpit. "Well, I can imagine some of you are wondering whether your pastor stands by every word my sister in ministry just stated." He paused for effect, and the sanctuary felt like it swelled at the thick silence he let gather. "I don't, for the record. My God, and the Scripture I interpret, tells me that those who live the gay lifestyle are clearly sinning. I'm sorry, it may sound harsh, but when God called me to preach, He didn't tell me to spoon out feel-good theology. *He told me to preach the Word!*" The church erupted in fierce applause, but he quickly quieted the congregation.

"With all that on the record, I see no place in Scripture that tells me Rising Son should work with less effort to save the souls of homosexuals than it works to save liars, cheaters, fornicators, or criminals. So I am here to say in solidarity with Reverend Dionne, who has already opened our eyes about how we can welcome in those of different ethnicities, that this church is going to actively reach out to you if you're gay. We're going to stop reminding you that we find your lifestyle an abomination, not because we don't, but because by this point you probably know that . . ."

The air crackled as Pastor announced his plan to set up a ministry aimed at members involved in homosexuality. Seated in the pulpit, watching him stroll the floor and press home his extemporaneous points, I was more comforted in my soul than I'd thought possible that morning. While Pastor Norm had grudgingly approved my sermon as submitted a few days earlier, I'd had no idea he would back me up this way. A group like GET UP wouldn't be endorsing Rising Son's new ministry anytime soon, but for this church the simple acknowledgment of sincere gay Christians was a step forward.

Despite myself, I felt a wide smile break out on my face, and when I dared to look out into the audience, the first pair of eyes I connected with were the most familiar in the room. There, three rows back and to the right from me, sat Jesse. Samuel lay across his lap. He had agreed to keep the baby that morning so I could focus on my last-minute preaching preparations, but I could hardly be surprised that he'd made the trip over.

With the baby cradled in his arms, Jesse extended a thumbs-up, his mouth wide with a smile second only to my own.

The remaining moments of service were almost surreal as Pastor Norm's invitation brought forward three new members, all of whom prayed with me to accept Christ. When the benediction ended and Pastor and I hosted a receiving line in the lobby, I was surprised at how positive everyone's attitude was. Granted, people who felt that my message of tolerance was heresy probably weren't likely to come shake my hand, but no one who came through the line was angry or judgmental. A few whispered that they wanted to speak with me privately, which probably meant they were also adjusting to the realities of gay friends and loved ones, or maybe even struggling with their own sexuality, for all I knew. As much as I had agonized over the sermon and rewritten it with input from Larry Sr. and Junior and even Jesse, one thing was certain: God had used me to touch a nerve that needed some scratching.

When I arrived at my office, Jesse and Samuel were there. Jesse sat on my small couch testing a bottle as Samuel piped up and reached his little hands toward his precious "moo juice." As my husband patiently plopped the bottle's nipple between Samuel's quivering lips, Jesse looked up at me with a proud smile. "God filled you, and the entire sanctuary, with his Spirit this morning. Dionne, that was beautiful."

I hovered over Jesse and the baby for a second, my loyalties divided. As estranged as my husband and I were, I was grateful to him and his family for their help in crafting a sermon message that had dealt honestly with the challenges of a complex issue. And now, seeing him attend so lovingly to our child, well, it just plain got to me.

"Why are you crying?" The way Samuel was intently sucking back milk, Jesse couldn't rise to hug me, but his eyes said it all. "Have a seat, girl. Please."

I settled in beside the two of them and began wiping my eyes, when the sound of a deep voice clearing its throat cut through the air.

Turning toward my doorway, I tried harder to dry my eyes as I met Earl's skeptical gaze. "Hey, there."

"You said to meet you here." Earl's matter-of-fact tone needed no elaboration.

"Yes, I know," I said, standing and feeling guilty for some reason. "I—I didn't know that Jesse would be coming here with the baby."

"I just came to hear the sermon, Earl," Jesse said, his eyes on Samuel's wavy strands of hair. "Nothing more to it than that, brother."

Earl glanced at his leather dress shoes before reaching suddenly for his cell phone, drawing it from the pocket of his overcoat. "I need to make a few calls," he said. "I'll be out in my car, so just page me when you're ready for me to come back."

"Hey, Earl," Jesse said.

Earl turned back to face us, his hand on the doorknob, but said nothing.

"First, I wanted to apologize for my behavior outside of your church that day," Jesse said, his gaze moving between me and Earl. "Secondly, I understand you've accepted Jesus Christ."

Arms hanging at his side, standing as if poised for an attack, Earl nodded affirmatively.

"Well, congratulations. Hands down, that's the best move you'll ever make in your life."

Earl looked at me, instead of Jesse, but said, "Thank you."

"Tell me if I'm out of line," Jesse said, easing the empty bottle out of Samuel's hands and shifting him to his opposite arm, "but is there any reason why you weren't at GET UP's press conference the other day?"

Earl's temples pulsed noticeably, as they always did when he got defensive. "Those jokers said it themselves, if I read the papers right," he replied. "They're about using Adrian's disappearance for a cause, man. I just want my brother back."

"I understand," Jesse said, eyes still on me as I remained standing, rooted to a spot in the middle of the floor. I probably looked like a hostage in my own office at that point. "You didn't hear it from me," Jesse continued, "but I have a sense there will be some good news about your brother very soon."

"Really?" Earl shrugged as if Jesse had just predicted the point spread for a big college football game. He looked at me again, clearly uninterested in baring his emotions in front of someone he viewed as a rival. "Rev, I'll be out in my car. Take care, Jesse."

When Earl was gone, I shut the door behind him and collapsed back onto the couch. Despite myself, I punched my husband in the shoulder, my touch almost as playful as it had been in smoother times. "What was that about? As if things weren't awkward enough, you're trying to be his friend or something?"

"I just need a couple more days," Jesse replied, passing Samuel's sleeping little body over to me. "But trust me, God has opened some doors for me, Angie, and Coleman to get to the bottom of things. I'm confident our investigator will have good insight on Adrian's where-abouts in another week's time."

I opted to take Jesse at his word—as the Gospel of Matthew says, each of my days already had enough trouble of their own. Unfortunately, I had one more bit of unpleasantness to raise. "So Daddy says you reached out to him."

"I had some extra tickets, is all," Jesse replied, referencing the Orioles tickets he had offered my father. "I wasn't crazy enough to offer to take him to the game, I let him take some of his fellow retirees so he could enjoy himself."

"He said you told him that he'll have to get used to you, regardless of what happens with us."

"Scary thing is, he barely fought me on that," Jesse said, chuckling. "Whenever you tell him the whole truth and nothing but, that'll probably change, but you know what, Dionne? It's taken all I have to accept God's forgiveness for my role in all this, and more still to really cleanse myself of the sin that moved me to lie to you in the first place." Jesse leaned forward, clasped his hands. "After going through all that, I don't have time to live in fear of your father's judgments anymore."

For a moment Samuel's coos were the only sound in the room, until I spoke. "You committed a horrible act, Jesse, but you're not the same man I met that day in the shower." I took a breath, then said, "And so that you know, if I decide that it eventually makes sense to tell the rest of my family that you're Samuel's biological father, I will make it clear that God alone can judge you. It's none of their business. Their only responsibilities are to love Samuel and to respect you in your role as his father, as long as you do right by him."

"I can't tell you how much I appreciate that," Jesse replied, his eyes downcast and his voice suddenly hoarse. "And for the record, if you decide to choose Earl over me, all I ask is that you give me generous joint custody rights."

Jesse's stark words and calm tone stabbed me in the pit of my stomach, and I flicked my eyes up to his. "What?"

"You heard me," he replied, a more transparent film of emotion seeping into his tone now. "I want you back so bad, Dionne, it embarrasses me. I don't have the right to press you on it, though."

I wasn't sure what I had expected Jesse to feel all this time, but this wasn't quite it. I felt my eyes narrow as I asked, "How can you want me back, but not act on it?"

"I just acted on it," Jesse said, his eyes meeting my stare now. "But you see, my father acted on it, too, every time Mama caught him laying up with a new girlfriend, including my own mother, of course. And every time Mama took him back."

"Jesse," I said, wondering if I was being roped in against my will, "you're not your father. If history's any indicator, you're much more likely to change your behavior than Phillip Sr. ever was."

"Prayerfully so," he replied. "But I can't expect you to take that chance."

"Well, I'm not ready to make that call, anyway," I said, sighing and focusing on Samuel again. "Whether we raise this child together or separately, though, I have prayed about one thing. We should have his paternity tested, Jesse. I know there's no reason not to believe you're his father, but women lie to the men in their lives about that every day. We need to know both sides of Samuel's genetic roots, so we're aware of what illnesses and things to look out for as Samuel grows up."

Jesse ran a hand over his brow and slowly said, "No."

Processing his brusque reply, I stood and walked to my desk with Samuel enveloped in my arms. "I'm not sure where this is coming from," I said, "but it's not so simple as you just stating your wish. I just explained my logic."

"I'm still convinced I gave my mama ulcers," Jesse said in reply. His chin tucked in toward his chest, he continued without looking up. "She loved me like I was her own, baby, you know that. She still does. But when I was little, there were more than a few nights I caught her sitting up staring at old photos of me with Cassie," he said, surprising me because Jesse rarely referred to his natural mother by name. "The look in her eyes, Dionne . . . I've never really gotten over it."

"She took you in, Jesse," I said, "because of Christ and the Holy Spirit's power in her life. She said so, the first time she told me how she decided to adopt you after your parents were killed."

"I know," Jesse replied, clearly struggling to keep his composure. "That didn't keep me from struggling with guilt over my simple existence for years. Dionne, I don't want to do anything to tempt you to feel the same type of resentment toward Samuel. You really think it'll help you to see it confirmed in black and white that he's mine?"

"Jesse," I replied, unable to find words. "Jesse, I don't know—"

"God will keep his hand on Samuel," he said, massaging my shoulder and placing a hand lovingly to the baby's head. "We have to take that on faith."

"Jesse, I just think that—"

He quieted me by placing two fingers against my lips. "We don't have to decide right now. Just enjoy the moment today, and thank God for His work in you this morning." He extended his arms. "Give me the little guy. He'll be waiting on you at your parents' house."

"Thanks," I said, handing over our little bundle of joy. "I really appreciate you coming today."

"It was my pleasure," he replied, stroking the back of Samuel's head. He held my gaze as he spoke, his eyes radiant with selflessness. "I love you, Dionne."

When I climbed into Earl's truck, he glanced over at me with grudging eyes. Ending a cell phone discussion, he cleared his throat. "I guess you only got a couple of minutes before the next service."

"Yes," I replied, my hands in my lap. "I'm sorry about all that."

"No worries," he said, a playful snort baring his sarcasm.

"Jesse was just here to support me through a controversial sermon," I said, "and frankly, to talk about family matters involving the baby."

"So, are you going back to him, or not?"

"I don't know," I replied. "Honestly."

Earl turned toward me and grabbed my hands with a gentle touch. "What do you need to help make up your mind?"

Something broke loose in me, and the combination of Earl's cologne, his hungering stare, and our growing bond took hold. In seconds I was palming the back of his head as we dove into another of what were now dozens of torrid kisses. When I felt his hands on my chest, I pulled back violently.

Earl nearly reached for me, then seemingly thought better of it. Pulling back to his side of the truck, he eyed me suspiciously. "What's that about?"

I looked away, unable to explain myself.

"You know," Earl said, "I have broken up a marriage or two in the not-too-distant past. I'm supposed to be past that now, right, now that I'm saved? So you need to tell me, are you still Jesse's wife or not?"

"Jesse's not rushing my decision" was all I could mutter as I prayed for God's forgiveness.

"Oh, so I shouldn't either, huh?" Earl laughed out loud, slapping his steering wheel. "If I wasn't saved, Rev, I'd tell you it's time to piss or get off the pot."

I stared back into Earl's large, fetching eyes, feeling as if my life might be defined by the next few minutes.

40

Jesse

The minute he crossed the threshold into Rachel's GET UP headquarters office, Adrian surveyed the room with a lazy, confident gaze. Dressed in a navy blazer, a striped turtleneck, and a pair of ratty jeans, he had let his hair grow out into what looked like the first phase of dreadlocks. Looking about the room and nodding slowly at me, Rachel, Coleman, and Coleman's pastor, Reverend Willis, he gave no evidence of shame or embarrassment. It was only when he pivoted to see the other person in the room—Earl, who sat in a separate corner chewing his top lip—that Adrian cracked.

"Oh God, Earl!" Adrian nearly leapt into his big brother's arms, knocking Earl back into his seat before he could rise. "I am so sorry," Adrian said, his voice nearing a whisper. "I know you were looking out for me—I would have clued you in to everything! It was just that we couldn't risk you giving anything away to Coleman and his crew. I'll explain everything, I swear."

Earl was still chewing on that lip as he wrapped his brother in a tight embrace. Holding Adrian back at arm's length as if to check him over, he finally spoke. "If I wasn't so glad to see you in one piece, little man, I'd bust your head open right about now."

Rachel let the brothers have their reunion for another minute before saying, "Adrian, I think Coleman, Jesse, and the pastor should hear the entire story from your side." This had been one of the conditions under which we'd agreed not to alert the authorities about GET UP's deception.

Adrian walked to Rachel's desk, shoved aside a ream of folders, and plopped himself on the edge. "So," he said, looking around at each of us with hardening eyes, "you wanna hit me up with questions or just have me take it from the top?"

Coleman managed a second's eye contact with his ex as he said, "Begin at the beginning."

"The root of all this," Adrian said, shrugging, "goes back to your attempt to shut me up, Coleman. D-Boy? He found me, sent his goons to intimidate me, just like you asked them to. I was walking back to my condo after a day down on the Mall, when they pulled alongside and grabbed me into their truck." The rest of us stayed uncomfortably silent as Adrian recounted the threats, his smart-mouthed responses, and the punches he'd taken to the face and stomach in return.

"They dumped me way down on Georgia Avenue, almost out in Maryland," Adrian said, his voice betraying residual bitterness. "I was dizzy, bloodied, and knew I had to look a mess. They'd cleaned my wallet out too, so I had no ID, no money, and no credit cards. I was gonna have to walk all the way home.

"Fortunately, I was able to go into a nearby McDonald's and talk up a cute little brother working the register. He hooked me up with his cell phone, and the first call I made was to Rachel."

"Adrian's proud," Rachel said, her intent gaze moving from one of us to the next. "I'll fill in some color for you. He was crying like a baby when he reached me."

Adrian nodded. "Whatever, yeah. I hadn't been that humiliated in a long time. It's one thing to be attacked for being gay, it's one thing even to be attacked by a lover's silly wife," he said, cutting his eyes in Coleman's direction, "but to have a bunch of brothers tell me I have no right to speak out for truth, to challenge a closeted brother who's harming the cause?"

"Adrian, stop," Coleman said, his voice even more husky than usual. "We agreed to let this slide if you'd stop lying about me. I'm not *closeted*. I love my wife and I'm faithful to her."

"So why did you kiss me, then? And so everyone's clear, Coleman, I'm referring to three months ago, not back when those photos were taken!"

Several throats were cleared as everyone processed Adrian's accusation. "You're the one here to explain yourself, not Coleman," I said finally, glancing sideways at Earl to make sure things weren't going to deteriorate totally.

"He's right," Earl said, his tone noncommittal. "Finish the story."

"I was pissed," Adrian said, "feeling like three-fifths of a human being, a status my people supposedly transcended decades ago. So I decided to strike back." He glanced around the room proudly. "Rachel supported me, but my disappearance was my idea."

"You had a lot at stake," I said. "A successful political consulting practice, for one. I would think your Republican clients wouldn't be too thrilled to have you openly flaunt your sexuality."

"Please," Adrian replied, waving my words off as nonsense. "Those Republicans could care less about anybody's sex life as long as they're helpful to the cause—low taxes, small government, and the freedom to make war whenever we choose. The antigay thing is just window dressing for the yahoos." He looked between me and Coleman as he said, "As long as this little fraudulent incident stays among us, I'll be welcomed back into the Grand Old Party, living proof of the 'big tent.'"

"You understand," I said, "that in order for everyone to keep you out of jail, Adrian, not only is Rachel resigning from GET UP, but when you return to work, you'll have to force your clients to personally support a 'big tent.' No supporting anyone who opposes civil unions or who wastes time trying to hold votes on antigay marriage laws. No support of people opposing gay adoptions, no pushing legislation that subordinates the rights of homosexuals to the rest of us."

Adrian grinned wickedly. "Well, haven't we been transformed into a flaming activist, now? Who knew, pretty boy, who knew?"

"Don't get it twisted," I replied. "This isn't about my personal beliefs. This is about you being true to your own stated cause. Pastor Willis, however, has agreed to help all of us find a positive way out of this." I turned to the preacher. "You want to break the news?"

"After consultation with Brothers Law and Hill," Pastor Willis said, standing and looking over the room as if he were in a pulpit, "I am going to build a ministry that will generate edifying conversations between Christian heterosexuals and our homosexual brethren. We're calling it 'Across the Void,' because Lord knows many of us are so separated on this issue, we can't even talk to one another."

Adrian frowned, wearing his skepticism like a badge of courage. "Are you gonna encourage closeted gay members—and by that, I'm including those with opposite-sex spouses—to take part, open up about their true desires?"

"Young brother," Pastor Willis replied, chuckling, "I can't force my members to do anything, so, no, I can't promise that this ministry will draw out any more than a handful of folk initially. Matter of fact," he said, leaning back in his seat, "if I really think about it, the first meeting will probably do well to have two or three of our openly gay members and another two or three conservative members eager to tell them they're headed for hell!" He shook his head as Adrian shrugged in an "I told you so" way.

"That doesn't mean it's not worth trying, though," the pastor continued. "The one thing I've come face-to-face with while counseling Brother Hill here is that most believers have a major problem in this area. And the only way we're going to address it is to have some honest dialogue."

Adrian raised an eyebrow. "Honest dialogue in the Church? I'd pay good money to see that. When's the first meeting, Pastor?"

"We'll need a few weeks to get it under way," Pastor Willis said, pointing a finger toward Coleman and me. "Brothers Hill and Law have agreed to serve as co-chairs of the ministry. I figure their influence with the youth should help get teens and college students of both persuasions interested. I want some of the older folk too, but I can recruit them on my own."

We talked for a while about exactly how the pastor should structure the Across the Void ministry, which, of course, erupted into more of an argument. Predictably, Adrian and Rachel's idealistic expectations clashed loudly with my, Earl's, and Pastor Willis's realism.

Coleman, for his part, said next to nothing the entire time.

By the time we finished our arguments over the ministry, as well as the details of Adrian's "homecoming"—he would magically appear at Earl's front door the next morning, after which Earl would call the police with the blessed news—Coleman looked as bushed as I felt. As we walked to our cars with Pastor Willis, I waved a hand in front of his face. "You in there, man? I know you're tired, but we should be praising God right about now!" I looked past Coleman at the pastor, who had already slowed his pace as we neared his Escalade truck. "Am I right, Pastor? The drama ends now."

"Well, in life the drama never truly ends," Pastor Willis replied, laughing as he turned to put his key into the Escalade's door. "But I agree, there is much to be thankful for today. Brother Adrian is safe and sound, Brother Earl has his family member back, there's no more cloud hanging over either you or Coleman, and, most important, Coleman here can see evidence that God has forgiven his past sins." He reached over and clapped Coleman on the shoulder. "You can make a fresh start now."

As Coleman looked down into his pastor's gaze and thanked him for the reassurance, I felt the question in my soul. *Will I get a fresh start?*

Once the pastor had said a prayer with us there on the street, Coleman and I watched him drive off before speaking. "Jesse," my old friend said, a tear slipping down his cheek and onto his chin, "I don't know who God used more mightily to save me from my past—Pastor, Dionne, or you."

"Hey," I said, holding Coleman's eye contact as his pain filled the air between us, air we shared with the shoppers and college kids slowly populating the surrounding blocks. "You have the right focus. God did it, not any of us. And you could argue that while she helped get you into a jam publishing those photos, Angie's the one God finally used to end the media nightmare we've all been living."

"Yeah, for real, for real," Coleman replied, glancing toward his car, which was parked across the street from where we stood.

"I'll see you, bro," I said, extending a hand and shaking vigorously when he took it. "Now go get your butt into a recording studio. I'm expecting great things."

Coleman gave me a mock punch to the chest before turning to cross the street. "Hey, what are you gonna do now, anyway?"

"What am I gonna do?"

"Yeah, I mean with your talent. I know you're keeping the lights on at home by teaching at Howard and doing more work for the music ministry. But you have writing and performing talents, man!"

I shook my head. "You know, Coleman, I've spent basically half my life on stage, projecting an image that too often didn't match up to the real Jesse Law. And that applies to my pre- and post-Christ days, frankly."

Coleman stopped where he stood, one foot poised over the street curb, then whipped back toward me. "I know you're not hanging up your microphone. The world needs to hear that voice, Jesse, needs to hear it singing about Christ."

"I'm not so sure," I replied. "I guess I think too much, but even now I get some of our younger fans—the teens and twenty-some-things especially—who walk up to me and ask if the rumors about my divorce are true." My voice cracked a bit as I said, "That's a scary feeling, man. I didn't become a gospel performer to tempt others to stumble, or to think that because Jesse Law couldn't stay on the right path, they never can either."

Coleman was in my face now, pointing to accentuate his words. "Nobody's perfect, brother," he said. "Come on, if every talented Christian artist took that view, there'd be very little praise and worship music on the market, touching and saving lives. I mean, can you name me a major gospel artist who *hasn't* been through a divorce lately?"

"Well," I said, "I can name you." I paused, letting the question sink in, even though Coleman could just as easily have whipped it around on me. "Right?"

"Yeah, right." He tossed his keys into the air and caught them again. "Never mind, then. Later."

"I'll see you at Pastor's first Across the Void ministry meeting, right?"

"Oh yeah, about that," Coleman said, turning back to face me with eyes incapable of hiding his annoyance. "I didn't have the heart to tell Willis just now, but I've decided it's best for me to sit that business out. I may be switching churches, actually. One of the key shareholders of my new label pastors a church down in Alexandria."

I said only one word, one word which said it all: "Coleman."

"Hey, look, it's just that At His Word has its own ideas about how I should address the homosexual issue. The executives want me to stick to a pretty tight script, Jesse. And leading some ministry that gets people baring their skeletons and thinking outside the box about the gay thing? It can't lead anywhere good."

I stood there and shook my head. "The only reason I'm in the middle of this is because of you."

"Don't you judge me!" He jammed a finger toward my cheek, and for a rare moment I was reminded that my good friend could easily knock me out. "You want me to help lead a ministry about gay issues? Fine. Just as soon as you lead one for sex addicts."

God forgive me, but the first word that popped out was not fit for print. I followed up with a stunned, "What are you talking about?"

"Well, everyone knows the saying about men who get women other than their wives pregnant," Coleman said, his eyes ablaze. "Nobody's that lucky. I never got Suzette pregnant with just one try."

My fists were balled, but I was praying for peace with each passing second. "Don't go there, man. I have plenty to be ashamed of, but not as much as you're trying to imply."

"There," Coleman said, raising his hands and stepping back from me. "See how it feels to have someone else decide how *you* should react to issues in your own life?"

I crossed my arms and let him talk.

"Why's it *my* responsibility to try and counsel all these confused brothers and sisters who like living gay? They're *weak*, Jesse!"

"Weak?"

"Yes!" Coleman took a quick look around, then leaned in close. "I was born gay, right? No secret there. You wanna know something else? Adrian wasn't talking smack back there just now. I did kiss him three months ago, the first time he called and asked to see me. This was before he told me about Angie's article and the old photos."

As far as I had come the past few months, and as huge of a sinner as I was myself, I'd be lying to say Coleman's confession didn't fill me with nausea. "Dionne and I," I said, stumbling over my words as I competed with the thumping hip-hop coming from a passing car, "we worked hard to save you and Zette's marriage, because you swore that you hadn't been involved with a man since—"

"And that was technically true," Coleman shot back. "It was one weak moment, Jess. I hadn't seen Adrian in years, Zette and I were in a bad patch sexually, and he was so smooth and charming at first." He looked at me triumphantly as he said, "I didn't sleep with him, though."

I replied with the only question that made sense. "Was Suzette proud of you when you shared that?"

"Yeah, right," Coleman said, nearly snorting in disdain. "She wrote me off even before I confessed that to her last month. It's okay, though, because we've made a deal."

An open marriage? The Spirit slapped my hand before I could speak the words, so instead I asked, "What sort of deal?"

"Never mind," Coleman said, looking away and shaking his head as if frustrated with himself. "Bottom line, Suzette and I will be a couple this time next year, peacefully raising our children." His eyes were clear as he asked me a parting question. "What about you and Dionne?"

41

Dionne

I was seated in a hard wooden chair, my hands and feet bound, a rope around my waist binding me to the chair. My father entered the dark, desolate room first.

"Pumpkin," he said, his arms crossed even as he sighed, "we had to do this for your own good. I mean, a parent sometimes has to save his child from herself."

"Daddy," I said, gasping for breath as the rope cut a burn into my chest, "please just untie me. I'll hear you out."

"Oh no." Daddy smiled patiently and took a seat in a chair that was a few feet in front of me. "Do I really have to spell it out for you, baby? You'd be a loon to take Jesse back. It took a while, see, but he ultimately proved your dear ole daddy right. He's a no-good hustler! And he hustled you on the one thing in life you wanted most—a child."

"I have a beautiful son now, Daddy." Angling my head toward the door through which my father had walked, I nodded weakly. "C-can I see Samuel now?"

"No, he's safer with his grandparents until you come to your senses." Daddy reached for a cigarette from his pocket and continued speaking as he lit it and took a first puff. "The man lied to you about that precious little boy's identity. Do you understand how serious a deception that is?"

"Mr. Favors, no offense, but she's heard enough." Suzette seemingly appeared from out of nowhere, standing behind Daddy as he stared me down from his chair. She tapped my father on the shoulder, working her neck as Daddy glared back at her. "Get up, old man."

After Daddy gave her a cross scolding and slipped out the door, Zette walked over to me. "I wish I could untie you, girl, really," she said, "but everybody out there made a deal. They said you had to hear everyone's opinion before you choose between Earl and Jesse."

"Why is this anyone's business besides God's, mine, Earl's, and Jesse's?"

Suzette smiled sheepishly. "I wish I could say. God knows I don't let anyone tell me whether I should stay with Coleman. He and I are just fine with our arrangement."

I frowned up at her, my question obvious.

"Girl, I only took part in this so I could make sure somebody spoke up on Jesse's behalf," she said. "I mean, okay, he lied to you about the pregnancy. But don't forget, it happened after *you* kicked him out and insulted his manhood. And, as soon as you said you wanted him back, he told you that he had slept with one woman during the separation."

"So this is all my fault?" I shook my head in disgust. "Give me a break, Zette. I was depressed, girl, dejected after years of unanswered prayer."

"You don't think Jesse was suffering all those years, right alongside you?"

"Okay, loudmouth." My sister Lisa was suddenly seated in the chair Daddy had vacated. "I already had to elbow my way past Mom and three of our aunts to get in here next." She leaned forward, looking into my eyes as if Suzette were invisible. "Don't fall for the okeydoke, girl," she said. "I think you're on the right track, seeing what's up with this Earl fellow. He may not be as fine as Jesse, but he's got quite a way about him. And I see how he looks at you," she said, grinning.

"Your sister is a God-fearing woman," Suzette said, her hand on my shoulder. "The most Spirit-filled woman I know, in fact. She knows the Word calls on her to forgive Jesse and give things another try."

Lisa frowned, her pert little nose scrunching up. "Um, hello? I really don't think my sister needs the advice of a woman whose husband is openly gay."

Suzette's nostrils flared, but the cool, calm look in her eyes made me proud. "Oh, Lisa, that's all right," she said. "Make your little Satan-fueled cracks all you want. You don't have to walk in my shoes, raise my children, or sleep with my husband."

Before I could tell them both to shut up, a young boy bound through the door and suddenly we were alone in the room. Standing not much more than four feet tall with saggy cheeks, curly hair, hazel eyes, and skin the color of heavily creamed coffee, the little cherub could have been five, six, or seven.

One hand in the pocket of his denim jeans and the other hanging coolly at his side, the little guy walked up to within a few inches of my chair. "Mommy," he said, sending a spike of shock through me, "who's my real daddy?"

I awoke screaming, my forehead clammy and hot as I slowly got my bearings. I was in a nightgown, in a strange bed, in a darkened room. A crack in a window shade betrayed that it was late morning, the sky likely just beginning to brighten with sunlight.

"Hey, hey," said a strong male voice as I lay there shuddering. A warm embrace enveloped me and I recognized both Earl's scent and his voice. "I'm right here, Dionne," he said, his use of my name still sounding surprising after two weeks of him banishing the "Rev" nickname.

After kissing me on the cheek, he slid back off the bed and turned on a lamp on the nearest nightstand. I looked up to see him observing me from the side of the bed, his hands stuffed into a silk house robe, which he wore draped over a matching pair of pajamas. "Are you okay?"

"I-I guess," I replied, feeling too shy to match his eye contact. "Earl," I moaned, "what am I doing waking up with you?" I was praying that I hadn't indulged my sexual attraction to him; for weeks I had teetered on the edge with Earl, but something inside had kept me from making that ultimate commitment with him.

"Calm down," Earl said, smiling. "You didn't get into any 'big girl' activity last night, if that's your concern. Is your recall really that fuzzy?"

"No," I said finally, recalling the night on the town I had spent with him and Adrian in celebration of the brothers' reunion. I had agreed to go along both in support of Earl, but also so that I could pick Adrian's brain for ideas on how best to reach out to gay and bisexual teens as part of my Rising Son ministry. Although Pastor Norm had decided not to devote a formal ministry to homosexual issues—when rumors circulated that he had that in mind, he had nearly been canned by the church board—he had given me permission to quietly recruit teens struggling with their sexuality, for whatever reason. I wasn't going to endorse the gay lifestyle—I had to respect Rising Son doctrine—but I was allowed to take a strong stance against homophobia in any form, including callous joking, and I was allowed to have gay kids talk openly in front of straight ones about their urges and whether they felt they were biological.

Adrian was still a skeptic, challenging me on every aspect of my plans, but over the course of the night, he began to charm me in his own way. The next thing I knew, I had indulged in a rare glass of wine—or maybe two—and been quickly reminded that while I was not convicted that drinking was itself a sin, it was something I was better off avoiding. As I'd learned one night in college, a couple of drinks was all it took to leave me disoriented.

Once I'd reconstructed the night before with Earl—including the fact that I had called my parents to tell them I was up late talking with Earl, and would be home early in the morning as a result—I hopped into the shower while he made coffee and eggs.

When I sat down at Earl's breakfast table to eat, my hair pulled into a ponytail and the same set of clothes from last night on my back, I sighed and said, "We need to talk."

"No, we don't," Earl replied, his back to me as he stirred some cream into a coffee mug. Turning to me and placing the coffee before me, he bit his lower lip. "After all we talked about last night, Dionne, don't try this."

"It's because we had that talk that I had that crazy dream," I said, taking the mug from him. "It's clear to me now, so please understand. I definitely have strong feelings for you, Earl Wilkes, but there's a problem."

"Don't tell me. You like me, but you love Jesse."

My heart nearly broke at the sound of the admission. "I do love Jesse. And to be honest, I don't know how to compare what I feel for the two of you. All I know is that I have to choose. My son deserves that much."

"And you're choosing Jesse."

"For now," I said, "I'm choosing Jesus."

• • •

When I walked through my parents' front door into the foyer, Daddy stood there holding Samuel, both their smiles aimed expectantly in my direction. "Hey, there she is, pardner! How's Mommy?"

"Just fine," I replied, kissing Samuel's forehead as I took him from Daddy.

Mom emerged from the kitchen as I playfully hoisted my son in the air. "Welcome back," she said, her voice taking on an edge that took me back to my teens. "I won't show out in front of my grandson, Dionne, but if you're going to be under this roof, I'd eventually like a better explanation of your whereabouts last night." She pushed Daddy aside playfully so she could get close enough to kiss me on the cheek. "You may be a grown woman, but your virtue is still a treasure. I hope you haven't given it away to someone besides your husband, especially as long as Jesse wants you back."

"She's through with the hustler now," Daddy said. "Stay out of your daughter's business, please."

"Oh, will you please go out to your wood shop!" Mom's barely repressed rage was almost comic, and she even chuckled out of embarrassment. "May I just have a moment with my daughter, please?"

"I have plenty to do," Daddy replied, turning to one of the closets and grabbing a jacket. "You ladies go ahead and have some tea or whatever you do." He kissed Samuel's forehead before heading out toward the garage. "And you," he said, pointing at Mom, "you think about how you're gonna make up with me when I get back."

"Ooh, stop Daddy," I said, shuddering playfully and cracking both of my parents up. "That's the last image I need to see in my head."

When Daddy had rounded the corner, Mom smiled at me. "I'm glad you got back before Jesse showed up." I had forgotten that I'd agreed to let him keep Samuel for the day, so they could go to a church revival in Virginia with his mother.

"What," I replied to Mom, "you figure he'd write me off if he learned I was at another man's all night?"

"Dionne, seriously," my mother said, her eyes grave, "as a woman of God, it doesn't pass the 'appearance of evil' sniff test."

"I know, Mom, trust me, I know," I said. I thought of the pained look in Earl's eyes as I had left, and prayed once again that I hadn't done anything to damage his newfound walk with Christ. As I had told him, as big a factor as my lingering feelings for Jesse and my loyalty to Samuel were, the ultimate reason for my ending things was to ensure that a romance with me didn't derail Earl's newfound relationship with Christ. It just wasn't the right time.

The doorbell rang, and Mom let Jesse in as I placed Samuel into his favorite swing, which sat just off the foyer in the living room. Jesse stepped into the room a minute later, after making some small talk with Mom, who had quickly made herself scarce.

After some standard pleasantries, Jesse took a seat on my parents' couch. "So the question, Dionne, is when will you take me up on my offer? I moved all my stuff out a month ago." He had offered to clear out of the house and rent his own apartment so that Samuel and I could move back in. "I'd rather have you back with me, don't get me wrong," he continued, his glance falling to the carpet, "but I'm trying to be realistic, leave the ball in your court."

I didn't really want to move back to the house for one reason—I didn't want to feel lonely, and I didn't want Samuel infected by any such emotions of mine. At least at my parents' we were always surrounded by loving energy. As much as I sensed God's love and provision these days, I had feared having to test it so thoroughly.

My relationship with Jesse had improved enough that his persistent

296 • *Xavier Knight*

questioning eventually wore me down, and I admitted some of my fears to him. "There's a really good answer to that problem," he replied. "You two won't be lonely if I'm there."

I wasn't going to let him off that easily. "We wouldn't be lonely if Earl moved in either."

The quickened look in Jesse's eyes told me what he was really thinking—*You wouldn't!*—but his mouth said, "I'm offering you the house without any strings. All I'd ask is that you don't let any other man actually move in until our situation's resolved." He glanced at the baby. "Let's not pass our problems down to him."

"I hear you," I said, focusing my gaze on Samuel, who had fallen asleep in my arms.

"I think you should pray and claim the promises of Deuteronomy 31," Jesse said. "You, of all people, know that God will never leave nor forsake us." He leaned back against the couch, his gaze resting squarely on Samuel. "You're blessed, Dionne, really. You've got a beautiful son you've already bonded with, a home that's paid for, and Earl is frankly just the first of any number of men who'd be honored to take my place."

I realized that my eyes were burning with tears, which I tried to wish away as my emotions got the better of me. "Just stop, Jesse. You sound like a man looking for a way out." My chin dipping toward my chest, I hung my head and began to weep.

I sat there, resenting my lack of self-control, when I felt Jesse settle in beside me and Samuel. Throwing his arms around me, he kissed me on the cheek, then turned my face until it was flush up against his. After drawing me in for a deep kiss, he pulled back suddenly. "I don't want to take advantage," he said, his eyes on the floor. "I hope I made my point."

Wiping my eyes, I looked frantically toward the clock over my parents' fireplace. "You two are going to be late. Didn't you say you were picking your mother up at noon?"

"Yeah, thanks," Jesse said, a sudden look of relief washing over him. I sensed that like me, he didn't want to rush things. "You need help packing his diaper bag?"

"No, everything's ready," I said. "What you can do, though, is go ahead and pack up whatever you need tonight. I think Samuel's ready to move into his real home."

Epilogue

Dionne and Jesse's was not a storybook ending, at least not in the conventional sense. If Jesse had been granted his wish, Dionne's decision to end her budding romance with Earl would have been final. If he had written the story of their marriage, the months following Samuel's birth would have been a short-term valley lasting forty days and nights, one during which Dionne flirted with experiencing another man, but quickly chose to do as so many other wronged wives did every day.

Dionne's memory, however, turned out to be longer than Hillary Clinton's. Even after she had sincerely forgiven Jesse for his deceptions and invited him to join her weekly counseling sessions with Pastor Norm, she was unable to convince herself to just traipse back into a badly damaged marriage. Honest prayer and meditation failed to change this, and over time she explained it clearly enough that Pastor Norm, her parents, and even Jesse had to respect her reasoning.

For close to two years, Dionne and Jesse lived life as a legally separated couple, and unlike the few weeks before, this time it was public knowledge. Dionne spent some of this time dating Earl, who told her from the start that she would wind up with Jesse. That did not stop him from opening his heart and his bed to her. Dionne and Jesse never

spoke about the exact ways in which Dionne and Earl expressed themselves with each other; in kind, she never asked Jesse how successful
he'd been at his proclaimed period of celibacy—one he promised
would not end until she took him back. If she had asked, his answer
would have made her proud.

As for little Samuel Law, it wasn't until he was nearly three years
old that he developed some sense of confusion about his mommy and
daddy's relationship. The more he compared notes with other play-
mates whose parents were married, the more it struck him that most
daddies didn't kiss their kids good night and then disappear out the
back door, and these kids' fathers didn't have their own apartments
with a second bed for the child either.

By the time Samuel was ready to speak the questions forming in his
head, Dionne beat him to the punch with a surprising announcement
the morning of his third birthday. "Your Daddy and I are taking you
shopping today," she said as she sat on the edge of his bed. "We need
to get you a new suit."

"For what?"

"Mommy and Daddy are holding a special ceremony, and we need
a little ring bearer."

Samuel inhaled suddenly, the combination of words sparking his
memory. "A-are you and Daddy getting married?"

The Laws' wedding renewal ceremony was performed jointly by Pastor Norm, of Rising Son, and Pastor Hicks, of Metropolitan. Held in
the family's backyard, the audience was a select group that included
not only Coleman and Suzette, but also the couple's parents and most
of their siblings, nephews and nieces, including Lisa, Carol, Harry,
Larry, and Larry Jr.

From Rising Son Church, Dionne's fellow associate ministers were
in attendance; from the reconfigured version of Men with a Message,

Frank and Isaac came out in support of their old friend. Turning more heads than any of these, though, was the sprinkling of secular music stars arrayed throughout the audience. With each passing year, Jesse was in increasing demand as a writer, arranger, and producer for "worldly" singers looking to prove that they hadn't forgotten their gospel roots. He usually cranked out two songs per artist—each one powered by the smooth contemporary style and emotionally intimate vibe that had put Men with a Message on the map. As the songs hit the airways, his manager inevitably got new calls from better-known artists.

Jesse, now dressed in his newly purchased gray tuxedo, followed the pastors and his brother Larry, his best man, to the front of the specially constructed gazebo. Reflecting on the many familiar faces whose eyes were now affixed on his back, Jesse could hear them buzzing about the well-founded rumors. For the first time in three years, he would be performing live this afternoon, taking time after "saluting" his renewed bride to serenade her with a newly written song expressing his gratitude to God for bringing them across so many rivers. Kenny Lattimore, Anthony Hamilton, or Brian McKnight would eventually sing it to the top of the charts, but Jesse was determined that its debut travel straight from the song's creator to its muse. There would always be a side of him that missed performing, but aside from the occasional guest appearance with a gospel industry powerhouse or an up-and-coming choir, Jesse was at peace with his decision. While temptation awaited him each day he stepped out the front door, he found it much more manageable without the baggage of being an entertainer.

As Dionne and her father stood in the tent from which the bride would emerge, she thanked the "old man." In the weeks since she and Jesse had made their decision public, Mr. Favors had made not one smart remark, not a single reference to her intended as a "hustler." The truth was, Dionne's father had seen his daughter endure enough quiet meditation, prayer, and pain as a legally single mother to know she had not chosen her course lightly.

Earl had called to thank her for the invitation. "A class act" was all he had said when she first picked up. "You didn't have to do that."

"I didn't want you to hear from anyone else," she had explained.

"I appreciate that," he replied. They talked for a while about his and Adrian's lives—Earl was going back to school to bone up on business education and eventually buy out the owners of Therapy Café, and Adrian had left the political arena to become a public relations VP for a gay cable channel—before acknowledging they were unlikely to talk again.

Suzette grabbed Dionne's hand suddenly, bringing her back to the present moment. "Hey, girl," she said, her voice a whisper as she kissed her good friend's cheek. "It's time for your matron of honor to haul *my* butt out there. That means you're up next."

As Dionne hugged her good friend close, she thanked God that while she wouldn't want to emulate their marriage, she and Jesse were blessed to still have Suzette and Coleman in their lives. Coleman, who was still with At His Word Records and carrying the water for the label's evangelical politics, seemed fulfilled, and his work was touching even more hearts than it had in his Men with a Message days. Some loyal fans complained that his music was losing its "soul," but no one could say he had taken Jesus out of the lyrics. And Suzette, who was now much more tight-lipped about personal issues and bodily functions, remained the most loyal friend Dionne knew.

The one thing the Hill and Law families rarely discussed, still, was Jesse and Dionne's continued involvement in Pastor Willis's Across the Void ministry. Now numbering two hundred members, the ministry led frequent seminars on self-esteem, sex education and counseling, HIV/AIDS prevention and treatment, and tolerance, throughout the Washington-Baltimore metropolis. Though it continued to draw fire from both right-wing and even some progressive Christian camps, a national support group for families of gays and lesbians had just honored Across the Void for "elevating the Church's approach to sensitive issues."

Coleman, however, showed little interest in the ministry's progress, a fact Jesse prayed long and hard about before deciding to respect his friend's decision to keep his own battles private. Together, Jesse and Dionne prayed daily for the Hills' marriage, warts and all.

When Dionne, leaning heavily on her father to buttress her rubbery knees, stepped onto the flower-strewn path leading to the gazebo, she was met by a surprise. Little Samuel, who unbeknownst to his parents had broken free of Grammy Favors's loving grasp, hopped into the aisle, blocking his mother and grandfather's path. "I want take Mommy up," he said, looking up at Dionne's father with a pouty lower lip.

Mr. Favors cast an embarrassed glance over the crowd, then looked over at his daughter. "I'm sorry, baby" he said. "I can't tell Little Man no. Looks like this is as far as I take you."

Dionne glanced down at her son in his pin-striped navy blue suit, wondering again at the fact that she was staring into a guileless version of Jesse's eyes. And as much as she loved Jesse, as much as she had finally made peace with the hills and valleys behind them, that recognition filled her with more hope than she could communicate. (Three years later, that same hope would help her eventually convince Jesse that they should introduce Samuel to his birth mother. Her husband would be unable to counter Dionne's strongest argument: "If Samuel never gets to know Vanessa, it's no different than if she died the same way your birth mom did. Do you want that for him?")

When Dionne and Samuel finally reached Jesse, the boy ran into his father's arms. As the crowd erupted in joyous laughter, Jesse hoisted their son in his arms, then pulled Dionne into a combined embrace. With tradition already thrown aside, she whipped back her veil and locked eyes with her husband. As they leaned into each other for an eager kiss, the same thought comforted them both. *With God, all things are possible.*

Reading Group Guide

Discussion Questions

1. According to strict interpretations of Scripture, Dionne had every right to divorce Jesse given that he had committed adultery. Should she have? Why or why not?

2. If his sister Carol had not appeared at Vanessa's bedside when she did, do you think Jesse would have followed through with his plan to confess the truth about Samuel's paternity on his own? If he had confessed on his own before Dionne figured it out, should she have forgiven him any more quickly?

3. Did the fact that Jesse took so many months to seriously consider confessing prove that his spiritual rebirth was as phony as many outsiders always assumed?

4. If you or any close friends or family have ever struggled with infertility in the way Dionne and Jesse did, how did your real-life responses differ from the Laws'? How much responsibility, if any, does Dionne bear for driving Jesse away and setting off the chain of events that led to Samuel's conception?

5. Did Vanessa make the right choice in giving Samuel up for adoption? Couldn't she have followed through with her medical career and still raised the baby with financial help from Jesse?

6. After Samuel's birth and during her long-term separation from Jesse—which included her relationship with Earl—should Dionne have stepped down from her ministry position at Rising Son? Why or why not?

7. Put yourself in Jesse's shoes: A close friend like Coleman comes to you, confesses a homosexual past, but insists he or she has been healed and is free of that lifestyle. How do you react? What types of questions do you ask? How do you pray for that friend?

8. In your opinion, did Suzette and Coleman make the right decision by keeping their family together? Whose sin was more wounding to the marriage—Coleman's keeping his past a secret, or Suzette's impulsive decision to have an affair as retaliation? Why?

9. Although Jesse still hadn't figured out all the answers, he decided to support his gay nephew, Larry Jr., in an attempt to get more Christians to speak frankly about the issue of homosexuality. Do you have gay friends or family who are sincere Christians and believe their orientation is a gift from God? How have you responded to their convictions? Have you drawn on your instinctive reaction, your lifelong beliefs, or further study of Scripture when speaking with them?

10. Some would say that neither Jesse and Dionne nor Coleman and Suzette's marriages were worth saving. Do you agree? Have you faced situations in your marriage that had others telling you to just quit? What decision did you make, and why? Would you make the same decisions today?